RAVEN

Wolfmoon Book III

NIKKI BROADWELL

AIRMID PUBLISHING
TUCSON, ARIZONA

Airmid Publishing

This is a work of fiction. All names, characters and ideas presented here are a product of the author's imagination.

ISBN-10: 0997994118
ISBN113: 9780997994117

Dedication

To my parents, who allowed me the freedom to run wild and the time to read.

"A thrilling and satisfying conclusion to this magical trilogy. Danger, mystery and the ultimate power of love take us on an engrossing journey with the characters we've come to know as friends and those we are glad are only fiction. The author deftly weaves the storylines begun in the first two books into a tale you won't want to put down."

~Christine Myers, Proofreader, Lady Myers' Wordsmithing

Acknowledgements

My deep gratitude goes to family members and friends who have stood by me in bringing this story into print, most especially my husband who has read and re-read and suffered through every incarnation.

Thanks especially to my most recent proofreader, Christine Myers, as well as Karalynn Ott of Verve Editorial and Lisa Constantino who was there at the beginning.

And thanks always to Emily Trinkaus who has used her amazing

astrology talents to guide and encourage me from day one.

Heart-felt thanks go to my website designer, Steph Wilder of Kismet design for the most amazing and beautiful cyber site ever!

And credit goes to Matthew Wood, author of "The Book of Herbal Wisdom", from which I borrowed liberally.

And lastly, I can't forget my on-going support from the many Celtic goddesses who have imbued this narrative with their mythos.

"There is no use trying," she said: "one can't believe impossible things."

"I dare say you haven't had much practice," said the Queen. "When I was your age I always did it for half-an-hour a day. Why, sometimes I've believed as many as six impossible things before breakfast."

~Lewis Carroll-'Through the Looking Glass'

Chapter

Scotland, 2009

Maeve Lewin stared out the plane window, her thoughts miles away. It seemed amazing that just a few short weeks ago she had been blissfully unaware of her Scottish mother. If it hadn't been for Finna's paintings arriving at the art gallery where she worked she would still be in the dark about all of it. How could her father have kept this woman a secret all these years? She thought about the beautiful artwork her mother had done—the familiar landscapes from her childhood. No wonder her dreams had been so weird lately. But several things had happened that were unexplainable—like the dream she had of walking into her mother's painting and merging with the figure that looked so similar to herself. How had her mother managed to do such a likeness without seeing her daughter for over twenty years? But that wasn't the half of it.

Coming back to the present, Maeve watched the men by the cargo hold unloading the cart of suitcases; heavy thumps reverberated under her feet as they were thrown in willy-nilly. They would be taking off soon. How would it be to meet this long lost mother—to be in the place of her birth? A part of her was angry with both her parents—at Alex for keeping her mother a secret and at Finna for not claiming her child. What kind of mother would allow her child to be taken and never take the time to search her out?

Her thoughts went in circles, going over everything that had brought her to this point—the camping trip with Harold during the full moon. *Samhain*—the time when the membrane between the living and dead was the thinnest. A shiver went down her spine as she remembered the sense that they were being watched and the strange peyote induced dream about the dark man who wanted to kill her. At the time Harold was just a good friend, but after the two of them shared a vision, things had changed between them—they were lovers now and leaving him back in Milltown had been very hard for her. To her great relief he had purchased a ticket and would join her over the New Year, only two weeks away.

A flutter went through her midsection as the plane began to taxi down the runway. As it built up speed she gripped the armrests.

"Flying frightens you."

Startled, Maeve turned. She hadn't heard this man arrive next to her. He wore a long hooded robe like a monk of some kind. His deep-set eyes had fastened on her knuckles, which had turned white. "I've never been on a plane this big."

"Believe you may not, but these silver beasts of the air are quite safe. Traveled to Scotland, have you?"

His unfamiliar accent and odd way of speaking made him difficult to understand. "Well, I was born in Scotland, but I don't remember it. I was very young when we left. I've been living in Milltown, Massachusetts since I was three. You see, I didn't even know my mother was alive until recently...and this visit will be a reunion for both of us..." she babbled on nervously, listening to the change in the engines as the plane lifted into the sky. "My father kept her a secret for some reason I can't fathom." When Maeve met the man's deep indigo eyes she felt lost for a second, her mind a blank.

He watched her, a smile playing around his lips.

"MacCuill," he said, holding out his hand.

"Maeve Lewin," she managed to mutter, grasping his rough hand in hers.

"The family resemblance is remarkable."

"Resemblance? Do you know my mother?" Maeve examined the well-worn face, the gray beard that he now pulled his fingers through.

MacCuill nodded, bringing his hand back to rest in his lap. "The first time I saw your mathair, she was a wee babe in the arms of your seanamhair, Catriona."

"So you're Scottish? Your accent seems different."

"Mine is an ancient dialect. I am very old, you see," he added, chuckling to himself.

Maeve had no idea how old he was. To her he seemed ageless and yet his deeply lined face suggested he was somewhere in his seventies.

"Worry not about my age, Maeve." MacCuill frowned, turning toward the aisle where an older woman had paused next to their seats.

Before Maeve could get a good look at her, she was hurrying away.

MacCuill put a hand on her shoulder. "You need to rest."

"Oh, I'm fine," she said, because she had been very much awake just a moment before, but as soon as these words were out of her mouth, her eyelids grew heavy and she had an overwhelming desire to close them.

She was in a dense conifer forest on a narrow trail. A white-haired man carrying a walking stick was ahead of her, moving quickly away. "Wait!" she cried, running to catch up.

3

"MacCuill!"

"Whom were you expecting?"

"I don't really know. Where are we?" A bright glow surrounded the trees despite the gloom of the forest. She looked up the trail to where the tree line ended, opening onto a wide valley.

"We are in the Otherworld. I thought you could use a bit of preparation."

"Preparation for what?"

"This is a place where time stands still, where magic still exists. Look around, Maeve, and tell me what you see."

By now they had reached the edge of the trees. In front of her a flat plain covered in thick purple heather, bracken fern, and yellow gorse stretched into the distance. *"Everything's lit up."*

MacCuill nodded. *"How it should be here, the way it once was."*

When the soft breeze touched her cheek, Maeve breathed deeply, savoring the sweet scent riding the air. Bees buzzed through the flowers, delicately picking up nectar.

MacCuill touched her arm, pulling her attention away from the pastoral scene. *"You have been summoned here to restore the balance."*

"Me? What do you mean?"

"You are part of an ancient prophecy, Maeve—I witnessed the ceremony to name you. Not name you in the way you imagine, more like naming the force you would become—a blessing bestowed by the moon goddess."

"This is a dream—I mean it has to be, doesn't it?"

When MacCuill turned his deep blue eyes on hers, her mind cleared. Her thoughts cascaded back to a recent experience where she felt the same way—the dream of merging with the painted figure that looked so much like her. Running down a wooded path, her mind had opened, expanding into a new and vivid reality. He watched her, as though he knew where her thoughts had gone.

"Do you understand now?" he asked.

At Maeve's nod MacCuill turned, striding away from her.

Maeve followed, carefully stepping into his footprints as they made their way by burbling streams hidden under thick clumps of heather. Sun warmed her bare arms as she gazed across the radiant landscape.

"See those mountains in the distance?"

Maeve squinted toward the horizon where massive snow-covered peaks lifted into the sky like shining beacons.

"That is the Caer Sidi, where the moon goddess, Arianrhod resides. I have been guardian of her domain for more years than I can count."

Maeve listened to his deep voice, registering the mingling scents of flowers, the hum and buzz of bees, birdsong in the distance. She was too taken with the scenery to put her questions into words. Instead she bent to touch the heather, feeling the roughness of the coarse bush under her fingers. If this was a dream, it was one of the most real seeming ones she had ever had. When MacCuill spoke again she noticed a change in tone, the sadness behind his eyes.

"What you see here is how the Otherworld was. Now I must show you what it has become." Before she could protest he grabbed her hand and she felt herself spinning away in a rainbow of color.

When he let go they were not far from where they'd been standing a minute before, but this time there were no bees, no sun, and no flowers. A dark and ominous sky hung low over the flat and frozen plain. Above the peaks to the north, the sky was filled with roiling black clouds.

"Despite my best efforts, the protections are lost and darkness threatens to overtake the Otherworld. The moon goddess is alone in her castle without the safeguards she has always had. I fear for her and all the creatures and plants that live here. The gods and goddesses have grown weak, and the water and tree spirits wait in another realm, wondering if they will ever be able to return."

Maeve felt a sinking sensation in the pit of her stomach. What could she do about any of this? As she turned to say as much, she woke up.

"Glad to see you're awake in time for breakfast." The flight attendant's teeth looked unusually white as she smiled, deftly pulling the tray holder down and placing the food tray on it.

"Where's the man who was sitting next to me?"

"What man?"

"There was an old man dressed in a robe in the seat next to me."

"I haven't seen anyone fitting that description and as far as I know this seat has been vacant for the entire flight."

"But I was talking to him, you must have seen him. I think he was some kind of a monk."

"Maybe you were dreaming. You've been asleep for most of the flight."

She had? Maeve thought about the vivid dream. She could still see MacCuill's indigo eyes and feel his dry hand in hers.

"Even that elderly woman couldn't seem to wake you," the flight attendant continued. "Is she your grandmother?"

Maeve frowned in confusion. "My grandmother? No. I don't know anybody on this plane." Except the monk, she thought to herself, wondering how she could have dreamed all of this up. Maeve was still pondering MacCuill's disappearance when they landed. Reaching for her carry-on under the seat in front of her, she was surprised to find a walking stick next to it. She pulled it out, examining the intricate knot carved into the top. It was made of a wood she couldn't identify—not any that her father used in his furniture making.

Maeve's nerves were at a fever pitch as she approached customs. It would only be a minute or two before she was reunited with her mother. She readjusted her pack and tucked the walking stick under her arm, scanning the area just beyond the barrier. A crush of people waited, and Maeve watched the tearful reunions with trepidation. Would she and Finna like each other? *I should call her mother*, Maeve thought to herself. But that didn't seem right either. Working her way around an embracing couple she heard her name being called and glanced over her shoulder to the right. A small woman with dark hair smiled her way, gesturing excitedly. As their eyes met Maeve dropped her bag and the walking stick, tripping over them in her haste to reach her mother. When Finna's arms went round her, Maeve burst into tears. It was a long moment before she could force herself to let go.

"My dearest, Maeve!" Finna exclaimed. "What a welcome sight ye are and exactly as I pictured ye."

Maeve gazed into the gray-green eyes, the light Scottish trill touching some deeply buried memory making her throat contract. "I was afraid you wouldn't be here. I left the flight information on some answering machine that wasn't yours—someone named Lily?" "Lily is my oldest friend. She's kind enough to allow my friends to leave their messages with her. I dinna have a telephone."

"No telephone? Not even a cell?" A flutter went through her. How could they keep in touch when she went back to the States?

"Not even a cell." Finna bent to pick up the bag that Maeve had dropped. "Where did ye get this?" she asked, lifting the walking stick.

"It's a strange story," Maeve began, as they walked together toward baggage claim. "It was on the floor next to my seat and no one claimed it, so I decided to keep it."

"It looks like one an old friend of mine uses," Finna observed, looking carefully at the carved knot.

"Is this friend an old man with gray hair and beard?" Maeve joked.

Finna's eyebrows went up. "Aye. He's called MacCuill, the druid."

"A druid? I didn't know they still existed. Are you saying he was real? I mean I thought I was dreaming. He said he knew you and my grandmother…and then I fell asleep. Oh, never mind—it's all too weird."

"Please go on, I'm always interested in what MacCuill is up to."

Finna looked so attentive that Maeve related the entire sur-real experience, glad that she was being taken seriously. "And when I woke MacCuill wasn't there."

"He's capable of all sorts of, what ye might call, magical phenomena. He can project himself from one place to another and so I dinna doubt for a minute that he was on your plane. He left that walking stick so ye would remember."

"Do you mean he can be in two places at once?"

Finna nodded.

"But none of the flight attendants saw him. I asked."

"If he wishes, he can cause people to forget they ever saw him. But more importantly, what did ye think of your experi-ence with him?"

"I've only had one other dream anything like that." Maeve recounted the experience of walking into the painting Finna had sent her, the painting that had brought Maeve to Scotland. Her experience of merging with the figure that looked so much like herself, plus following wolves down a forest path and coming upon her mother and her grandmother asleep on the ground, had shaken her. Especially since her mother was hugely preg-nant at the time. They reached baggage claim and lowered their voices.

"Ye were in the past, Maeve, the past that existed before ye were born—my past. And I think ye may have inherited your grandmother's connection with wolves." Finna linked her arm through Maeve's. "Let's collect your bags and go home and settle in. I have much to tell ye."

On the way out of the airport Finna stopped abruptly, a warning hand on Maeve's arm. Her mother's face was blanched of color, all the ruddiness gone from her cheeks. "What is it?" Maeve whispered.

Finna pointed toward the escalator where an older woman dressed in a tweed suit had just stepped on.

"Who's that?"

"Someone I hoped I would never see again."

Maeve looked again, paying closer attention to the ordinary looking woman who appeared to be in her late sixties. She was facing them now and seemed to notice their stares. Just before reaching the top of the escalator, her lips curved into a delighted smile and she waved.

"She seems friendly enough."

"That woman is very dangerous. And if she's here ye can be certain Brandubh is close about. That's Adair, your great-grandmother." Finna scanned behind them and then grabbed Maeve's arm. "Let's get out of here."

Hurrying along with her mother, Maeve thought about Brandubh and the little she knew of him. He was a priest, her grandmother's twin brother, and was somehow involved in several depraved sounding acts. Several weeks before Maeve left on this trip she had had a very strange visitation in her bedroom that she was fairly certain was Brandubh. He had nearly smothered her. Her hand went unconsciously to her throat as she recalled the horrible feeling of being enveloped in airless darkness. Later, when she shared it with her father, he told her a vague story about a town being burned—that the priest was responsible. And now her mother was telling her that Adair, Brandubh's mother and her great-grandmother, was also dangerous? A shiver snaked down her spine. Many questions circled in her head.

Finna drove out of the Edinburgh airport heading west on the A71. The heat was cranked up all the way in her ancient Mini Cooper, but it still wasn't enough to keep cold air from blowing in around Maeve's feet. December in Scotland was definitely not tourist time.

"There's a rug in the back seat if ye wish to cover your legs," Finna said, turning around to reach for the plaid blanket.

"I'll get it," Maeve said quickly as the car swerved sideways.

"I don't drive much. I guess ye can tell." Finna laughed, pressing down on the gas as they barreled up a hill, the engine straining.

Finna seemed normal again, her face filled with color, her eyes sparkling. Maeve had a million questions on the tip of her tongue but didn't want to put a pall on the upbeat mood. It could wait.

"I'm so glad you're here in time to celebrate the winter solstice."

"That's the longest night of the year, right?"

"Aye. We have a bonfire every year to dance the light back." Finna grinned, glancing at Maeve. "'Tis always full of music and with your arrival we will probably have quite a crowd."

"Who else is invited?"

"Well, your grandmother, Catriona and Eron, your grandfather, and of course, MacCuill, since he's a wee bit of a pyromaniac and likes to set off fireworks and such..."

"Dad told me my grandfather's name was Angus," Maeve interrupted.

"Angus did raise me but he isnae my real father. I didna find out about Eron until just before ye were born. By that time Alex was determined not to believe anything I told him."

Maeve thought about how little she knew about her mother's life. It was frustrating and she felt a twinge of new anger at her father. He had been lying for over twenty years and had barely filled Maeve in on the Scottish contingent of her family. "If you're his daughter, didn't Eron want to raise you?"

"Eron was married to someone else at the time of my birth. I knew nothing about him for many years."

"But...that means...your mother..."

"Aye. Your grandmother is what I would call a free spirit." The car swerved again as Finna turned toward Maeve. "Eron's wife is dead now and Eron and Catriona are finally together. I know 'tis difficult at your age to imagine someone in their sixties being that much in love, but believe me, they are. And they want to make the most of their time together."

Maeve had no picture in her mind of her grandmother. Her father had called her a witch, intimating that Catriona had powers. "Will Dad's mother be at the party?" Rose had been in touch by letter after Alex had been forced to tell his daughter the truth. If it hadn't been for Finna's paintings arriving at the gallery where Maeve worked, who knows when, or even if, she would have learned the truth. Maeve had been astounded by her father's behavior and although she loved him, something had changed in her as a result of finding out about her family in Scotland.

"Rose does nae attend these gatherings, although she's come to accept what she calls my pagan ways." Finna chuckled. "She's a staunch Catholic."

Maeve gazed out the car window. Sheep with curled horns that looked too heavy for their heads grazed on the little bit of grass remaining, but mostly the landscape seemed cold and barren. It was barely four in the afternoon and already growing dark.

A short time later they left the main road and entered the small town of Bailemuir. Finna navigated the narrow lanes through the shopping district and then left the city limits, driving for a couple of miles before turning into a rutted driveway. When she pulled up behind a small house and turned the car off, Maeve's excitement rose. Before her was the cottage she had been dreaming about for the past several months, its whitewashed walls glowing in the dusky light.

"I'll get your bags, Maeve."

Maeve jumped out of the car, grabbing the suitcase out of her mother's hands. "That's way too heavy for you," Maeve said, dragging it across the gravel toward the flagstone path.

Finna laughed. "I'm stronger than I look." She hoisted the duffel, disappearing around the corner of the house while Maeve stopped to breathe in the sea air. The hill sloped away from the where the cottage stood, ending at a horseshoe-shaped cove. Although night was upon them, Maeve could still make out the white foam of waves rolling in and out. A childhood memory surfaced—the simple feeling of being safe and happy. Tears filled her eyes and trickled down her cheeks. Her heart felt so full she thought it might burst.

Maeve wiped at her eyes and then hurried after her mother. She waited in the doorway while Finna went inside to light the kerosene lamps. Something pulled her eyes upward to the sign above the lintel—**Cead Mille Failte.**

"It means 'a hundred thousand welcomes'," Finna explained, reappearing beside her. "How many times I had to repeat the Gaelic words to ye when ye were a wee lass! Come inside, my daughter."

The interior glowed warmly—not at all like the bright incandescent bulbs Maeve was used to. Glancing around the room, she saw herself as a toddler, walking unsteadily across the wide floorboards—she recognized every knothole and striation. The familiar patchwork quilt covering the four-poster bed against the far wall brought jumbled memories, one on top of the other—snuggling with Finna, birdsong waking her in the early morning, being lifted in her mother's arms, laughter. Glancing to the left she spied the rustic table where she had eaten oatmeal filled with raisins and sweetened with honey.

"I added an extra bedroom a couple of years ago. 'Tis more private for guests." Maeve followed her to a door on the far side of the fireplace. Lifting the old-fashioned iron latch, Finna led the way down two shallow steps into a room with a steeply pitched roof. She lit the lamp and then placed Maeve's duffel on a cedar chest at the foot of the antique wooden bed. On the wall next to the front-facing window, Maeve noticed a painting she was sure was one of Finna's. Like a fairy-tale scene, it depicted snow-covered mountains with a castle built into its base that appeared to be made of ice. Beneath the painting, a table held an old-fashioned plain crockery pitcher and bowl for washing. A shallow fireplace was set into the formerly exterior wall that separated the rooms.

"Can ye be comfortable here?"

"I love it."

"I'm sure 'tis rustic compared with what you're used to, but it has its charms. It stays very warm once we get the fire going—but try not to let it go out." Finna sat on her heels to place kindling and small logs on the low grate and then stuffed paper underneath. A box of fireplace matches leaned up against the plaster wall and she removed one and struck it against the box. The paper caught quickly and the dry logs began to sputter.

"My bedroom at Dad's has some antiques that remind me of these."

"I suppose I'm nae surprised. Your Da and I always had the same taste in furniture. I must tell ye that I dinna have an interior bathroom." Finna pointed toward a small recessed door on the east-facing wall. "Through there ye will find the outhouse."

She must be kidding. An outhouse? Maeve must have had a shocked expression on her face because Finna looked embarrassed, her gaze going to the floor as she spoke.

"Everyone tells me I should put in a bathroom, but 'tis terribly expensive, and where would it go? 'Twould also entail a lot of digging for the septic and this cottage sits on bedrock. This one is nae so bad as all that—'tis a compostin' toilet. All ye need do is throw in a handful of peat moss from the bucket after ye use it."

Maeve stared at her, unable to utter a word.

"Dinna worry, Maeve, in a couple of days ye won't even notice. 'Tis insulated, by the way. I covered the entire inside with felted wool."

Maeve was already planning where a bathroom could go. And how was a little bit of felted wool going to keep out the freezing temperatures?

"If ye wish to freshen up there's water in the pitcher and now ye know how to get to the 'necessary'." Finna laughed, turning to go.

"What about a shower?"

"That I do have, but I hope ye can wait until the morrow. 'Tis a bit tricky to use in the dark."

What in the world did that mean? Oh well, she could take a sponge bath tonight—it was too cold for anything else. She was glad she packed her flannel pajamas.

"I'll just go make a fire in the other room and put the kettle on." Finna left the room and closed the door.

Maeve opened her suitcase and pulled out a sweater and a pair of thick woolen pants before stripping down to wash. Shivering, she hurried through the process, dressing quickly before opening the door to the outside to throw out the murky water. When she happened to look up, she was awestruck by the billions of stars blinking across the night sky. Even at her father's house there were too many streetlights that interfered with stargazing. She stood for a long moment breathing in the fresh sea-tinged air before heading across the crisp grass toward the outhouse. Opening the door expecting pitch black, Maeve was surprised to find a skylight built into the roof, the stars winking blue, bringing their brightness with them. The wool that covered the walls smelled faintly of lanolin—there was not the unpleasant odor that she associated with outhouses.

She followed her mother's instructions to the letter, and then left, closing the door and heading back to her room. One last peek at the stars made her realize how happy she would be to use an outhouse every night if it meant a view like this. Before joining her mother in the other room, she added a couple of logs to the fire and then placed the screen carefully in front.

"What kind of fuel do you use?" Maeve asked, walking into the other room. "Do you even have electricity?"

Finna turned from the stove. "Nae electricity. The Aga and refrigerator are both propane. It gets delivered every three months. The tank is at the back of the house. When I was first here I had only a woodstove for heat and cooking. I kept my perishables in the root cellar."

Living without electricity meant no computer, no Internet, no e-mail—something Maeve could not imagine. "How did you manage? It must be so much work."

Her mother smiled, carrying a covered dish to the table. "In the beginning I made weekly trips to the village for supplies. I had a vegetable garden out back, but I was nae here that long before…" Finna paused, her gaze going to some undefined point in front of her.

"Before what?"

"Before Catriona, your grandmother, arrived."

"Did she stay here until I was born?"

"Your Da hasna told ye much, has he? Did the man even mention where ye were born?" Finna sighed, shaking her head. "Let's have our dinner. I'll answer all your questions in the morn."

Finna ladled the stew, pouring steaming vegetables and meat into two earthenware bowls. Just before Maeve picked up her spoon she heard Finna's voice and noticed that her head was bowed. She put her spoon down.

"I give thanks to the goddess and to the spirits that dwell in all things for this food and the arrival of my dearest daughter." There was a moment of silence and then Finna said, "I try to remember to give thanks every day for what I have. It connects me with the spirits of this place. When this cottage was originally built, several hundred years ago, it was just the one room with a fireplace. About a hundred years ago or so the stone was re-pointed and then covered over with plaster. I built the extra bedroom and the counter to separate the kitchen from the rest of the room. And on the other side," she said, pointing to the wall behind the AGA, "I added another shed room for the shower and some storage. I feel the spirits in this house."

Maeve looked up, surprised. "What do you mean? Like ghosts?"

"Not exactly, 'tis hard to explain, more like a good presence that enfolds the place. Do ye have any memory of livin' here?"

"A few things, but they're kind of muddled."

"The morrow we will take a walk around the cove. It might jostle the memories of your time here with me."

"Did you know I thought you were dead?"

"Aye, child. Ned—ye ken Ned Gordon, right? He let me know that Alex had told ye that lie. But in some ways 'twas necessary."

Maeve opened her mouth to ask a question but before she could form the words, her mother continued.

"Ned's been a blessing. Brought me news about ye over the years. I dinna ken how I could have coped without him."

"Why didn't you get in touch if you knew where I was?"

Finna shook her head. "I specifically asked Ned not to tell me. 'Tis a long story that can wait until you're more rested."

Maeve's confusion mounted. She wanted to hear about it all, right now, but her head spun from jet lag and everything she had already heard. "Okay, but if you forget, I'll remind you."

Maeve woke with her heart pounding. She had been dreaming about the heather-filled valley where she'd gone with

MacCuill, but in this dream there was something lurking in the background—something dangerous. But as soon as her eyes opened the images disappeared. The bedroom was filled with greenish light and she went to investigate, gasping as her bare feet hit the cold floorboards. On the other side of the window, a swirling mass of snowflakes moved erratically, melting as they came in contact with the glass. Pulling on her robe, she ran into the other room.

"Ach, good mornin' to ye, Maeve! What do ye think of the snow?"

"It's beautiful! Do you think we'll be snowed in?"

"If we are 'twill be a perfect winter solstice." Finna was dressed warmly, in black woolen pants and a fleece tunic that came down over her hips. Her brown hair hung in two loose braids on either side of her face. "I've made some coffee for ye and the remaining bread is warming."

"How did you know I prefer coffee?" Maeve asked, sitting down at her place from the night before.

"Ye didna tell me?"

"I don't think so."

"Just a lucky guess then." Finna poured the dark liquid into a cup and brought it over.

Maeve added cream from the flowered pitcher on the table and then took a sip, gratified to find that it wasn't half bad. She smiled to herself thinking about how spoiled she was living in a town that had a good coffee shop on every corner. "Did your paintings make it back in good shape?" One of Maeve's responsibilities at the art gallery in Milltown was to pack up artwork after a show and have it shipped back to the artist. Her mother's show had been such a success that only two paintings had to be returned.

"Aye. And they were delivered right here to the house. Thank ye for that."

"Since I wasn't sure of your address I only sent them to the post office in town—they're the ones you should thank for that. Your work is so beautiful and ethereal. Everyone loved it." Maeve thought about the day her mother's paintings arrived at First Street Gallery. She hadn't known at the time why she had such a strange reaction to the mystical landscapes and figures. It was only after describing the landscapes and the title, '*Saille, the Willow*', to her father and sharing the artist's initials, F.L., that she learned the truth. For some reason he had neglected to ever mention that her middle name was Saille. And when she pressed him, his explanations for why he stole his daughter away from Finna when she was barely three years old had been lame and evasive. Anger flooded her, making her cheeks hot. Her mother's voice brought her attention back to the here and now.

"I have to say 'twas gratifying to sell so many. I painted those a long time ago, at a time when I was quite desolate. I started them after Alex took ye away."

Maeve didn't know what to say and wished she could quell the emotions that were creeping around her heart. "I'm still so mad at him. But how did you know about the gallery, that I was working there?"

"I dinna ken anything about ye being there. A woman I know here, a fellow artist, saw my work and suggested that I show it. She was the one who got in touch with whoever either owned or managed your gallery."

"Maybe she knew Sandra Brighton." According to the gallery owner, Carol Susskind, Sandra was someone Carol often consulted regarding new artists to book.

"Brighton? Aye, that sounds right." Finna refilled her cup and took a long swallow. "I thought 'twould be fun to apply, so I sent some slides, and surprisingly I was accepted."

"Don't you think it's strange that your art ended up at the gallery where I worked? I mean what are the chances?"

"Have ye nae noticed other coincidences in your life?"

"What's strange to me is that I didn't work there when your show was arranged. I didn't come in until a month or so later."

"Ye see? The universe was definitely trying to bring us together."

Despite Maeve's acceptance of serendipity, the scenario seemed implausible. Ned must have played a part, even if Finna didn't remember it. "You started to tell me something last night about Ned."

Finna collected the cups, carrying them over to the sink. "Before I get into all of that, would ye like a bite to eat?"

"I think I'll just stick with coffee. My appetite seems a bit off, probably from the time change."

Finna buttered a piece of bread and then searched in the cupboards. Finally finding what she wanted, she turned toward Maeve. "Ned and I grew up together. We knew each other long before I met Alex." Finna paused, staring at Maeve with her brows pulled together, as though she was trying to make a decision. When she continued, her voice had taken on a different, more somber tone. "I must tell ye that I arranged to have Alex take ye away from here, 'twas the only way I knew to keep ye safe."

"*You* arranged it? Why?" An image of a sneering face, eyes black as coals, appeared in Maeve's mind. "Is this something to do with my great-uncle and his mother?"

Finna nodded, sitting down across from Maeve. She placed a jar of honey between them and then used a spoon to scoop some out, spreading it on her bread. "Ned convinced Alex 'twas a good idea to move ye to the United States. Ye see Ned has always known about Brandubh and Adair and the evil they are capable of. Your Da knew too, but he chose to ignore it and accused me of making it all up."

"I think he believes it now." Maeve thought about her Dad's unexpected visit to her apartment to warn her that Brandubh might be stopping by—he clearly felt terrible about giving the man Maeve's address. "He remembered some conversation between you and Catriona—something about a town getting burned?"

Finna looked surprised. "I'm glad to hear that, Maeve. Alex must have changed a great deal." Finna seemed thoughtful, her eyes cast down. "Alex was referring to an incident years ago when Brandubh set fire to a settlement in the Otherworld. Eron's wife and child were burned to death, along with many others."

"I'm so sorry to bring it up," Maeve said, dismayed to see tears in her mother's eyes.

Finna shook her head, wiping her eyes on her sleeve.

Maeve wanted to ask why Brandubh would do such a despicable thing, but she didn't want to upset her mother anymore than she already had. Instead she got up and cut herself a piece of bread, buttering it before she came back to the table. "So Ned knows all about the town and whatever else Brandubh is up to, and he helped you get Dad to take me to the States?"

"Ned planted the idea in Alex's mind. He encouraged your Da to think I was crazy and that he needed to get ye away from me."

Maeve thought about what her father had said about Finna being 'a bit off'. It was his justification for why he did what he did. Things were starting to make sense. "When did all of this happen?"

"Six months before your third birthday. It didna take much for Alex to believe Ned's stories—he already thought I was half-crazy. And I knew he would never have believed the truth since I had already spoken with him about what was going on, that ye were in mortal danger. I bless Ned for taking matters into his own hands. Ye could nae stay here under any circumstances."

Maeve frowned. *Mortal danger?* "I'm still not clear about Brandubh. I know he's a priest and he's responsible for some horrible fire—but he's your uncle, right? He's part of the family— why would he want to hurt me?"

"Do ye have any idea why you're here, Maeve?"
"To meet you, of course."

Finna and Maeve stood on the beach in ankle deep snow. The sea was milky green and rough, filled with rocks and coarse sand beneath the foamy waves that piled in, one after the other. As they broke, they left behind bright pebbles and shells that chattered against each other as the water receded. It had stopped snowing for the time being, but the sky was still a menacing shade of gray.

On the right a sandstone cliff rose out of the water like a pale monolith, a rocky path leading up its steep sides. A mid-sized heather-covered bluff sloped down on the far side of the cove, ending at the water's edge. In between a curve of sand formed a shallow U. From where they stood the islands of the Inner Hebrides could be spotted, dark lumpy shapes in the distance. She never wanted to leave this place; it felt like home. It was home. Now she knew that all the recent dreams had been about trying to find her mother, as though she had known deep inside that Finna was alive.

Tears filled her eyes and she turned to look at her mother. Finna's cheeks and nose were red from the cold—her reflective eyes, the color of the sea. There was a stillness about her that Maeve craved. Her gaze went out to sea again, hoping to find words to continue the conversation that she and Finna had begun, the lost years that needed to be explored. She wanted to know more, but at the same time she was afraid. Finna had touched on some things that did not make any sense. She now knew there was more to this trip than merely connecting with her mother. But what was it all about?

Chapter

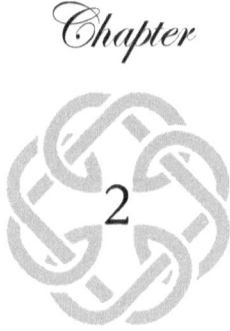

2

Sometime after lunch there was a sharp rap on the door. Startled, Maeve glanced toward Finna who jumped up and hurried toward the door. Maeve watched her fling the door wide to embrace the man standing there. When they pulled apart he scanned the room, his eyes coming to rest on Maeve. He wasn't a stranger after all, she realized, recognizing the deep-set, indigo eyes of the man on the plane. She stood up and smiled his way, wondering why she was so pleased to see him.

"Hallo, Maeve. I told you we would meet soon again."

He came toward her and before she could utter a word he had enfolded her in his arms. Scratchy wool rubbed against her cheek as she took in the scent of fresh air that clung to him. After he released her she felt more awake, as though all her senses had come alive at once.

"Come and sit, MacCuill. I think there's coffee left. It so happens that Maeve is also a coffee drinker."

When Finna went to the cupboard to fetch a mug MacCuill's worried gaze traveled across the room ending at the open door into the other bedroom. "Catriona? She is not yet here?"

"She comes the morrow. Did ye see Herska and Mikdal on your way?"

"Chan eil. You have not heard the news of Clachencreid?"

Finna's face paled. She shook her head.

"The entire place has been burned to the ground—all the villagers have left. I have no idea where Mikdal and Herska have gone or even if they are safe."

"Ach!" Finna's hand went to her mouth. "'Tis as before."

"This act of destruction does have shades of the past about it. But I cannot say for sure this was Brandubh's doing; there were no crows or ravens involved this time. But then again perhaps the Morrighan will no longer tolerate the man's arrogance. I will rest easier once Catriona arrives."

Maeve observed the expressions of concern and worry on their faces, wondering what they were talking about—was the 'past act of destruction' the fire that killed Eron's wife and child? And who was Morrighan? "Where's Clock and cree?" she finally asked.

"'Tis a wee town in the Otherworld," Finna answered distractedly, her attention on the druid.

Before Maeve could form another question the druid cut in, his booming voice echoing off the walls. "Do you recall our short trip, Maeve?"

"Well, I…um," she stammered, looking down at her feet. "I thought…I mean I didn't know…"

"I took you there to give you a taste of what is going on. Every day I am faced with new challenges." His eyes narrowed. "It is time I had your help."

"*My* help?" Maeve shook her head in confusion, glancing toward her mother, but Finna was drinking tea, her gaze fixed on the table.

"You have been called upon to bring balance into the Otherworld at a time when the dark is near complete. Think of the painting your mother sent you, the wolves. Remember your dreams, your visions. This might be hard for you to comprehend but you soon will." His eyes held hers in a mesmerizing gaze. When, after a moment, she looked away, it was as though a thread of energy had been severed. She shivered violently, wrapping her arms around herself.

"Come by the fire." MacCuill took hold of her shoulder, steering her toward the blaze. Maeve sat down in the ladder-backed chair, watching the druid head to the kitchen. He filled the kettle with water and set it on the Aga, throwing in herbs that he got from a basket under the sink. A few minutes later he brought over a large steaming mug.

"Drink this, it will help."

From the table Finna's lilt drew Maeve's gaze. "I know 'tis hard to accept and will take some getting used to. Ye've come to us without the proper preparation."

Maeve opened her mouth and closed it. She took a sip of tea, letting the warm liquid slide down her throat before she tried to speak again. "So what I hear you saying is that I'm supposed to help with…this… whatever is going on in the Otherworld? What *is* this *Otherworld*? It sounds like some made up place."

"I spent many months there when I was pregnant with ye, Maeve. Do ye recall the dream ye told me about at the airport? From my recollection ye came upon me and my mother and 'twas right before your birth from your description of where we were. The birth pains began only hours after that sleep. Ye were born near Clachencreid with your grandmother, Catriona, as midwife."

Maeve's mind went to the dream, the strangeness of coming upon the two women. Something in her had known that the dark-haired pregnant woman was her mother. "Dad never said…"

"He wouldna speak of it, would he? He hated the idea that his child was born in a place he didna believe in, the birth helped along by a woman he detested and didna trust."

25

Finna came over to Maeve's chair, kneeling next to her. When she placed a hand on Maeve's head, stroking her hair softly, Maeve was propelled into the past. This was her mother's way of soothing her when she was a baby. Her breathing slowed and she relaxed, leaning her head onto her mother's shoulder.

"I better fill ye in on some things before Catriona arrives," Finna added. "If it helps at all, I was also brought up without a mother. Your grandmother left me with Angus and I didna see her again until I was eighteen."

"Why did she leave?"

Finna sighed. "I have never truly understood. Angus told me she was dead, so ye see, we have a lot in common."

"So what happened? She just showed up one day?"

Finna nodded. "Catriona arrived here without warnin' and told me she had received a message from the 'ether' that I was pregnant."

"And it was true—did she explain how she knew?"

Finna stood, turning her back to the fire. "She has visions, my mother. There is no real explanation for it. That very day she handed me the moonstone and insisted I accompany her to the Glass Mountain to have the stone blessed by the moon goddess—told me that the child I carried was the focus of an ancient prophecy."

Maeve's mouth fell open. "But that child…I'm that child. Why would you believe that? You didn't even know her—and an ancient prophecy? You mean like Edgar Casey? No wonder Dad said…"

"I didna believe her at first, Maeve, but Catriona has a way about her—she can be very persuasive. In the end I had to take it all on faith—for what purpose would she lie? And people in town knew her, which made me realize she was telling the truth. That trip was one of the hardest things I've ever gone through—but she convinced me that I had to for your sake and for the sake of the Otherworld. I wondered many times if I would make it back alive."

"Your mother is a strong woman," MacCuill added, his eyes focused on Maeve. "Finna may not have liked what she had to do, but she did it and brought you into this world. Do not allow her to diminish her own courage." From a pocket in his robe, MacCuill removed a small pipe. A moment later he was puffing on it, fragrant smoke spiraling up toward the ceiling.

"The blessing ceremony took place at the castle of the moon goddess, Arianrhod," Finna continued. "Have ye noticed the landscape in your bedroom? I painted it from memory."

Finna rubbed her lower back, gazing into the distance. "The ceremony was magnificent—I was surrounded with gods and goddesses as well as all the animals who came to be part of it." She turned back to Maeve, a smile softening the worry lines in her forehead. "At the end of it, the moonstone disappeared. And when I asked Arianrhod where it was, she told me all the magic of that stone was inside my baby. Inside you, Maeve, the child of the prophecy."

Child of the prophecy. All the things her father had told her about Finna and Catriona swirled around in her brain. Maybe her mother really was crazy. Right now she wished she were home in Milltown and not thousands of miles away with a woman she didn't know and a druid who seemed to think she was some powerful priestess. If it wasn't for all the strange happenings of the past few months she wouldn't believe a word of this. Maeve sucked in air, wondering how long she'd been holding her breath.

When she glanced up, MacCuill was staring at her. "Remember what I have already shown you," he said solemnly. "Remember the wolves, the dreams, the ravens all around you."

Maeve lowered her gaze to the scars on her forearms from her encounter with the huge crow. It had been locked inside her next-door neighbor's apartment and when Maeve tried to let it out, it attacked her. The malevolent look in that bird's eye still haunted her. "How do you know about that?" she asked, thinking about the many times the dark birds had come out of nowhere. They had been in the woods when she and Harold were camping, they had been outside the shop where she had her Tarot cards read, and on her way home from her Dad's house, one had hit her windshield, causing her to run off the road.

MacCuill was silent, the piercing gaze he fixed her with his answer. When he spoke again his voice seemed to resonate inside her. "Crows and ravens are linked to Brandubh, a manifestation of him. The word brandubh is Gaelic for 'black raven'."

Maeve tried to think of something to say. "So the crows were...what...under Brandubh's control?" Maeve tried to laugh but it stuck in her throat.

MacCuill watched her, his eyebrows pulled together. There was a softness now behind his eyes, as though he felt sympathy for her confusion. "What was your explanation?"

Maeve frowned, thinking about the darkness Gertrude, the Tarot card reader, had indicated might be in her future. Was the prophecy part of this? And if so, why hadn't it showed up in the cards? "I tried not to think about it because it made no sense. But then, after I found out about my mother, I assumed it was all related to her and the lies Dad had told me."

"And the ravens?"

"Just a coincidence—although the one that attacked me was very scary. I've never been afraid of them before." When her eyes met MacCuill's, her mind was flooded with images, ones from her recent past and others she didn't recognize that seemed related to her trip into the Otherworld with the druid. She put her fingers on her temples, wondering if he was communicating telepathically. "I'm just a woman, not some sort of goddess," she muttered. "I haven't had any special training. And besides that, no one has explained what's really going on—you just keep alluding to things that don't make any sense!"

Right after she said this, Maeve had a vision of herself running, a long red velvet dress swirling around her calves—her dream of being inside her mother's painting. *Saille, the Willow*, it was titled, her doppelganger. For just an instant she was infused with the strength of that woman who looked so much like her.

MacCuill nodded, watching her. "What you're seeing and feeling is exactly what I am talking about."

"Are you reading my mind?"

MacCuill smiled. "You could say I'm sending your mind little reminders. In that experience you were in the Otherworld." MacCuill turned toward Finna. "Your daughter *is* prepared, Finna. Her intuition is strong but she does not yet trust."

Maeve's thoughts were spinning now, a headache brewing behind her eyes. She tried to make sense of the interchange between her mother and MacCuill, but fuzz seemed to have settled over her thinking processes.

"This is not about physical strength," MacCuill continued, answering the question she was about to ask. "As you tap into the buried parts of yourself, you will know."

Maeve picked up her cup and took a long swallow.

"The moonstone energy is inside you, Maeve—the magic and power of generations of strong women who came before. The stone will keep you safe while you travel."

"But I still don't understand. If I had never come here, never found my mother, what would have happened?"

Frowning, Finna glanced toward MacCuill. "Perhaps we should let Catriona explain it all when she arrives."

"I don't want to wait for Catriona!" Maeve shouted.

MacCuill's mouth quirked. "I can see the tea is working. With that energy, some instruction may be in order."

"Today? But I just got here and I was planning…"

"To get to know your mother. Unfortunately this takes precedence. And you and your mother will have more to talk about after we take another little trip."

His changeable eyes were stern again and she withered under his gaze. "A trip?"

"Into the Otherworld as we were before, in the dreamtime. Time is not linear, as you have been taught, but more like a ribbon that wraps back and forth. The dreamtime is as potent as this world, if not more so."

Maeve stared at him, knowing she could not refuse. Adrenaline raced through her, making her dizzy. "What do I need to do?"

"Just close your eyes and relax."

Relax? Yeah, right. But a second later Maeve's eyes closed. His warm hand gripped hers and she found herself floating on a swiftly-moving current of air.

MacCuill touched Maeve lightly on her cheek. When she opened her eyes he nodded, pointing toward the landscape below. It was a desolate place, the dark sky making it even more so. Large sections of the forest had been burned, the open spaces filled with hacked off stumps of trees. The hills were bare and dry and erratic cracks snaked down their sides.

"This is evidence of Black Raven and his armies. They destroy the land in search of precious ores—gold and silver that they sell in the outside world. The people here have always lived in peace and harmony. All the love and appreciation that the plants and trees received every day has been taken away by the fear and hatred that Black Raven and his minions have been fomenting, and this has weakened the spirits. Remember how the plants glowed on our first trip? Well, no longer. This world cannot survive the loss of love."

They flew on, arriving at a wide river in which no water flowed. Below them crows fed on scattered animal carcasses. Maeve's stomach churned.

"They have closed off the animals normal water supply and are killing them for food, wasting a lot of the meat and leaving them to rot. The water supply has always served the people here as well as the wildlife but now the priest controls it in order to keep the people working. He has made them into slaves. Look." MacCuill pointed toward

an enormous animal pen where people were chained, huddling together to stay warm, their clothes ragged and filthy. A group of grotesque troll-like creatures lounged around a fire on the outside of the fence.

"The guards are the Oillteil, underworld dwellers brought forth to help Black Raven in his exploits. Villagers have been captured as well as the small ones known as the Crion. They work in the mines—if they refuse, they are killed."

Maeve's mouth went dry. "Can we go back now?"

"There is one more place I need to take you."

They flew on over more eroded hills covered with stumps, finally arriving at a wide valley. "Remember this place—the heather and the bees? This was once the home of the Crion."

Below them the ground had been ripped apart. Large slashes, like wounds in the earth's skin, looked dark against the massive piles of rubble. Not one living thing could be seen and all the streams had dried up; the entire area was frozen solid.

"See that hole over there?" MacCuill pointed. "That's the First Village of the Crion."

Maeve followed his gaze. It was as though huge hands had ripped into the earth, pulling it apart and scattering everything they found. Parts of looms and colored wools were strewn about, bright spots of color in an otherwise gray and dismal landscape.

Maeve's stomach twisted in alarm. "Where are the people who lived here?"

"Most have been captured and the others have gone deep underground. Their tunnels are vast—far beneath the surface of the earth. We will visit them now."

They flew low for a while and then descended rapidly to end up at a flat round stone set flush with the ground. Maeve looked around nervously as MacCuill rapped three times in quick succession with his staff. The hollow sound reverberated, echoing deep inside. It was only a moment before the stone was lifted, revealing three small figures. Maeve backed away as she took in their alien features.

They chattered excitedly in a foreign tongue and then rushed to embrace MacCuill. Once he released them he reached back for Maeve's hand, pulling her forward. "These are the Crion I was telling you about."

The druid spoke to them in their language, gesturing toward Maeve. She watched in bewilderment as they turned their triangular faces toward her, their hands in prayer position. Their large amber eyes held an expression of awe as they bowed low before her.

"What are they doing?"

"They honor you, the one in the prophecy. I have just told them who you are."

"But I'm not anybody special!"

"Yes, Maeve, you are."

His eyes met hers and she felt again the charge of energy. Looking down, she noticed she was wearing the red gown from Finna's painting. For a moment she tried to figure out how this was possible and then gave up, allowing her thinking mind to fall away as she accepted the new sensations of strength surging through her.

"I'm Saille," she said in a voice that didn't sound at all like her own. They raised their heads in acknowledgement and then she held out her hands. Their delicate fingers clasped hers.

The tallest of the three said, "I am Corey and this is Aila, my mate," pointing to the small woman with bright copper hair next to him. "And this is our daughter Dervla." Dervla held out her hand and knelt down in front of Maeve.

"Please don't!" Maeve cried, reaching to pull her up. "I feel so foolish I..."

MacCuill's booming voice cut in, "Accept who you are!"

They followed the Crion down stairway after stairway waiting every so often for Corey to roll a stone into place, sealing off the tunnel behind. These rolling doors could only be opened from the inside. Finally the stairs ended and she and MacCuill followed the small ones into darkness.

A few minutes of walking brought them to a large room with a high domed ceiling. Orange and blue rugs covered the packed earth floors and lit torches cast flickering shadows against the curved walls. The sound of bells could be heard coming from somewhere close by. "What's that?" Maeve whispered.

"The Crion raise sheep. They dye the wool and weave it into rugs and clothing. Look there." He pointed into the shadows where a door-way led into another room. Maeve turned her head, breathing in the musky odor of droppings and hay. As her eyes became accustomed to the darkness she could make out their milling shapes. Every movement of their heads brought out the dull clank of the bells hanging around their necks—a symphony of sound.

"Do they keep them inside all the time?"

MacCuill shook his head. "This practice is useful in the colder months since they burn the dried droppings for heat. And it keeps the sheep safe from the marauding Beithir and wolves."

Maeve started to ask what the unfamiliar word meant, but was distracted by the loud clang of a gong. She looked toward the corner of the room where Corey was holding a wooden mallet. He hit the brass disc a second time, the sound deafening in the enclosed space. It was only a few moments before the room began to fill with Crion, their eyes going wide as they took in Maeve and MacCuill.

Once the last stragglers came in, MacCuill addressed the assembled crowd. "I want to introduce Saille, the Willow, the one we have all been waiting for. We have come to the Otherworld through the dreamtime but the next time will be to gather the forces to fight for this world."

When MacCuill finished speaking, a shout went up. To Maeve the word sounded like 'bway'. She looked over at MacCuill and mouthed, "What does that mean?"

"'Buaidh'," he answered, "is the Gaelic word for victory."

A moment later MacCuill went down on one knee, pledging himself to Maeve and to defending the Otherworld. Around him all the Crion bowed. At the edges of the room stood creatures that looked like large upright apes. Seeming shy, they held back. Maeve was struck by their

*oddness and also a little afraid, since there were many of them. "Who
are they?" she asked, trying not to point.*

*MacCuill looked their way, nodding in greeting. "They are known
as the Amuigh. Together with the Crion they are the keepers of the
wisdom here in the Otherworld. They will never fight but they pledge
to help in whatever ways they can." Maeve watched them, mouthing
the word,' amoo', to herself and wondering how they came to be. They
looked back with their intelligent deep brown eyes and Maeve felt their
goodwill even though they didn't smile. She nodded to them, acknowledging their presence.*

*By now Maeve was very close to tears, overwhelmed by the ceremony
and what MacCuill had done. He was now like her knight. How
strange all of this was. It felt like a dream, but then again it seemed too
real to be a dream.*

MacCuill turned toward her. "It is time for us to go."

*Maeve looked around at all the shining faces, the feeling of love
and joy here. She didn't want to leave. They smiled, calling out a word
that she couldn't understand. She put her hands in prayer position and
bowed her head before she turned to follow MacCuill.*

*"What were they saying at the end?" she asked, as they headed up
the tunnel.*

*"'Taing', it means gratitude. They were thanking you for what
they know you will accomplish here."*

*Maeve's face went hot. This was not fair to expect of her. How
could she possibly...?*

*MacCuill's hand came down on her shoulder, startling her. "Do not
think about it, just let it all be. You will be ready when the time comes,
rest assured."*

*Outside, the sky had turned the color of iron. The clouds rolled and
bumped as a storm approached from the north, cold wind catching at
their hair and clothes.*

*MacCuill glanced from left to right, his thick eyebrows pulled to-
gether in concentration. He pulled his billowing wool robe around himself, and then touched Maeve on the shoulder. Maeve kept her eyes open*

this time, watching as their surroundings went out of focus and disappeared. Swirling colors were all around her and then they were back in front of the fire inside Finna's cottage.

"I can't believe we weren't really there!"

"Oh, we were there all right."

"But not really there, more like a facsimile."

"A what?"

"You know, a fax, a copy of something."

"I have not heard that word but I assure you we were not copies just now. We moved through the dreamtime, a different reality."

Maeve thought about everything she had seen and felt. A new kind of knowing was making its way into her psyche, coming from...she didn't know where it was coming from, she just felt it. Kind of like when her father put the dried flowers in her room and she knew that lavender was for luck and yarrow was for healing. According to Gertrude she had a lot of knowledge buried in her subconscious mind. And now all these new revelations about the moonstone and the prophecy—this entire experience reminded her of some sci-fi thriller in which she was a leading character.

"Soon after the solstice celebration we should consider beginning our journey."

Maeve frowned, staring at the druid. She thought of her boyfriend at home, the plans they had made for him to be here in Scotland for the New Year. "But Harold arrives on the thirty-first and we're only staying for a week after that. We're flying back home on the eighth." Maeve glanced toward her mother. "I forgot to ask if it was all right for Harold to stay here. He told me to get him a hotel room but..."

"Of course he's welcome here, Maeve."

Maeve noted her mother's serious tone and expression. She glanced toward MacCuill, who stood with arms folded, watching her.

"I thought you understood," he said.

Something heavy seemed to be pressing against her chest. She couldn't catch her breath.

"Think, Maeve. What have you been doing today?" Finna's voice was soft but there was steel beneath the words.

"We went to the Otherworld. Yes, I got that. I do understand, at least more than I did, but I can't go anywhere and help anyone now. How am I supposed to know what to do? Maybe after a few months of training or in the spring...or I don't know...I can't imagine ever being ready for this!" She looked from one to the other, trying to discern some softness or the hint of a smile. Tears pressed against her eyelids as the image of the Crion came before her mind's eye. They were counting on her.

"There is no time to waste."

When MacCuill moved toward her she backed away, hitting the chair behind her and knocking it over. "But what about Harold?" she cried.

"Maybe ye should take a walk. I think the fresh air will help clear your head."

Although Finna said this gently enough, sobs bubbled up before Maeve could stop them. Tears were already running down her cheeks as she grabbed her coat. She opened the door so violently that it slammed against the wall.

As the door was closed behind her, Maeve heard her mother's voice through the open kitchen window. "This is too much too soon. She's nae ready."

"She *is* ready, Finna. I have great faith in her and you should too."

"But she's just a green girl! What does she know of this danger? Her life has been so sheltered, ye said so yourself. And she has no idea what she's up against!"

"I was concerned as well but she has connected with that part of her that knows. Her arrival at this time was no coincidence."

There was silence and Maeve held her breath. When Finna spoke again her voice was more distant, as though she had moved away from the window.

"She's my dear daughter and I dinna want to lose her again just as we've found each other. And MacCuill, how will ye break it to her what's at stake? Brandubh and his mother want to..."

"You will not lose her, Finna. This is her destiny. You have known this was coming for all these many years. Catriona will explain things to Maeve—you know your mother's special abilities in that department." MacCuill chuckled. "And she's met the Crion and Amuigh now and seen how things are."

"Is it possible? I mean will this modern, unschooled girl be able to fulfill the prophecy?"

"She's hardly unschooled, Finna. These past months have brought an understanding in her that I can see very clearly."

"But if she...I mean..."

"Then all will be lost."

In the silence that followed, Maeve headed away from the house. *The prophecy.* Her mind reeled. This was not how she had pictured her reunion with her mother. More tears spilled over and trickled down her cheeks and she wiped them away with the back of her hand. Sitting down on a weathered cedar log she stared across the turbulent sea until her tears dried and her heartbeat returned to normal, but her mind was still a whirl of contradicting thoughts and emotions. She breathed deeply, taking in the fresh salt-tinged air, trying to remember the little bit of meditation she had learned during her yoga class. What had she gotten herself into?

The light was fading fast by the time Maeve started toward the house. The temperature had dropped and she felt chilled to the marrow of her soul as she came up the path. Most of the snow had melted in the sun, leaving wet patches here and there that were becoming icy. The little cottage was surrounded with a pale rose aura; each branch of the bare bushes outside the front door looked as though they were on fire. She turned, wondering if this was some trick of the light, but the sun had already dipped below the horizon.

As she reached for the handle, the door opened abruptly, revealing Finna's worried face. Her mother held her arms out and Maeve walked into her embrace. It was a long moment before they released one another.

Chapter

3

"'**T**is another lovely sunny day, what would ye think about walkin' into Bailemuir to visit your grandmother Rose?"

Maeve looked up from her large mug of coffee. "When is Catriona arriving?"

"Today but not until late afternoon. We'll be back by then. And MacCuill will be here to greet her."

When Maeve turned toward the druid he was busy eating his oatmeal as if nothing out of the ordinary had transpired. The day before had been deeply disturbing, last night's sleep filled with nightmares that woke her nearly every hour—cold, bleak landscapes covered with ice lay all around her and she was paralyzed with indecision about which way to go.

So far this morning nothing had been said about the prophecy or her part in it. MacCuill had appeared in the kitchen from wherever he had spent the night, acting like a kindly grandfather, making Maeve wonder if she had imagined it all. But she knew deep inside that she had not.

The two women left the house before the sun had reached the tops of the trees, hiking up the rocky trail away from the beach. From the ridge they turned to wave to MacCuill who watched them from the doorway, and then Finna led the way into the trees, walking quickly through the deep snow. Maeve stumbled as she ran to catch up, her heavy sweater already too hot.

"Why didn't take the road?" Maeve turned her gaze to the right, looking down on the flat snow-free driveway. She pulled off her sweater and tied it around her waist.

"This path is shorter and much more beautiful. And I have some things to tell ye that are better spoken around the trees."

Spoken around the trees? When Maeve glanced her way, Finna was concentrating on the path. After they crossed a small bridge, Maeve turned to see the sun peeking over the treetops, shining down on the thick thatch roof of Finna's cottage. A tendril of smoke emerged from the chimney, dark against the muted morning light. Still in shadow, the ocean looked opaque, a flat sheen of silver. The sound of the waves was muffled, a dull rhythmic thump; wind moved lightly through the branches of the conifers, making them sway. The pake sky made shifting puzzle shapes where it jig-sawed through the dark canopy.

Today seemed like a normal day, walking into town with her mother to visit her grandmother. "What a lovely day!" she cried, reaching to pull her mother into a hug.

Finna laughed. "Aye, Maeve, especially with ye here with me."

But her light-heartedness disappeared when Finna began to talk in low tones. What her mother said made the hair on the back of her neck stand up.

"Maeve, ye must ken the magnitude of what lies afore ye.
Ye've met the Crion and seen the Amuigh now, but there are
many things about the Otherworld that ye do not ken. 'Tis
nothing like this world. I wish ye could have come here when
ye were younger so that ye could have learned about it all before
ye had to face the perils of the place. I have nae been back since
your birth. 'Twas once most beautiful, but now..." Finna shook
her head. "There are forces at work there that will pull at ye, try
to make ye do things that will hurt ye. The winds have a mind
of their own and they can suck your thoughts right out of ye,
leave ye helpless as a newborn babe."

"But..."

Finna held up her hand. "MacCuill will explain it all and
train your mind a bit before ye go, but ye have to have your wits
about ye at all times. I dinna wish to scare ye, but ye must be
prepared."

It was close to an hour before they reached the end of the
path. The village of Bailemuir spread out below them, its winding cobbled streets somehow reassuring. There had been no further discussion of the Otherworld, but Maeve had not been able
to stop thinking about her mother's words of warning. At street
level, they followed the curve of the road until it opened out,
revealing houses with small front gardens blanketed in white.
Maeve's heartbeat quickened when she recognized the house
from the photo her grandmother Rose had sent her: white pick-
et fence, rose bushes that had been full of blooms, now trimmed
back and bare. Snow covered the small front garden that had
been lush and green in summer.

"That's the one," Maeve said with assurance. I recognize it."

Finna nodded and opened the gate, going ahead of her up the shoveled flagstone path. "Maeve, please dinna mention our talk to your grandmother. 'Twould only worry her."

Finna lifted the brass knocker and let it fall. A moment later the door opened, revealing a hollow-cheeked gray-haired woman. Maeve recognized the narrow nose and shape of the mouth so similar to her father's. And her grandmother's eyes were the same shade of pale blue. Over her collared shirt, Rose wore a threadbare gray sweater that she pulled around herself defensively.

"Finna, my dear! I didna expect ye!" she cried.

"Rose, look who I've brought with me." Finna stepped to the side, allowing Maeve to come closer.

"Maeve?" The older woman's eyes filled with tears as she reached to draw Maeve into a warm embrace. She smelled like mothballs mixed with the scent of faded roses. "I canna believe it. I didna ken if I would ever meet ye. Please come in out of the cold," she invited, standing back to let them pass.

They entered a narrow hall with closed doors on both sides, steep stairs leading up to a second story. Rose gestured to the right. "Make yourselves comfortable in the livin' room. I'll just go prepare the tea." She disappeared through the door on the other side, closing it after her.

Finna led the way into a room filled to overflowing with heavy furniture and knick-knacks. It had a musty smell, as though it had been closed up for too long. The upholstered chairs and couch had worn through to the stuffing in some places, the crocheted antimacassars doing little to cheer the place up.

Framed photos sat on every available surface and Maeve walked to the various tables to examine them. Against the wall, a gate-legged table held a large photo of Alex and Finna. Inside the sterling silver frame Finna gazed at Alex, her expression filled with love. And the rapt look in her father's eyes said that the sun rose and set in this woman. Maeve felt a twinge of sadness as she replaced the photo carefully.

Rose emerged through the doorway carrying the tea tray. "I did send ye some photos, I hope?" she asked, placing the tray on the coffee table.

"Yes. Thank you. Some of them seemed like they were taken around the same time as these," she said, pointing to several pictures of her as a baby.

"Those were taken right after ye were born and before Alex moved out."

"He didn't leave for the States until I was three, right?"

"I meant when he…" Rose glanced at Finna.

"'Tis fine, Rose. I have nae secrets. Maeve understands that we lived separately for some time."

Rose sighed, letting her shoulders sag. She shook her head, her eyes sad as though revisiting the past was a burden that she had to bear. "Alex could go on the bash but his Da—well. Alex got the bree o't. Malcolm could tak a guid bucket and when he did he was mean. I dinna like to speak ill of the dead but he beat Alex and hit me more times than I wish to remember."

Maeve recoiled. "I never knew that! Dad has never mentioned anything about his father." Or his life here, she thought angrily. Why hadn't she thought to ask about her grandparents? Maybe she had and maybe he had told her something early on—some other lie that had taken root in her subconscious.

"That does nae surprise me. He wouldna wish to revisit that time in his life. My poor Malcolm's Da was a laird but Malcolm was the shakkins o' the poke."

Bewildered, Maeve turned toward Finna.

"That means the last born, the son who inherits nothing. Go on Rose."

"Malcolm couldna abide it, made himself sick with wantin' what his brothers had, 'twas why he died so young—that and the drink. Ah'm certain Alex took his Da's frustration on himself. He tried, Alex did, but he couldna keep himself away from the pub. I had hoped with your birth, Maeve, but..." Rose looked into the distance for a moment. "Well. Shall we speak of more pleasant things?"

"You do know that Dad's in AA now," Maeve said, reaching for the teacup Rose handed her.

Rose smiled. "Aye. He's told me as much. I pray for my son near every day. And to look at ye here Maeve, 'tis obvious he's been a good Da to ye." Rose reached across the table to grasp Maeve's hand. "Ye are a lovely and well-mannered lass."

"These are so pretty!" Maeve said, trying to steer the subject away from herself. She held up the porcelain cup, examining the interwoven design of roses and vines, a pattern very similar to Harold's dishes.

"I inherited the set from my mither who inherited them from your great-grandmither, Fiona. They will go to ye, Maeve, when I die."

Maeve was unsure how to respond and felt odd at the idea of inheriting anything from a grandmother whom she had only just met. "I'm overwhelmed, Rose," she managed to mumble.

Rose gazed at her fondly. "Well, dear one, ye are my only granddaughter, ye ken."

"Is that you?" Maeve pointed to a large portrait above the fireplace.

"Yur dear mother painted that when I was a lot younger."

Rose looked lovely, seated in a large wicker chair, her shoulders covered with an embroidered maroon silk shawl over a dark dress. The low-cut front showed off the pale skin of her collarbones and décolletage, her soft blue eyes fixed on some point in the middle distance.

"It's beautiful. You're beautiful," she added, her gaze going to the older woman. Compared to the woman in the paiting, Rose looked drained now, like another person, and it wasn't just her age.

"'Twas the artist who made it so."

"Nae Rose, I only painted what I saw."

Rose looked embarrassed, her pale hand fluttering to her neck to straighten her collar. "Maeve do ye have the latest paintin' your mother did? The bonnie lass lookin' like yourself in medieval claise?"

"Do you mean the one with the willow tree?"

Rose nodded. "Your Da sent me a recent picture of ye, ye ken, and I gave it to your mother."

"I wondered how she could do such an amazing likeness."

"Aye. 'Tis a true work of art. I hope the gallery didna sell that one."

"Don't worry, there was no way I was going to let that one go. It's hanging in my bedroom at home." Maeve thought about all her weird experiences with that painting: the wolves disappearing out of the canvas and then re-appearing the next day; a necklace suddenly hanging around the figure's neck where it hadn't been the day before; and of course her dream of following Marmalade the cat inside the painting—her first experience with the Otherworld, she realized with a jolt.

"Enough about my paintings," Finna said, raising her hands in protest. "I have more pressing things on my mind. I need to go into town and do a wee bit of shoppin' for the solstice celebration. Could I leave Maeve here for an hour or so?"

"I would be delighted! I hope 'tis all right with ye, Maeve," Rose added, with a worried frown.

"Of course, Rose. I've been looking forward to meeting you for a long time."

"Ye can call me Nanna, Maeve. Take all the time ye need, Finna."

"I'll see you at the back o' thrie," Finna said, opening the door.

45

Finna arrived at midafternoon, emerging through the door carrying a basket full of various jars, a loaf of bread, butter, some leeks and a bag of flour. "If we dinna want to be walkin' in the dark we best be on our way."

Maeve rose from the couch and bent to hug her grandmother. "I'm sure I'll see you again soon."

"I certainly hope so, Maeve. 'Tis been an unexpected delight."

Rose's eyes filled with tears giving Maeve an acute understanding of how lonely she was.

Walking down the street a few minutes later, Maeve turned toward Finna. "What happened to her? I mean the painting you did wasn't that long ago, was it? She looks so much older now."

Finna frowned and shook her head. "At first I blamed it on Alex leavin' Scotland but this decline is more recent. I asked her if she had been to the doctor and she said, yes, that her check-up was fine." Finna stopped to face Maeve. "She told me she's been goin' to church, the little Catholic chapel in Bailemuir, to pray she would meet ye before she dies. My first thought was, good, 'tis always helpful to sit in a sacred place and pray. But then she told me she's been going to confession, that she really liked the parish priest who was so full of good advice. When I asked her to describe him..." Finna stopped speaking and looked away.

"It's Brandubh, isn't it? Brandubh has been doing something to her." Maeve's insides felt cold, icy with anger.

"In the past two years Rose has gone from a vibrant woman to withered and old. And aye, the priest she described sounded very much like Brandubh. At the time I dismissed it, since I was sure Brandubh was livin' in the Otherworld. But now I realize he comes and goes, doin' goddess knows what on his trips here."

"Do you think it's possible that Brandubh found out where we lived from Rose? He just showed up, walked into Dad's house in Halston and asked all sorts of questions. And he also found his way to the gallery in Milltown. I didn't recognize him at the time."

Finna's lips pressed together. "If Brandubh was her confessor, aye, I'm sure of it. Things said in the privacy of the confessional are not to be used, but in this case..." Finna looked down. "For years I've been blamin' Alex for Rose's decline...I wish I could tell him how sorry I am."

"Dad hasn't exactly been the model son though, has he? As far as I can tell he's neglected Rose. He hasn't even written."

Finna sighed. "I still feel badly that he's become my scapegoat. He's had his own reasons for how he's behaved and since I havna spoken to him in over twenty years, I dinna ken what those reasons might be. He did seem to have an odd attitude about his mother, maybe because of how she doted on him. When your father and I lived together in town before ye were born, Rose came by every day. I think it embarrassed him and at times put him in a mood that I can only describe as rageful. I think his drinking was more to do with Rose than with Malcolm, who died when Alex was fifteen. Rose means well—she's just one of those mothers who canna let go."

There was silence for a few moments as they walked down the road side-by-side. "Mother, you haven't explained why my whereabouts had to be kept secret—why you sent me away."

Finna opened her mouth, a look of surprise on her face. "I'm amazed ye would ask such a question after the past couple of days. Brandubh knows all about the prophecy, Maeve. If I had kept ye here with me he would have found ye before ye could fight him off. Catriona and I placed stones around the cottage when ye were a wee bairn to ward him off, but by the time ye were three the magic was broken. He would have killed ye."

Maeve felt a sudden sharp pain in her chest. A prophecy, destiny—all of it seemed absurd. Brandubh was certainly corrupt, but killing a child of three? That sounded more like a psychopath.

After they climbed the ridge, Maeve turned back for one last view of the village below. It was picturesque with the snow and the winding cobbled streets. Her mind spun in circles, far away from what her eyes were focused on.

"'Tis a sweet little town. Next time I'll make sure to take ye shopping with me. We'll need to stock up for your upcoming trip to the Otherworld with MacCuill."

The assuredness with which Finna said this set Maeve's teeth on edge, making her blurted answer sharp. "If there is to be a trip, it can't happen now. Harold will be here in just over a week and we have tickets to go home on the eighth. I'm sure I mentioned this to you several times already."

Finna gazed at her without speaking for several long moments. When she spoke her tone was soft as though she recognized Maeve's distress. "I dinna think ye can put it off, there are too many lives hanging in the balance. Ye do know enough now to realize this?"

"But how can it matter? I mean, what's a month or two in the scheme of things? And why did you say 'with MacCuill'? Aren't you planning to take me like your mother did with you?"

"This trip is very different from the one I made. Mine was all about the child I carried and the blessing ceremony. Ye have been named in a prophecy."

Maeve opened her mouth, words tumbling out before she could stop them. "I'm not sure I believe any of this—it's just too far-fetched."

Finna's eyes narrowed. "So you're callin' me a liar?"

"No...not really...but can you prove any of it?"

Finna opened her mouth and closed it. She shook her head and moved quickly away, lengthening the distance between them.

"Wait, Mother! I can't go that fast."

Finna turned. "I had hoped ye understood the severity of the situation, 'tis why I spoke with ye on the way to town. MacCuill has been insisting that you're ready but ye have nae understood anythin' we've said. Maybe Catriona will have some influence on ye."

When Maeve met Finna's annoyed gaze, she felt chastised and embarrassed. She followed her mother down the path again, her mind on the dreams of the past few months that seemed almost clairvoyant after being in the Otherworld with MacCuill. And what about the wolf outside her apartment she had locked eyes with and felt like she knew? There were no wolves anywhere close to the city of Milltown. None of her recent experiences could be explained rationally.

It seemed impossible that she was on some sort of predestined path, but inside a little voice murmured, 'you know it's true.' And now her mother, who she just reconnected with, was angry with her. And what about Harold? Would they be able to have a life together if she was really meant to do this...this saving of the Otherworld? She had a sickening thought of being lost in some dark and terrible place and never finding her way home.

It had begun to snow again and she looked up to see the small swirling flakes being blown around by the wind. She felt just like the snow, blown in every direction with no will of her own.

The two women walked in silence, Finna slightly ahead. When they reached the end of the trail above the cottage, they paused, gazing down at the scene below. The druid was standing in front of an enormous pile of wood and beside him was a hatless, gray-haired woman dressed in a dark cloak. They were deep in conversation, seemingly oblivious of the thick snow falling all around them.

Maeve grabbed Finna's arm before her mother started down the path. "Mother, I don't like you being angry with me. I don't even know you yet, nor you me, and yet I'm supposed to accept that I've been named in a prophecy and that I'm supposed to accomplish…what? Even if I accept this, I need a lot more explanation and time to think about it all, not to mention some training." She didn't want to cry but tears trickled down her cheeks.

Finna grasped her hand, turning to face her. "I'm sorry, Maeve. This is too much for ye to take in so quickly. I said as much to MacCuill but he thought he could whisk ye into the dreamtime and circumvent your training. I think his plan has backfired. I'm sorry I was frustrated earlier; I'm not sure what got into me, possibly nervous anticipation about Catriona arriving. She can be trying, my mother."

"In what way?"

"She always seems to have the last word and she's very sure of herself. She can make me feel like an inept child."

"Maybe it's just a mother-daughter thing."

Finna laughed. "Ye may be right about that. Come along, Maeve, 'tis time to meet your other grandmother." Finna took off down the hill at a run, her basket swinging. Maeve followed at a distance, not at all sure she was ready to meet the formidable Catriona.

Maeve watched the two women greet one another, heard Finna's laughter and Catriona's foreign sounding chatter. A moment later Catriona waved in her direction, gesturing for her to come down. Maeve waved back, wondering how she was going to make it through the next few days. What she needed was time to process this new role she seemed to have fallen into, but every reluctant step brought her closer to the intimate group on the beach. She had never felt more like an outsider as she walked toward the three of them. Drawing closer she noticed that the snow, which had already soaked her hat and her sweater, fell all around Catriona but did not land on her.

"Maeve!" Catriona hurried toward her with arms out-stretched. Maeve let herself be hugged by the older woman. When they pulled apart, Catriona grasped her by the forearms, her green gaze searching Maeve's features. "Ye are the perfect image of myself when I was your age! Do ye see it, MacCuill?"

MacCuill nodded, running his fingers through his wet beard. "Variations on a theme, you three," he said, and then put his head back and laughed.

Maeve smiled and nodded, at a loss for words, but Catriona paid no attention, linking arms with her and chattering excitedly. When MacCuill led the way to the cottage, they followed, waiting while he opened the door. Inside, Maeve pulled off her hat and ran her fingers through her curls, untangling the ends.

"My hair was once that exact russet color." Catriona wound her fingers through her long gray tangle, pulling it away from her face. "Tis faded now," she added, her mouth in a moue. She removed her cloak and hung it on the coat hook by the door. Maeve glanced at her belted wool tunic, the high boots of deer-skin that hugged her shapely calves. Despite the gray hair, she hardly looked fifty, much less sixty years old.

"Ach, 'tis lovely to be here, Finna. I love this time o' year and the celebrations! And now," she turned to gaze at Maeve, "with my granddaughter here, 'tis better than ever."

Maeve was beginning to feel uncomfortable under the older woman's scrutiny and asked Finna if she could help in the kitchen.

"Visit with your grandmother, I'll just tend the fire," Finna answered, kneeling to add another log. "That should do for a while. It feels good to get out of the cold. MacCuill, could ye please put the kettle on?"

"The tea's steeping. It should be near ready."

Moments later he brought over four mugs, handing them around and then sitting agilely on the floor next to Catriona.

Catriona leaned toward Maeve. "Seanamhair is Gaelic for grandmother but the informal is Mamo."

"Shannuh-ver," Maeve intoned, trying out the foreign word. "I think I'll go with Mamo. So, Mamo, how far away do you live?"

"Many a days walk. 'Tis braw for herb gathering, although now things are changing…" Her gaze went into the distance for a moment before she turned back with a smile that seemed forced. "Are ye interested in herbology, Maeve?"

"Funny you should ask since I just bought a really good book called, 'The Book of Herbal Wisdom.' Do you know it?"

"Nae, but maybe I can add a bit of my own knowledge. I've studied herbs since I was a wee bairn."

Catriona proceeded to describe herbs to treat wounds and broken bones, tree bark for fevers and stomach ailments, herbs to use for stamina and sleep and many others. Maeve tried to keep the information straight but it was a lot to take in. "I think I need a notebook."

"Dinna worry Maeve, ye will remember. All the women in our line have special abilities in the healing arts."

That night MacCuill took over Maeve's room and Catriona and Finna shared the double bed. A cot had been produced and Maeve lay a few feet away listening to the rhythmic breathing of her mother and grandmother. This evening Catriona had talked about past trips to the Glass Mountain, stories that sounded made up but that Maeve now knew had to be true. Catriona had mentioned gods and goddesses she and Finna had encountered, as well as confrontations with mysterious sentient winds and other fantastic things. Her grandmother made it sound like a lark but when Maeve glanced at her mother, Finna's expression had been somber.

A pang of longing went through her as she thought of Harold. At this moment she felt estranged from this group, freaked out by all the things she'd been told. She could use the comfort of someone she knew and trusted. There were still ten long days until his arrival. She needed to get in touch to verify his plans as well as call her father whom she had completely forgotten to contact. He was probably mad at her by now, either that or worried. Maybe after the solstice she could drive the little mini into town and use a phone box. No one here seemed to have a cell phone.

As night deepened she heard the low ping-pong sound of screech owls, a pair calling back and forth. Moonlight made a bright patch on the floor. Her thoughts began to drift...

She wasn't sure if she was awake or asleep as she got out of bed, walked to the front door, opened it and went outside. The slight breeze felt balmy on her skin. As she walked down the hill toward the water, her pajama bottoms dragged through the snow. The reflected moon made undulating lines of light in the water as waves coursed gently in and out. The moon seemed impossibly close, giving her the sense that she was drifting upwards through the warm air. Long smoke-like filaments of light waved toward her as the bright orb moved slowly toward the horizon, the tendrils wrapping around and through her, suffusing her with energy. She moved into the sea, walking further and further out until her feet no longer touched the bottom. Floating on her back, she let the waves rock her as though she was a baby in a cradle. Her arms were wide, embracing the moonlight, hearing the silent message it sent deep inside. An enormous owl flew soundlessly across the sky, blocking the moonlight for a moment before disappearing into the darkness.

When Maeve woke, Finna and Catriona were already busy in the kitchen. There was no sign of MacCuill and the door to the other bedroom was open so she went in to get dressed. Pulling off her pajama bottoms she was surprised to see damp sand clinging to them. Her dream came flooding back and with it a momentary uneasiness. The moon…before she could recall anything else she heard her mother calling her.

"I'll be right out!"

She changed quickly, noticing that the bed was neatly made, MacCuill's walking stick propped in the corner. This one had a wolf's head carved into the top. Without bothering to comb through her tangled hair, she pulled it back, securing it with a scrunchy and then hurried into the other room.

Catriona looked up from where she was rolling out dough. "A bheil an t-acras ort?"

It wasn't until after Maeve shook her head, no, that she realized she understood the Gaelic words asking if she was hungry.

Catriona smiled, watching her for a moment. Turning back to the counter, she pushed her hair away from her rosy face, leaving a smudge of flour on her forehead.

"Come have some coffee at least," Finna urged, gesturing to the chair next to where she sat. "There's a lot to get done today."

Maeve ran her hand across her face, feeling the salty film. "I really need a shower."

"Aye, of course ye would." Finna pushed her chair back. "Come, I'll show ye the set-up."

Finna led the way out the door and turned right. Before she reached the corner of the cottage, she opened an inconspicuous door leading into a narrow room under the eaves. Several skylights had been placed at intervals, providing the only light. Shelves were filled with gardening tools, potting soil, clay pots, pruning shears and trowels. Canvases of different sizes leaned against the wall amid jars of brushes, turpentine and assorted oil paints. At the far end a showerhead jutted over a small metal tub with a series of handles and valves below it.

"Two pots of water is all ye need—one hot and one cold, but the water grows cold fast, so be quick about it. In the warm months I have gravity feed from the spring at the top of the hill and ye can shower, but this time o' year 'tis closed to protect the pipes from freezin."

After filling the tub Maeve climbed in, marveling at Finna's ability to deal with the rustic living conditions. Finna's warnings had been correct, the water turning cool before she finished rinsing the shampoo out of her hair. Five minutes later she had dressed and was heading outside. Entering the cottage she realized the druid was still conspicuously absent. "Where's MacCuill?" she asked, pulling the towel off her hair.

Catriona looked up from a pile of half-peeled apples. "He's outside doing some more preparations for tonight. I think he wants it to be a surprise."

Finna was at the sink where a stack of dirty dishes had accumulated. Maeve watched in amazement as she worked the hand pump adding hot water from the kettle to fill up the sink. Every task was complicated here.

After washing a few dishes Finna turned, wiping her hands on her apron. "To fill ye in on the history of this day, 'tis ten years we've been holdin' it here. I'm glad of it since I didna attend before that—I had to make due with Catriona's accounts and our own small celebrations the day after."

"Why didn't you go?"

Finna shook her head, her glance going toward her mother.

Catriona smiled at her daughter and then addressed Maeve. "Finna is a homebody. If I wish to see her I ken I must travel here. And in addition Brandubh has been an issue. He has made it quite impossible to gather at the stone circle—he detests the pagan festivals, thinks they are blasphemous. Ye will meet the ones who come here on the solstice but most have given up the rituals that always marked their year."

"I don't know much about the Celtic holidays. Dad never mentioned it."

Catriona came over with a big mug of coffee and a hunk of bread and butter and put it on the low table next to Maeve and then sat down cross-legged on the floor. "It seems there is much for ye to learn. Where should I start?"

"Why did you leave your daughter with Angus?" Maeve blurted out before she could stop herself.

Catriona laughed and then turned to gaze at Finna. "To be quite honest I just couldn't imagine bringing up a child."

"I wouldn't have thought ye'd be afraid of anything," Finna exclaimed, staring at her mother with a surprised expression.

Catriona seemed almost embarrassed for a moment her, lips pressed together. "That trip your mathair and I made when she was barely eighteen was an eye opener for both of us. Finna was so young and naïve. I'm afraid my behavior shocked her more than once."

"Tell me," Maeve said eagerly. She picked up the fresh bread and took a bite.

"Do ye mind, Finna?"

Finna shook her head, but the expression on her face said something different.. "I want Maeve to understand the past. It connects us to now and what is to come."

"Remember Duncan?" Catriona twisted to look at Finna who was taking something out of the refrigerator.

"Of course, how could I forget him? Have ye seen him recently?"

Catriona shook her head, and then addressed Maeve, her gaze intent. "Duncan was one of my lovers. We met when I was seventeen. When Finna and I traveled through his village of Tiadhan he offered to put us up for the night. We hadn't seen each other for a long time and so we weren't as discreet as we should have been. But I have to say in our defense that Finna was very prudish back then and we both thought she was asleep in the other room." She laughed, gazing in Finna's direction.

"Mother, weren't you married at the time?"

"Aye, Maeve, but I had been sheltered, ye see—brought up by a man and then married to another without livin' on my own

56

at all. Alex and I...well let's just say, since we're givin' away secrets, that my understandin' of what goes on between a man and woman was less than complete."

"But you were pregnant..."

"Aye." Finna didn't say anything more, turning toward her mother.

Catriona chuckled to herself, breaking the tension. "That man brought out the hedonist in me. He loved to dance. Remember, Finna?" As she spoke, Catriona stood and began to move about the room doing a sort of waltz step, her arms held out as though clutching another person. Her full skirt flowed around her calves as she whirled.

Finna grinned. "The two o' ye were waltzin' all over the square."

Maeve tried to imagine the scene—her mother, impossibly young, inexperienced and pregnant with her, and wild Catriona, beautiful and full of life. Her grandmother would have been around the same age Finna was now. Maeve looked toward her mother whose face had lit up as she watched Catriona's antics.

"I hope he's all right," Catriona murmured, coming to a stop. "'Tis many years since I've laid my eyes on the man."

"So tell me more, Mamo. This is getting interesting."

"Mother," Finna's voice cut in sharply. "I think we need to curtail the musings from the past now and focus on Maeve."

Catriona turned in surprise, seeming taken aback. "I suppose it does nae good to relive the past now, does it?"

"No, and it wasn't the lark for me that it was for you."

Catriona poured herself coffee from the carafe. "It was nae such a lark for me either, Finna. I spent most of my time worryin' about ye and feelin' shame at what I'd done."

Maeve thought about all the parallels—the lies her father had told, his reluctance to reveal the real truth.

"I've loved Eron since I was fifteen," Catriona continued. "I would never have had a child with him if it hadna been so— there are many herbs to prevent that."

"Mother, Maeve needs to hear the prophecy." Finna looked angry now, a frown of annoyance between her brows.

At that moment the door opened and MacCuill appeared. "What do we have here?" he asked, looking curiously at the three silent women.

"I'm about to recite the prophecy," Catriona answered like a reprimanded child.

MacCuill nodded, settling into a chair as Catriona stared into the distance. "This is the way the original went," she said, folding her hands in front of her before she began to recite the ancient text.

> "It has been foretold and will come to pass
> in the dawn of the darkest year, that the
> girl-child, born of Brigid, will return to the
> Otherworld. She will be joined by many, but
> only one of noble birth shall stand by her
> side—part of a new life.
> It will be at the time of the wolf moon,
> when the full moon rises twice and the wa-
> ters surge in anger and the earth trembles.
> She will ride the wild wolf and carry the
> staff of justice. With eyes the color of spring
> she will be known to all as Saille, the willow,
> and her fiery hair will be her flag of truth.
> Her strength will be tested against the sor-
> cery of the dark man, her power from the
> tree that bends but does not break. If she
> accomplishes the task set before her, this
> world will again fill with light, restoring
> balance. If she should fail, the darkness shall

spread throughout this world and into the
next, plunging all into darkness."

All of a sudden Maeve was shaking, her earlier calm completely gone. "Who exactly is this Brigid? Seems like it would
say 'child of Finna', if it really referred to me. There are lots of
women with red hair and green eyes—you could have been the
one," she added, pointing toward Catriona.

Catriona shook her head dismissively. "Brigid is our ancestor, the first woman of our line to have her unborn child blessed
at the Glass Mountain. I suppose you're right in the sense that
we are all 'born of Brigid', since we are in the same family, but
there's more to the connection between you and Brigid."

"Brigid, our ancestor, was named for the goddess of fire,"
Finna added. "Because of the prophecy I wanted to name ye
Brigid, but Alex balked at having his child named after the
first woman to use the moonstone. He hated that stone."
Finna's laugh sounded bitter. "The prophecy seems to point toward ye being a reincarnation of Brigid. In Gaelic Brigid means
'bright flame'. As a goddess she represents rebirth, fertility and
inspiration—'the fire of the soul'. Of course once the Christians
took over, they claimed her, turning her into a saint."

Reincarnation as well as gods and goddesses and alien beings—
was she supposed to accept what they said without question? "How
do you know all of this? I thought Brandubh was the main problem
but it sounds like this has been going on for centuries."

"Brigid mentions the prophecy in her writings. Before that
it was passed down by word of mouth."

"But you haven't said what was going on back then. What
was the original purpose of the blessing ceremony?"

"'Twas a way to protect our line knowin' 'twould be one
of our own who would save the Otherworld," Finna answered,
glancing toward her mother.

Catriona nodded. "Light and dark are both necessary for existence—just as night follows day and so on. For everything there is an opposite—hot and cold, sweet and sour, female and male. For many years there was no darkness in the Otherworld. It seemed a wondrous place with everything growing and moving toward the light, but what no one realized was the dark had been buried. If we refuse to own the shadow inside each and every one of us it *will* be projected out, onto someone or something else. This is what causes wars. It leads to religious persecution. 'Tis the reason Brandubh and the Oillteil were able to take over so easily. They filled the void. The balance was already off but now it has shifted so far the other way that it threatens to annihilate the entire place."

"Can I read the journals? I would love to know what my multiple great-grandmothers had to say."

"I have them in safe keeping," Catriona replied. "As ye can imagine they are very fragile."

During the lengthy silence that followed, Maeve wondered if the prophecy was actually written down anywhere—Catriona had a funny look on her face when Maeve asked about the journals. Her mind went to the trip to the Crion tunnels, and the way the Crion had greeted her—they knew all about the prophecy. "What does the 'wolf moon' refer to?"

"The wolf moon is about protection and confidence," MacCuill answered. "It is a strong portent for good. And remember also that the prophecy mentions 'many'—you will not be alone. You must keep our trip to the Crion village in your mind."

"You don't have to remind me of that," Maeve muttered, as a heavy feeling descended onto her shoulders. Those people seemed so helpless and fragile. There was no way they could fight a war.

"To answer your first question, Maeve," Catriona added, "'tis not only the mention of the red hair and green eyes, 'tis also timing. This year is the darkest yet and this coming January has two full moons. This is a very rare occurrence."

"Your seanamhair has many gifts, one of which is second sight," MacCuill added.

"So, Mamo, are you a witch like my father told me?"

Catriona laughed. "I have visions, things that have not yet occurred. I suppose ye might call it clairvoyance if ye wish to assign a name to it."

"So what's going to happen? Will I save the Otherworld?" Maeve joked, trying to lighten the mood.

There was a long uncomfortable silence and then Catriona said, "That I cannot see."

Maeve watched her grandmother, waiting for more, but Catriona only stared into the distance, a slight frown furrowing her brow.

"Tell us what other experiences you've had these past months, Maeve—aside from the ravens and the dreams," MacCuil asked a moment later.

Maeve's mind cascaded back to all the odd happenings of the past month. Where to begin? "Something happened regarding the 'Saille' painting a few days before I left for Scotland." She looked down at her hands, surprised to see them twisted together. When she looked up again MacCuill was watching her, a questioning expression in his eyes. "The wolves disappeared."

"Are ye sure about that?" Finna asked.

When Finna glanced toward MacCuill, Maeve noticed the knowing smile that curved at the corners of his mouth. "They were definitely gone," Maeve answered. "I checked carefully under the light because it freaked me out so much. But the next morning they were back."

"Possibly they had other business to attend to," Catriona muttered.

Maeve stared at her grandmother. "Other business?"

Catriona shrugged. "It seems as though those wolves are more than oil paint. Ask your mother. She's the one who painted it." Catriona laughed. "Finna is always saying how the psychic abilities skipped a generation."

"I had nothing to do with that painting other than putting oil to canvas. I painted it because my spirit guides told me to."

"The spirit was able to come through ye because of your open heart, Finna," Catriona said, placing an arm around her daughter's shoulder. "And ye, Maeve," she continued, "you're getting in touch with your deeper knowing. Your gifts will be far greater than mine."

Maeve shook her head.

"Dinna doubt yourself, child. I can see it beneath the surface."

Maeve laughed. "What does this new me look like?"

"'Tis nae physical, 'tis more an internal shift. Do ye nae feel it?"

"All I feel is nervous." The words were automatic, a quick response to the question, but as Maeve took a look inside, she felt the steadiness of her heartbeat, a calm feeling that had not been there the day before.

When Catriona laughed, Maeve was about to share her insight but another question popped up in her mind instead. "Mamo, what is going on with my great uncle? I understand the light and the dark thing, the shadow, but that doesn't explain the horror of what he's doing. Haven't you talked to him at all?"

Shifting emotions moved across Catriona's mobile face. It was a long moment before she responded. "He was corrupted when he was very small. Some say he didn't belong here, that his birth was an anomaly. Ye see there have only been girl children born in our line and never twins. When we were bairns our minds were linked—we were as close as two people can be. But then..." Catriona's eyes darkened, as though a shadow had come across her vision.

"MacCuill told me about the Oillteil. Is that who corrupted him?"

Catriona shook her head. "'Twas mainly Adair, our mother. My brother was vulnerable because of the darkness he carries within. There's a part of him that went into the priesthood for the right reasons but temptation was just too strong."

"But why? What was going on with Adair?"

"Adair has an evil inside her that is inexplicable. From the moment of our birth she rejected me and took Brandubh to her heart. She trained him in the dark arts, sorcery, turning the kind and loving part of him into something else. Because of her influence my brother has convinced himself that he's doing the right thing in bringing Christianity to the Otherworld but truly, 'tis all about his own power. He quotes the part of the Bible that speaks of dominion over the earth, that it's his duty to bring God to the, in his words, 'backward' people. He has twisted the goodness of the teachings to suit himself and what he wants. And 'tis all for the sake of money and power--the two strongest seducers in the world. With the help of the Oillteil and Adair, he's raping the land, taking things that dinna belong to him and selling them on the outside. 'Tis the worst sort of desecration."

Maeve waited to hear more but Catriona went into the kitchen. "Well then, I guess we better begin our preparations," she said, gulping down the rest of her coffee as though they had been discussing grocery prices. "Maeve, dear, would ye mind cutting some branches of holly? And some ivy and mistletoe as well---they all grow up the hill under the trees there. Holly is the sacred plant of protection and ivy represents life enduring and the mistletoe...well...it stands for fertility, among other things. Druids regard mistletoe as a magical plant—it has many healing qualities."

"Alban Arthan, the druid name for the winter solstice, is when we cut this sacred plant. The berries contain the sperm of the gods," MacCuill added, winking.

Maeve pulled on her jacket and left the house, welcoming the cold air. Catriona's stories plus the revelations about Brandubh and Adair had given her an unsettled feeling. It was hard to imagine anyone being like that. Arriving later with an armload of greenery, she had no memory of gathering it. When she came through the door, the two women and MacCuill were sitting at the table deep in conversation. MacCuill jumped up to help her with the prickly branches.

"Finna is the decorator so I'll let her figure out what to do with them," he said, placing them in piles on the counter.

"I'm making apple and mince pies, anyone want to join me?" Finna pushed back her chair and headed into the kitchen.

"I love making pies," Maeve offered. When she gazed his way, MacCuill smiled and then got up and left the house, letting in a blast of cold air before he closed the door.

"Good then. The dough for the second pie is cooling in the refrigerator. It needs to be rolled out. Can ye manage that?"

Maeve joined her mother, glad for something useful to do. She rolled out dough, placing it carefully into the festive crockery pie dish Finna produced. When she finished with that task she looked around—her mother and Catriona were working on the pie filling and there didn't seem to be any pressing need for her help. "Do you mind if I join McCuill outside?" she asked, heading to the coat rack.

Finna waved a hand in her direction. "By all means. I'll call ye if we need your help." As soon as Maeve headed through the door she heard the murmur of conversation start up between Finna and Catriona.

Down the hill the druid was sitting on his heels in front of the woodpile. The sun had already set, leaving a thin line of pale orange lingering above the ocean horizon.

"What are you doing?" she asked, puzzling over the odd sticks poking out here and there.

"You will soon see." He grinned, straightening up.

"Do you think Eron is on his way?"

"He will certainly be here if he can. He never misses a good party. Shall we take a stroll down to the cove?"

She glanced at him, trying to discern his expression. It was hard to tell when he was teasing and when he was serious. "Sure."

They walked in silence along the beach, the only sound the waves rolling in and out. A seagull flapped by, flying erratically as the wind came up. When MacCuill headed back toward the cedar log, Maeve followed, sitting down next to him. She stole a look at him, wondering what he was thinking, but his face was in shadow. In the velvet sky stars began to wink alive, one by one.

"What are your thoughts about everything you've heard so far?"

Maeve startled, turning toward him. His eyes looked very dark and it scared her for a moment. "I certainly don't feel like someone who can solve the problems in the Otherworld, if that's what you're asking. What about my life?"

"This *is* your life, Maeve. If you close your eyes what do you see?"

Maeve obeyed, her mind whirling with scattered fragments of conversation and images.

"Go into the whirlpool but do not try to figure it out."

She imagined herself inside the whirling storm of thoughts and as she did so she came to a still point right in the center.

"Listen only to my voice," MacCuill ordered. "Look around and tell me what you notice."

"I see light going around me very fast."

"And where are you?"

"I'm in the center."

"The center of what?"

"My thoughts."

"Are you in the thoughts?"

"No."

"Step through into the light, Maeve, into the thoughts."

Without thinking she did as he asked, entering the whirling mass.

"What now?" MacCuill asked.

"Light is going through me."

"Do you have control of it?"

"Yes… no… I mean it isn't really bothering me."

"But do you control it?"

Maeve looked around and held up her hand. The movement stopped immediately and she was within a vast silence. "Yes!"

"Good. Now open your eyes."

"How did you do that?"

"I didn't do anything, you did."

"But…"

"All I did was give you directions. You did all the rest. This was your first lesson and you managed very well. You have everything you need within you; it is only a matter of tapping into it. You stopped your thoughts. Try to remember this when you feel afraid—the fear will block your abilities. Any fear begins with a thought, and these thoughts are not the truth. The truth lies within the silence."

His lined face was in shadow so she couldn't see his expression. Maybe he had hypnotized her, or maybe not, but whatever had happened, she trusted him.

When MacCuill and Maeve entered the cottage a short while later, the holly branches and ivy were arranged on the mantel over the fireplace, red candles placed artfully every five or six inches. Mistletoe tied with red ribbon hung from a couple of strategic places above their heads. The table was covered with a simple white linen tablecloth and each place setting held a crystal goblet and lace napkin. Handwritten place cards lay on each plate and at the table's center, a circle of holly with seven white candles cast a festive glow. Dishes of food covered the counter and mouth-watering smells filled the house.

Finna had changed into a white velvet gown with sleeves trimmed in hunter green. Combs held her long hair back from her flushed face. Maeve wished Alex were here to see her.

"If ye would like to dress up, Maeve, now is the time."

"I didn't bring anything dressy except a black skirt and a nice sweater."

Catriona appeared from the bedroom in an emerald green velvet dress. Her braided hair was wound into a low bun intertwined with sprigs of holly. She looked ageless in the soft light. "I've put a dress on your bed," she said, gazing at Maeve. "But dinna feel that ye have to wear it."

"If it's anything like yours and my mother's, I'm sure I'll love it."

Finna turned from where she was adding the finishing touches to the table. "There's a small gift there from me, as well. I meant to give it to ye sooner but there's been so much going on that I havna had the chance."

The gown lying on the bed was a deep rich shade of red with gold trim. The tight-fitting bodice had a square neckline and long sleeves that buttoned at the wrists. After slipping it on and fastening the tiny moonstone buttons, Maeve twirled, feeling the fabric lift and then settle softly against her hips. It was as though the dress had been made for her. Her eyes lit on the small velvet bag—the present from her mother. Knowing what it was before she reached inside, her excitement rose. In her palm the moonstone shimmered, feeling almost alive as she turned it over to examine the Celtic knot setting done in gold. A fluttery feeling went through her as she thought of all the women who had touched and held this magical stone—she was now part of the lineage. It felt good lying lightly in her hand but it did not reveal its secrets.

A black velvet ribbon ran through a small gold loop at the top and she pulled the necklace over her head, letting the stone rest at her breastbone. When she looked into the mirror, a stranger's face stared back at her with eyes so green they startled her. She felt transformed, not only in her appearance but deeper, as though she was shedding some outer skin like a snake, revealing something completely new, a present that was hidden inside.

When she stepped into the other room an older woman with wiry gray hair had come through the door and was greeting Finna and Catriona. Maeve stood back, listening to the lift and cadence of the three women's words, wondering at her newfound understanding of the language she was sure she had never heard before her arrival in Scotland. After Finna had taken her cloak, the woman looked around the room, her worried gaze coming to rest on Maeve. When she smiled, raising her hand in greeting, Maeve moved toward her.

"I'm Maeve, Finna's daughter?"

The woman nodded, her smile growing wide. "I would have known ye anywhere." She leaned forward, pressing her cheek to Maeve's. "I am Herska."

"Where is Mikdal?" Finna asked, peering out the door.

Worry lines appeared again on Herska's small features. "I dinna ken, 'twas hopin' he would find his way here. The man has been gone near two weeks. After the fire in Clachencreid we hid in the mountains, but a few days later Mikdal went back to see if he could help. I have nae seen him since. I stopped on my way here but the village was deserted aside from the dead. I said a few words to speed them on to their next life, but the ground was frozen hard and so I could only pile rock and make the Cairns." Herska began to cry.

"Who did this horrible thing?" Finna asked.

Herska glanced sideways at Catriona across the room and then spoke in a whisper. "'Twas Dark Raven and his minions. There have been many attacks of this type in the past few months."

"I'm so sorry." Finna put an arm around the woman's shoulders. "I'm certain Mikdal will show up. I know how much he enjoys this night."

"Herska!" boomed MacCuill coming to embrace the small woman. "I am glad to see you safe, but where is your husband?" Herska shook her head, wiping her eyes on her sleeve. "If he doesn't show, we'll find him," MacCuill said decisively.

Maeve didn't know what to add in the face of what she had just heard. She finally managed to gesture toward the table, finding the place card with Herska's name.

"Where's Eron?" Maeve heard Finna whisper.

"I dinna ken," Catriona replied. "He should have been here hours ago."

"Do ye think we should wait for him?"

"Nae, we should eat our supper."

Maeve felt a growing anxiety about the night and her own upcoming responsibility according to the prophecy. She couldn't imagine what a solution would be based on from what she'd heard so far. Someone better fill her in soon, although there was hardly time between now and her flight home. When she envisioned getting on the plane with Harold, relief coursed through her.

Everyone found their seats and had settled in when the door flew open, hitting the wall with a bang. All eyes turned to see the man who strode in. He gazed around, his warm brown eyes coming to rest on Catriona.

"Eron!" she cried, jumping up to greet him.

He put his leather satchel down and kissed his wife thoroughly before turning toward the others. "I'm afraid I bring disturbing news."

MacCuill's chair scraped back. "What is it?"

"Brandubh followed me part of the way here. I managed to elude him by taking a circuitous route. I doubled back a couple of times—this is why I'm so late."

"I doubt he'll have the nerve to disturb us on this night. The spirits are strong here and especially during the oak moon of the solstice."

"I hope the protections we placed will hold," Catriona muttered.

Maeve turned to stare at her grandmother wondering what she meant. Had she and Finna placed stones again or was this some other witchery?

Eron came to the table, the scent of pine and wood smoke wafting around him. He bent his head to Maeve's. "My granddaughter, daughter of the moon," he said, clasping her hand firmly. He pulled out a chair, sitting between Maeve and Catriona.

Maeve took in his coppery sun-drenched skin. His brown eyes regarded her calmly despite his unnerving pronouncement.

There was a solid feeling about this man—he reminded her of a tree with roots that went deep into the earth. Maeve's intuition told her that he was not easily pulled off center; whatever was going on out there was deadly serious.

"I'm so very glad you're here. The last time I laid eyes on ye, ye were only a wee babe in arms." He smiled, studying Maeve's face. "I'm sorry to bring such news on this important night—I hope we will have no further disruption."

A moment later Finna bowed her head and the room became quiet. "I thank the Cailleach and all the spirits of winter for this feast and having such close friends and family to share it with, especially havin' my grown daughter here for the first time in so many years. Thank ye all for bein' here." She linked hands with Maeve and Herska and the others followed suit. A long moment went by and then Finna broke the silence. "Now, let us eat this lovely food!"

"Slainte mhor agad!" MacCuill cried, holding his glass of mead high. Everyone lifted their glasses in the toast for good health.

As they began passing dishes and returned to conversation, Maeve thought about the possibility of Brandubh lurking outside in the dark. The mood of the little party had taken on a somber tone. Trying to let go of the uneasy feeling in her solar plexus, she added her voice to the different topics that drifted around the table.

When the last piece of mince and apple pie was eaten and they had finished their goblets of mead, Finna and Catriona began to clear the dishes. Maeve rose to help, carrying the leftovers from the counter to the refrigerator. She joined them at the sink as they set to work with a pan of water. Herska, MacCuill and Eron remained at the table talking in low voices.

"D' ye like the dress, Maeve?" Catriona asked.

"It's beautiful!" Maeve moved from side to side to swing the long skirt. "It feels like it was made for me."

"In a way it was. That dress was a gift from the moon goddess, Arianrhod, twenty-four years ago. It was for me to wear to your blessing ceremony, so ye see it rightly belongs to ye. I knew 'twould fit. I've grown too stout for it," she added, her hands going to her midriff.

"Thank you for lending it to me. I feel different in it."

"I'm nae lendin' it to ye, child—'tis yours now. This dress has magical properties and will keep ye warm even in the coldest temperatures. And the color suits ye with your hair. Not everyone can wear that shade of red, ye ken."

Finna laughed. "Mathair, ye are incorrigible."

Maeve hugged Catriona and thanked her again before she went to collect more dishes. As she reached the table MacCuill looked up. "I see the moonstone is where it belongs."

"The moonstone!" Maeve turned. "I forgot to thank you, Mother—it's really special. But you told me the moonstone disappeared."

"It did. But a month or so ago I was going through a drawer in my dresser and there was the little velvet bag. I have no idea how it got there." Finna chuckled, raising her hands. "I nae longer question what happens regardin' that stone. I had the setting done in a shop in Bailemuir in honor of your arrival."

Eron pulled something out of his satchel and held it out. "I brought these for ye, Maeve. I hope they fit."

Maeve took the soft gray-brown boots from him and sat down to try them on. They came to just below her knee with straps that could be tightened or loosened across the front. "I love them! Did you make them?" she asked, noticing the neat stitching of the deerskin tunic he wore.

72

"Aye. I used Catriona's feet as my model." He smiled. "I'm glad they fit ye so well."

"Thank you." Maeve reached up to hug him, breathing in the woodsy smell on his fringed tunic as he pressed her close. "But I have nothing for you."

" 'Tis enough to have ye here, moon granddaughter."

"Why do you call me that?"

"Because of your link with the moon. Have ye felt it?"

"Maybe I have," she said, "but only when I'm dreaming."

He nodded. "Dreams hold the secrets that we cannot see when we're awake."

The waxing gibbous moon had risen and was emerging over the roof of the house when the group gathered around the bonfire. MacCuill seemed unconcerned about the possibility of Brandubh lurking close by. He told everyone to stand back as he held his walking stick out, lighting fireworks that he had placed at strategic spots around the circle of logs. White, green and blue sparks flew into the sky, hissing and murmuring like something wild and alive. There was an exalted expression in the druid's eyes as he watched the fireworks. Everyone else stood transfixed, mesmerized by the dazzling display.

As the fire blazed higher, the sound of drums, stringed instrument, and flutes, floated eerily out of the darkness. The music grew louder and then a parade of Crion appeared within the circle of light, each one playing an instrument. The dissonance of the melody, and the strangeness of the night triggered a sense of dislocation in Maeve, causing her to shiver for a moment. Her fingers grasped the moonstone, which seemed to pulse in rhythm to the sound.

Catriona began to dance, moving sinuously and weaving her way through the group of people. A second later Finna turned and followed her and then Herska, all of them forming a winding line of movement. Maeve wanted to join in but still felt too shy, but as the tempo of the music increased she was unable to resist. Euphoria stole through her as she moved her body with abandon. She had never felt so free.

The minor notes of the flutes gave way to the rhythmic syncopated beat of drums and the dancing grew even wilder. The line broke up, each person caught up within their own unique movement.

MacCuill was playing a flute now and Maeve could hear the deeper tones harmonizing with the others. Eron, who had been playing a drum, now joined in the dance and Maeve watched as he bent his knees and lifted his feet up and down in sync with the beat of the bodhran played by one of the Crion men. Catriona danced next to him, her body flowing moodily to the drum, her movement liquid, as the flickering firelight cast odd-shaped shadows against her cheek.

The night wore on and the dancing continued. Maeve began to lose any sense of herself. The filaments from the moon reached toward her, long silver strands that disappeared into her body, suffusing her with a curious energy. The resonant sounds of chanting wafted through the cold night air and she looked around, noticing the other beings that had joined the dance—men with wolf and deer heads complete with antlers, the spirits of winter as well as members of the tribe known as the Amuigh. She didn't question their arrival, just took their presence in, continuing her own motion in time to the music and letting herself go completely. Her eyes closed as she swayed to and fro, her arms and fingers weaving circular patterns through the air.

When the music stopped abruptly Maeve opened her eyes. Everyone was focused on the shadows beyond the fire where a tall figure in black stood, his fingers curled around a long barreled pistol. When he stepped into the light the animals at his heels circled around him, their lolling tongues dripping saliva. Rough yellow-brown fur stood up from their hunched, hyena –like backs, their red eyes searching hungrily through the crowd.

"Happy solstice!" Brandubh cried, opening fire.

At the same time the beasts hurled themselves into the crowd, their gaping mouths finding the nearest bodies. Screams pierced the air, the noise deafening. The attacking beasts brought shrieks of pain and tearing fabric, black smoke billowing and blocking the view. When Maeve ran frantically toward where she had last seen her mother, an arm like a vice grip took her round the neck.

"And where do you think you're going, my little niece?"

The silky voice made her skin crawl as she tried to slip out of his grip, but the more she struggled the tighter it became. Through the smoky haze a horrific scene of fallen and bleeding Crion came and went. Several Amuigh were limping away, their furry backs hunched in pain. A sob erupted from her throat.

"Shut up!" Brandubh said harshly. "You are nothing but a sniveling girl, aren't you? I should have known you were powerless. That prophecy is rubbish." His grating laugh filled Maeve with revulsion.

"You're coming with me my little faker. It's time to put a stop to all this pagan nonsense once and for all." His breath was hot in her ear as he crooked one elbow around her neck and dragged her backwards. He clamped his enormous hand over her mouth as his other arm held her round the middle. If she didn't get his hand to move she was going to pass out from lack of air. They were beyond the cottage now; he dragged her easily through the snow like a rag doll. The excited barks and snarls brought shouts and high-pitched screaming—the beasts were still attacking. "Watch out!" she heard someone yell and then, "Get him off, he'll kill her!" Maeve pictured her mother in the

75

jaws of one of those horrible things, her eyes filling with hot tears, which slid down her cheeks.

"I'm surprised at how weak you are, I was expecting more of a fight." Brandubh laughed, the fetid air finding her nostrils and making her gag. Bile rose into her throat and she swallowed, trying to keep from throwing up. Anger welled up from someplace deep inside, giving her a tiny bit of strength. Her free hand went to the moonstone as she struggled and writhed to get away from him; she couldn't loosen his grip. Once he had pulled her away from the noise and confusion around the bonfire, a man appeared out of the shadows. He stared at Maeve with a look of utter loathing. It was John, her neighbor's boyfriend—how could that be?

"Hey there, Maeve. Bet you didn't expect to see me. I got recruited to the cause and you will be the second casualty. The first one is over there in the woods." He laughed, pointing toward the trees. "They're going to wonder about that one."

"What the hell are you talking about?" Brandubh snarled.

"The woman over there. The beasts helped me kill her. Didn't you hear her screaming? It was loud enough. I guess you were busy with your own killing, weren't you? I added a small decoration, one that I think you would approve of: a cross, right in the middle of her forehead."

"John, this is not part of my plan. What do you want to do—get the authorities on our backs? We need to be able to come and go without being noticed. Do you understand? Do *not* go off on your own again. And hide my gun—it's useless where we're headed."

"What do you mean? You can't use a gun in the Otherworld?"

"No, it doesn't work—believe me I've tried."

Maeve saw the feverish look in John's glittering eyes as Brandubh used one hand to dig the gun out of his belt and hand it to him.

"Track down the beasts and the deacons and then put the gun somewhere we can find it."

Shooting pain went through her neck as Brandubh's fingers dug deeper into her windpipe. A gagging sensation made her choke—she was afraid she was going to faint. She held tightly to the moonstone, feeling the heat building in it. The whirring in her ears made it hard to hear John's mumbled response as he walked away. In the distance the sounds of snarling and screaming went on unabated.

"Hurry, John! We don't have all night! Goddamn that idiot! I should never have brought him along."

Something was happening to her—she must be passing out—colors whirled by her eyes making her dizzy. The last sound she heard was fabric ripping as the necklace was torn from her neck and then Brandubh's angry voice yelling, "I've got the stone now, you little witch. Next time you won't be so lucky."

Chapter

4

There was no light, no road noise, no voices, no drone of planes—the silence was so absolute that it hurt her ears. Brandubh was gone, as well as the cottage, her friends, family or anything familiar. As her eyes adjusted she began to notice shapes around her—trees so close together that the darkness between them looked impenetrable. Above her was an overcast sky. She distinctly remembered the moon and a sky full of stars. Her hand went to her throat as the memory of Brandubh's cold fingers sent a shiver through her body. The moonstone was gone.

The still bodies of the Crion came into her mind and before she could stop it a sob rose and echoed into the silence like an animal howl of pain. Her hand went to her mouth—what if Brandubh heard her? With the moonstone in his clutches it was very likely he was on her trail. The dark forest stood silently neutral with only a whisper of wind in the upper branches of the conifers.

On the other side of the clearing she discovered a narrow deer trail and followed it into the shadows. A scuffling sound came to her ears as she moved down the path, making her heartbeat quicken. The image of Brandubh's wild beasts was still fresh in her mind—for all she knew they were right behind her. Adrenaline raced through her veins and she sprinted into the darkness. After catching her clothing on low-hanging branches and stumbling over roots for what seemed like hours, she stopped again to listen. Her breath was coming in gasps—it was hard to hear anything. She put her hands on her knees sucking in air noisily until her heartbeat returned to normal. When she looked up a few seconds later, two sets of amber eyes stared into hers. She shrieked, scrambling behind a tree, but the wolves didn't move. "What do you want?" she asked loudly, trying to sound brave and in control. They didn't speak but she heard their answer in her head: *We are here to help you—follow us.* This was getting stranger by the minute. Did she really just get a clear message from an animal? She felt dizzy for a second—everything seemed surreal, kind of like Alice falling down the rabbit hole. The wolves padded away and then turned to glance back at her expectantly. "Okay, I'm coming," she said. And the sound of her voice was somehow reassuring as she followed them down the twisting trail.

After a while they left the forest, heading down a steep bank toward a stream. The gurgling water rushed by, barely discernible in the moonless night. The wolves headed downstream and she struggled after them, trying not to slip in the mud along the bank. Twice she went down as her boots went out from under her, the long skirt tangling around her legs when she tried to stand. Both times the wolves waited patiently until she was on her feet again. The landscape changed as they followed the downhill slope of the streambed. Sandstone cliffs loomed up on her left, the pale stone visible despite the darkness. Soon the wolves slowed and headed up a twisting trail, disappearing from view. Maeve quickly scrambled after them. They waited for her by the entrance to a cave. Inside she found a thick sheepskin on the floor and sank down, exhausted. She fell asleep with the warmth of their bodies lying close beside her.

When Maeve woke, the wolves were gone. It was somewhat light now and she could see the recently ransacked shelves that lined the rounded walls. Shards of glass and pottery were scattered across the floor. A broken flute lay in two pieces, impossible to mend. The acrid smell of burnt wood and decay filled the air. Outside the cave she couldn't tell the time of day. The sky was a solid gray mass. Looking around for her wolf friends she wondered if she had dreamed the entire bizarre experience. But then icy wind hit her cheek and as she wrapped her arms around her body she noticed the mud-spattered dress and filthy boots—this was no dream.

Maeve headed upstream, retracing her footprints from the night before. Her only thought was to find her way out of here, back to Bailemuir and her family. When the stream disappeared under the bank, she climbed across, finding herself in an open space where a spring bubbled into a deep natural pool surrounded by rocks. Steam rose from the surface and she tested it, finding the water enticingly warm. Before she stripped off her clothes she listened carefully and then peered into the trees that circled the clearing. Part of her was very nervous about placing herself in such a vulnerable position, but in the end she couldn't resist the call of the water. Once in the pool she sank gratefully beneath the surface, letting her mind empty. Once she had bathed she would find the way back.

Sometime later an odd sound brought her out of repose. Orange eyes peered at her from a shimmering feathery shape across the pool.

"I am Corra the goddess of prophecy—I bring the Willow a message."

Maeve sat up, focusing on the bird/woman, her heart doing weird somersaults.

"I know it is hard to hear me or see me now because of the changes that have been wrought here. You must travel to Rhiannon's castle as quickly as you can. We are all depending on you. Follow the trail on the other side of the glade to the edge of the forest. Once there you will turn to the left, following the rise of the hill until you see the towers in the distance. Rhiannon will give you further instructions. And thank you for being here."

Maeve opened her mouth to reply but the apparition was already becoming translucent and then faded away completely. Her mind reeled as she replayed the message from what—a bird? A line from *Alice in Wonderland* came to her and her manic laughter accompanied the words she said out loud, *'curiouser and curiouser'*, that seemed to describe her current situation. Her plan to find the way back to Bailemuir receded from her mind as she replayed Corra's message: *we are all depending on you.* But how could she help? Best to follow Corra's instructions and see what came up next. Maybe Rhiannon, whoever she was, would explain things.

After climbing out of the pool she noticed a finely carved bow and quiver of arrows lying on the ground next to her clothes. She was certain they had not been there before. She dressed quickly and then pulled out an arrow and nocked it, focusing on a large knothole in a pine tree forty feet away. Taking a deep breath she let the arrow fly. When she went to retrieve it she was pleased to see that she had not lost her touch. Slinging the bow and quiver across her shoulder she hurried across the clearing.

It was not far to the edge of the woods. The valley lay below, a bleak and frozen wasteland. She recognized it from her time with MacCuill, but now a dark fog spiraled from the ground like something alive. Panic rose in her throat as the view was obliterated. Hugging the safety of the trees, she headed to the left, following Corra's directions.

Another wave of panic went through her as she reached up and registered the absence of the stone but then she remembered MacCuill's instruction and his prophetic words. She slowed her breath, concentrating on clearing her turbulent mind but all she was able to manage was a deep anxiety about what she was doing here at all. And Brandubh had the moonstone. At least she had gotten away from him, but she couldn't say how.

She was running now. When had she started to run? The last thought that had gone through her mind was Brandubh's scowling face, his hands clutching her neck. Now she felt like her body belonged to someone else; her feet barely touched the ground. Had she magically transformed into the person that everyone kept telling her she was? Ahead was a narrow cliff edge where she would need to make a choice: continue along the edge of the woods or go down the hill and into the black fog. In the distance, tall spires rose out of the mist. She squinted, recognizing remnants of a castle that immediately reminded of a picture in a fairytale she had read as a child: a fortress with golden spires reaching into a cerulean sky. But this castle was in ruin and the sky here was anything but blue. After a moment of deliberation she headed down the steep and rocky incline.

Attempting to keep the castle in her sights, she ran straight into the fog and across a sheet of ice. Soon the battlements came into view: tall turrets at each of the four corners of the outer walls, barely visible through the thickening haze. They looked partially demolished with large pieces missing from their base.

Inside the keep, the castle was in the same shape, with crumbling towers and rubble in other places. Dread crept around her heart and she tried to ignore the sensation of icy fingers clawing at her as the fog closed in. A deep chill entered her chest and with it her mind went numb. Her body was so weak...so tired. The last thing she remembered was looking up to see a monstrous face coalescing within the cloud above her, before paralyzing cold sucked away her breath.

Chapter

5

Gertrude drove out of Bailemuir in her rental car. Her bag sat on the back seat and she held a sheet of paper in her hand with directions to Finna's house she had gotten from the pub on the main road. The icy roads made for treacherous driving and she took her time.

A few miles out of town she made a right onto the narrow driveway next to the rosehips she'd been told about. The car tires slid as she made her way down the muddy lane that came to an end at the back of the cottage. She parked behind an ancient Mini, turned the car off and sat for a moment, wondering how to explain her sudden appearance.

When she headed around the house toward the front door, she heard voices coming from down the hill. Turning she was surprised to see two women and a man near the little beach. From her vantage point it appeared they were placing bodies on canvas litters. They were dressed oddly in medieval looking clothes, the man wearing a long gray robe. Maybe she had stumbled onto some kind of pagan ritual. "Hello?" she called out, hesitantly.

All three looked her way and then one of the women started up the hill.

"Can I help ye?" The green eyes were bloodshot, her nose red from the cold. Untidy gray strands of hair fell across the older woman's face and she brushed them back in an irritated manner as she peered at Gertrude curiously.

"Sorry to barge in like this but you have no phone. My name is Gertrude Russo and I'm trying to find Maeve Lewin. Is she here?"

"I'm afraid not. I'm her grandmother, Catriona." She held out her hand.

Gertrude tried to quell her uneasiness. "I'm a friend of Maeve's from Milltown."

"You do not look like a Gertrude," the robed man remarked, joining them.

Gertrude laughed. "I do have some German blood but mostly I'm Italian and Middle Eastern. The name comes from a distant relative who needed to be remembered, I suppose."

The man smiled but Gertrude could see pain behind his eyes. "Aye, the gods of the past need to be appeased. I am MacCuill," he added, holding out his hand. "And this is Herska." He gestured to the slight woman with wiry gray hair who headed toward them.

Gertrude nodded to her, trying to ignore the tug of fear that had taken up residence in her stomach. Dark circles lay under Herska's eyes, her special dress muddied and torn. What was going on here?

"I know why ye've come," Catriona remarked suddenly. "Ye ken about the prophecy."

"That's right," she said. "It came up in the cards. But how did you know?"

"I'm a seer."

Gertrude nodded as she met the older woman's eyes. "Maeve came to me for a reading and some things showed up in the cards, the Tarot. I was worried because Maeve…Maeve didn't recall anything. And then I began having dreams about monsters and other unexplainable things and what she might be up against. I just had to come." Gertrude felt she was babbling but couldn't seem to stop.

"I understand perfectly," Catriona remarked. " I know what a burden psychic abilities can be. Last night two of our dear friends were killed and another was severely injured. Maeve disappeared at the same time." Her eyes clouded. "Come inside and meet my daughter, Finna. We can tell ye the rest over a cup o' tea. We've been up all night."

Gertrude was at a loss for words. The situation she had walked in on was dire. She followed them into the cottage.

Finna came across the room from where she had been tending a small white-faced form on the bed. "Maeve has spoken of ye," she said, after being introduced. Worry lines etched her pale face. "I guess ye've heard about what happened last night." Finna gestured toward the bed. "Aila was lucky to survive."

"Yes. Catriona told me about the two people who were killed. I'm so sorry. How did this happen?"

"Three," MacCuill amended. "Do not forget that poor woman I found in the woods."

Gertrude stared at him. "Someone else as well?"

He nodded. "A person we have never seen before. I assume she was in the wrong place at the wrong time."

"But who did this terrible thing?"

"Have you heard the name, Brandubh?" Finna asked, staring at Gertrude with a look of fury on her face.

Gertrude startled, trying to regain her composure. What should she say? She took in a deep breath, her mind going to the few days spent with the very attractive priest back in Milltown. It was all she could do not to blurt out everything. But something inside her told her it was better to keep this to herself, at least for now. "The name is not familiar but I had an image of a dark man during Maeve's reading. Is he a priest?"

"I guess ye might call him a false priest since he disnae follow the tenets of the kirk. He came last night and shot these people and then kidnapped my daughter."

Gertrude put her hand to her mouth, shocked into silence. She watched Catriona bring a tray from the kitchen and put it down on a table. "Please help yourself to tea."

She picked up a mug and took a sip, trying to marshal her thoughts. People had been shot, killed—Maeve had been taken by the man she had nearly slept with, would have slept with if he hadn't stopped her advances. "If I can help in any way, please tell me what to do."

"We're preparing to take the dead home for burial and I canna see Maeve at present. 'Tis as though a curtain has fallen between us." Catriona glanced worriedly at MacCuill.

Finna picked up a mug. "I hope my dear one is still alive." Tears welled in her eyes.

"She is not dead, Finna—Maeve is in the Otherworld." MacCuill picked up a mug. "But where, I do not know."

"I don't have children but I can imagine how distressing this must be," Gertrude said, putting a hand on Finna's shoulder.

Catriona looked around the room and then turned toward the window, peering through the antique panes. "Where has Eron gone now?"

"He's probably headed off to find his granddaughter," MacCuill answered calmly.

"Why would he go without saying anything? I wish he had waited for us." Catriona fussed with her shawl, wrapping and rewrapping it around her shoulders nervously.

"So, Eron is a family member?"

Catriona frowned. "Eron is my husband and Finna's father and that makes him Maeve's grandfather." Now the older woman seemed more irritated than sad, pulling angrily at her hair that was falling out of some intricate configuration. A moment later she had unbraided it, letting it hang untidily around her tired-looking face. "I canna imagine why he would take leave of us without a word," she muttered, heading to the kitchen. She bent down, searching under the sink. When she stood again her hands were wrapped around a small wooden box. "I shall consult the oracle before we leave." Catriona brought the box to the table and then pulled off the lid. Inside were many dowel-like pieces of wood, each about six inches long.

"What is this?" Gertrude asked, pulling one out to take a better look.

"'Tis the Ogham tree oracle," Catriona explained, "a very old form of divination used by the druids. This set was made for me by Roc, a wood carver I know."

"I've never seen anything like it. Is each one made of a different wood?"

"Aye. Each represents a certain tree." Catriona held up one of the sticks, pointing out the markings carved into it. "This one has one horizontal slash to the right. That's the birch or Beth in the old language. Each tree has certain unique properties and wisdom to impart. There's a circle of cedars at the top of the hill where I cast the oracle. The spirits are strong there. Do ye wish to join us?"

"Yes, of course." Gertrude stared at Catriona who in the last few minutes seemed to have turned into some warrior goddess, her eyes full of fire.

MacCuill stood with arms folded, a sentry waiting for the moment to act.

Finna turned from where she was leaning over the bed. "I think that is an excellent idea, Maithair."

Finna was drawn and pale, her eyes tired, but Gertrude could see the strength in her. It was different than Catriona's intensity, more hidden. "I shouldn't have descended on you like this, and I appreciate your allowing me to be part of the... the search for Maeve. I feel connected to her, I'm not really sure why...I've only met her a few times, and yet...there was something about her...and then of course what I saw during her reading." She looked up, unable to go on, overcome by an emotion that she couldn't name.

"Ye've come for a reason," Catriona said. "I trust whatever it was that brought ye here to us."

"And what an auspicious time for your arrival," Finna added. "Just when Maeve has disappeared and we need all the help we can get."

"There is no such thing as a coincidence, Gertrude," MacCuill added, "as you should well know. We will all be grateful for your help whether it be through your psychic abilities or your caring heart."

Herska stayed behind to watch over Aila while the rest of them followed Catriona to the top of the hill and into a grove of ancient cedar trees. Catriona took off her wool shawl and laid it on the damp ground, inviting everyone to sit.

"MacCuill? Do ye nae plan to join us?" Catriona called, after the women were settled.

"I will stand if you do not mind."

"But I need your interpretation!"

"I can hear and I am very familiar with the different essences of trees. That is what we druids are all about." He stood ramrod straight with his back to them, gazing out of the clearing.

Catriona sighed and then opened the box. "First of all I want to thank the oracle for it's help today and I give thanks to this ancient grove for protectin' us." When she closed her eyes and bowed her head an answering whisper of wind rustled through the upper branches of the trees and then all was silent.

Catriona mumbled some words under her breath and then pulled out three sticks and laid them on the ground in a vertical line. She bent over them, her eyebrows drawn together in concentration. "The one in the middle is the rowan. This tree represents magic and the lord of the hunt. Hmm, if I didn't know better I would say Eron is either with Maeve or on his way to her."

"Why do ye say that?" Finna asked.

"According to the Celtic moon calendar, he was born in the month of this tree—December. And as ye ken, he's a hunter."

"I would like to think Eron is with her," Finna mumbled, a catch in her voice.

Catriona continued. "The rowan is known as the tallest tree in the forest because of its search for light. Maeve is engaged in the struggle to bring the light back into a dark world, the same way the rowan is trying to reach for the sun. MacCuill?" she called. "Anything to add? You're the tree expert here."

MacCuill turned toward them. "The rowan is an auspicious tree. It has magical properties to ward off evil. The Ogham is saying that what Maeve's engaged in requires tremendous inner effort. She has escaped from Brandubh and is safe for now."

There was silence as everyone absorbed the druid's words and then Catriona looked down. "The one on the left is the elder," she said, looking down at the five lines cut across the single line. "This placement represents the dilemma she's faced with. The elder can have to do with shame." Catriona paused for a moment. "Possibly she's being faced with her own inadequacies."

"Elder can also refer to one's elders and the realization that we do not know what we need to know. I would say she's at the spring," MacCuill observed. "She's bathing there to prepare herself for her destiny even if she's not conscious of this."

Gertrude stared at him in surprise. "How do you know that?" All of this was so far removed from the Tarot that she had nothing to contribute. And she knew next to nothing about trees.

"Because this tree represents cleansing and purging. Transformation. The elder brings clarity about one's task as an individual and also as part of a clan."

"I do agree with MacCuill about the spring, which is close to Eron's cave. If I close my eyes I can see her there, but this may be wishful thinking on my part," Catriona added, glancing up at the druid. "I do hope you're right, MacCuill, about her getting away from my brother."

"What about the third one?" Gertrude asked, pointing to the last stick that had two short horizontal lines connected to one vertical line.

"The oak, formidable and strong. This has to do with the solution." Catriona smiled, her features relaxing for the first time.

"Isn't the oak the tree of the druids?" Gertrude asked. It was the one thing she had read somewhere having to do with magical trees.

"Aye—higher powers at work," MacCuill answered. "*Arddam Dossa*, which translates roughly to mean the highest of defenses. Maeve will find someone to help and protect her. Someone who is like a king or queen or possibly a goddess."

"Or a druid," Finna added, staring hopefully at MacCuill. "The only problem with this oracle is we dinna ken the time frame."

"That is true. This could be something far in the future or just a few days from now. In any case I would say from this reading that the outlook is positive. The oak is a mighty tree. Help will come." MacCuill sat down next to Finna and put his hand on her shoulder. "I do not think you should worry so much, Finna, Your daughter is stronger and more resourceful than you know and she has many to help her. Think of the wording of the prophecy."

"What shall we do now?" Gertrude asked. She had never expected anything like this. This was entirely new and rather frightening if she let herself dwell on it for too long, especially from what she'd gleaned from her own visions. And Brandubh's involvement was even more disturbing—the man she had been attracted to back in Milltown didn't seem to bear any resemblance to this depraved person. Better to play dumb and just follow along.

"The first order of business is to get Aila and the dead back to their clan as soon as possible. After that we can search for Maeve." MacCuill turned toward the hill, heading away from them.

"But MacCuill..." Finna cried, running after him, "the first order of business should be to find Maeve!"

"No, Finna, we must honor the dead and help Aila." His tone brooked no argument and Gertrude watched the woman crumple. But a minute later Finna squared her shoulders and followed the druid down the hill.

As Gertrude rose, Catriona put a hand on her arm. "Gertrude, I hope ye are prepared for what lies ahead. The Otherworld is an extremely dangerous place. There are forces at work there that ye are nae prepared for no matter how many dreams ye've had. If ye truly want to come along ye must know ye will be stuck with us. Ye will nae find your way out again without help and none of us will be willin' to spare the time. D' ye understand?"

Catriona's tone was somber, the question almost harsh. Gertrude thought about it. Did she really want to put herself into this situation? But after coming all this way, how could she back out? "I know what I'm getting myself into," she answered, hoping fervently that this was true.

Chapter

6

Maeve's eyes opened, traveling across a partially burned out ceiling. An acrid smell lingered in the air, making her want to sneeze.

"You are awake," a reedy voice murmured.

A filmy, wavery figure came toward her. Eyes the color of lilac became clearer as the woman drew close.

"I am Rhiannon. I found you on the ice in a very bad state. How are you feeling now?"

Maeve gazed at the apparition that seemed to move in and out of focus. For a moment she could see dark hair and strong features, a tattered golden gown covering a voluptuous figure. "I feel okay, but what is that out there...that weird mist?"

"The fog is a malevolent force that would have killed you if I had not found you when I did."

"Corra told me to come here. I have no idea what I'm supposed to be doing. I'm..."

"I know who you are. Corra has sent you here for the wolf."

"The wolf?"

Rhiannon nodded. "The wolf will take you to the boatman. He has the key."

"The key for what?" Maeve put her hand on her forehead where a headache had started behind her eyes.

"Follow me."

Rhiannon headed for the door. "Do not forget your bow," she called over her shoulder. "You may need it."

Maeve swung her legs off the bed, standing unsteadily. The bow and arrows lay on a small three-legged chair and Maeve picked them up, her mind whirling in several different directions. She followed Rhiannon down a decrepit stairway, taking care not to trip on the cracked and broken stone while she sorted through her limited knowledge of Celtic myth. It was obvious that Rhiannon was a goddess even though the woman hadn't mentioned it, and from Maeve's recollection she was a horse goddess, among other things.

The room they entered looked as though a bomb had hit it. A crystal chandelier had fallen and splintered into a million shards. Upholstered chairs were ripped, with stuffing and springs showing, and the once beautiful marble floors were cracked and split. Without a word of explanation Rhiannon navigated carefully through the destruction and went through another door, entering a rustic kitchen.

"My father and mother lived here and this is where I was born. It breaks my heart to see it in such shambles but I can do nothing until the balance is restored. I no longer have the power."

Every time Maeve focused on Rhiannon her image grew a bit clearer. Now she could see the strong jaw line and wide shoulders, the gloss of black hair cascading down her back. Rhiannon seemed familiar to her and then she remembered the night Harold and she did peyote together out in the woods. In her vision brought on by the buttons, Harold had been kneeling before this very same woman. And he had been wearing a crown.

Before she had a chance to puzzle this out Rhiannon said, "I lived in this castle with my husband, Pwyll, a mortal. I gave up my powers for many years to give him a son. But Pwyll has died and I am now married to Manawydan, the god of the sea. He does not like this dry place and chooses instead his castle under the ocean where I must soon join him."

Rhiannon sighed heavily and then went through another door that led outside. A small path headed downhill to the keep below. Maeve looked out beyond the crumbling castle walls at the swirling dark fog. An involuntary shudder went through her body.

The goddess hurried toward a long barn where several horses were housed. A soft-eyed gray mare nickered as they passed and Rhiannon stopped. "My mare will call to Finiche. Although they are not the same species, they have become friends." Rhiannon whispered some words and a moment later the mare put her nose in the air and neighed.

Before Maeve could frame a question a large gray shape loped up the hill. Maeve sucked in her breath as she came face to face with a gigantic wolf. "This is Finiche?" She looked into the familiar amber eyes—this was the very same animal that had appeared below her apartment in Milltown.

"You must go quickly. I fear there is danger heading this way. Finiche will take you to the boatman."

Maeve's heart seemed to skip a beat. "Is it Brandubh?"

"I do not know. It could be Oillteil or even my son, Pryderi. All I know is that it is time for you to go." Her tone was urgent.

"Pryderi?"

"Yes, my son is allied with the dark forces. I coddled him after his father died and because of this he grew to have no re-spect for me. I am afraid of what he has become because of my indulgence. You must take care not to get into his clutches."

Maeve adjusted the bow and quiver of arrows onto her back and tried to quell the terror building in the pit of her stomach. Her mind had not caught up with what was happening to her—everything was going too fast.

"Go now, Saille. I will keep your safety in my heart. You are our only hope. Follow your heart and you will succeed." Rhiannon gave the wolf a pat on his neck and opened the gate.

Maeve grabbed his thick ruff and pulled herself onto the wide back, tucking the skirt around her thighs. Her legs were long but she was dwarfed by his size. Before she had a chance to say goodbye or thank you, he began to run, heading into the fog and across the ice. As she felt the powerful muscles working under her and watched the scenery fly by, Maeve was overtaken by a wild exuberance. When she let out a whoop Finiche answered with a haunting howl that made the hair on the back of her neck stand up.

It was a long time before the wolf finally came to a stop. A sharp twinge of pain shot through her lower back as Maeve slid to the ground. Rhiannon's words reverberated in her mind, *'You are our only hope'*. Nausea overcame her for a moment and she pressed her fingers into her temples. How in the world was she supposed to accomplish anything—she knew nothing of this place, nor what her mission actually was. Was she supposed to recruit an army to fight Brandubh? And if so who? So far she'd seen no one who fit the profile other than the two goddesses, and they had both told her that they were powerless now.

Above the hill of oak trees where they rested purple storm clouds gathered in the early dusk. A strong cold wind whistled through the bare trees. Without the magical properties of this dress she would freeze, she thought, pulling the skirt folds around her lower body where she crouched by the wolf.

Their route had taken them by two newly-erected forts where Maeve had caught sight of many Crion prisoners. They were not dressed properly for the cold and were chained, huddled close together for warmth. In the second fort, hundreds of humans languished, watched over by wild looking men in animal skins. The hyena-like beasts with rough spotted fur milled around the guards.

As the disturbing images faded from her mind, a feeling of futility entered her heart, riding on the chill wind that blew up from the valley. A river lay snake-like in the distance. That must be where she would find the boatman. Hunger gnawed at her and she wondered how long she had been in this alien world. It seemed like forever. Her mind drifted back to the celebration, her mother, Catriona and the others. Were they alive or had they been shot in the chaos before she was dragged away?

When Finiche padded up beside her she dragged herself onto his back and then used her dress to wipe the tears from the corners of her eyes. The wolf waited until she was settled and then trotted down the hill toward a narrow stream meandering along the bottom of the bank. At the water's edge, Maeve jumped off, eagerly heading to get a drink, but as she went by him the wolf's nose touched her arm. When she turned, his lambent eyes stared into hers, communicating his message: this stream was clean but many were not, what the men were doing had contaminated the waterways and water had become very scarce. Maeve had seen evidence of the mines. They littered the landscape like open wounds.

He drank and then waited as she cupped her hands into the frigid water. After quenching her thirst, she got to her feet and then walked next to Finiche, following the creek's winding path toward the distant river. She wished she had a bottle to fill—who knew how long it might be before she came upon another clean stream? After walking for what seemed like hours, Maeve began to hear a keening cry. She stopped to listen. It was coming from somewhere above. Finiche kept by her side as she followed the sound up the hill and deep into the forest. When she finally came upon the source her heart nearly stopped. In front of her was an enormous creature that looked like an ape but not. She remembered that a few of these creatures had come to the cottage the night of the celebration. It sat on the ground, its long furry brown arms cradling another of its species. When the creature looked up and their eyes met, Maeve was instantly aware of the wise intelligence shining out from the deep-set brown eyes. This was a sentient being—a female Amuigh.

"Mena," the creature said in a melodic tone, long dark fingers pointing to her chest. "Beag," she added, gazing sadly at the dead creature whose head rested in her lap. "Mate," she added and then began the mournful sound again.

Maeve spoke her own name and then drew closer, no longer afraid. "What can I do?" she asked.

Mena shook her head, rocking Beag like a baby. When Maeve asked what had happened, Mena used a few words and hand gestures to indicate that Beag had worked in the mine on the other side of the hill. The only food provided for the workers was meat, animals that had died of hunger or thirst or ones the guards killed. The Amuigh were vegetarians. They were not capable of metabolizing this type of protein and so Beag had starved to death. Maeve was horrified, disgusted and appalled by such callous disregard for life and said so. Mena regarded her calmly, with no apparent malice or feelings of revenge. Maeve rose, realizing there was nothing more to be done for Mena. Before leaving Maeve vowed to release any and all Amuigh being held by Brandubh.

As Maeve and Finiche continued on, Maeve's thoughts were focused on the pens and how she would manage this dangerous undertaking. She was saddened by the terrible loss and despair emanating from Mena, the hideous cruelty of Brandubh and his men. Reaching the top of a hill, the smell of smoke rode the wind, emerging from the valley ahead of them. Maeve couldn't see an encampment, but these valleys were deceptive, hiding circuitous trails into protected areas. Finiche put his nose into the wind, his nostrils flaring. When a dark tendril of smoke appeared, Maeve ran back to where she'd seen a path. Finiche gave a bark of warning but she ignored him, starting down the steep hill at a crouch. Hopefully whoever had the fire would be friendly and willing to share some food, she thought, her hand going to her growling stomach.

A pinewood fire sent sparks into the air and voices could be heard speaking some guttural language. Cautiously she crawled downward until she was looking directly on their camp. Small squat beings with large, misshapen heads sat around the low flames. Maeve sucked in her breath, shaken to the core. She had seen these beings in the dreamtime with MacCuill and heard about them from Catriona—the Oillteil, dwellers from the underworld come to help Brandubh. Trying to move backward, she dislodged a rock, sending a small landslide skittering down the hill. One of the creatures looked up and let out a yell and then five of them started toward her. Backtracking, she pulled the bow off her shoulder and nocked an arrow, letting it fly before sprinting toward the wolf. She barely managed to pull herself onto his back before he took off at a gallop. When she looked over her shoulder, she was surprised to see one of the creatures on the ground. Her arrow had found purchase. Pride and then a sick feeling went through her as she realized what she'd done. Tears brimmed over and trickled down her face as the wolf galloped on. When he finally came to a stop she jumped off his back, stumbling away to be sick. She retched but there was nothing in her stomach to come up. Leaning against a tree she closed her eyes for a moment trying to let go of the image of the injured Oillteil. If killing these creatures was part of her mission she didn't think she was up to it.

Her eyes flew open when she heard the sound of frenzied yipping. Three wolves were greeting Finiche, their wagging tails the sign that they knew one another. They turned toward her, their golden eyes focused on her face and she heard the message deep inside. *Follow us to the one who searches.* She wasn't at all sure what that meant but by now she trusted Finiche, and so she nodded, following the four into the protection of the trees. Instead of sticking to a path, the wolves meandered through the brush, their noses to the ground. Where in the world were they taking her? When they arrived at a clearing, Maeve breathed a sigh of relief, brushing off the twigs and brambles that clung to her dress. Hearing the crackle of a fire she looked up, surprised to see Eron sitting cross-legged in front of it.

When their eyes met he smiled, rising to greet her. "I thought you might be along soon."

Her grandfather's strong arms came around her and she melted into his embrace, weak with relief.

"I'm glad you're safe."

Before Maeve had a chance to ask any questions, Finiche and the others headed away, trotting down a winding trail.

"Follow him," Eron ordered. "He's taking us to the cave." Maeve waited a moment while Eron threw dirt on the fire and gathered his gear and then the two of them hurried after the wolves.

The cave was dug into the scarp, a place where the pack raised their young and a safe haven, far enough away from the Oillteil to feel at ease. Other wolves were there, young ones as well as older. Maeve watched their ritualized greeting, glad to be allowed in their midst. Finiche was obviously the alpha male--not only was he much larger than the others, but also they deferred to him, ducking their heads in submission as he walked by. A large gray-black female was with Finiche now and they circled each other with dog-like behavior, their plumed tails wagging.

"She is his mate," Eron said, following her gaze. "Those two are their pups from last year." He pointed to two small wolves tussling on the floor. He laid out pemmican and bread and then made a fire with wood stacked by the entrance.

"So you've camped here before?"

Eron nodded. "It's on my hunting route."

Maeve watched him light the kindling with some home-made looking matches he carried in a small pouch around his neck. After it was going he added a metal grate, laying it across the rocks surrounding the pit. He poured water from a skin into an earthenware bowl and set it on the grate. "Oh, I almost forgot to give you this. I found it by the spring."

He reached into a pocket in his tunic and held out his hand.

Maeve took the necklace staring at him in surprise. "But... how? Brandubh had it."

"It will always find the way back to its true owner."

She retied the frayed ribbon ends and pulled it over her head, wondering if Brandubh had dropped it on his way to find her. The stone felt cool where it lay in its proper place in the hollow just below her breastbone.

"And I see you found the bow."

Maeve nodded and then began to cry. "I just shot one of those creatures with this bow. I think I may have killed him."

Eron's expression was full of sympathy. "The first time is the hardest. But be assured the Oillteil would have killed you if you had given them the chance."

Maeve wiped the tears from her face with the back of her hand. "Did you make the bow?" she asked, trying to let go of the image of the fallen creature, blood pouring from the ragged wound.

"It was made by a friend of mine who lives close to the yew forest in the northeast. Yew is the traditional wood for bow making."

Maeve ran her hand along the smooth surface. "It's beautiful. How did you know I've studied archery?"

"I didn't. I only thought you should be armed in this dangerous place."

Maeve wondered when he had left the bow. She hadn't heard him. Maybe he hadn't wanted to embarrass her while she was bathing in the spring. And how had the man known where she would be? She raked her tangled hair away from her face, trying unsuccessfully to tie it back. Bits of bark and twig had caught in the curls. "Eron, may I borrow your hunting knife?"

"Be careful, it's extremely sharp," he warned, pulling the knife out of the sheath on his belt.

Maeve took the sharp tool in her hands, examining the bone handle carved with unfamiliar symbols. It was well worn, imprinted with indentations from his hand. She looked up to see him watching her, his dark brows raised in question. With her left hand she lifted up a large swatch of her hair, bringing the blade against it. It cut through like butter and curls fell to the ground. Lifting the clumps one by one, she watched the pile at her feet grow. When there was no more hair to cut she laid the knife aside and ran her hands through the uneven tufts. "That feels better," she muttered. A shiver went through her as the cold air touched her bare neck making her move closer to the fire.

Eron picked up the knife and began to carve a small piece of wood. When their eyes met she saw a twitch at the corner of his mouth but he didn't say a word. He continued whittling, his gaze focused on what he was doing.

"I have so many questions I don't know where to begin," she started, wrapping her arms around herself. "I don't know how I got here. All I know is Brandubh had me and then I ended up in the forest." She gazed at him questioningly.

Eron nodded, putting the knife down. "You've begun the journey put into place many years ago. As for how you got here, I would say you brought yourself here with the aid of the stone."

"But Brandubh took the stone."

"Not before it worked its magic. You wanted to get away from him and you were taken to the safest place—the place where you belong."

"Were you still at the cottage when Brandubh was shooting? Did you see if my mother...?"

"Your mother is fine as is your grandmother. Two Crion were killed, another wounded. I left shortly after you disappeared, hoping to find you somewhere around the cottage, but when you weren't there I knew what had happened." He picked up the wood again, his attention going back to the small figure emerging.

Maeve stared into space, her mind traveling back to that terrible night. It seemed like weeks since she'd been wandering through the Otherworld. "At the spring, the bird goddess told me to find Rhiannon. She gave me directions to the castle but I could barely see or hear her."

Eron looked up from his whittling. "The gods and goddesses in the Otherworld are kept vibrant by people's belief in them. Now that Brandubh has taken over he discourages anything to do with what he terms the 'outdated beliefs" and speaks only of the 'one true god'. Many spirits have completely vanished, leaving the Otherworld even more vulnerable. You have arrived in the nick of time."

A wave of heat rose to her face. "Has everyone here just been waiting for the prophecy to come to fruition? I hope they realize I'm only one person." She turned away, tears pressing against her eyelids. Her short time in this place had given her a taste of what was to come and she didn't like it at all.

"Knowledge of the prophecy has not kept the people from trying to fight, Maeve. But Brandubh has recruited so many to his cause there are not enough left to make a difference. And most of those who are left are only simple farmers, not warriors. Of course I use the word 'recruit' loosely; Brandubh's way has been to offer them work or death. He's killed many. There are also those who believe in him and those who have the desire to become rich, but most are only trying to stay alive. The Crion and the Amuigh will never fight—many are being used as slaves to work the mines. Have you come upon the Wildmen on your travels? They are part of the duine fiain, the lawless ones who live in caves and have no leader. It is only during celebrations that they come together with others. Now they follow Brandubh, not because of what he preaches but because it suits their needs. Their hunting grounds have been diminished but Brandubh provides for them in exchange for their exceptional hunting skills. And they have the Beithir—the ferocious beasts you might have noticed on the night of the bonfire—the animals are a great asset to Brandubh."

"I did see some people who fit that description on the way from Rhiannon's castle, and I also met an Amuigh named Mena. Beag, her mate, died from starvation. Did you know they're vegetarians? It seems like Brandubh would know that and feed them something other than meat—it doesn't do him any good to have them die." Maeve felt tears building again and tried to stave them off.

"The Amuigh live as hunter-gatherers, gentle beings who will die out if this drought continues. Their home is far away from the fighting—I was glad to see the few that made it to the celebration. I was unaware that they were being captured, but I'm not surprised to hear it. I suppose to Brandubh they are disposable. It's easier to use them up than find the correct food for them. There is very little growing here now and grains are being hoarded."

"I thought it snowed here. The clouds certainly seem to hold moisture." Maeve gazed up at the heavy gray sky.

"The clouds hold only rage. No rain or snow or even sleet has fallen in the Otherworld for many months. Two springs are all that remain of the water supply. All the rest of the water has been dammed up for use in the mines or has frozen solid."

Maeve watched the light leach slowly out of the sky leaving a darkness that seemed dense and malevolent. She moved into the back of the cave. When Eron handed her his deerskin tunic she gratefully pulled it over her head. Finiche lay down beside her and she curled into his warmth. In the darkness behind her she heard the snuffling of the other wolves as they settled in for the night. The last thing she noticed before her eyes closed was the flicker of fire shadows playing across Eron's cheek as he sat cross-legged by the cave entrance.

*Sall—yaay...Sall—yaay...*Maeve woke with a start. Eron was asleep next to the entrance, his head cradled on his arm. All the wolves, including Finiche, had gone off somewhere. She pulled on her boots and left the cave trying to head in the direction of the melodic voice. *Sall—yaay....*there it was again. Listening carefully she moved through thick fog across the frozen ground. It was bitterly cold, her gasping breath white as she hurried forward. Trees suddenly appeared, their jutting roots making her stumble. A moment later she sucked in her breath as a ghost-like figure moved toward her from under the dark canopy.

"I am Airmid, the goddess of herbs and healing. You are a healer just as I am."

Maeve tried to bring the woman into focus through the fog swirling between them. For a moment she could see the wide belt encircling the woman's tiny waist, the many pouches tied to it, but a second later the figure had disappeared again. It was a moment later that she was able to discern a tangle of brown hair filled with bits of twig and leaves. Eyes the color of moss regarded her gravely as she exteneded her hand. Maeve gripped the cold fingers concentrating on Airmid's shining eyes.

"You know a lot of this intuitively but there is much more for you to learn. Listen to me very carefully."

Maeve felt rather than heard all that Airmid imparted. The knowledge came in the form of thought waves: where to find the herbs, what they were good for and how to prepare them. Catriona had barely scratched the surface in comparison to what this woman conveyed.

"There is a special herb that can help you at this crucial time. It is called werewolf root, named for the werewolf who shape-shifts from his human form. It will allow you to let go of the past to embrace your destiny. It will give you the strength to rise above the hopelessness here that rides on the wind. But you must be ready for it." She fiddled in one of the pouches and pulled out something that looked like a parsnip with a forked end and then waited with a questioning expression.

Maeve gazed into the luminous eyes. "I don't know if I'm ready," she answered truthfully. "How can I tell?"

"Tune in, Saille."

Maeve breathed deeply, letting her thoughts drift away as MacCuill had instructed her, only a few days ago she realized; it seemed like a year. As she breathed steadily in and out her mind cleared and after a few moments a voice in her head said *'yes'*. She looked up and nodded.

"Chew only a small amount as it can be toxic in larger doses. The rest you can save for a later time."

Toxic? What would the root do? Was she suddenly going to be ten feet tall or would she shrink down to mouse size?

"Do not be afraid, the root will only help you." Airmid held it out, her lips curled in a smile as though she knew exactly what Maeve was thinking.

When Maeve chewed off a tiny piece, the taste brought back the memory of the night she and Harold had done peyote together and all at once she wasn't here at all—she was with Harold again, kissing him with abandon under the trees. Her eyes filled with tears and she wondered how long it would be before they saw each other again. She heard the soft-spoken voice and turned her attention back to the healer, wiping at her face with the back of her hand.

Airmid watched her, waiting until she had composed herself before continuing. "I am the keeper of the sacred spring that brings the dead back to life. It is very far from here in the north-west. If you ever need me, you will find me there. Thank you for believing in me." Her smile transformed her face for a moment and Maeve got a glimpse of her ethereal beauty, the serenity and acceptance that lay within her lovely eyes.

A second later Maeve was overcome by an intense headache. She closed her eyes and when she looked up again Airmid had melted into the fog.

She put the rest of the root into her pocket and slowly walked back toward the cave, her thoughts churning in circles. "Did you see her?" she asked Eron, sitting down next to him.

Eron's brown eyes met hers. "See who?"

"The goddess, the woman—Airmid."

"I have not seen Airmid for many moons. Have some tea, granddaughter. I think you've been dreaming."

"I was just with her—look what she gave me." Maeve pulled the root out her pocket.

Eron turned it over in his big hands. "Werewolf root."

"Airmid thought it would be good for me."

Eron stared into the distance. When he turned back his eyes were clouded. "I have used this in the past. It helped me through a very bleak time. Its effects are subtle. You probably won't notice right away, aside from the headache, but then you'll realize that a shift has taken place."

Maeve looked down, her eyes coming to rest on the long red scars on her forearms—the crow attack she had cured with several herbs that had just popped into her mind. And that was before coming here, before hearing from Catriona and Airmid. Now her brain was chock full of herbal information. In the distance she heard a wolf howl and the mournful sound put her back in the woods with Harold, his arms tight around her, his lips on hers. If she didn't get out of here soon she wouldn't be able to meet him at the airport. Before she could stop herself tears were rolling down her cheeks.

"What is it, moon granddaughter?"

"Harold, my boyfriend, is arriving on the first."

"Ah...well that is a conundrum. I doubt you will be there to meet him." Eron stirred the embers with a narrow stick, encouraging the newly added wood to catch fire.

"But what will he do?"

Eron sat back on his heels. "If Harold is part of your destiny, he will find you. If not, you will have to find each other after your job here is completed."

In her last Tarot reading, Gertrude had warned her that something was going to happen regarding Harold. All she could think of now was how much she loved and missed him and wished he were sitting here beside her. Gazing at her grandfather she thought the two men were a lot alike—calm and capable.

Maeve thought about everything that had happened since she had been catapulted into the Otherworld. It seemed much longer than three days. Her father was back in New England celebrating Christmas Eve. Since she was a little girl it had been a time when they shared a meal and opened presents. Sometimes they would go to the little church in Halston to listen to the music and sing along. She had a sudden image of the snow, and yearned for the coziness of his living room with the fire going, the house where she had grown up. How long would it be before she saw her family and friends again? It was still a week until Harold's arrival; maybe she could manage to meet him after all.

Looking up, she reached for the tea her grandfather was handing her. She took a sip, a strange feeling stealing over her. It was as though the past was fading into a sort of tableau in sepia. She watched it move backward in her mind, growing smaller and smaller until there was nothing there. "I have to find the river and get the key from the boatman," she found herself mumbling. "I have to release the prisoners."

"The river is half a days ride from here. It is too late to start. Have some food, you need to keep up the warmth in your body." Eron handed her a piece of bread and some cheese. "As long as we are together I could share a bit of family history. Are you interested?"

Maeve nodded, her mouth full of cheese.

"I'm sure the others have filled you in on a lot of it but maybe I can add some pieces to the puzzle. For instance who your grandmother really is and what happened to her brother."

"Catriona told me that Brandubh was an anomaly, that only girl children had been born in the line."

Eron nodded. "He and Catriona were extremely close growing up. They could read each other's minds. They were in constant communication." He turned to pour tea for himself, taking a sip before continuing. "It was your great-grandfather, Fergus, who twisted the boy's mind."

"I heard it was Adair who did the damage."

"Adair has influenced him more recently but what I'm about to tell you happened when the twins were only twelve. Brandubh came upon his father forcing himself on Catriona. He attacked the man, pulling him off, but in the process Fergus fell and hit his head. He died instantly."

Maeve recoiled, visualizing the gruesome scene.

"Adair blamed Catriona for Fergus's death, and accused Catriona of seducing her own father. Fergus was an evil and cruel man but Adair was worse in some ways because she knew the truth and did nothing about it. The abuse had been going on for years. After the death, Brandubh disappeared. Catriona had thought to stay to help her mother, but after the accusations began to fly she ran away. She tried to find her brother but when she used her mental telepathy it was as though he had cut himself off from her completely. No one saw him again until he showed up in Bailemuir around the time Catriona moved in with Angus."

"Why did she do that? It doesn't fit with my picture of her, especially after the stories about her wild, free-love sort of attitude."

"She was that. I met her when she was fifteen and it was love at first sight. I've never felt that way about anyone—as though the sun was gone when we were apart. Catriona felt badly about my wife, Grita—neither of us wanted to hurt her." Eron looked away for a moment. "I hope all this doesn't shock you."

"It doesn't. And I've already heard most of it from my mother."

Eron nodded. "Well...when your grandmother realized she was pregnant she took off. She didn't want me to be concerned about her and the baby."

"Why didn't you stop her?"

Eron shook his head. "Catriona has a mind of her own and I suppose I knew she was right. It would have hurt Grita too much if I had told her the truth. She was a very fragile soul."

"But what about Finna? How could you stand it?"

"Mikdal and Herska acted like go-betweens during that time. Catriona had lived with them off and on for several years and they were very close to her. I thought she had decided to stay in Bailemuir with Angus. I tried to forget her and concentrate on my own family, but I was deeply depressed without her. I hadn't laid eyes on my daughter until the two of them showed up at the spring on their way to the blessing ceremony—the very same one where you bathed, Maeve. By that time Finna was already a grown woman and pregnant with you."

Maeve stared at her grandfather. "So all those years you just stayed away? I mean you loved each other and you knew you had a daughter—I just don't understand."

"I decided I had to wait for Catriona to search me out. It was her decision to leave me and it had to be her decision to find me again. From what I heard from Mikdal and Herska she was doing all right in her new life. After my wife and child were killed in the fire I went into an even deeper depression. I felt responsible, you see, because I wasn't with them. I had moved into the cave by that time. I had finally come clean to Grita about Catriona and so to punish myself I decided to become a hermit."

"This sounds very much like one of those horrible Victorian stories where people sacrifice their lives so as not to hurt others."

Eron grinned and then laughed. "I'm glad I grew out of that phase. Your grandmother and I didn't get back together until I met her on that trip to the Glass Mountain. My wife and child had been gone for many years by that time."

"I can't believe you didn't meet your daughter until she was twenty!"

Eron nodded and looked down. His eyes looked dark now, filled with an old sadness. "Finna was furious—she couldn't believe that her entire life had been built on lies. And it was the first time she had heard about the prophecy. You can imagine how upsetting all of that was."

Maeve didn't have to try very hard to envision how her mother must have felt—the parallels were undeniable. At least she wasn't carrying a child right now—that would put her over the top. She ran her fingers through her hair, surprised when she felt the short tufts.

"I think I like this new you," Eron said, watching her. "Not the city girl anymore, more like what you're becoming. Cutting your hair represents a rite of passage."

"The hair was just getting in my way, that's all." When Maeve looked into Eron's nut-brown eyes she became aware that her answer had been automatic and not the truth at all. "No... you're right," she added. "Something came over me and I just had to cut it." She thought about the feel of the knife in her hand as it slid through her long curls. The act had felt violent and strangely out of control.

Eron stared at her for a moment and then smiled. "You are transitioning into your role here, Maeve. From now on you will notice other things, different ways of thinking, parts of yourself that seem alien."

Maeve tried to think about Milltown, her old life, but since taking the werewolf root her mind simply would not go there. She was here now, her thoughts on what was in her future. She stared out of the cave, watching clouds bump against each other in the heavy sky. "When I went into the dreamtime with MacCuill he took me to a time when the Otherworld was full of light and joy. But now I can't imagine it ever being that way again. In the Crion village the people were so happy. And then I saw them at the fort on the way here. It was terrible."

Eron nodded. "Much of the forest has been cut down or burned. The snows have always brought moisture for the spring thaw, filling in the aquifers. The Cailleach, the goddess of winter, is gone, and now everything remains frozen year-round. The underground rivers beneath the earth are being polluted from acids released from the mining processes, so even if we had running water it would be undrinkable. There are very few places to find clean water now. I hunt deer, trap rabbits and other small game. This is how I've always lived. But now game is scarce and the fish are being poisoned."

With no rain or snow and no water re-filling the aquifers there was not much hope of a future here. And if there weren't people to fight this battle how was her being here going to help? Then she remembered something that MacCuill had told her, that this fight wasn't about physical strength. She puzzled over that for a long time, coming to no conclusion.

Chapter

7

Maeve didn't hear the approach of the Oillteil until it was too late, waking to a rough hand clamped over her mouth and the aroma of unwashed flesh. The last thing she remembered was Eron telling her to rest while he went with the wolves to check his snares. He would be back shortly, he had said, hopefully with something to cook. Terror shot through her and she struggled until she realized her ankles and her arms had been tightly bound. Her body bumped painfully as they carried her roughly down the hill. A filthy rag was tied across her mouth, the smell of which was making her feel sick. When she began to gag, her face was slapped, bringing tears to her eyes. After that she worked hard to keep the bile down and tried to breathe shallowly.

Her mind had gone blank. All she could picture was Brandubh's horrible white face from the night of the bonfire. Were they taking her to him? Uncontrolled shivering racked her body. When they reached the camp she was dumped unceremoniously on the ground. She managed to rub the rag off her face so she could throw up. She rolled away from the stench trying to ignore the lingering taste in her mouth. A moan of terror escaped her lips as she heard one of her captors say the name, *Black Raven.* The hideously ugly creature came by her and kicked her in the ribs, sending a spasm of pain through her. From then on she tried to stay quiet although it was very hard since she was freezing cold and shivering violently. She could hear the crackling of a wood fire inside the animal skin tent about ten feet away; smoke was escaping out of a hole in the top. Rolling over gave her a view through the door flap and she saw one of the Oillteil doing something with a dark-feathered bird. A little later a crow emerged from the hole in the top of the tent. He fixed her with his bright eye before lifting into the sky and flying away. He was a messenger, she realized, sent to fetch Brandubh. Her arms burned suddenly, the remaining welts seeming to react to the sight of the black bird so similar to the one that had attacked her in Naomi's apartment. Her stomach filled with fear.

The misshapen and grotesque faces of the Oillteil heading toward her looked off center, with mouths that turned down on one side, up on the other. Their tiny eyes were too close together and not lined up. Large ears stuck out from bald flat heads, their overlong arms ending in stubby hands and twisted fingers.

"Not very strong, why he so excited about this one?" one of them said, looking down on her. He kicked her, connecting with her already sore ribs and she let out a moan. As he bent toward her, his putrid breath assaulted her nostrils making her gag.

"I like to kill you but priest want you for himself." He made a weird repetitive grunting sound that Maeve thought might be a laugh.

"What is going to happen to me?" she asked in what she hoped was a strong voice.

"The priest take care of that. He come soon."

When the Oillteil walked away, Maeve worked her hands frantically back and forth, the ropes biting into the broken skin.

"I don't deserve to be tortured or killed. Why do you serve this man? He is evil!" she called out.

The creature turned, fixing her with a malevolent stare. "He give us food he give us power. We help him get power—dig gold."

"He is not going to give you power. He will use you and take all the power and gold for himself."

"Why I listen to you? You work for other side."

"I don't work for anyone. That's the difference between us. I want what's best for all the beings here, including you. I want everyone to have their own power. I want this place to be restored to what it once was."

The creature cocked his head as though listening and then said, "The priest come—too late now." He began the repetitive grunting again, watching her. When there was a loud shout from down the canyon, he picked up a massive wooden club and lumbered away.

Another Oillteil appeared, apparently sent to keep an eye on her. This one was smaller, his beady eyes filled with hate. "Please let me go, I don't want to die." Despite trying to seem strong, tears rolled down her cheeks but the Oillteil had turned away, interested in the shrieks and shouting coming from the canyon. Maybe he couldn't understand her.

She worked her wrists back and forth trying to keep from crying out from the pain. An image of Brandubh sent adrenaline rushing through her—she had to get away before he arrived. He would surely kill her. One hand was free now—had the guard noticed? No, he was staring away with his back to her. She reached around with her free hand, her fingers clutching the moonstone.

"Ahhiiiee…" the guard said. The Oillteil glanced toward her and then pointed down the hill where a horse with a dark-cloaked rider was approaching at a gallop. He turned back to her, recognition widening his eyes and then headed her way. He was hoping to be given the credit for her capture. She could hear the hooves pounding the ground as Brandubh headed up the hill. He was nearly there. The stone burned her hand but she tightened her grip—something was changing in the air around her. "Grab her!" she heard the priest scream. She could see him now, his eyes intent on her as he grabbed the Oillteil by the neck throwing him aside. His hand reached out and she felt the brush of his fingers just before she whirled away into the colored mist.

Maeve landed hard, hitting her head. When she sat up she thought she might have been unconscious for a minute or two, dizziness accompanying a raging headache. Her wrists were bloody and she had nothing to treat the cuts although she knew without having to think about it that Elder would heal them. Too bad Airmid hadn't given her some of those little bags hanging from her belt. Her fingers went up to the necklace—the moonstone had saved her once again, because now she was positive of the power it carried.

When she stood up the world spun for a moment. When she was steady again she took a look around, dismayed to see eroded hills covered in hoarfrost stretching for miles in every direction. Clouds scudded by like dark birds. A knot formed in the pit of her stomach as she realized she was truly alone in a place where she didn't know the rules. There was no map and no way to get back to Eron or the wolves.

Her skirt was torn, the hem trailing strings from the encounter with the Oillteil. She brushed the dirt off the back and pulled Eron's tunic down over her hips, glad for the extra layer. Turning in a circle, she waited for someone or something to tell her which direction to go, but when nothing happened she began to walk.

It wasn't long before a river valley came into view in the distance, and beyond that a flat icy area led toward higher hills capped in white. Nothing looked familiar, but why would it? Winds whipped around her, entering her mind like shadowy beings, taking her thoughts and tossing them away. Idly she wondered if this was some aftereffect of the werewolf root. It was as though her mind had been scoured.

The wind abruptly stopped, the meager light draining quickly from the sky. Night fell over her like a dark curtain. Despite the darkness she continued on. The smooth-looking hills were deceptive, with sharp rocks hidden in the weeds and patches of ice, and she tripped often, bruising her already sore ankles. It was completely silent; no nighttime scuttling of animals, no dark-eyed bats above her in the night sky, no calling owls.

At the river she bent down to rinse her mouth and wash her face. After that she drank until her thirst was quenched, hoping that it wasn't polluted. When she searched for a bridge or some way to cross, all she found were dead weeds and brittle cattails. While she stood there wondering what to do she heard water slapping against wood and looked up to see a small walnut-shaped boat appearing out of the dark mist. A white-haired man stood in the middle, using one oar to steer the coracle toward her. He approached the shore and then let the boat drift into the weeds where it came to rest.

"Hello!" she called.

His milky eyes glowed out of the dark as he drew closer. "Who is there?"

"I'm Maeve. Can you take me across the river?"

"What is your reason for crossing the river?"

Maeve wondered if this was some trick question. She thought about it for a moment and then she answered, "I need to find my way but I don't know where I'm going."

"What do you expect to find on the other side?"

"I don't know, but the river is a sign and I need to cross it."

121

"Climb in," he offered, moving to the back of the boat to give her room. "Normally I exact payment for my services but you are Saille, the one from the prophecy. It is an honor to take you across."

"What do you know of the prophecy?" she asked, sitting down on the small wooden seat. The little boat was made of split and woven willow and covered in animal hide. It bobbed in the water like a cork.

He switched the oar from one side to the other, somehow keeping the odd-shaped boat going in a straight line against the current. His arms were hugely muscled, as though he had done this a thousand times.

"I know you are the one to bring the balance back and I also know that you have come too early, that your true power arrives with the wolf moon."

"What do you mean? When is the wolf moon?"

"The wolf moon begins at the full moon. It is still many days away. How did you get here?"

"I don't really know. I...I was trying to get away from my great-uncle."

"Ah yes, the priest."

"Who are you? How do you know about Brandubh?"

"Everyone in the Otherworld knows about Brandubh, if not directly then through someone who has had bad dealings with him or his mother. This man was brought forth by the under-world." His voice softened. "Do not fear me Saille, I am the boatman, nothing more."

The boatman. She shivered and pulled Eron's tunic closer. "Rhiannon told me to get the key from you to release the pris-oners," she said through chattering teeth.

He turned his blind eyes on her, staring straight into her soul. "I have this key you ask for, but you are far from where these prisoners languish. How will you find them?"

"I don't really know."

"If you wish it, I can take you there."

Maeve thought about that for a moment. She was separated from Finiche and Eron, maybe if he took her back she could find them as well. But she had a feeling the moonstone had brought her here for a reason. She wasn't sure what to do. "What is your name?"

"I have no name, I am merely the boatman. I've been here for a thousand years."

"But how did you know I was here?"

"This river is long and meanders around and through this world. I go where I am needed. You needed to cross here at this time and I am the boatman. Do you understand?"

"No, but don't try to explain anymore, my mind feels muddled enough."

"You will come to understand the way things work here after you have been in this world for a while. Now what is it to be? Shall I take you back or do you wish to go to the other side?"

"I think I'm meant to be here but I also need to release the prisoners as soon as I can. What do you think I should do?"

He took a small golden key out of his pocket and handed it to her. "Guard this, it is the only one." When the boat glided through some reeds and came to rest against the far bank she climbed out.

"Thank you."

"Do not lose the key…" When she looked back he had already disappeared into the mist.

Chapter

8

Gertrude tripped over a tree root and twisted her ankle. It hurt like hell, but she would be damned if she was going to be the one to hold up the group. It was bad enough that her reactions to everything strange they had seen were always high-pitched shrieks of terror or surprise. She had embarrassed herself more than once. This trip in the dead of night, following wolves through the forest, was more strange than anything she could have conjured up—occasional fire erupting from MacCuill's fingers when they couldn't see well enough to get around brambles and fallen tree limbs, not to mention the eerie howling of the wind that sounded almost alive. But would she rather be back in Milltown? Heavens no, she had decided that this was much more interesting, even with the awareness of very real danger around every corner.

What they had gone through to get to this place had been something she would never have believed if she hadn't experienced it. The four women had followed MacCuill up the path away from the cottage and then into a wilderness that ended at the edge of a river. A mist hung over the water despite the clear blue sky, and there was something unsettling about the quality of the silence at the edge of the bank. But it was when the boat appeared out of the mist that her heart began to beat erratically. The person steering the craft was not of this world with his milky, unseeing eyes and white hair that flowed to his waist.

As they crossed, Gertrude stared into the opaque looking water, imagining she saw eyes peering up at her. She was glad when they arrived on the other side. But this place did not bear any resemblance to the other shore. It was bleak and cold, the dark sky full of threatening clouds.

By the time they delivered the two fallen Crion to their village and said goodbye to Aila, Gertrude was succumbing to jetlag and nerves. Her coat wasn't warm enough and she felt chilled to the bone. Outside the Crion tunnels, Herska said goodbye to them, heading off to search for Mikdal.

Gertrude's thoughts had been miles away when MacCuill abruptly stopped in front of her. She very nearly ran into him.

"From here on we need to be very careful," the druid whispered. "We are close to one of Brandubh's forts. No more talking and try to go as quietly as you can." He moved silently away from the trees, following the wolves down a steep hillside.

Brandubh. My God, was he really living out here in this desolate place? Gertrude thought back on her time spent with the priest. How smitten she had been. And that man had enjoyed the lap of luxury with his fine wine, gourmet meals and palatial hotel rooms. Thinking about it all now it seemed strange that their paths had crossed in the coffee shop in Milltown. Could it really have been coincidence? And now he had shot two Crion and wounded another and worst of all, kidnapped Maeve.

This Brandubh did not bear any resemblance to the charming and solicitous priest in Milltown, who had taken her out to the most expensive dinner of her life. The only chink in his armor had been finding out that he could read her mind, a fact he had kept to himself for the entire three days she spent with him. And of course the night he chose to divulge this, all her thoughts had been centering on the two of them in bed together. She shook her head. This was not the time to revisit that particular evening.

She followed the others down the hill, her ankle protesting painfully as it bent to accommodate the grade. She hopped on her left leg trying to spare her right one the worst of the descent. No one had even noticed that she was hurt. Maybe they couldn't see her, it was certainly black as pitch out here. She stopped for a moment to pull up the hood of her jacket and then hurried to catch up as the small group moved away from her, disappearing from view.

Just as she was about to call out, a hand clamped over her mouth. She tried to scream but a rag was stuffed into her mouth before she could emit a sound. Then she was picked up by strong arms and carried silently away. It was too dark to see her captors. Her eyelids felt heavy and her body went limp as she fell into a drugged torpor.

Gertrude stared into dark hooded eyes peering down at her where she lay on the frozen ground.

"Gertrude! What in hell are you doing here?" a familiar voice said.

"You tell me. One minute I was walking down the hill and the next...well, someone grabbed me. Wasn't it you?"

Brandubh bent down and unhooked her from the chain that connected her to several other prisoners. Grabbing her arm, he dragged her into the log fort, leading her into a rectangular room with a long table and chairs. A threadbare carpet lay on the wood floor in front of a wide stone fireplace. "Stand by the fire and get out of those wet clothes. I'll get you some dry ones."

Large aromatic pine logs burned hot, sending welcome warmth into the chilly room.

Gertrude stripped off her coat, shirt and jeans, leaving only her bra and underpants. When Brandubh came back in the room his eyes traveled across her body before he handed her a long woolen robe.

"So, my dear, you didn't tell me how you ended up in the Otherworld. Last I heard you refused to come with me." His dark eyes regarded her coldly.

Gertrude thought back to his invitation and her decision. She had very much wanted to travel to Scotland with him but his deception had hurt her and made her refuse. "You know very well why I said no. And if you remember I mentioned coming at a later date. But this trip had nothing to do with you. I...I had some strange visions about Maeve. Did you really do those terrible things I heard about?"

"If you're speaking about the night of the solstice, yes. But they had it coming. I cannot tolerate the pagan celebrations. They go against everything I stand for."

Gertrude watched his eyes darken, a scowl bringing his eyebrows together. She realized she was trembling and she pulled her arms around her nearly naked body, pulling the robe across her chest to cover herself.

"You should take a warm shower before putting that on," he said.

"That would be wonderful."

He crossed the room and opened another door. "Don't be too long, there isn't much hot water."

When she walked past him he closed the door, leaving her alone in the small bathroom. She heard a click and when she tried it, the door was locked. Her teeth chattered so hard they hurt and her throat ached every time she swallowed. She took off her underclothes and turned the knobs, stepping under the warm stream. Ah, heavenly, she thought, trying to remember the last time she had taken a shower. She found a small bar of soap and lathered her hair and body. As she was rinsing, the hot water supply began to run out, and she hurried to get the soap out of her hair. By the time she had dried and put on the robe she was certain she had a fever; her cough had deepened and now her head was throbbing.

It took knocking loudly and calling out to get someone to unlock the door. The man who finally opened it scared her with his dreadlocks and dead eyes. He led the way back to the room with the fire where Brandubh was sitting on a chair with his back to the flames. The priest looked imposing and powerful, his feet planted on each side of the chair legs, hands on his thighs.

"Feel better, Gertrude?" His eyes focused on hers, the gaze intimate.

"Yes, it was wonderful but I'm certain I have a fever. Also my ankle is throbbing."

"Come sit in front of the fire. I'll get you some soup and hot tea. And you need to dry that hair." He put his hand on her forehead before he disappeared through another door. A few minutes later he was back, carrying a mug and a bowl. "So, if you're not here because of me I want to know everything you saw in your visions and how this prompted you to make a trip across the ocean."

She took a sip of tea, an herbal blend that she didn't recognize. "I read Maeve's cards right before she left for Scotland and what I saw…well…now I know what's going on." She looked at him pointedly but he didn't return her gaze.

"Do not jump to conclusions about what you've seen. Things are very different in this world."

"Did you kidnap Maeve?"

Brandubh shook his head, turning toward the fire again. "She managed to escape. I'm in the process of searching for her."

"And what do you plan to do if you find her?"

"Don't ask questions about things you don't understand. My plans have been in place for many years and I won't let your arrival pull me off course." He ran his fingers through his hair, showing his agitation. "The people here are very superstitious but I'm managing to bring them into the fold."

Gertrude watched his face for signs of the man she knew from Milltown but couldn't find him. She shivered again and moved closer to the fire. "I don't feel at all well."

Brandubh looked up. "The tea will help you sleep."

Shortly after she finished eating Gertrude was taken over by extreme exhaustion—she could barely keep her eyes open. Brandubh pulled her up by her hand and put his arm around her waist. "You can rest in my room," he said, helping her out the door and up a flight of stairs. By the time they reached the little room at the top of the stairs she felt almost delirious.

"Lie down and let me take a look at that ankle before you go to sleep." As she sank onto the raised sleeping pallet, he reached down and took her leg gently into his large hands. "I have something that will help."

A strong and pungent aroma lifted into the air as he rubbed in a thick and gooey substance. He reached into a drawer and pulled out a piece of silk that he wrapped around her ankle. "This will be much better by tomorrow. Now go to sleep, I promise I won't disturb you. I need you to be well."

When she lay back on the thick mattress he covered her with a sheep's wool blanket. She barely heard the door close before falling into a dreamless sleep.

In the morning Gertrude was unable at first to remember where she was. Everything had a fuzzy quality to it. At least her fever seemed to have broken, her throat not nearly so sore. She got out of bed, testing her ankle; whatever he had used on it had worked. She walked gingerly to the window and looked out. The sky was the same shade of dark gray as the day before, the small people still chained in the courtyard below. A wave of pity went through her. Here she was ensconced in Brandubh's bedroom and they were still shivering in the cold. Maybe she could talk Brandubh into taking better care of his prisoners. They wouldn't do him much good if they were dead.

Carefully she headed down the stairs, hoping to find Brandubh in the main room, but when she got to the door, two guards barred her way. "Where is Brandubh?" she demanded.

"He go north," one of the strange looking creatures said.

"When will he be back?"

He shook his head.

"Can I come in by the fire?" They glanced at each other and then opened the door. Behind her she noticed a number of filthy men dressed in animal skins emerging from the back of the house and heading out the door toward the courtyard. Their pale amber eyes regarded her like a wolf regards its prey before killing it—she shivered and shrank away from them, hurrying into the room.

While she warmed herself in front of the fire, the door opened and one of the guards brought her a bowl of porridge and a mug of tea. Why was she getting this preferential treatment? It worried her, but she also felt grateful. She was sure she would have pneumonia by now if Brandubh hadn't brought her inside last night.

"Gertrude." Brandubh stepped quietly into the bedroom. "What are you doing up here?"

Gertrude turned from the window where she had been watching the comings and goings of his men. "I didn't know who those men were and I got nervous. Who is that?" She pointed to a gangly man with dirty blond hair dressed in jeans and a heavy modern-looking down jacket.

"That's John, my right hand man. I recruited him when I was in Milltown. Remember the man I went to visit? Well, there he is, ripe for my instructions. I have to say John's a wee bit bloodthirsty. The others down there are the duine fiain, the Wildmen." He looked her way and must have noticed her petrified expression. "Don't worry. They are all under my control. Come down by the fire, you're shaking." Brandubh took her hand and led her toward the door.

"It is chilly up here, but this room seemed safer somehow."

"Well, you're right about that, no one would disturb you up here. This is my sanctuary." He smiled. "Consider yourself privileged."

His smile was reassuring but there was something about him here that didn't fit with the man she knew from Milltown—his manner was hardly priest-like despite the dark woolen robes he wore. "Why was I captured?" she asked, following him down the stairs.

"The Oillteil thought you were Maeve. They are not the most intelligent tribe I've encountered, but now that you're here I think we can find a use for you."

So that's what the ugly creatures were called. When they entered the main room John and a group of Wildmen stood in front of the fire conversing in low tones. A number of Oillteil stood next to the door looking unhappy. As soon as the door closed behind them, everyone stopped speaking and turned, staring at Gertrude in surprise.

"This is Gertrude, my houseguest," Brandubh said, heading toward the fire. The group dispersed, their eyes wary. Only John remained there, his eyes fastening on hers with an angry glare.

132

"Get out of the way, John," Brandubh ordered loudly, pulling over a chair. He motioned for Gertrude to sit and then went to the head of the table. "Come everyone. We have plans to make." He settled his tall frame into the chair waiting for the other men to join him. John sat at the other end facing him, his back to Gertrude.

Once everyone was settled Brandubh gazed around the table. "John and I have just arrived from the Oillteil camp in the north. It seems our quarry has escaped once again. She seems to be able to do some sort of vanishing act. We need to find her. I want you to divide into groups and begin the search. I've already alerted the men in the barracks, some of whom will be joining you. One group will head north, one south and one east. I myself plan to head west with John and some of my men. Whoever brings Maeve to me will be rewarded beyond imagining. Does everyone understand?"

There was a mumbling of assent as the men glanced around at each other.

"Take the wild dogs and get on with it. I expect you to report back in a few days and I hope for your sakes that you are successful."

The Wildmen jumped up, exiting the room noisily and pushing roughly into the Oillteil guards on their way out. A few skirmishes started up before Brandubh bellowed, "Stop this nonsense! We need to be united in our cause! John, get the horses ready. I'll join you shortly."

Gertrude watched them, acutely aware of the tension between the men and Brandubh's thread-like hold on the proceedings. She did not want to be alone with the Wildmen. And those terrifying animal-like men were about to head off to find Maeve—she hoped MacCuill and the others had found her by now.

After everyone left Brandubh came toward her, placing his hands on her shoulders. "How about some dinner?"

An electric charge went through her body and she stood up, letting him steer her to the table. Even with what she knew about him there was this attraction between them—it was hard to understand. When she gazed up at him he was smiling down on her, his lips curved knowingly. Damn the man and his mind reading!

Brandubh turned to one of the guards. "Bring us some food and then tell Brug that we will be heading out within the hour." He turned back to Gertrude. "I'm sorry to leave you again, but as you heard I have matters of importance to attend to. Will you be all right here until my return?"

"As long as the Wildmen aren't around. They scare me."

"Aside from the Oillteil guards, they will all be with me—you'll have the place to yourself."

"May I use your bed again?"

"As long as you don't mind sharing it when I get back. I'll need to sleep for a couple of hours."

"What do you plan to do with me?"

"Nothing, my dear. I'm merely using you for bait. You understand that, don't you? You seem like an intelligent woman."

"So you're hoping that MacCuill and the others will come to rescue me?"

"I'm sure they will."

When the two guards returned with steaming bowls of stew and placed them on the table, Brandubh picked up a wooden spoon and began to eat. "Have some stew, Gertrude, I want you to be completely over your illness. You look pale."

When they finished eating Brandubh pushed his chair back. "I need to leave now. Make yourself comfortable. If you need tea or wine ask the guard to bring it. I hope to spend some time with you later on tonight." At her panicked expression, he smiled. "Don't look so worried, I promise not to hurt you in any way. After all, you are my guest. Sleep well, my dear."

Just before he swept from the room, pulling his dark cloak around him, he turned back to stare at her. She met his eyes, the attraction between them making her weak. This man was evil and planning to hurt or possibly kill Maeve. How could her body betray her like this? She remembered what he had told her back in Milltown, that here in the Otherworld he could break his vows. Would she stop him if he tried something? Hopefully MacCuill and the others would rescue her before he returned tonight, but there was a tiny part of her that wished for something quite different.

Chapter

9

Maeve spent a restless night under a grove of leafless birch trees. But despite the layer of frost all around, she had not been cold. The answer lay above her in the trees where a web had been woven in between the branches. It was not made by a spider and seemed of some protective fibrous material. She puzzled over this, wondering who or what had woven it. Had it happened before or after she laid down the night before, she wondered, because it was completely dark when she finally succumbed to exhaustion.

A buzz and tinkling sound had her searching through the trees, but she found nothing—maybe the profound silence was doing something to her hearing. Her mind felt blank and fuzzy, with no energy for figuring things out. She was alive at least, and thankful for that. Her scan of the bleak landscape stretching in every direction brought no insights. She chose a direction at random and began to walk.

Time seemed different here. It was nearly dark again after what seemed to be only a few hours of walking. Her muscles ached from navigating the uneven ground and there was a painful twinge in her right hip joint. In the distance, rocky hills rose out of the valley and she headed towards them. Hopefully there were caves there or at least crevasses where she could get out of the cold and go to sleep. By now the shivering had her teeth chattering and if it wasn't for whatever magical properties this dress contained she would have long ago given herself over to the cold. The idea of death didn't really disturb her. Her mind was not working well and she had the strangest impression that she was having some kind of terrible dream that she sincerely wanted to wake up from.

Ahead of her hills rose and fell in endless waves of ochre and brown. The air was still, the sky a forbidding shade of gray, but no moisture had come out of those heavy clouds. No trail to follow, no people, no animals, no birds, just the countless hills stretching endlessly into the distance. It seemed as if she had been walking for days.

She ran her fingers through her hair. It seemed like a lifetime ago she had cut it. Looking down she noticed more tears in her beautiful velvet skirt—covered with grime, the entire hem seemed to be unraveling. She must look like some kind of crazy street person with her chopped off hair and ragged clothes. What would Harold say if he could see her now? She laughed, the echo of the alien sound bringing back to her how far from her normal life she had traveled.

The wind came up, sending sharp bits of dirt into her face and making her eyes water. A steep hill led toward the valley, but the hill on the other side was just like the one she was on—no trees, just bracken fern and dead heather. Was she in some kind of weird loop where the same landscape kept repeating, or was she traveling in circles? Her stomach clenched at the thought. She knew very little about how this "Otherworld" worked, pretty much anything was possible. Isn't that what the boatman had conveyed? Better to just keep going and not think about it. There had to be something different on the other side of the next hill.

With the simple rhythmic act of putting one foot in front of the other, her mind grew calm, so when she had the vision it didn't seem at all odd. At first she heard Catriona's voice in her mind, calling to her. Maeve answered, letting Catriona know that she could hear her. After that Maeve began to get flashes. They were disturbing but she tried to keep her mind clear so as not to block them. Her grandmother had lost the bond with her twin brother, a connection they had shared since birth and maybe from when they were in the womb. It was like losing a part of herself. Catriona felt guilty, as though what Brandubh was doing now was related to her inability to reach him. She blamed herself for everything Brandubh had done and was racked with guilt because she had turned away from him. And yet from Maeve's point of view this had not been the case; it had been Brandubh who cut himself off from his sister, severing their bond with knife-like precision. The conflict Catriona felt rolled through Maeve's consciousness making her dizzy. Why did Catriona want Maeve to know all this?

After these flashes and thoughts, something changed. Maeve now experienced Catriona's current vision, *running as a wolf, with far-seeing eyes, her ears attuned to distant sounds, nose to the wind, picking up the many varied scents coming to her, the information flooding her consciousness.* Maeve wondered for a moment where Catriona was—was she in the Otherworld, and if so how far away? But before she could think about it any further she was taken into her grandmother's mind again, pulled into the wolf's senses that Catriona was experiencing. Maeve gave herself over to it, allowing Catriona full rein. *Her padded feet flew across the earth, light as a feather and fast, while she catalogued the different smells, searching for the ones that led her to the man, her brother. She*

*now stood on a high hill and could see Brandubh and another man ap-
proaching a wooden structure in the valley miles away. As she looked toward the north she saw a huge army marching. Reluctantly she turned
her wolf mind away from the armies and concentrated on her brother,
probing his mind carefully so as not to alert him of her presence. His
rage rode red on the surface, covering everything he did and thought;
Catriona's wolf mind could see it like a veil of death. He had desecrated
the sacred places, telling the people who worshipped at these sites that it
was blasphemy, a word they did not know the meaning of.*

Maeve could see the specific fort in Catriona's wolf mind,
knew now that Brandubh planned to organize the Oillteil and
the many soldiers he had recruited. He was training them in
his dark magic, teaching them to want power the way he did,
as well as the gold and silver that lay beneath the ground. He
promised them land and dominion over it. Two hundred men
were housed at the fort, thousands more were ready in the
north. He planned to find Maeve, to bring her there, hurt her.
Maeve recoiled as she saw the blackness and evil in his mind and
turned away, severing the psychic connection with Catriona.

A sob escaped from her throat, echoing into the silence.
Why couldn't Catriona have told her all of this when they
were together? It was too much to take in all at once. She felt
weak and shaky thinking about what she now knew for certain.
Brandubh was still on her trail, and if he found her there would
be no mercy.

After she regained her composure, if you could call it that,
Maeve concentrated on opening her mind once more. She hoped
for a clear message about what she should be doing, but nothing happened. All she knew for certain was that she must close
her mind to Brandubh. If she couldn't accomplish that he would
find her for sure.

In the meantime it had grown completely dark and as she
scanned the immediate area she realized there was no place to
shelter for the night. Even with the magical dress there was no

way she could survive this frigid night out in the open. A moment later there were dancing lights all around her, like tiny fireflies. At first she figured she must be hallucinating from lack of food and dehydration but as she watched in amazement, they formed a circle and then fanned out in a line. A high-pitched buzzing seemed to be coming from them but she was so tired and light-headed she didn't know what to think.

The line of lights led her across the darkened terrain, up and down rocky hills, finally arriving at a cliff face. Maeve followed them through a gap between rocks, her arms straining as she pulled herself onto a narrow ledge. With a sigh of relief she levered herself into a cave, sinking out of breath onto the dry dirt floor. Shaking with cold and fatigue, she pulled her knees up and under Eron's tunic. It wasn't long before she fell asleep.

In the morning Meave woke with the remnants of a dream lingering on the edge of her consciousness—the sinking feeling that time was running out. Her mind went to the key and the decision she had made to continue going forward instead of going back to help the prisoners. She wished she had chosen differently because she had no sense of where she was or what to do.

The events of the day before had a dreamlike quality—the endless walking, Catriona's vision and the little light beings that she was sure she'd imagined. Her teeth were already chattering from the cold. She thought about her grandfather, wishing he were here with her, handing her a hot cup of tea. She could see him so clearly in her mind's eye, his dark eyes, the calmness that emanated from his being. If nothing else she was happy to have met these relatives of hers who had been missing from her life.

Maeve sat on her haunches, staring out at the bleak landscape, stretching her tight calves and Achilles tendons. Every muscle in her body hurt and she was so thirsty all she could think of was water. But everything in the immediate vicinity was frozen and dry. Her stomach rumbled as her belly complained about its emptiness. Today she was unable to imagine taking care of herself, much less having the wherewithal to bring the balance back to this strange world, whatever that meant. She turned away from the desolate scene and studied the inky blackness at the back of the cave. It seemed deeper than she originally thought.

A faint breeze brushed her cheek as she crawled into the darkness. The tunnel narrowed almost immediately and she found herself flat on her stomach, inching her way along in the pitch black. She had never liked tight places—closets with the door shut or elevators crowded with people—and panic rose in her throat. She was crawling out backwards when she saw the little lights coming toward her from deeper within the tunnel. Almost immediately her spirits lifted. When they reached her they hovered around her head and then turned and headed down the tunnel. She followed them, hoping it would widen soon. When the tunnel made another sharp bend, she felt the wind again, stronger now. The roof widened out and she stood up, following at a crouch as they led her downward. What if this was some kind of a trap? But a little voice in her head assured her that they were looking out for her, they were her allies. She continued on, wondering how long she had been in here. The muscles in the middle of her back were protesting and she reached around to rub them. It was then that she noticed the slight lightening ahead. "What now?" she wanted to ask them, but when she arrived at the opening, the light beings had disappeared.

From just outside the tunnel opening Maeve could hear the distinctive sound of burbling somewhere below. Water! There were trees here, and although they were leafless they did offer a modicum of protection from the cold and wind. She scrambled down the rocky hill, hoping this stream wasn't filled with poisons. At the stream edge she kneeled, looking carefully at the water and sniffing before drinking. But as she leaned over, a stranger's face stared back at her. Gasping she turned to look behind her but there was no one there. She breathed in and out for a minute to calm herself before trying again. This time she was prepared for the gaunt-eyed woman with the uneven tufts of hair whose pale face was covered in mud, but the brooding expression on this face was very different from the Maeve she was familiar with. Giddy hysteria came over her and she laughed out loud, thinking, *who have I become?*

Using a small piece of hem for a washcloth, she washed the mud and tears off her face and then scooped cool clear water into her mouth, savoring its sweetness as it slid down her parched throat. Downstream the bank had been dug out and piles of slag littered the edges. Her gaze traveled uphill to the rough-hewn tree trunks that had been cut as supports for a mine. Muddy rivulets of dirt and pebbles ran into the stream, clogging the flow. With her hands she cleared the mud dam that had formed and dug out a trench to divert the water. When she finished she walked up the hill, looking back to admire her handiwork. The water leapt downstream with a happy gurgling sound and she had the distinct impression that it was thanking her.

Shrieking pierced the momentary serenity, jarring her into action. It was coming from the hill above and she began a careful ascent. At the top an intricate and unusual wooden fence came into view. She followed its graceful contours with her eyes until it disappeared over the rise. From here the yelling was louder and there were shouts of pain and high-pitched screams. Goats and sheep grazed calmly along the grassy hillside, seemingly unperturbed by the noise and chaos.

As she crept along the fence line the silver glint of a knife caught her eye and a second later a terrible sound rent the air as it found purchase. Maeve skirted the hill making her way by the fighting. She climbed through a break in the fence and then hid behind a thick grove of rowan trees. Her heart thumped unevenly, her rasping breath loud in her ears. From her hiding place she had a clear view of bodies and blood. She crept toward the closest one and reached out to check for a pulse.

"Who are ye?" The man's eyes were wide with terror and pain as he tried to sit up.

"I'm Maeve. I'm only here to help you. Where are you hurt?"

He searched her face and then fell back. "I think my leg is broken."

"Can you walk if I support you?"

"I can try but I suggest we do this quickly before the Oillteil see ye." He looked nervously in the direction of the noise.

Maeve grabbed his hand and pulled him to a sitting position.

"There's a small building back there where we will be safe," he told her, gesturing toward a narrow path. Maeve helped him stand, supporting him as he put his arm around her shoulders.

They worked their way slowly toward a small wooden structure flanked by two rowan trees, their interwoven branches forming an elaborate arch.

"The spirit house is a sacred place," he said, watching her closely as he opened the door.

Maeve pushed it the rest of the way with her foot and helped him inside.

As soon as they were over the threshold he let out a heavy sigh. "Well, at least I know you're not one of them. Evil canna cross this threshold."

Maeve looked around, her gaze coming to rest on a wooden bench running along the wall. She supported him there, helping him to sit down. From the center fire pit, the pungent scent of sage and burning wood reached her nostrils. Smoke rose delicately, exiting through a small hole in the roof.

"Is Brandubh involved in what's going on here?"

"How do ye know about Brandubh, girl?" His eyes were wary, a frown on his face as he looked her over.

"Well, I…I've seen what he's been doing. He's holding people hostage and destroying the land."

The man stared at her for a while as though assessing whether she was telling the truth. Finally he seemed to come to a decision. "Brandubh is not here at the moment but these Oillteil who fight us are in his employ. Some people in town dismantled part of the fence to let them in. They will not get away with this again," he mumbled, his face grim. A second later he turned pale, a moan escaping his lips.

"You should stretch out for a moment. I need to take a look at your leg." Maeve rolled up a piece of burlap, placing it near his head for a pillow. "It must be terrible to know that your friends have been conspiring with the enemy."

"That's the worst part of it." He lay back with his eyes closed, his mouth a line of pain. After a moment he continued. "Many years ago we had the same sort of trouble. The people responsible were punished by the villagers and vowed to never do anything like this again and yet they were the very same ones who helped the Oillteil."

"Why did you trust them?" Maeve asked, carefully rolling up his pant leg to examine the wound.

"Because they assured us of this."

"And the entire village believed them."

"Of course, why wouldn't we? Brianag was and is a healer and part of our community. Pryderi is the son of a goddess. And besides that, there was some magic at play the first time around—some sort of sorcery. We all know each other here and we have to trust one another. Without that we have nothing."

145

He closed his eyes, his forehead furrowed in pain. When he opened them a moment later he held out his hand. "I'm Roc."

Maeve grasped his warm fingers, gazing into pale blue eyes. He was older than she had at first thought, his skin deeply lined beneath the thick gray beard. "So what finally happened to Brianag?"

"She was banished to the outside of the fence but over the years her transgressions were forgiven and she moved back inside. Ye must understand that it was another entity that came through her the first time—an evil that none of us could have predicted, 'twas not her own doing."

"And Pryderi?"

"Aye, he is Rhiannon's son but ye would never know it from his actions. We have nae control over him. With his powers he comes and goes as he pleases. I havna seen him for years but by the looks of it, he was instrumental in this break-in."

"How long has the fighting been going on?" She felt carefully along his leg. The bone was broken but not all the way through.

"Many years, but this attack, only a few days. We've barely managed to keep them from gainin' control of the village. I'm nae sure what it is they want. They seem to be in a kind of frenzy."

Maeve wondered if this could be a plot to capture her. Maybe Brandubh was on his way—maybe he had seen inside her head and knew exactly where she was. Her hands went up to press against her temples, a feeling of futility clamping around her heart. "What is this village called?"

"This is Rowan. I thought ye knew this. Where did ye say ye came from?"

Maeve shook her head, ignoring the question. Her mind spun in circles. She breathed in and out, trying to place herself in the center. "But what do they gain by attacking here?"

"This hill is a strategic spot and the rowan trees have many magical properties. 'Tis how we've kept ourselves from harm. Ye must have noticed that we have water here. Most springs are polluted or dammed up." Roc winced as he tried to shift his position. "Rowan is one of the last bastions in the Otherworld that hasna been mined or clear-cut. The trees will nae permit it.

"But I saw a mine just down the hill," Maeve said.

Roc looked her way with a puzzled expression and then his eyes lit up. "Aye, 'tis an old one from early days. Not in use now."

Maeve thought about the dammed up streambed, the evidence of recent activity. Perhaps Roc hadn't left the village for a while. "What would happen if they tried to cut down the trees?"

"They wield their branches like weapons."

In her mind's eye Maeve pictured angry trees pulling up their roots, their limbs swinging like clubs. She turned back toward Roc, watching his face contort again in pain. "Try to relax now. I'll see what I can do for your leg." Despite her lack of knowledge in the healing arts, Maeve placed her hands around his calf and closed her eyes, concentrating on drawing out the pain. Energy coursed beneath her fingers.

"That feels better. Are ye a healer?"

"No, I mean I didn't think I was... but I seem to have acquired some abilities. It comes as a complete surprise to me."

Roc stared at her for a long moment and then his eyebrows lifted in recognition. "Now I ken who ye are. Your mother and grandmother came through here many years ago, another time when Brandubh attacked. Ye take after your seanmhair. You're the Willow from the prophecy." He smiled, his over-bright eyes trained on her.

She smiled back. "The light beings led me here. Have you ever seen them?"

"Only once a very long time ago. Ye may have been brought here to stop the Oillteil from takin' over the village."

147

"I don't see how that could be. It's more likely that my being here will bring Brandubh. I'm sure he's tracking me."

He shook his head. "Since ye just now arrived here, I dinna think this attack has much to do with ye. Brandubh is nae here nor anywhere close. If he were, we would have seen him by now."

"I really hope you're right. I would hate to be the cause of more injury."

Roc gazed at her as if in awe. "I've been hearin' about ye for a very long time. The Otherworld has been waitin' for your arrival."

Maeve stared at the fire. "The boatman told me that my power comes during the wolf moon."

Roc nodded. "Tis foretold in the prophecy. In two days time 'twill be full moon but this year's month of the wolf is special since there will be another at month's end."

"Where I live two full moons in the same month are known as a blue moon. We have a saying, 'once in a blue moon'. It means something that almost never happens. What is the significance of the wolf moon?"

"'Tis a time to work on new goals. Literally the wolf moon refers to the coldest time of the year when the wolves come into the villages to find food. Because of the prophecy the two full moons might represent doubling of power—your power."

Maeve sighed. "I hope you're right. I got kind of shoved into the Otherworld before I was ready." When she bent over him and felt his leg again, she noticed the swelling had diminished considerably. "I need to make a splint." Ignoring the doubt that arose about her diagnosis she set to work ripping off part of her trailing hem. "Where can I find a straight branch of rowan wood?"

"Around back you'll find a grove of small trees. Just give thanks before you break a twig—the rowan is sensitive and doesn't like to be desecrated without a reason."

Behind the house the trees had formed a small circle around some very old standing stones. Their limbs were leafless, covered in reddish-orange berries that stood out against the glowing cinnamon-colored bark. She placed her hands on a trunk and asked permission to cut a branch for Roc. The answer came in the way of a wind that bent the branches toward her. She grasped one and waited again, thanking the tree for its graciousness. Before she snapped the branch, she heard a whisper in her ear—a *yes* without words.

"My leg pains me again," Roc complained on her arrival back inside.

"This should help." Maeve found a hatchet in the corner and managed to split the wide limb into two fairly even pieces. She took one and placed the flat side under his leg and then ripped a small piece of hem to tie it in place. When she was finished, she held her hands lightly on the break, visualizing golden light all along the leg.

"That feels much better," Roc mumbled with a sleepy sigh. "If you don't mind I think I might take a short nap."

She watched him for a minute and then the name of an herb popped into her mind. "Before you go to sleep, Roc, do you know where I might find Solomon seal?"

"Aye," he answered, his eyes drooping. "Just along the street two doors down you'll find the healer's house. I dinna ken if he's there now, but his name is Janus. Just ask him for what ye need."

Maeve left the spirit house, following the path to the street. The fighting was far away now—just a low din in the distance. When she came to the house Roc had described she knocked and when there was no answer she opened the door. "Halloo, anyone here?" Along the wall a wide shelf held tinctures, jars of herbs and salves labeled neatly in black pen. This Janus must be a very organized man, she thought, moving down the line to the S's.

The root needed to be boiled in milk and she searched the house in vain, finally concluding that there must be a spring-house close by where the cheese and milk were kept. Sure enough, a short trip behind the house revealed a small chamber dug into the hill. As she opened the latch a mossy earth smell wafted out from the dark empty hole where water should be bubbling up from the underground spring. Hadn't Roc mentioned that the springs here were intact? He hadn't known about the mine at the bottom of the hill either. What else was the man in the dark about? Maybe his assurances that Brandubh was nowhere around were also not true. Behind the spring a dirt shelf held several jars, and she lifted one and pulled off the cloth top to check the contents. Her nose wrinkled in distaste—definitely goat's milk.

Back in the spirit house, Maeve sat on her heels next to the fire. A few dried cedar limbs had been stacked by the wall and she placed them in the coals, watching the sparks fly up and out the small hole in the center of the roof. The air filled with the aroma of burning needles. Once the flames had settled down, she placed an iron pot on the hook over the fire. Dropping the root into the milk she waited for the mixture to come to a boil.

"It's almost ready," she said as Roc began to stir. Another piece of hem became an oven mitt as she lifted the pot off the fire. Once the concoction had cooled sufficiently, she undid the binding on his leg and smoothed on the warm paste.

"Can you rest a bit more? It's the best thing for you."

"Aye, I'm sure I can. The fire is warming up my old bones."

After she spread all the paste and tied another strip of hem around his leg, Maeve left Roc, heading down the street in search of more wounded. Many houses were burning and she could hear hysterical shouting coming from within. It was impossible to help since the doorways and windows were impassable. She watched in dismay as the wind picked up burning cinders and carried them from house to house, quickly catching the neighboring thatch on fire. Where was the well? There needed to be an effort to stop the spread of fire. But then again if the spring was dry the only source would be the stream at the bottom of the hill and that was just too far away for a bucket line.

Through the billowing black smoke Maeve saw a woman emerge from a doorway and run for the trees. She followed, getting there just as the woman collapsed. "Let me help you," Maeve said, kneeling next to her.

"Who are ye?" Her eyes were wide with distrust, her clothes covered in soot with red blistering burns lining her arms and neck.

"I'm Maeve—also known as Saille. The one from the prophecy?" she added, as the woman continued to stare at her suspiciously.

"Hanna," she finally said.

Maeve helped her up and they made their way slowly to the healer's house. Settling Hanna on the floor next to the fireplace she set to work building a fire. Once the logs caught, Maeve searched through the jars, looking for nettle. As she was kneeling down to treat her, the door flew open and a man entered, making her jump. "Sorry to startle ye. I'm Janus. I live here," he added, his eyebrows raised. "Where did ye appear from?" Grey eyes regarded her curiously.

"I'm Maeve. I...I didn't know where else to take Hanna since the other place is so small."

"Glad to make your acquaintance," he said, holding out his hand. "Have ye laid eyes an old man with a beard?"

Maeve smiled. "You mean Roc? He's the one who pointed me here. He's resting in the spirit house."

"Ye are a healer," Janus said with surprise as he watched her place nettle leaves on Hanna's burns.

Maeve shook her head. "Sometimes things come to me..."

Recognition lit up his eyes. "You're Finna's daughter! It was over twenty years ago that she and your seanamhair were here. She was pregnant and very sick at the time."

"My mother didn't tell me about that," Maeve answered, feeling uncomfortable under his scrutiny.

"Ye resemble Catriona," he added. His eyes went wide. "The prophecy! I should have known from the first moment I laid eyes on ye."

Maeve ignored his stare, turning back to Hanna. "Do you have herbs for her chest? Possibly agrimony—she's breathed in a lot of smoke."

Janus pulled his eyes away from her face and went to the shelf. He searched for a moment and then brought over two jars, setting them on the floor by where she knelt.

Maeve grabbed a pillow off a chair and folded it in half, placing it under the woman's head and upper back. "This should ease your breathing a bit."

Hanna's face was white with pain, her eyes wild. "My husband...my bairn...have ye seen them?"

"Not yet. Janus will take care of you and I'll go look for them. How old is the child?"

"She's eight—long blonde curls, ye can't miss her, and my husband, Jake, he's..."

"I know Jake," Janus interrupted. "Maeve, ye stay here, I'll find them." Janus left quickly, slamming the door behind him.

"Do you mind if I rub some salve into your chest? It will help your breathing."

Hanna shook her head and closed her eyes. Maeve unbuttoned the top of her dress and rubbed in the salve, glad when the woman's labored gasps became more even.

"Thank ye," Hanna mumbled, turning on her side.

A few minutes later the door flew open and Janus entered, his arm supporting a man carrying a sobbing little girl.

"Dana, here's your mother...see?" Janus coaxed.

When the man put her down she let out a happy cry, rushing to cuddle with her mother, but the fabric of Hanna's dress on her blistered cheek had her screaming in pain. "Dana, Dana," Hanna cried, "my bairn…"

"Come, Dana," Maeve urged gently, arranging a place for her on the rug close to Hanna. "We need to treat those burns." Maeve applied nettle leaves directly to the girl's skin, gratified when she began to relax. A few minutes later the child was fast asleep.

On the other side of Hanna, Janus worked on Jake who had a deep wound between two ribs. A jagged line of flesh oozed blood from where an arrow had been roughly pulled out. He glanced at Maeve. "I need yarrow and could you heat up some water?" He pointed toward the fireplace where an iron rod supported a kettle.

"Where's the water?" Maeve asked, hoping she wouldn't have to travel down the hill to get it.

Janus pointed toward a heavy crock on the counter. Maeve filled the kettle and built up the fire, swinging the iron arm over the flames. It wouldn't take long. When steam began coming from the nozzle, she looked around for tongs or something to keep from burning her hands. How did these people manage, she wondered, ripping another long piece of velvet from her hem. Doubling it over she reached for the handle, bringing the kettle over by Janus.

"Pour," he ordered, pointing to a small bowl next to him.

Maeve did as he asked and then stood next to him, watching as he cleaned the wound. "That needs to be stitched up."

Janus nodded. "I'll get ye what ye need."

"Not for me…I've never stitched up a wound."

Janus smiled. "'Twill be your first time then. I can assist." He went to his shelves, bringing back a wooden box filled with thorns and bone of various sizes that had been fashioned into needles. "I'll fetch ye some clean flax," he said, rummaging through another small box.

Maeve picked out a narrow thorn that had a small hole drilled through it. "This seems about the right size," she said, holding it out.

Janus nodded and raised his eyebrows, watching her with amusement.

"So you really think I can do this?"

"First time is the hardest—'tis a good skill to have here with all the fightin' goin' on. It may come in handy."

Maeve sighed, turning back to Jake who seemed not to have heard the interchange. Either that or he chose to ignore it. Janus helped Maeve clean the wound and staunch the blood, and then encouraged Jake to take a good swig of the brandy he brought over from a cabinet by the wall. When Jake handed the bottle back Janus poured some of the amber liquid directly on the wound. "All ready for ye now," he said, moving aside.

Maeve's hands shook as she pulled the flaps of flesh together, lining them up correctly. She breathed deeply in and out until her hands were steady and then set to work. She knew that every time she pushed the thorn through his skin she caused the man great pain, but Jake did not flinch or cry out. When she finished and looked up Janus gave a nod of approval. "Now we must look for others," he said, heading toward the door.

"Isn't there some way to put out the fires?" Maeve asked as they headed down the street. Many of the houses had already succumbed to the flames and were now only smoldering hulks. A few pieces of bright cloth lay here and there, testament to the people who had lived within their walls. But there was no sign of life.

"Until the Oillteil leave I'm afraid there is nothing to be done. Our wells have dried up and we canna waste what little water we have. We rely on the small stream at the bottom of the hill for all our needs."

When they came upon an injured Oillteil, Maeve moved off the path, kneeling next to where he lay under the trees. The creature was barely conscious, his breathing shallow. When she looked around for Janus he was several yards away, walking quickly down the street. "Can you help me?" she called out.

He turned back, shaking his head in protest. "What can we do for him?"

"Take him to your house where the supplies are."

His mouth fell open. "We canna do that. We have villagers there, what do ye think they'll do if we bring in an Oillteil?"

"Don't you have an extra room? He's severely injured." Maeve pointed toward two deep gashes in the creature's arm that were still bleeding. "He'll bleed to death if we don't get this stopped." Maeve ripped a piece of hem and tied it tightly above and over the wound. "We need to hurry."

Maeve stared at Janus pointedly until he turned back. When he reached her his face was closed and angry.

They had raised the creature to a sitting position when a voice seemed to come out of nowhere. "What are ye two doin'?" A soot-covered man stood next to them, his eyes wide with horror.

"He's injured. We can't leave him here to die."

"He's the enemy. Look how many of us he's killed." The man gestured wildly, pointing out several motionless bodies lying in the dirt.

"He's a living being. I don't care if he's the enemy or not. Maybe you'd like to assist in finding other *villagers* who need our help. If you choose to do so, bring them to the house just there," Maeve said, pointing back up the street. Without answering, the man turned away. Maeve watched him for a moment and then turned back to the problem at hand. "If you can take his shoulders, I'll get his feet."

Janus didn't say a word as he reached his arms underneath the Oillteil's back. The creature grunted once as they lifted him and then seemed to pass out.

In the cottage they carried him into another room, placing him on a rug by the fireplace. Janus left the room, letting Maeve build up the fire. The Oillteil looked green and she didn't know if this was his normal color or if it was due to blood loss. He had regained consciousness and watched her warily as she worked to get the logs burning.

"What is your name?" she asked, wondering if he spoke English.

"Name, Oak."

"Well, Oak, do you feel dizzy?"

He nodded, his eyes darting from side to side.

Maeve worked on the deep gash in his upper arm, cleaning it with hot water that Janus brought in. She placed agrimony leaves directly on the wound. "Oak, I need to get a blanket for you. I'll be right back."

In the other room Janus whispered, "How is he?"

"I don't know. He's lost a lot of blood."

"I still think this was a bad idea."

"I'm surprised to hear you say this since you're a healer."

Janus didn't answer and a long moment went by. "Where did ye obtain your knowledge of herbs?" Janus finally asked.

"You won't believe it if I tell you."

"Try me."

"I studied a bit on my own but my grandmother Catriona told me all sorts of things and then Airmid came to me and kind of put information into my brain. Now I just seem to know things, things that I never had any inkling about before."

"Airmid, the healing goddess," Janus said thoughtfully. "I have yet to meet her. I had to learn the old-fashioned way."

"Where do you keep the blankets?"

When she went back into the other room Oak had fallen asleep. She covered him with a blanket and closed the door softly behind her.

"Janus, I'm going to look for others who might need our help. Will you come with me?"

He nodded, his eyes on the closed door between the rooms. "There are friends of mine still out there, but first I want to check on Roc."

"I'll be down the street."

"Be careful Maeve, the Oillteil are still burning houses, try to stay out of sight."

He turned to the cabinets and pulled out a heavy padlock. "This will assure safety," he muttered, placing it around the latch. "I woudna wish trouble before we return."

Maeve shook her head in exasperation. There was no way Oak would have the strength to do anything. They exited the house together, Janus turning right and Maeve left.

"I'll catch up with ye," Janus called over his shoulder. "Be careful."

Maeve headed down the street toward the fire and smoke. In her fervor to help she had lost any lingering fear. And from what she could see and hear, the fighting had moved at least a mile away.

"The old man's fine," Janus said, joining her a few minutes later.

Maeve glanced his way, noticing the deep lines on his face, the thinning gray hair. Could Roc be that much older than Janus? She wanted to question him about her mother's illness and what Roc had told her about that long ago visit, but now was not the time.

This time when they came upon more injured Oillteil, Janus made no comment, only bending to help her carry them back to the cottage. They made several trips.

"I'll just take one more look around," Janus said from the doorway after they had settled another villager in front of the fire. "Ye look worn out, lass. Stay here and tend the wounded. I'll be back shortly."

Maeve was happy to comply. Her arms and shoulders ached from the heavy lifting and she felt exhausted beyond measure. She checked on the four Oillteil, glad to see that the valerian tea she had administered had put them to sleep. In the main room several small children were crying—more frightened than hurt. Some of their parents had not yet been found.

Maeve was attempting to soothe them when Janus burst into the cottage, his arm around a young woman. A dress hung in tatters around her thin form, her legs and arms covered in cuts. Despite her injuries she brought the welcome news that the remaining Oillteil were gone, defeated by the villagers at the outskirts of town. The hole in the fence had just been repaired, she told them, but there were many people who had been burned trying to escape the fires that still raged on. After the woman finished her tale, she slumped into a chair, her face haggard.

"This is Sara, for any of ye who might not know." Janus smiled toward Maeve, his hand protectively on the woman's shoulder.

When Maeve came close to examine Sara's wounds, the woman told her that she'd lost her five-year-old child in the chaos and didn't know if the little girl was alive or dead. She wanted to look for her but could not walk on her own. Janus tried to comfort her, assuring her that he would go and find the little girl. He left the house looking determined. As soon as the door closed, Sara began to cry.

"He'll find her," Maeve assured her, placing comfrey leaves on the many cuts covering her legs. She helped Sara stretch out and then treated her arms, rubbing salve into the burns. But Sara couldn't settle, her gaze on the door. Her eyes were wild and bloodshot, her face pinched with worry. Maeve put her hand on the crown of her head, pressing down firmly. "Try not to worry. You need to concentrate on your own healing." Maeve lessened the pressure, feeling energy course into her fingers. "Imagine all the pain and worry going into my hands," she whispered, placing one hand on each side of the woman's head. Sara gazed up at her and then closed her eyes.

By this time the room was full of bodies, the pungent odor of salve and herbs heavy in the warm closed-up space. Maeve cracked a window and then checked the fire in the other room, adding another log. After that she busied herself chopping vegetables for soup. She tried to ignore her burning eyes and the shakiness in her legs. Soon the aroma of barley, onions, carrots and potatoes mingled with the strong scent of medicinal herbs.

Just as she was about to serve the soup, Janus came throught the door looking disheveled and upset. He had not been able to find Sara's child and clearly felt terrible about it. He went to kneel by Sara who threw her arms around his neck and burst into tears. Maeve heard him say something about being glad that he hadn't found the child hurt or dead but those words, meant to soothe, only made her cry harder.

Maeve served soup to all who could eat, helping those who were too weak to raise a spoon to their mouths. The Oillteil were still wary and afraid of her, she could see it in their pig-like eyes, but she put on a friendly expression and tried to ignore the sour smell coming from them. She spoke in a soothing tone to the ones who didn't speak her language, using gestures to encourage them to eat. Once she had served Sara and Janus she ladled a small bowl for herself; it had been a long time since she had eaten anything warm or substantial.

Gazing around the room filled her with a deep sense of gratitude and peace. There was a faint glow shimmering around each person. Was she imagining things? Surprised, she glanced at Sara sitting next to Janus. They were conversing in low tones, their heads close together. Pale rose light surrounded them, becoming stronger every time their eyes met. As they talked he placed his hand on hers. They were in love—and love was a powerful force.

Chapter

10

Gertrude finally fell into a restless sleep only to be awakened by the sound of a heavy boot on the floorboards. She sat up and looked toward the door.

"Sorry to wake you, my dear, although I am glad for some company at this moment." He lit a candle and brought it over by the bed.

"Were you able to find Maeve?" she asked, afraid of the answer.

"No, that woman is quite elusive. Eventually we will find her." Brandubh sat down on the bed and took his boots off. He turned toward her but the candle was behind him and she couldn't discern his expression. "If I were a gentleman I would sleep on the floor, but we both know that is not the case, don't we?"

A shiver went through her. What should she say? She smelled his musky odor and felt weak and bewildered. An image of his arms around her went through her mind and she sucked in her breath, trying to will it away.

He raised his eyebrows suggestively, leering at her as he removed his cassock, placing it carefully over the chair. When he pulled off his wool undershirt and long johns she couldn't keep her eyes off him.

He smiled then and moved toward her. "I see your attraction has not diminished," he said, sliding in next to her. Heat rose from him, along with the scent of healthy sweat. She tried to move away, but he was too close now, inside her personal space, and electricity sparked between their bodies. "So, Gertrude, you're here now, where I told you things would be different. Are you ready for this?"

Gertrude tried to speak but nothing would come out of her mouth as she stared into his hooded eyes. A long moment went by.

"Well, woman, what is it to be? I don't want to take you by force but I think I might have to if you don't give me permission." His eyebrows lifted in question.

Tentatively she placed her hand on his wide chest. He shivered and then his arms came around her back. He pulled the robe she was wearing over her head, pushing her gently down. His eyes slid across her naked body, coming to rest on her face.

"I've been waiting a long time for this," he pronounced, lifting her like a doll and pressing her body against his.

Waves of desire coursed through her as she felt the press of his skin, his hands moving across her back. He pulled her closer, his lips on her neck. When she moaned he pushed her away to lie on her back. He watched her, his eyes dark. She moaned again, reaching up to pull him toward her.

"I would say the answer is a resounding yes," he whispered, and then his lips were on hers and she opened to him hungrily. The current reality disappeared—they were in a sun-drenched meadow lying naked in the grass. She knew this man so well. "My love," he mumbled into her neck, sending little shock waves across her skin. She was under him now, his chest pushing against her breasts, his hips against her hips, they fitted together perfectly.

Later he gave her tea and stroked her like a cat—she almost purred as his hands moved lightly along her skin. He told her she was beautiful with her olive skin and dark eyes, she had a sultry look that he found irresistible. As he lifted her long hair and kissed her neck, he mumbled that he could not afford this kind of distraction right now. Before she could catch her breath to answer, his lips found hers. And this time there was no hesitation as their bodies met, devouring each other as though they had been lovers forever.

When it was over and they lay spent in each other's arms, he told her he might need her help in the future, that the two of them were connected now, their minds linked. Would she mind? She gazed into his eyes—this was the man she had been searching for, her soul mate. They had been together through many lifetimes—how could she deny him? Fate had brought her to him. "Of course not," she answered.

"In that case I have a gift for you," Brandubh told her. From a drawer he brought over an exquisite necklace made of silver— she recognized at once the symbol for the triple goddess inside a circle. At the very center lay a red jewel. When he hooked it around her neck it fell heavily into the hollow between her breasts.

She ran her fingers over it, touched by the gesture. "It's beautiful, where did you get this?"

Brandubh smiled. "It's just something I picked up along the way."

A short time later she fell asleep in his arms.

When Gertrude opened her eyes again she was lying on the ground next to a fire. The flickering light cast shadows against the standing stones that ringed the campsite. As her eyes adjusted she recognized the sleeping faces of Finna and MacCuill. Catriona's head rested on the chest of an unfamiliar man, his arm circling her shoulder. On the other side of the fire huddled shapes slept under blankets. She had been 'rescued', she thought wryly—this was not the outcome she had hoped for. Before she could register what she was doing adrenaline brought her to her feet, her legs tangling in Brandubh's long robe. The tea Brandubh had brought her had been drunk sans clothing for both of them. It must have been very late by that time—they had fallen asleep and then wakened once more to rekindle their passion. A little thrill went through her as she recalled the glow of his skin in the candlelight—like alabaster. How could this be the man everyone spoke of—the evil force in the Otherworld?

A flush came into her cheeks. Had they found her like that—naked in his bed? Good God—how could she explain this? And what had they done to Brandubh? He didn't seem the kind of man who could be easily outwitted. The tea must have had quite a sedative effect for her not to awaken en route. Why would Brandubh sedate her like that?

She moved out of the protective circle of stones, heading toward the trees to relieve herself. Four wolves were there, and she heard a low rumbling growl coming from one of them. She wondered if the animal knew what she had just done. *Don't be silly*, she said to herself. But it was looking at her with what she would call a relatively unfriendly expression. "Hello wolf," she whispered. "Good doggy." She reached down to pat the large gray head, but when her hand came close to his muzzle, he snarled, exposing large white teeth. She pulled her hand quickly away and then moved behind a tree, keeping an eye on them as she raised the robe. When she walked by them a few minutes later, they ignored her, their eyes closed. She took her place back by the fire, settling down to think.

A little later the stirrings of the others woke her—she must have fallen back asleep. Her insides churned when they turned their expectant faces toward her.

"Good morning, Gertrude. Glad you're with us again." MacCuill smiled, his gaze warm. "How are you feeling?"

"I think I'm all right," she stammered, trying to sound normal.

"Come over by the fire, we've made tea," Catriona invited, motioning to a spot next to her. The Crion passed a cup between them, sipping delicately.

Gertrude took the cup and sat down, concentrating very hard on her tea.

"Did ye see Maeve?" Finna asked nervously.

"No. She wasn't there. I overheard talk about her escaping from some camp."

"I'm Maeve's grandfather, Eron."

Gertrude turned to the dark-haired stranger leaning forward with his hand extended. She took it, trying to smile.

"Maeve was with me when she was captured," Eron continued. "I'm afraid it was my fault, I shouldn't have left her alone."

"I didn't know—she wasn't at the fort." Gertrude pressed her released hand into her other palm. She looked down.

"Eron, dinna blame yourself," Catriona admonished. "At least now we know she escaped." Catriona frowned, casting a sharp look at Gertrude.

"I'm so sorry ye had to go through that ordeal," Finna said, her eyes searching. "Did Brandubh hurt ye?"

There was silence as they all waited for her response.

Gertrude drew in a breath. "No, he didn't. He was very kind to me. I don't know why…"

"We found you, umm, in a rather compromised state," Eron interrupted. "Do you have any recollection of what happened—why you were in his bed unconscious and unclothed?"

"I think he gave me some kind of sleeping potion," she answered quickly. "It must have been in the tea." Her cheeks burned.

"He didn't…I mean…did he …?" Finna seemed embarrassed as she struggled for words.

"I don't think he did anything." Gertrude tried to maintain a convincing tone. "All I remember is drinking tea and then I woke up here. My clothes were wet. That must be why…" But that didn't explain why Brandubh was undressed.

All eyes were on her. Even the small Crion were staring at her now. Catriona watched her, her head cocked to the side as though she was listening to something. Gertrude tried desperately to clear her mind as she smiled around at the group. "Honestly, I feel pretty good. Brandubh put some salve on my ankle and it feels completely healed." She picked up her leg and moved her ankle in a circle but then realized that no one knew about her injury. She was captured right after that. "By the way, what happened to him when you rescued me?" she asked, trying to sound nonchalant.

"I knocked him down and put a short spell on him while Eron carried you out of there," MacCuill answered. "Surely you can tell us a bit more about what happened during the two full days you were there."

Was that a suspicious look she saw in the druid's eyes? Her insides quivered. "He was making plans to go after Maeve with the Oillteil and those other wild-looking men. They all took off but they couldn't find her and he came back. He left me alone at the fort for most of the time. I was sick after being out in the weather and when he brought me inside I just rested and recovered until you rescued me." That was mostly true, she thought, wondering why her heart was beating so fast.

"Sick?" Catriona asked, looking skeptical.

"I got a fever from being out in the freezing cold. I thought I was going to get pneumonia." She coughed to prove her point.

"And where did ye get that necklace? I dinna remember ye wearin' it earlier."

Gertrude's fingers went up to the spiral. If she'd been thinking clearly she would have removed it earlier to avoid questions. Her face reddened as she tried to come up with a good answer. Finally she went with the truth. "Brandubh gave it to me. He said he found it somewhere and had no need for it."

Catriona shook her head. " 'Tis awfully fine to be given freely to a complete stranger."

Gertrude stared at her, trying to will her features into neutrality. "I thought so too but he insisted." Gertrude tried to laugh but it sounded forced. "I just couldn't turn down such a nice piece of jewelry."

A long moment of silence went by.

"Well, I'm glad he took you inside, Gertrude," MacCuill finally remarked. "It's more than he did for these poor Crion."

"We need to get these people back to their home," Eron added. "As you can see a few of them are not at all well and the rest have been severely stressed from lack of food and water. And as you mentioned, being exposed to the cold for days on end."

Gertrude met the man's eyes, hoping she imagined the accusatory look there. Why

hadn't she tried to help the Crion? Surely she could have convinced Brandubh to bring them under a roof. There was a stable for the horses where they could have stayed dry. She looked into their pale faces and heard a lot of them sniffling and coughing. Two of the women were still lying down, curled up close to the fire. She felt a pang of regret at her selfish behavior. She should have mentioned something the first day—before their physical encounter wiped all reason from her brain.

Catriona pulled a bag of herbs from her pack, placing leaves into a shallow bowl of water over the fire. When they had soaked for a moment, she pressed them onto the women's upper chests. "They all have chest colds, but Mira and Tari are the hardest hit. This catnip should help." She murmured something to the two women in their language and then went back to the fire to brew more tea.

"Isn't this close to the time when the Crion were planning their burial ceremony?" Finna asked, looking toward the druid. "I hoped we would have found Maeve by now," she muttered. "Goddess knows where she is." Finna's hand went up to wipe the tears from her face.

Gertrude had a pang of remorse. Maeve was her client and a friend, a young and vulnerable woman in a very dangerous situation. Brandubh would kill Maeve if he found her. A shiver went down her spine when she recalled the Wildmen and the horrible beasts that traveled with them.

MacCuill turned to the Crion man behind him, conversing quietly. At the end of the conversation he translated for the rest of the group. "The ceremony is in two days time. Their tradition is to carry their dead on ceremonial beds that will be burned in the bonfire. But first we need to get these people home so they can rest. They will insist on being a part of this tradition and the Dolmen is a long way from the second Crion village."

They left camp around midday, going slowly because of the sick and injured Crion. As the day passed, Gertrude struggled to put her mind on other things but could not get the image of herself and Brandubh out of her mind. She was positive everyone knew what had happened between them. Scenarios kept popping into her mind, stories she could tell them to explain why she had been undressed--she was asleep when he got there, she had nothing dry to put on, it was hot in his upstairs room— all were completely implausible. And behind all her thoughts was the memory of their connection, her feeling that he was her soul mate. Physical longing plagued her constantly and she wondered if Brandubh was feeling the same way. He had warned her that their minds were linked now. And yet underneath all of this was the horrible guilt for what she'd done. She had never felt so conflicted in her life.

This disoriented feeling was not one she was used to. In her life at home it was she who read the cards, interpreted what the fates were saying. Now it was as though all her self-control had disappeared, blowing away with the strange energy-sapping wind they had encountered on the long walk. This turn of events was not at all what she'd expected when she made the decision to fly to Scotland. Maeve had been first and foremost on her mind and now she couldn't stop thinking about Brandubh. Maybe he was doing this to her, placing himself in her mind to keep her under his control.

By the time they reached the Crion village it was nearly dark. They were warmly welcomed, the sick ones fussed over and then taken away to the healers. Gertrude and the others were shown into a room with soft sheepskin beds covered in bright woven blankets. Food was brought on trays—soup and bread—and shortly after that they all went to bed.

In the morning the village was bustling, shrill voices echoing off the tunnel walls as the Crion prepared for departure.

"Today we will accompany the Crion north to the Dolmen," MacCuill announced, translating what he had learned from the woman who had brought the morning tea. "The ceremony will take place tomorrow." He looked around. "Is everyone feeling up to the trip? How about you, Gertrude? Your cough seemed worse during the night."

"I'll make it," Gertrude replied. "But I wonder…can we borrow some clothing from the Crion? One of those warm wool ponchos would be nice to have on right now." Gertrude had changed into clean underwear and another pair of jeans and a sweater but her other clothes and warm coat had been left behind at Brandubh's fort. The robe lay on the bed.

"I'm sure they have something for you to wear, but don't leave that robe behind. It's warm and you never know when you might need it," MacCuill urged.

Gertrude picked it up, bringing it to her nose. A faint musky odor clung to the wool, bringing a sense memory with it. She rolled it into a tight ball and stuffed it into her pack, a blush creeping up her chest and neck. When she looked up, everyone was busy packing their belongings. She released a long breath and turned to finish her tea.

It was late afternoon by the time they arrived at the sacred spot. The ceremony had been planned for the following evening so Gertrude and the others made camp under spindly trees on the downward slope of the hill. The Crion took shelter under and around the Dolmen.

That night the temperature dropped below freezing, turning the fog to hoarfrost that sidled its way under blankets and clothes. When morning finally arrived, the weary travelers woke to a sky full of dark clouds. The Crion were already busy gathering firewood for the bonfire, the unearthly silence broken only by the snap of twigs and limbs as they were taken.

Gertrude huddled next to the meager fire MacCuill had managed to coax into existence, wondering why she had been so excited to come into the Otherworld. At this moment she longed for the comforts of home and if it wasn't for this obsession with Brandubh she would certainly try to find her way out of this dank and dreary place. The cough was still with her and had kept her up for most of the night. Catriona had not offered to help her in any way. She knew the woman was an herbalist, she had seen her treat the Crion.

After a breakfast of tea and stale bread, the search for wood for the bonfire began in earnest. After laying a hand on her forehead, MacCuill told Gertrude to take it easy, saying that she might have a slight fever. But after an hour or so of watching the others struggle through the frozen trees, she felt guilty and got up to help. The search took them far from the hillside and was made difficult by the ice that lay across the ground but despite that, the pile at the top of the hill grew. MacCuill used his magic to dry the wood so it would burn easily once the time came. The horrid frozen landscape, her worsening cough and the idea of burning people up in a bonfire had Gertrude's thoughts traveling backward to the horror stories her mother had told her about the gypsy holocaust during the second world war—this entire scenario seemed repulsive and macabre.

The Crion were fasting and meditating in preparation for their ceremony and because he was officiating, MacCuill did not partake of the bread and cheese Catriona offered him. He left them to their lunch and disappeared toward the top of the hill to speak with the elders. Gertrude's stomach contracted when Catriona held out some cheese. She shook her head, no, leaving the fire to escape the accusing looks. She wandered under the trees, her arms hugging her body. When the tears started she didn't try to stop them, letting them flow down her cheeks unimpeded.

At dusk the procession started up the hill, MacCuill in the lead. He wore his white robes, ghostly in the swirling mist and fog. Behind him came the elders, holding their burning torches high, and behind them the Crion carried the beds of woven willow supporting the tightly wrapped bodies of the dead.

Eighteen stones made a ring big enough to hold a hundred people. The burial chamber stood on a small rise above the circle, comprised of two ten-foot high standing stones with

an enormous slab across the top. A wide altar stone lay on the
ground beneath. After the day of silence, the chanting voices
of the hundred Crion seemed deafening. Many piercing cries of
sorrow were interwoven within the song that was repeated over
and over, their special way of singing the dead into their next
life. Gertrude, Finna and Catriona followed behind the Crion as
MacCuill made his way through a gap in the stones toward the
center of the circle.

Once the willow beds were placed on the pyre, the wood
was lit with rush torches, bursting immediately into flame.
MacCuill offered the sacred words about their journey into their
next life being swift and then he knelt on the ground in front
of the conflagration and played his flute of alder, a song full of
aching sadness. After he put his flute away, the keening voices
began once more, mingling with the sound of crackling wood
as the blaze burned hot, flames lifting into the dark sky. The
mourners continued their song until everything had burned
away, leaving only ash. Once the ashes had cooled, the elders
scooped them into ceremonial vessels that they placed on the
altar stone.

As if on cue, the wind came up, lifting the ashes in a swirling spiral and dispersing them in the four directions. It was at
that moment that the moon goddess, Arianrhod appeared, at
first as an owl and then as a woman, her golden hair a shimmering nimbus against the darkness of the night. At first her figure
looked faint and indistinct, but as the Crion acknowledged her
with shouts of joy and awe, she became more solid. It was her
job to take the souls to the stars until their rebirth, Catriona
whispered. This was the night of the full moon, she added,
although no one could see it. The time of the wolf moon had
begun.

Chapter 11

h arold drove on the A71 toward Glasgow. Maeve had
not been at the airport to pick him up, which was odd,
to say the least. And her cell phone didn't work here
so he couldn't get in touch to find out if she was all right. The
directions Alex had given him were definitely outdated. More
modern roads had been built in his absence and it was getting
confusing as hell. He pulled off on a side road and consulted the
map the rental agency had given him, trying to get a handle
on which route to take. He finally decided to pick up the A82
outside Glasgow, hoping he wouldn't be caught in some snarl of
city traffic.

He arrived in Glasgow before rush hour and sailed through,
turning off at the exit for the A82. It was an A road but only
two lane and by this time it was growing dark. There were no
streetlights and he was becoming increasingly tired. He needed
to stop somewhere and get a cup of coffee or find some place to
spend the night. He had seen a sign for the small village of Luss
on Loch Lomond and thought he would check it out, see if there
was a motel.

When he turned off the main road it dawned on him that, unlike the U.S., there were no cheap motels stuck out on the roads and lit up with bright neon signs. It was then that he remembered the GPS that came with the car and he switched it on, giving the satellite a moment to connect. There was quite a list of hotels in the area and he ran down it, checking the prices. The dollar-pound ratio was not in his favor. He finally found a youth hostel on the other side of the Loch at a reasonable price and turned his car around to head toward Rowardennan.

Driving through the villages he came upon revelers carrying torches and singing as they walked along the narrow streets. This was the first of January, was it still the New Year celebration? He finally stopped to ask and the man told him that this was Hogmanay, a Scottish celebration that went on for two to three days. Harold wondered what hogs had to do with anything—he had smelled whiskey on the man's breath. Harold decided to find out more about this tradition in the morning. Right now he was too tired to try and make sense out of it.

In the morning Harold looked out his picture window at a breathtaking view of the Loch. The area around Loch Lomond was mountainous, with high peaks covered in snow, the dark water reflecting them back like a mirror. A slight mist lay over the still lake, giving it an otherworldly feel. He stood there for a long while feeling lost in time.

While eating his breakfast of ham and eggs in the dining room, he was regaled with all the customs related to the Hogmanay celebration. The word had various meanings from derivations in other languages, including 'holy month' and 'new morning'. It dated back centuries and was solely a Scottish tradition that had come about because of the distrust of Christmas, which in the early days was seen as 'popeish and full of superstitions'—in other words a purely Catholic holiday. It wasn't until the 1960s that Christmas was celebrated in Scotland. Before that, the gift giving and feasting had taken place between the thirty-first of December and January second. When he asked about the name and if it had anything to do with hogs his question was met with raucous laughter.

He left Rowardennan around nine, the helpful proprietors giving him directions and shortcuts to Bailemuir. The day was chilly and overcast with a slight mist that caused him to turn on his windshield wipers every few minutes. He felt wired from coffee and couldn't seem to contain his excitement about being reunited with Maeve. The two weeks apart had seemed endless and this place had a romantic feeling about it that only heightened his anticipation.

He drove fast once he got on the main road and made good time; by ten-thirty he was turning off the A83. From here he estimated another forty-five minutes if he didn't run into slow traffic. The countryside was criss-crossed with low stone walls behind which many different breeds of sheep grazed. It was cold but the early morning frost was already long gone and pale sunlight was sneaking through the dispersing clouds.

As he drove through the picturesque villages he thought about Maeve, and how she fit into this landscape. In his mind's eye he could see some distant relative of hers working in the fields, hanging up laundry, red curls tied back under a bright headscarf. He had the distinct impression that he was heading back in time and was somewhat unnerved by all the images that raced through his mind. Some deep part of him seemed to recognize the terrain. Maybe it had something to do with his own Scottish heritage.

His mother's maiden name was MacAlpin so it was possible that he had some distant relatives somewhere around here. He knew his mother's family lived in the district of Argyll, but not exactly where. Or possibly the images were from reading the historical novel, *Kenneth,* about the first King of Scotland. The book had been recommended by his parents to give him a taste of Scotland's distant past before he embarked on his trip. On his last visit to their house, his mother had entertained him with tongue-in-cheek tales about King "Cineath" MacAlpin's exploits and the fact that she was related to royalty. She had also told him that the succession to the throne in Scotland had always been matrilineal, gazing at him with a sly smile. MacAlpin's mother was thought to have been a Pictish princess.

Harold had taken a lot of what she claimed as harmless story telling. But he didn't think the scenes in his mind came from the book or her tales, they were too clear—sword fights, wild looking half-naked men painted blue running across green fields, men dressed in chainmail with spiky light-colored hair, mud, large scruffy hunting dogs, horses—a muddle of unconnected events. The weird thing was that they seemed like memories rather than something he had read. And the closer he got to Bailemuir the stronger they became.

He tried to concentrate on where he was going after he swerved off the road to avoid hitting a rabbit. He didn't want to miss the sign for the small side road that led to town. There had been snow here recently, he noticed. Most of it had melted away but fields were still partially covered in white and muddy where it had thawed. He slowed down just in time to glimpse a tiny wooden sign pointing to the right, **Bailemuir** printed on it in small block letters. He took the turn and drove down a narrow one-lane road with turnouts for traffic coming the other way. When he finally drove into the town it was larger than he had imagined. He looked for a parking place in the main square and parked the car. He needed to find Rose's house to get directions to Finna's cottage. There must be a city map in one of these little stores.

After asking in a couple of stores for a map, Harold went into the local pub. The smells coming from the kitchen convinced him to have a quick bite. It wouldn't do to arrive starving at Finna's house. While he ate at the bar, he asked the proprietor if he knew Finna or Rose Lewin. The man knew them both and gave Harold explicit directions to Rose's house. She lived only a half a mile from the pub. The man, who introduced himself as Calum, was probably in his late sixties, heavy set with many broken blood vessels in his ruddy face. He had curly white hair cut short. It was a slow time in the pub so Calum poured them both a pint and then entertained him with stories about Rose's husband Malcolm and how he had spent many a night hanging out in this very room drinking beer. Calum laughed then, and said it was a good thing he lived so close by because some nights he could barely walk when he left the pub.

Calum told Harold that this very pub was where Alex and Finna had first courted. He would have continued talking forever if Harold had let him. He tried not to be rude, saying that he was anxious to find Maeve, explaining who she was. Calum seemed quite excited by this news and offered Harold a couple of free pints if he brought Maeve back. He said he would love to meet Malcolm and Rose's granddaughter. Harold thanked him with assurances that he would try to get back very soon.

It was after two in the afternoon by the time Harold reached Rose's cottage. He was becoming increasingly anxious to see Maeve and knocked rapidly with his knuckles before noticing the brass knocker. He waited, uncertain whether he should use the knocker, when the door opened. A pale pinched face peered out at him.

"Aye?" Rose asked tentatively from behind the door.

"Mrs. Lewin, I'm Harold Fitzhugh, a friend of Maeve's. I need to get directions to Maeve's mother's house."

"Harold! Maeve has told me all about ye. Please come in! Maeve didn't pick ye up at the airport?" Her thin shoulders were hunched against the cold breeze blowing through the open doorway.

Harold stepped across the threshold and she closed the door, throwing the bolt lock across.

"No, she didn't. I can't stay long, Mrs. Lewin. I need to find Finna's house before it gets dark."

"Please call me Rose. The last time I saw Maeve, I'm sure she mentioned that she would be pickin' ye up. I do understand your excitement but surely ye can stay for a cup o' tea? 'Tis close to teatime and I cleaned the house from top to bottom for Hogmanay. 'Twould be nice to have someone see it this way, it won't last long." Her face held a bright hopeful expression.

"How far is it from here to Finna's house?" Harold asked, lowering himself onto the couch.

"Not far at all—'tis only a ten minute drive. Ye have plenty of time. 'Twill take but a minute to brew some tea. If ye wouldn't mind could ye make a fire while I prepare the tea? 'Tis rather chilly in here. I spend most of my time in the kitchen with the Aga. 'Tis the warmest room in the house."

When Rose left the room Harold knelt by the hearth. He was anxious to go, but Rose seemed so lonely and needy that he didn't have the heart to rush off. He moved the tapestry fire screen, noticing the intricate design of roses done in needlepoint in the center. A copper bucket sat on the stone hearth next to the fireplace holding logs of different sizes as well as discarded newspapers. He began stacking kindling on top of balled up newspaper, placing a couple of larger logs on top.

As he pulled out part of the paper he noticed an article about the odd death of a local woman. He scanned down the page. The authorities thought the woman had died from wounds incurred from some kind of wild beast-like dog that had been spotted in the area around the solstice. Apparently the woman had gone for a walk the morning of December twenty-first and had never returned. Some local teenagers had found her body just recently and according to the article, the authorities were continuing to investigate. A cross had been carved into her forehead, which suggested some sort of ritualistic murder, possibly a satanic cult. Until they figured it out, they warned people to stay out of the woods. At the bottom of the page the article mentioned that a younger brother and a husband survived the twenty-five year old woman. She had been an herbalist and owned a small shop in town.

Harold shivered as he put a match to the fire, waiting for it to catch before going back to the couch.

"Thank ye, dear boy," Rose said, arriving with a tray. "The fire makes this room so much more cozy." She placed the tray on the low coffee table and sat down in a wingback chair. "'Tis nae often that I have company for tea. I managed to find some biscuits, I hope they aren't too stale."

She poured tea into a cup and handed it to Harold and then poured her own. "Something probably happened with Finna's mini. 'Tis old and frequently breaks down. 'Tis the problem with nae havin' a phone, ye have nae way to let people know these things. In any case I'm sure there's a good explanation for Maeve not being at the airport." She took a sip of tea. "Now Harold, I want to hear a little about ye. I know you're pushed for time but if you're seein' my granddaughter, I feel I have a right to find out a wee bit about ye." She smiled and held out the plate of biscuits, gazing at Harold expectantly.

"Well, I live in the same town as your son Alex."

Rose's eyes widened. "Oh do ye? Do ye see him often? I miss that boy."

"I've had more contact with him recently since Maeve's been gone. He helped me with directions to Bailemuir and so on—told me a little about the area. We met a couple of times at a restaurant we both like." Harold felt nervous for some reason, afraid he might say something that he shouldn't.

"Do ye think there's any possibility he might visit? I havna laid eyes on him for such a long time."

Rose's eyes had filled with tears. Harold had an overwhelming urge to run through the door. But in the next moment all he felt was sorrow for this lonely woman. It must be so hard to have her only son across the ocean, so far away. He was so close to his own parents and visited often. "I don't really know, maybe you could take a trip to see him. Would that be possible?"

She shook her head. "I live on a stipend that I get from the government, I could never afford a trip like that."

"Good biscuit, Mrs....I mean Rose."

"I'm glad ye like it. 'Tis a recipe I've used since Alex was a bairn."

Harold ate another biscuit and finished his tea. "I really should be getting on my way," he said, glancing out the window at the darkening sky. "Can you tell me the best way to go?"

"There's only one way to Finna's house. Ye take the main road out of town heading southwest toward the harbor. A couple of miles out you'll come to her driveway. You'll know you're there by the hedgerow." Rose smiled, dabbing her eyes with a handkerchief she took out of her cuff. "Finna planted the rose bushes when she finally bought the place about fifteen years ago. Anyway, the bushes are covered in bright orange rosehips at this time o' year so ye canna miss them. As soon as ye see them, look for the turn to the right. 'Tis a narrow road and ye can easily miss it. If ye do, just turn around about a half-mile up in Mr. McGregor's driveway. That will be the first turn to the left. Ye should have nae problem at this time o' night."

"Thank you so much for the tea," Harold said, getting up. "You know Rose, I could buy you a ticket while I'm here. I have some miles saved up now and if we get it soon, it shouldn't be too expensive. Why don't you check on dates that you might be able to go?"

"That is the sweetest offer I have ever heard but I don't think I could."

"But why not? I'm sure Alex would chip in once all is said and done. He's been talking about getting you over for a visit."

"Well, thank ye, dear boy. I'll think about it. Now don't forget your hat," Rose said, holding out the tweed cap he'd left on the couch.

"Thank you. I need that in this weather. When Maeve and I come back you can let me know what you've decided."

Rose brightened. "Will ye visit again soon?"

Harold smiled. "We'd better since we're flying out in a week."

"That will be nice. I havena seen her since before the solstice."

Before the solstice? That was close to two weeks ago. "Haven't they been to town for groceries?"

Rose shook her head. "I thought they might come to visit after Gertrude arrived. Do ye know her?"

"Not really, only what Maeve has told me. I'm surprised she's here in Scotland."

"Aye. She arrived soon after the solstice. A very nice woman and quite striking with all that dark hair."

"Do you know how long she plans to stay?"

"She didna say."

Harold wondered why Gertrude would be here. All he knew about her was what Maeve had told him regarding the Tarot reading. If she was staying at Finna's house he doubted that there would be room for him. Maybe he should book a room in town.

"Now dinna forget my invitation."

"I will bring Maeve back to visit before we head home," he promised dutifully, heading toward the front door. "Don't forget to check on tickets and thank you again for your hospitality."

As Harold opened the door, Rose gave him a firm hug, pressing her cold cheek against his. "I think my granddaughter is very wise to be seein' ye."

Harold laughed. "Well I'm glad you think so, but I'm the lucky one."

"Good-bye, dear boy, and I hope to see ye soon again," Rose called as Harold headed down the flagstone path.

As soon as he was out of sight he began to jog. He felt more anxious than ever after hearing that Finna and Maeve hadn't been in contact with Rose—and why was Gertrude here? The news article about the dead woman hadn't helped. When he gazed up at the dark clouds a gust of cold wind hit him, the bass drum of thunder rumbling in the distance. He began to run, hoping to get to his car before the rain hit. He didn't want to get lost on one of these unlit country roads in a storm.

He pressed down on the accelerator as he left the city limits. Wind began to blow, and then the sky opened up, sending ice pellets down to slam against his windshield. Foreboding had adrenaline racing through his veins. He turned on the wipers, peering into the darkness, his tires slipping as he rounded a sharp corner. Presssing his foot on the brake, he searched for the hedgerow Rose had mentioned, sure he had driven past it. But then he noticed the bright orange rosehips and slowed down, turning into the narrow unpaved lane.

Behind the cottage he saw the infamous mini and another car parked next to it. He slid his rental into the remaining space and shut off the engine. He sat for a moment trying to bring his heartbeat to normal, watching ice coat the windshield. Finally he pulled his coat on and opened the door, pulling the hood up before reaching into the backseat to get his backpack and guitar. The duffel would have to wait.

There were no lights showing in the windows. All he could hear was the hiss of the ice hitting the flagstones and the low roar of the ocean. His mind took in the eerie silence, the dark cottage. All of a sudden he was running, his feet slipping on the wet grass at the front of the house. He reached the door, knocking hard, surprised when it opened under his hand. He pushed against it and called out, "Hello? Anybody home?" The interior was dark as a tomb, his search for a light switch futile. He pulled matches out of his pack, lighting one and looking around. A kerosene lamp sat on a table next to the fireplace and he removed the chimney and lit the wick.

It was warm inside the house, which he took to mean that the inhabitants must be close by. After he had a look around he noticed the AGA against the wall in the kitchen that served as both heater and stove. He was familiar with this appliance since his parents had one when he was growing up. He lit another lamp noticing that the bed against the far wall was unmade. When he examined further, he saw stains on the sheets that looked like blood. He didn't want to think about what this might mean. There were partially filled cups and dishes left on tables—the place looked as though everyone had left in a hurry. From the amount of dishes it seemed as though several people had been here. Well, that made sense—Maeve, her mother and her grandmother. Feeling a need to be active, he carried the dishes to the sink and used the hand pump to wash them. The water was ice cold but he continued, not wanting to stop to figure out how the hot water worked.

As he worked he tried to make sense of things. The amount of blood on the bed was negligible but still, it was blood. Something had happened here. Where was Maeve? It was too stormy now to go back into town and maybe, just maybe, Finna and Maeve were simply out for a walk and would arrive home shortly—but as soon as that thought registered he discarded it, gazing out the sleet-covered window and listening to the howl of wind. After cleaning up, he made a fire and sat cross-legged staring at the flames. He opened his guitar case and pulled out his old Gibson, checking the tuning. Not too bad considering the atmospheric changes the instrument had just been through. He tuned it and then began to play a few chords of a blues riff he knew, letting his mind drift as his fingers sought out the familiar progression. An hour went by as he waited, hoping for someone to arrive home. Finally he put the guitar down and went to look in the kitchen for something to eat.

While the storm raged outside, Harold sat in front of the fire eating cheese, stale bread and part of a pie. He made himself a cup of tea and sipped slowly, letting his mind wander down strange roads. He was extremely unsettled by the empty cottage, the extra dishes and the blood. His eyes began to droop from jet lag and coming down from the excitement about reuniting with Maeve. Where should he sleep? Somehow lying down in that unmade, bloody bed didn't appeal. It was then that he noticed the small door to the left of the fireplace.

As soon as he opened the door he smelled Maeve's citrusy perfume and for a moment was afraid she lay hurt or worse in the rumpled bed. Her suitcase was on the floor, clothes strewn all over, lying over chairs and on the bed. He puzzled over this, trying to make some kind of sense of it all, but he was just too tired. There was nothing more he could do tonight. Maybe in the morning he could take a good look around and figure it all out. He took off his clothes and crawled into the bed, pulling the down comforter over him, breathing in Maeve's scent from the pillowcase. He fell asleep to the sound of the wind and rain beating against the windows

Chapter

12

"I see you're still working. I hope ye got some rest yourself, you're going to wear yourself out, lass."

Maeve turned at Roc's voice, glad to see a sparkle in his eyes. He seemed a lot better this morning, without the gray pallor of the day before. "I slept, don't worry. And you appear to feel better too."

Roc smiled, his blue eyes lost for a moment in the wrinkles. "If I could walk on this leg I'd get back to my studio."

"Studio? What do you do? I forgot to ask."

"I'm a woodworker."

"Ah, now I know why your hands are so rough. What kinds of things do you make?"

"Furniture, jewelry, ye name it, all out of rowan wood."

Maeve smiled and then turned back to the fire, adding a couple of logs. The stack was dwindling; she would need to gather more. "How about some tea?" she asked, standing up and rubbing the sore muscles in the small of her back.

"I would love some, but I dinna wish ye to wait on me. Perhaps ye could find me a walking stick and I could get around on my own."

"Not yet. Your leg needs to be immobile for at least another day or two before you start putting weight on it. If you need to use the..." she couldn't think of what to call the toilet, "Um...I could..."

"Aye, I take your meanin'," he said smiling. "Thank ye, but I'll get there on my own. If I canna manage that, then...I should be put out of my misery." His eyes twinkled and then he laughed.

"All right, I'll find you a walking stick. Too bad I don't have the one MacCuill gave me." As Maeve spoke his name, the door flew open and MacCuill was standing there, a walking stick in his hand.

"Wow! How did you do that?" she asked, staring in amazement.

"Timing is everything," MacCuill chuckled. "And how are you, my old friend?" he asked, heading over to the bench. He handed Roc the walking stick and then sat down, his back to the wall.

"Could be better but without Maeve's help I would be a lot worse off."

"So Maeve, it looks as though your powers have kicked in, yes?" He watched her, his eyes bright.

"I do seem to have some healing ability. I guess it's from Catriona and Airmid. She came to me when I was with Eron and gave me all sorts of information."

MacCuill snorted. "This is your own, Maeve, inherited from your grandmother and grandfather."

"Eron's a healer?"

MacCuill nodded. "He uses herbs but also his hands."

"But he never said a thing, even after I told him about Airmid!"

"That is his way. He wouldn't want to interfere in your development. What about your ability to move from place to place?"

"So how do you know about that?"

MacCuill gazed at her without expression.

"Okay, I get it—just another druid thing, right?"

He smiled.

"It only seems to happen when my life is in danger."

"I can help you with that. You must learn to focus on where it is you want to go, to concentrate with all your mind."

"That would be wonderful, MacCuill, if I knew where I wanted to go. Mostly it's just a way of escaping. I feel at the whim of whatever is happening to me, although I'm very grateful for these gifts." Maeve thought about the key, her pledge to help the prisoners.

"One of the reasons I came is to warn you that Brandubh and his men are riding in this direction. You will need to leave here before they arrive."

"He won't be able to get in, will he?"

"I cannot say for sure. He has his ways and you should not take chances right now. Your mission is too important."

Maeve looked into his dark eyes. He wasn't going to take no for an answer. "What about all the people here? I haven't had a chance to find the rest of the injured—there must be many around the houses that burned. And what if he gets in and hurts more of them?"

"Are there others you have not treated? I was in Janus's house and saw all of your good work. Those that you healed are on the mend. The few left will be in Janus's capable hands. Without you here Brandubh has little reason to fight these people. You are all he wants."

Maeve sucked in her breath—she felt winded as though she had run up a steep hill. Her being here could put these people in even more danger. "I don't have a plan."

"No plan is good, Maeve. Your intuition is strong as well as your link to the spirits. You must trust that you will find the correct way. I will do whatever I can for you, but I cannot tell you how to proceed. Just know that you have all the power within you to accomplish this. Have you felt your connection with Brigid? Your talents are only beginning."

Maeve opened her mouth to ask, 'what connection', but the door opened before she could get it out.

"I brought your morning tea," Janus announced, kicking the door shut with his foot. "Sara is preparing porridge for breakfast." He handed Roc a mug and then held one out to Maeve. "Everyone in my house is feeling better this morning but I havna divulged to the villagers that there are Oillteil in the other room. I'm afraid of what might happen." He glanced toward Roc, as though to ask for his support in the matter. "I have to say when I checked on them they seemed less hostile. They're still weak and Oak needs stitches—I plan to do that after breakfast if he'll let me." His eyes went to Maeve. "Ye might have a better chance since he seems to trust ye, lass. Come over for porridge when ye finish your tea." He started toward the door and stopped, turning to face them. "I almost forgot the best news of all—we found Sara's daughter early this morning and she's fine." His smile was wide and happy. On his way out he nodded to MacCuill.

Maeve sat down next to the fire. She whispered a small prayer of gratitude to the universe about the child before she took her first sip. "I really need to find my way to the holding pens where Brandubh keeps his workers. The boatman gave me a key to unlock the chains." She pulled the ribbon out of her sweater, showing MacCuill the golden key.

He nodded, sitting on the floor next to her. "You will manage all of this in good time. After breakfast I will teach you how to keep Brandubh from seeing into your mind. You can be on your way as fast as the wind if you learn this one simple lesson."

"On the way here I had a vision—but it was Catriona's vision not mine. I think she sent it to me, but I could have been tapping into her thoughts. It was horrific, all about her father and Brandubh—I guess you know everything she went through."

"Yes. Fergus hurt Catriona on many levels. When did you have this vision?"

"It was a couple of days ago."

"Catriona's vision came to you because you're linked with her. Your grandmother has much wisdom to impart, my child. This vision of yours shows that your gifts grow stronger."

Maeve looked toward her lap where her hands twisted together. "How are all the others?"

"They are trying to connect with you. Eron is now with them. I had to leave because I've been summoned by my queen, Druantia."

A moment of silence went by and Maeve glanced back toward Roc. He was resting again, his eyes closed. She turned back to MacCuill. "I saw what was happening with the Oillteil camps while I was traveling with Finiche. It's not safe for my mother and Catriona to be wandering about." *Without you,* she finished silently.

"I am aware of this, Maeve, but Catriona is a seer and has lived here her entire life—they will be fine until I rejoin them. Did you know Gertrude is here?"

"Gertrude? From Milltown?"

"She told us she had been having dreams about you—she was so worried she felt compelled to come."

"That is the strangest news yet. And she's with my mother and Catriona?"

"As far as I know."

Something about his tone alerted her. "What aren't you telling me?"

MacCuill stared at the wall for a moment before he answered. "Gertrude was kidnapped by Brandubh..." When Maeve opened her mouth MacCuill held up his hand. "We got her back, but something happened between them."

"Something? Like what?"

"I think she's infatuated with the man."

"What?"

MacCuill didn't answer and then he said, "Maeve, I must leave soon. We need to begin."

"You're not going to elaborate?"

"There's not much more to say. She will try to find him again and I sincerely hope she doesn't get herself killed."

Maeve was quiet, trying to take in what MacCuill had told her. She tried to picture Gertrude with Brandubh and strangely enough was able to see them together. But with Gertrude's psychic abilities why couldn't she intuit how evil the man was? "I have another question before we start. Has anyone heard from Harold? I'm sure he's arrived by now."

"You can check on him yourself."

Maeve stared at him in surprise. He had a sly smile that lifted one corner of his mouth.

"What do you mean—transport myself to the airport?"

"He's no longer at the airport, I'm sure of that. He's gone to Bailemuir to find you, wouldn't you say?"

Yes. Harold would have found a way to get himself to Finna's house. If he was at the cottage, he was probably very worried by now. "If he's there, do you think I should bring him into the Otherworld?"

"You need to be the one to decide that. It depends on him and what he can accept. If you think his being here will be an impediment to your own path, I would say no."

Maeve thought about what she knew of Harold. She doubted that he would be an impediment, but he could be a distraction and it would take time for her to explain things to him, time she didn't have. And would he believe her? As the two worlds collided in her mind her brain seemed to fog over. She couldn't afford to do this right now. She needed her wits about her. "I don't want to lose my focus, but I can't just leave him out there at Finna's empty cottage."

"Maybe he can be of some use here. What are his special talents?"

Maeve considered for a few moments. "He's very level-headed. He can build anything with his hands. He's used to being out in the wilderness."

"Sounds like he will fit right in," Roc offered, from the other side of the room.

"I will give you directions for Harold if you decide to go and find him. He needs to know how to follow the path to the river that runs between the two worlds. I'll draw you a map." The druid dug inside his robe, producing a piece of paper and a pencil and began scribbling down instructions. "This will get him to Corra's spring. After that it's up to him." MacCuill handed the paper to Maeve and then steered her outside, walking with her to the small grove of rowan trees. "Now it's time to get to work. First of all I will give you the details of how to move from place to place. Concentrate on where it is you want to go. You can practice by moving yourself into the roundhouse and back out here."

"I don't want to disturb Roc."

MacCuill chuckled. "That old man has seen plenty of this sort of thing, don't worry about him. Just breathe deeply and try to clear your mind. Let your thoughts drift away with the wind."

Maeve tried to do what he instructed but kept seeing Harold at Finna's cottage with a worried expression on his face.

MacCuill's powerful voice intruded into the whirl of images racing through her mind. "Clear your mind of what was and what will be. See only the task before you. When your mind is completely clear, like a running stream, concentrate on the roundhouse. See the inside of it, all the little details, the fire pit, the hole in the roof, the smell of the cedar, focus on it as if you were there."

Maeve attempted to let go of Harold's image, but the harder she tried the more it took over her mind. Maybe he was communicating telepathically and she needed to do something to help him. When her fingers curled around the moonstone, she felt a charge in the energy around her, as though the air had thickened. She could no longer see the trees or hear MacCuill's voice. Within this opaque space there was a high-pitched whirring and then she was taken into the void, an overwhelming desire to see Harold the only thing on her mind.

Chapter 13

harold woke in the morning with an overpowering urge to pee. He jumped out of bed, wondering where the bathroom was, and then decided to do the easiest thing, opening the door to the outside and pissing into the cold morning air. He stood there for a moment, breathing in the smell of the sea. Above him the sky looked ominous and gray— another day of storms. He shivered, closing the door, and went to get his clothes, pulling them on quickly. In the other room he put the teakettle on and searched for something to eat. As he made himself oatmeal he thought about what might be going on here, glad to see his mind was willing to grapple with the problem now. From the little fridge, he pulled out a jar of milk. Before pouring it on the cereal he sniffed it, wrinkling his nose. He tossed it down the sink in disgust.

If Maeve left her clothes here, she must have expected to come back soon. He had no real way of knowing when they had left, it could have been yesterday or days ago. Judging by the sour milk though, they had probably been gone longer than a day.

After the unsatisfying and over-dry oatmeal he opened the front door, taking a look around. Small waves coursed in, breaking gently on the sand and in the distance, whitecaps rode the dark water. Further out, sky and sea met with little difference in color.

Examining the area in front of the cottage revealed the remnants of a bonfire, an enormous one by the looks of it. Because of the storm, any footprints were long gone, but the smell of burned wood lingered, mixing with the damp salt air. He poked around but all he found was charred wood and ash and something that looked like spent fireworks.

When an object outside the fire circle caught his eye, he went over to examine it—a wooden flute with a simple carved fetish, well made, a piece of art, really. He picked it up and wiped off the mud and snow on his jeans, and then placed his fingers on the holes and put it to his lips, blowing softly. A clear note lifted into the air. He moved his fingers, playing a few notes in sequence, amazed by the crystalline tone. It was in the key of G, he thought, tuned in the pentatonic scale like a Native American flute. Something dire must have happened here to cause this valuable instrument to be left behind. He scanned around, becoming more and more afraid for Maeve and her mother. And then he remembered the newspaper article about the poor dead woman with the cross carved into her forehead. The hair on the back of his neck stood up as he envisioned Maeve and Finna lying wounded somewhere in the woods above the house.

He turned and ran back to the cottage. There must be a first aid kit her somewhere, he thought, searching frantically through the cupboards. Under the sink he found some gauze and a jar of salve. The contents smelled vaguely mentholated. He put them in his backpack, left the cottage and ran toward the wooded path that led up the hill away from the sea.

Harold quickly became out of breath. His apprehension, accompanied by jet lag, had taken a toll on his normal stamina.

Every so often he checked the muddy and snowy ground for prints but so far he hadn't seen anything other than rabbit, squirrel and raccoon tracks leading across the trail and into the woods. He stopped and called a couple of times but heard nothing in return, just an eerie stillness. He walked, letting his heartbeat return to normal, and tried to marshal his wild thoughts. Rose had told him that there was a walking trail that led to town and he was pretty sure he was on it. If he continued, he would eventually end up in Bailemuir and then he would go to the police and report Finna and Maeve missing. It felt like a good plan and he sped up again, finally having a sense of purpose.

Harold stopped, his hands on his thighs. The adrenaline had long since worn off. He squinted, trying to see the end of the trail. How long could this take? It seemed as though he should have reached town by now. Maybe he took a wrong turn—but thinking back he didn't remember any other paths that he might have missed. He squatted on his heels, leaning against a tree trunk. As he closed his eyes, Maeve's face loomed into his mind and he had such a pang of longing that he almost doubled up. Where was she? He couldn't lose her—his stomach clenched. He heard a faint sound in the distance and got to his feet. There it was again, coming from the trail behind him. He walked back, stopping every few seconds to listen. When he didn't hear anything he yelled, "Halloo!" as loud as he could. He heard a faint response—a woman's voice. He called out again and then began to jog back along the path.

Another minute or two went by and then he distinctly heard his name being called—his heart sped up and became erratic. He broke into a run, retracing his steps and then halted, watching an unfamiliar woman heading toward him at a run.

"Harold...Harold!"

Harold stared, trying to make sense of what his eyes were telling him. Could this be Maeve? She looked emaciated, a ragged and filthy dress hanging in tatters around her calves, her hair sticking up in spikes. When she flung herself into his arms a moment later, all thought left him. He breathed in her spicy scent, tears welling in his eyes. He hugged her close, feeling every rib, the bones of her back. They stood pressed together for many minutes before he pulled away and looked into her face.

"My God, Maeve! What have you done to yourself?" Harold stared in disbelief at the short red tufts, the hollow cheeks, and the violet circles under the familiar green eyes. He reached out and placed his hand gently on her cheek. She looked ethereal, fragile and beautiful, and there was a very different expression in her eyes.

"Oh Harold! I have so much to tell you!" she cried, pressing into his arms once more.

He folded her against him, registering the need that rose. "I was so worried, there was an article in the paper about a woman killed by some beast and I thought…not that it was you because she was identified, but…there was no one at the cottage and…" His face was buried in her hair now and he felt the warmth of her body. "Where's your mother?" he asked, pulling away again, his hands clutching her forearms.

"It's a long story—let's go back to the cottage," she urged, tugging him by the hand. "I don't have much time to fill you in on everything that's happening here."

"So…how do you feel about everything I've told you?" Maeve asked thirty minutes later.

Harold brought his attention back to her face. His thoughts had been chaotic, churning about things he couldn't even re-member now. "It's a lot to take in. I'm having a hard time as-similating all the information and I…don't know…it's not that I don't believe you, it's just so…"

"Weird?"

"Well, yes—and frightening. I don't want to lose you, and this place, the Otherworld, sounds incredibly dangerous."

"I guess it is, but honestly I've only been really afraid once or twice and now that I know I can transport myself I feel a lot safer."

"About that—how did you say this works?" Harold shook his head. "At least with the two of us I can feel better about it all. I'm glad I'm here."

Maeve looked out the window and there was a long moment of tense silence. When she turned back her eyes glistened with tears. "That's just it—you can't. I need to do this on my own."

Harold stared into her unblinking green eyes. "What are you talking about? Of course I'm going with you."

Maeve put a hand on his arm and shook her head. "You can't because it's just the beginning of the wolf moon. I hate to say this, but being with you now would only be a distraction."

"Maeve, you can't be serious. And what's the damn wolf moon got to do with it? I'm going whether you like it or not." He turned to the sink and pumped water into the tea kettle, and then clunked it loudly down on the AGA. He couldn't believe this. There was no way he could let her fight these battles alone. It hurt him deeply that she referred to his presence as a distraction. What she had just told him about what she was up against made his blood run cold.

He was watching the kettle when he felt her arms come round his back. He didn't move or respond to her hug. She slid around to face him, her eyes on his as she brought her face close. "Damn it, Maeve, I'm not in the mood for this right now!"

Maeve paid no attention and when her lips touched his there was no more resisting. His body took over. She tasted so sweet, and all the love he felt poured out of him, making him almost cry out. When they pulled apart he took her small face between his hands. "God, Maeve. How can you expect me...?"

"Please, Harold. We don't have much time."

Her pleading look, the unshed tears in her eyes made his heart turn over. He loved her. His fingers shook as he unfastened the many buttons and then pulled the velvet dress off her shoulders, letting it drop to the floor at her feet. His eyes traveled across her body—she was so thin. He picked her up in his arms, startled by the lightness of her, carrying her to the rug in front of the fireplace. Just then the kettle whistled, making them both jump. "I'll be back in a minute—don't move," he said, hurrying across the room.

On the way back he unzipped his jeans, nearly falling as he hurried to get them off. He met her gaze as he pulled his sweater over his head. She looked so sad. He came by her but before he could lie down next to her she was on her knees reaching for him. He kneeled in front of her, laughing as he ran his fingers through her short hair. The hair changed her, made her seem different, boyish. Her face was close to his now and he bent to kiss her. Their lips met and he searched for her tongue—urgency had taken over his brain but he tried to go slow, letting the tension mount. As his hands moved across her, he smelled the musk of her unwashed hair, felt the smoothness of her skin. When she pressed against him he could feel her heart beating in time with his own. His hands went to her hips, feeling the jutting hipbones and the hollow of her belly against his. He sucked in his breath. And then he was lost, gone into their combined breath, the rhythmic sound like waves moving into shore. It felt like a prayer as their kneeling bodies joined.

Maeve left the cottage before dawn, closing the door quietly behind her and heading up the hill toward the cedar grove. This time she had thought to put extra wool pants and a warm wool coat in her pack, as well as matches and a flashlight. Jeans over long johns and a heavy wool sweater over a waffle weave under-shirt had replaced the ragged and filthy dress.

Once inside the circle of trees, she stopped and sat down. Her heart felt heavy. She hated leaving like this, but there was no other way. Right now she felt stuck, caught by her love for Harold, the physicality of him still alive on her skin. She shook her head. It was a distraction that she couldn't afford.

Maeve dug through her pack, finding the little piece of root. She had to do this, had to put Harold behind her and embrace her destiny—tears streamed down her face as she bit into it, tasting the earthy flavor. It was only a few minutes before the headache began—the splitting of her mind. She sat still and let the herb do its work. After a short time she got up and walked out of the grove. Her mind was clear now, her thoughts lucid. Her hand went to the moonstone and hanging beside it, the little key from the boatman. Now was the time to release the prisoners. The stone grew hot as she concentrated, *to go where she was needed the most.* It was no surprise when the strange whirring began. The next moment she was traveling, the now familiar vertigo making her dizzy as wind rushed by her ears.

Right after she landed, she had a moment when she thought she might be sick, but luckily it passed. She was about midway up a steep hill, dark conifer forest to her left, and a dry riverbed along the bottom. Raised and threatening voices could be heard from an area beyond the trees. As she made her way cautiously toward the sounds, a small rustic village came into view. An imposing house with a wide chimney of river rock sat at the very top, and next to it stood a church of equal grandeur with a great iron cross on its steeple. The area of forest behind had been clear-cut, leaving at least a hundred stumps behind.

Tentatively she moved closer, trying to hear what was going on. This landscape wasn't familiar—didn't look like the area of the holding pens she and Finiche had ridden past. Where had the moonstone taken her? She hung back behind a spindly pine and peeked around the trunk. Going closer would put her out in the open and she needed to get her bearings before she approached. From here the only people she could see were women and they did not look well. She heard deep coughing and noticed that many faces were red and splotchy. The arguments seemed pointless, almost like the people were just arguing for the sake of arguing. Okay, she thought, her fingers on the moonstone, these people must need her healing abilities, such as they were. She patted her pack where she had stuffed bags of herbs, tinctures, gauze and salve, taken from her mother's cottage. Time to make her presence known.

When Maeve stepped out and called hello the women looked up, staring at her suspiciously.

"I'm Maeve," she called as she walked toward them, hoping her smile would put them at ease. But their expressions were terrified now, as though they didn't understand English—and that was certainly possible.

"I hope I can help you in some way, you see, I'm a healer." Maeve heard her own words, surprised at the certainty in her tone. Perhaps the werewolf root had done more than leave the past behind—it had given her a surety she had not had before.

"We take care of our own here, we dinna need anyone from outside tellin' us what to do. The priest, he will be back to help us soon enough."

Maeve scanned nervously up the hill. "Where are your men?"

"They went with the priest. They work in the mines and they fight with him against the badness, the pagans."

Maeve felt tingling on the back of her neck. This priest wasn't just anybody, it was Brandubh who presided over this place. Did they know who she was? And if so, would she tolerate her presence here? A clear image of being tied to a tree and stoned to death appeared in her mind. "A lot of you seem sick.

I can help until the priest comes back. I have herbs with me, healing herbs. When do you expect him?" Maeve tried to keep her tone even, resisting the urge to look up at the church.

"He didna say. Why should we trust you?"

The woman who spoke seemed to have some authority here. In her mid to late thirties, she held herself stiffly, as though her back hurt. When she grimaced and reached for her hip, Maeve's suspicions were confirmed.

"Is there no healer here?" From Maeve's limited experience it seemed that each settlement had someone with abilities in this area. Probably Brandubh had banished or killed the woman, if there ever was one.

"She died a while back from the cough that has taken over the village."

"What's your name?"

"I am Sorcha." The woman glanced around at the others. "What say you to this woman, Maeve? Shall we see what she has to offer?"

There was muttering, their glances going to Maeve. After a few moments of deliberation one of them nodded.

"I will show ye the healing house," Sorcha said, leading the way toward a group of ramshackle huts. Maeve and the other women followed. When Sorcha entered a small house with a burlap sack for a door, Maeve headed in after her. It was freezing cold inside, no fire burned in the hearth. Bunches of dust-covered dried herbs hung from a small beam that ran across the ceiling, and there was a musty smell, like rat or mouse droppings. The other women waited outside, their whispered voices becoming louder.

"Do you really think they'll let me help them?"

"Tis difficult to say. More than likely they want to wait for the priest. He told them they will only get well when they stop sinning, but I dinna ken what he means by this." Sorcha's gaze went into the distance for a moment. Turning back she moved closer to Maeve. "I pray every day to understand. The women are good and do everything he asks of them," she whispered, her eyes troubled.

"How many live here?"

"Many of the women have succumbed to the illness but others have grown old overnight and died. We have nae understandin' of why this happens. It seems to take the younger ones. We are down to less than forty, including the men."

Grown old overnight? "Sorcha, where are the children?"

Sorcha gazed down, her hands coming to rest on her narrow belly. "We can nae longer bear children and our numbers have dwindled because of this." The woman's eyes filled with tears.

"Maybe it's because you haven't enough to eat," Maeve suggested. She knew that restricted diets could cause a drop in fertility and these women were all bone thin. As her eyes met Sorcha's, she remembered her first trip into the Otherworld with MacCuill. It had been a paradise before Brandubh took over. If this place and these people weren't healed soon there would be nothing to save.

Maeve put a tentative hand on her arm. "Sorcha, can you convince these people to let me help them? I know what the priest told you, but this isn't true, you are not sinners, you must believe this. I can heal them but we must act quickly before he returns." She pawed through her pack, bringing out the herbs and salve.

Sorcha watched her, trying to wipe the tears from her face with her apron. Muddy streaks remained, leaving her cheeks dirty and swollen. She stood straight again, her hand on her right hip.

"All I ken is that a number of years ago a flock of crows flew into the settlement here. They were frenzied and pecked two children to death and injured many others. The priest told us they came because of our sins and that if we didna do as he commanded they would come again. The elders of the village remember a similar thing happening twenty or more years ago, but that time was much worse—the villagers were burned up in a terrible fire. 'Tis why he chose this place to build the kirk. 'Tis hallowed ground now. We are privileged that he and his mother picked this spot for their home."

His mother. Maeve was suddenly on the alert, her hands tingling with nerves. Both of them lived here. Obviously the crows were under some enchantment. They weren't by nature evil birds. Her thoughts scattered back to the messenger at the Oillteil camp—how the bird had fixed her with his stare, a look of utter loathing, if you could say that about a bird's expression. The crows were intimately connected to Dark Raven and had been for many years.

"Are there any other priests here that you've encountered?"

Sorcha shook her head. "Brandubh is the only priest that I ken but he has many deacons in his employ. They come with him sometimes and visit us occasionally when the priest is gone."

Maeve stared into the distance. She hadn't come across anyone fitting this description nor had Eron or the others mentioned them. "Sorcha, what you feel in your heart is important, not what anyone else tells you."

"But I am a sinner."

"What makes you say that?" This conversation was going in circles, getting nowhere.

"I have blasphemous thoughts, I doubt things… I think badly about the deacons, what they do with the women, what they expect of me. I ken 'tis important for the continuation of the settlement but…" Sorcha's face turned red and she looked away, kneeling down in front of the firepit. She placed a few twigs on top of the cold ashes, getting soot all over her fingers.

"What do you mean? What do the deacons do?"

"They only want to help us," she mumbled. "Our men are gone…and the priest knows what's best for us," she added quietly, glancing over her shoulder at Maeve. "He wishes us to conceive."

"What are you saying? No, never mind, I know what you're saying." Maeve recoiled with disgust and outrage. Who were these so-called deacons? Had they come from outside this world? Maybe John was one of them. According to her neighbor in Milltown, Naomi, Brandubh had spent quite a bit of time mentoring the man. Maybe he had done the same with others and then brought them here to work with him.

"And besides we are all born sinners and we need to atone. This is why we have no bairns," Sorcha continued.

"We're innocent when we're born, how could it be other-wise?" Maeve's hands shook with outrage and frustration. They were brainwashed. "If I were to tell you something about why this world has grown so dark, why the sun never shines, why the women cannot conceive a child, would you listen?"

Sorcha gazed at her for a long moment, finally nodding.

"Brandubh and his mother have done something here, some-thing that has to do with black magic. They have made you believe things that are untrue, caused you to doubt your own wisdom. This is why the women cannot conceive. This thing with the deacons is reprehensible. They are taking advantage of you. Have any of you conceived as a result of this? If you let me help, I assure you that once these women have their men back they will be able to have babies."

Sorcha stood up, staring straight into Maeve's eyes. "No bairns have come yet but they tell us it takes some time to heal what ails us."

Maeve listened to Sorcha, the tone of confidence with which these words were spoken. A frisson of doubt went through her. How could she countermand the spell that Adair and Brandubh had cast? But then she thought about what MacCuill had told her, that she had all this power within her—maybe that com-bined with the herbs for fertility and some good wholesome food could start them on the road to recovery. Unfortunately from what she'd seen so far there was no food to be had. Searching through her pack again she pulled out what she'd taken from the cottage—several apples, a large wedge of cheese, a loaf of bread and a bag of oatmeal.

"Take this, Sorcha. It isn't much but maybe I can find a way to get you more." Maeve put three apples, half the loaf of bread and the cheese on the floor next to the fire, her thoughts going to her bow left behind at Eron's camp. It would have come in handy right about now, although she had yet to see a rabbit, a deer or a wild boar. A feeling of helplessness went through her as she realized the enormity of the task she was faced with.

"On second thought, will you and the others come with me? I can keep you safe. My grandfather is a hunter—he'll help us." Maeve wondered exactly how she would accomplish this but let the worry drift off—she would find a way. "You need to find yourselves again, to connect with the goddess and the earth, our mother." Maeve was astonished as this statement came out of her mouth—the words didn't seem her own.

Sorcha was kneeling again and had managed to coax a meager fire into existence. She rose and wiped her hands on her filthy apron and then turned to Maeve. "Ye dinna live here and havna authority. Without the priest everyone would have perished. He and his maithair helped all of us recognize the evil we carry inside, to repent and mend our foul and corrupt ways. We worshipped at the altar of false prophets before he led us to salvation. We must listen to him and do as he says."

"You're right, I don't live here, but I do know this priest. I know he's a bad man—you must believe me. He's not a true representative of the church. He's distorted the teachings to his own end. My grandmother is his twin—she's told me all about him."

"Your grandmother? I dinna ken the priest had a twin. He brings others who work with him but nae his sister. Is she a nun?"

Maeve sighed. The woman didn't seem to be taking in what she was trying to say. "No, she's not. The Otherworld has always been her home and she fights for this place, trying to bring it back to what it once was." Maeve looked down at her hands, wondering why they were tingling. A second later, words poured out of her mouth unbidden. "You must have noticed how the sun never shines, how scarce the water that used to flow abundantly. Look to the stream at the bottom of your hill—did it not rush with fresh clear water? Is that not where you filled your buckets?" Maeve was not familiar with this area or how much water they did or did not have. And the speech patterns of this entity were not hers. When she looked down again she noticed a faint imprint of another hand, the fingers adorned with several heavy rings. Before she could make sense of it, the image was gone.

"Hello. What do we have here?" The burlap parted revealing an older woman with gray hair done up in a bun. When her pale blue eyes lighted on her, Maeve recognized the woman from the airport—Adair, Brandubh's mother.

"Sorcha, what have you been saying? You know how we frown on this sort of thing."

Maeve stared at Adair, unable to utter a word. It was as though something had clamped over her mouth. She struggled to get control of herself to no avail. When she glanced at Sorcha, the young woman's face had gone white, her eyes wide.

When Maeve looked at Adair she smiled, showing straight white teeth. She addressed Maeve in a kind voice. "Ye are correct, little one. I am your great-grandmother. So sorry Finna couldn't be bothered to introduce us. I've been looking forward to this moment for such a very long time."

She reached forward to grasp Maeve's shoulder, sending a shiver down her arm. Maeve felt as though her energy was draining out. She pulled out from under the woman's claw-like hand, gasping for breath.

"What's the matter, dear? The cat got your tongue?"

Again the winning smile, the look of total innocence. Maeve stood transfixed, her mind telling her not to trust this woman but another voice assuring her that Adair was harmless. "I...I didn't expect to see you here."

Adair laughed. "This is my home. Didna Sorcha here tell ye this? These women are all under my care. What is it ye wish from them, Maeve?"

"They seem sick—I thought I might..."

"Ye might...what? Heal them?" Adair laughed again, a grating sound. "I told ye they are under my care."

Maeve glanced toward Sorcha who stood with her hands folded across her belly looking down. "Sorcha, do you want me to go?"

When Sorcha looked up her eyes were blank. "If Adair says so then I agree."

Adair was blocking the door to the outside, her arms folded across her chest.

"I guess I'll be going then," Maeve said uneasily, moving toward the opening.

"But my dear, surely ye ken that we canna allow that." Adair opened the burlap and called out, "This woman is a witch, and ye ken how we deal with witches!"

Somehow Maeve managed to get by her, stumbling toward the crowd of women outside.

"Stop her!" Sorcha yelled, heading out the door and toward Maeve with her fist held up.

Behind Sorcha, Adair watched Maeve, her lips curled into a delighted smile.

When a rock hit her temple, Maeve took off running, heading down the hill toward the dry riverbed. She crossed a rickety wooden bridge and headed up the path on the other side. A minute later a searing pain in her side had her doubled up. She frantically struggled to catch her breath, watching the women race across the bridge. The rocks they held were jagged and big enough to cause serious injury. Maeve took off, not waiting until they were in throwing range. The pain in her side felt like a knife blade—she gasped for breath—how were these weak and sick women managing to gain on her like this? But when she turned back again she noticed Adair, her hands weaving patterns in the air, her lips moving silently. Terror shot through her, sending adrenaline coursing through her veins. Maeve hurtled away, her fingers closing around the moonstone. The shouts were too close now—she couldn't outrun them. Another rock hit her square in the back, knocking her down.

Adair was suddenly there, her right hand reaching to help Maeve up. "I will nae hurt ye, my dear."

Maeve hesitated, her mind confused. The older woman looked so benign, her smile so sweet. They were of the same blood. But then she noticed the enormous rock in Adair's other hand. Feeling the energy draining from her body she tried to pull away, but the woman's grip was like iron. Adair's hand was coming toward Maeve's head, the rock ready to split her skull in two. But the whirring had begun, the sound loud in her ears.

"Brigid will nae save ye!" she heard Adair scream just before she was whisked away, safe inside a blur of color.

Chapter

14

h arold woke with a start. He had been dreaming
something important but it was now gone. He sat up
and then shivered—the fire had gone out. The blanket
they had pulled over themselves last night was not warm
enough without Maeve's body next to him. Where was Maeve?
She must have gone to the outhouse, he thought, pulling on his
jeans and sweater. His mind went to the night before, reliving
their magical reunion. He wouldn't mind repeating the entire
interlude right now, he thought, desire coursing through him.
He smiled to himself as he put the kettle on for tea, looking
around for something to nibble on. It had been many hours
since their soup.

When he turned to sit down at the table he noticed the
note. He picked it up, uneasiness making its way into his gut.

Dear Harold,

*I had to go. I didn't want to get into an argument
about this and waste even more time. I love you but I*

*must do this on my own. I'm sure we will be together
again very soon. Last night was about as wonderful as
anything could be and leaving you this morning was
the hardest thing I think I've ever done. Just please
know that if it wasn't absolutely necessary I wouldn't
be doing this.*

*Here are instructions on how to get to the Otherworld.
I will try to alert my mother and Catriona so they can
meet you at the spring. If you don't find them, head
north. I've told you all about what's going on there,
so be forewarned. If you decide to stay here, that's fine
too. Just know that I will find you when I can.*

I love you,

Maeve

At the bottom Maeve had written instructions about the
boatman, explaining that once Harold crossed the river he
would be in the Otherworld—she warned him about staying
out of sight and traveling by night. It wasn't safe for him to
wander around with all the fighting going on. She didn't want
him to end up being imprisoned with the others she'd seen.
Another scrap of paper covered in a foreign hand contained a
detailed map of the area surrounding the cottage and the trail
to the river and then from the other side of the river all the way
to the spring. This same hand suggested he wait at the spring
until Eron, Catriona or Finna arrived. *Wonder who wrote this?*
Distractedly, he folded both notes, stuffing them in his back
pocket.

A knot had formed in Harold's stomach. He could barely
stand the idea of Maeve out there alone. But then a little nig-
gling doubt entered his mind. Could all of this really be true?

It hardly seemed plausible. But he had never known Maeve to make things up. Her kisses had stopped his questions the night before—he'd basically forgotten everything in the throes of passion. Damn! Instead of letting his pecker take over he should have insisted on going with her.

He packed quickly, deciding to skip breakfast. He put in extra clothes and as much cheese, apples and bread he could fit, as well as his water bottle. He had a Swiss army knife, matches, and a coil of rope that he found under Finna's sink. Looking around his eyes lit on some candles on a shelf above the sink—he threw them in with all the rest of his gear, wishing he had his little lightweight camp stove but he had not thought to bring it along. He hadn't known at the time that he would be heading into some godforsaken wilderness.

Following the map he walked to the top of the ridge and through the cedar grove, heading past the holly trees and then across the hill on the other side. From here the river came into view, meandering snake-like into the distance. He found the footpath and headed down, feeling very apprehensive about what he would find on the other side of that murky looking ribbon of water; a wall of mist lay over the opaque surface, obscuring the far bank. Maeve had warned him about the boatman so he wasn't surprised when he saw the small coracle gliding toward him out of the fog.

He waited until the boatman was close before he called out, "Hello!"

The man didn't speak as he guided the boat into the little U in the riverbank where the path ended, his blind eyes glowing in the gray mist. Harold stepped forward but didn't attempt to board, afraid that the boatman didn't know he was there.

"Come on, Kenneth," the boatman insisted, gesturing for him to get on board.

"I go by Harold, but how did you know my middle name is Kenneth?" he asked, stepping into the boat and dropping down onto the narrow wooden seat.

"I am the boatman, I know these things. You are the one in the prophecy."

"The prophecy? I know about the prophecy but...I don't think I'm mentioned."

"Yes, Kenneth, you are. You are the one of noble birth to stand by the side of the Willow."

"I'm certainly not of noble birth," Harold declared emphatically, staring into the strange eyes. He tried to remember what Maeve had told him about the wording, but she was only able to come up with a few sentences—and nothing about a person of noble birth.

"Do you have something for me, Kenneth?" the boatman asked.

Maeve had told him about this part of the trip and he was prepared, taking a silver coin out of his pocket and placing it in the boatman's outstretched weathered hand.

"This will not do. I want something that is of value—this coin means nothing to you."

Harold took the coin back, realizing the man was right; money was only something he used because he had to, of no other importance. He thought for a moment and then pulled his Swiss army knife out of his pack. He didn't want to part with this. It had been a gift from his father and it was also extremely useful. Reluctantly he placed it in the man's hand.

"Yes, this is of value to you, I can feel it." His fingers closed around the knife before he pushed it into a pocket of his trousers. "Now, Kenneth, I must tell you a story."

Harold stretched out his legs and leaned back as the boatman pushed off and began to row across the river. The boatman's words drifted into his mind like a childhood yarn—far-fetched and whimsical. As they passed into the mist Harold felt dizzy for a few moments, disoriented. He missed a sentence or two as he tried to reclaim his equilibrium. From a distance he heard the boatman saying, "...it may take some time for you to remember me or the experiences we've had together but as you become oriented to this world your memories will return."

By the time they reached the other side, Harold was even more lightheaded, his thoughts scattered and erratic. He got out of the boat forgetting to thank the boatman or even to say good-bye. When he looked up again, the coracle had already disappeared into the mist. What the boatman had told him was unbelievable—that Harold had been Kenneth MacAlpin in a previous life. The boatman told him he had known Kenneth well and that he recognized Harold immediately. He and Kenneth had fought side by side and there was no doubt at all in his mind. Harold knew all about this first King of Scotland because he had just finished reading a book about him, but trying to swallow the news that he was this man seemed beyond preposterous. Kenneth MacAlpin had been alive a thousand years ago. When he mentioned this fact, the boatman had said, "Not quite. We fought together eleven-hundred and fifty-eight years ago, in 847 A.D." That would make the boatman how old?

This was not really worth thinking about and what difference did it make, anyway? *Only the fact that if he was mentioned in the prophecy he belonged here as much as Maeve—he had a job to do.* He stood on the bank staring into the mist. On the other side of the river everything had seemed somewhat normal but now... now he didn't know what to think.

15

The castle faced the sea on a slight rise, a wondrous monolith made of red stone in the northwest corner of the Caer Sidi. MacCuill walked through the enormous wooden doors, announcing himself to one of the guards standing watch and entered the hall to wait. In just a minute or two the guard was back and beckoning MacCuill forward into the room where the Queen of the Druids entertained her more personal guests. He felt privileged to be brought in here instead of the more forbidding throne room. The guard opened the door into the square room and backed away, closing the door after MacCuill went through. The Queen was seated next to the fireplace and looked up as MacCuill approached.

"Come and sit beside me, MacCuill, son of Hazel. I have missed your company."

MacCuill walked over to the fire and sat down on a wide chair next to Queen Druantia, but not before bowing down to her. He was glad of her tone since at times her anger could be crushing. "I am glad to see you my Queen," he said. "I have been away far too long." He gazed into her blue-violet eyes, noticing the firelight reflected inside them. He smiled inwardly, thinking about the fire that burned in this woman's very soul. In past years he might have mentioned this observation but now he was conscious of a strain between them.

Her golden brocade dress, studded with jewels, sparkled as she turned toward him, her expression serious. Her hair was almost all white now and lay in waves on her shoulders. She had not put it up for this meeting, another positive portent, he thought.

"Yes, MacCuill, you have neglected your duties here in the north and now the Caer Sidi suffers. I have had to summon Cathbadh and Abaris and although very high in rank, they are not of this time and have little understanding of what we are up against. The protections have been breached—soldiers march on the eastern hills and through the forests, disturbing the balance. They kill the reindeer and the aurochs, angering the god of the forest. You must return here to where you were born."

"But my Queen..." he started.

Her eyes flashed gold for a moment before she spoke in a commanding tone. "You will not raise objections to me! I say what happens and you will stay here!" She stared at him for a full minute and then continued more quietly, her mouth turning up a little at the edges. "At least until the meeting is over. I know what you feel for this girl they call the willow. Maeve has her path to follow and if you interfere she will not be able to accomplish her destiny. Her path has been clearly defined, although she may not be cognizant of this as yet. If and when you see her you must follow her orders explicitly, even if what she asks sounds like a fool's errand. Our own Brigid speaks through her and because of this her authority is above yours, even above mine. The time of the wolf moon has begun and the one named in the prophecy will decide the direction of this fight."

MacCuill stared at Druantia, surprised by her emphatic words. "I have pledged myself to her, my Queen."

"I understand this and it is right that you have. And there will be times when she will call to you and of course you must heed her call. However you are also needed here."

MacCuill watched Druantia, noticing a sudden drop in the queen's energy. Her skin seemed to sag as she turned her gaze toward the fire.

"There will be many diversions for you to accomplish here in the Caer Sidi when these troops come our way. There have already been many reports of animals slaughtered to feed the vast armies that are gathering. Cernunnos is very angry. Extensive sections of the forests have been cut down to make forts to house the workers, or slaves, I should say. Mines are being dug all over the Otherworld, decimating the landscape and disrupting the animal trails as well as their water supplies and grazing lands. Are Brandubh and his minions selling our precious wood outside this world, along with the gold and silver? These are the things you must find out for me. We need to be prepared. The earth cries out. Water is being diverted, springs are drying up and nothing can grow now that the sun no longer shines. We have had earth tremors here for the first time."

Druantia rose and went to a small table, pouring amber liquid from a pitcher into a glass. "Would you like a glass of mead? It is newly made. I fear there will be no more since the bees have deserted us."

"I would have done that for you," MacCuill said, standing. "It is not my intention to be waited on by my queen." He poured another glass and then placed his hand on her elbow, guiding her back to the chair.

Druantia sat down, and then took a small sip from her glass. "This comes from the last barrel—taste the sweetness and hold the memory of it. It saddens me that we will have no more." She held up her glass.

MacCuill clinked his glass against hers before taking a long swallow. He held it in his mouth, remembering the years of making mead, the festivals in which the honey drink was given in libation. Now every drop was hoarded.

A moment of silence went by, each one lost in their own thoughts and memories from the past as they sipped their drinks. When MacCuill heard the rustle of Druantia's dress he looked up to meet her gaze.

"I will require you and some of the others to act as scouts once our meeting is over. You must discover who is working with Brandubh and the Oillteil. I am certain he has promised great wealth to these strangers who have arrived from outside this world." She gazed off again, her eyes growing misty. "It used to be that only the pure hearted could enter—now, somehow, this has changed. You must find out how he has managed this. It must be stopped."

"You have not yet mentioned Adair. It is she who has connected with the power of the underworld and it might be through her that the protections have been breached. I fear what she has become."

Drantia turned, her gaze sharp. "That woman will not preside over this world. My power is still greater than hers."

MacCuill watched the years fall away as the queen's words poured forth. Her hands gestured wildly as she described her past encounters with Adair. It seemed they had long been enemies.

"All the druids here and even beyond our shores have been summoned to the castle for this meeting," Druantia continued. "Many will stay to protect the Caer Sidi. Until the meeting is over I want you here, by my side. But when the meeting is ended, you will go and find the answers to my questions. You are aware of what is happening in other parts of this world. I am no longer able to travel—you must be my eyes and ears. And when you return, you are to impart this information to all the druids. As you are aware, the gods and goddesses and all the spirits have grown weak—we must do everything in our power to bring them back. That will require a great summoning of spiritual energy."

MacCuill felt uneasy. There was no more time to lose. Cernunnos, the deity of the druids, kept the wilderness in balance. He had been present at the blessing ceremony so many years ago, but MacCuill had not seen him for many years. Cernunnos would not put up with the destruction of his animals and his forest unless he, also, had grown very weak. MacCuill's first duty would be to travel to the east and try to communicate with this 'honored god'. He turned to his queen. "Have you seen Cernunnos?"

"Yes. I have seen him and he grows weaker, just as the other gods and goddesses, but because of his animals he is not so diminished. The belief in him is still strong within the herds of sacred auroch and the deer.

"When will this meeting take place?"

"In two days time. In the meantime you and I will discuss strategies. I have much to tell you, my old friend." Druantia smiled, her hand on MacCuill's arm.

"What of Maeve's mother and grandmother?"

"What of them? They will be fine. Catriona is a skilled seer, her husband a tracker and hunter. Finna..." Druantia hesitated. "I would feel better if she was in a safer place but I suppose the others will watch out for her."

"Finna is strong in her own right. I have seen her strength, watched her grow over the years. She will be an asset to them." MacCuill put his hand over hers. "I will worry if I am not able to check on them once in a while."

Druantia pulled her hand away. "You will have your chance once the meeting is finished, " she said sharply. "You must look to the future, MacCuill. These people you love so much are merely human. They will soon be gone but you and I will remain. What happens here is not for them—it is for the Otherworld. The Willow has been called to bring this change but she will not live forever—perhaps she will be killed in the course of battle."

When MacCuill opened his mouth to respond, Druantia held her hand up. "No more. You will stay in your usual tower room. I expect you to be my spy once the others arrive. Although I trust most, there are some I wonder about. Come with me now, we will enjoy a meal together and then I will employ your younger eyes to go over some maps and plans."

With MacCuill's help, Druantia rose and walked toward the door. Her back was as straight as ever but as MacCuill lent her his arm, he noticed the tremor in her hands. The youthfulness he had seen earlier was gone now, replaced with an aging queen attempting to maintain her authority. The encroaching darkness was having an effect on them all.

As they walked down the hall together, MacCuill thought of the things he had not yet told her—the armies of Oillteil marching in the great middle valley, Brandubh and his recruits riding north, Gertrude's presence here, her involvement with Brandubh, Maeve's blossoming abilities. It could all wait, he supposed, as he opened the door into the elegant dining room. He stood aside, allowing the queen to go ahead of him. Seated at a long wooden table next to an open fireplace was the rest of her court, druids both young and old, their questioning eyes fixed on MacCuill.

Chapter

16

Maeve's heart pounded in her ears, her eyes closing as vibrant colors swirled by at an alarming rate. When she landed she didn't move for several minutes, her hands on her chest. The image of Adair was still vivid in her mind. She finally stood and brushed herself off, wondering where she was now. No thought had entered her head except *get me out of here* when her fingers closed around the moonstone. Was this yet another place where she would be rebuffed and possibly killed in her attempts to help? What was that saying? *No good deed goes unpunished.* She tried to laugh but her nerves were too much on edge.

Forest lay behind her, silent and dark. It didn't look at all familiar. She waited, her mind reaching out to the voice she'd heard earlier. After a few minutes she moved toward the trees, her thoughts going in circles. Now was not the time to be confused. She needed all her senses to find the holding pens and release the prisoners.

A very narrow path led into a forest of conifers. At least they hadn't been clear-cut. It was pleasant under the trees, the smell of pine resin sharp in her nostrils. She was just thinking about how safe she felt when a twig snapped. Turning she found herself face to face with a tall russet-haired woman.

"I decided I better show myself before you thought you had lost your mind." The woman smiled, pulling a dark shawl around herself. "'Tis difficult now to come here, to be present in the flesh. I do not have long."

"You must be Brigid."

She nodded, her pale hands fastening a brooch to hold her shawl in place around her wide shoulders. Her fingers were long and covered with rings of semi-precious stones. "I was the first one, you see. With your incarnation the circle has closed."

"Are you talking about the moonstone?" Maeve put her hand up, feeling reassured by its presence around her neck.

"The moonstone is the symbol of all that was to come. It has brought us to this point where the Otherworld is poised on the brink of destruction. You are the one, Maeve, the girl child born of Brigid. Not only are we linked but you are also linked to the goddess of fire for whom I was named. This next phase is for you and you alone to accomplish."

"But the prophecy said many—many would be by my side to help me."

"The many will only come because of who you are. I cannot say more than this. My ability to see into the future is limited and cannot be shared."

"But how do I do this? How do I save this place? It seems impossible."

When Maeve focused again on Brigid she was dismayed to see the woman growing less and less distinct.

"I must go." Brigid put her hand out, her fingers brushing Maeve's arm lightly. "Remember, we are linked," she said, just before fading away completely.

Maeve stared at the place where she had been, her eyes filling with tears. This woman was her ancestor. She felt connected to her as though they were mother and daughter or maybe even sisters. A sense of loss enveloped her. She sat down under a tree and put her head in her hands, mourning the loss of Brigid and wishing they could have more time together. But there was no time for wallowing, a little voice insisted. It was time to go. She obeyed, her thoughts scattered and diffuse.

After the encounter with Brigid, Maeve worked her way through the forest, trying to focus her mind on releasing the prisoners. There was no path to follow, no sunlight to clue her into what direction she was going, but she kept on, the image of the horrible holding pens clear in her mind. The forest ended, the path heading across a ridge and down the other side. Scanning the immediate vicinity, Maeve was not surprised by the denuded hillside with no signs of life. The area was familiar. One of the forts was around here somewhere.

Cautiously she moved toward the edge of the ridge. Her heart contracted as she made out the high fence below, the huddled people shivering inside the enclosure. Oillteil and Wildmen wandered around the outside, talking in low voices. There were at least six of them and maybe more. An image of Adair went through her mind, the rock poised to fly, the woman's uncanny ability to manipulate Maeve's thoughts. The effect of that encounter plagued her, undermining her confidence—she still felt weak, as though the woman had sucked out some of her energy. Brigid's cryptic messages had done nothing to help. And now there was no wolf by her side and no Eron to encourage her and make tea. Harold was far away, his reassuring presence only a memory.

She breathed in and out slowly, trying to let go of the defeatist thoughts crowding her mind and clouding her judgment.

You can do this, a voice whispered in her ear. Buoyed by the encouragement she assumed came from Brigid, she edged down the hill. Luckily some scraggly trees had been forgotten in the haste to cut down every living thing. Using the trunks for cover, she moved further down, getting close enough to watch the comings and goings. It was time to settle in and scope out the situation.

The moments went by slowly. Maeve was cold, her body uncomfortable where she sat hunched over on the frozen ground. Waiting seemed to activate her mind, her thoughts going in circles as she trained her eyes below. To keep her brain busy she tried to calculate how many days had gone by since Rowan— was it two or three? But time seemed different here and when she attempted to put it into a framework everything became muddled. Take now, for instance—hadn't it been light only a second ago? She sighed, rolling over on her stomach. It felt good to change position—her cold muscles were tightening and beginning to cramp.

She wondered where she was in relation to Corra's spring— if Harold ended up there, how would they reconnect? She was certain the man would not sit around waiting for her to come back—no, he was definitely on his way. She shook her head in frustration. Transporting herself all over with the moonstone was no way to get her bearings—she needed a map. But then an odd idea came to her—maybe she could just ask the stone where to take her—just say, *Corra's spring,* and focus on what she remembered of the place. So far her movements had all been accompanied by an urgent need to get away from something.

A yell from below startled her back to the present and she squinted into the darkness. Two more Oillteil guards had arrived and appeared to be arguing with one of the Wildmen. A deep growl had her sucking in her breath—the Wildmen's beasts had turned their heads in her direction, their noses in the air. She crawled behind the tree, holding her breath and hoping the breeze was going in the other direction. If they came up to investigate she could never outrun them. The beasts were fighting now, and their frenzied barking had her scrambling back up the hill. Getting herself killed at this juncture was not an option.

At the top of the ridge she paused, trying to take in enough breath to stop her heart from hammering. Her mind called out to Brigid, hoping for some insight—surely the goddess Brigid could help her, even if the woman couldn't, especially one so closely linked. But the only answer was a cold whistling wind that entered her mind, leaving her breathless and freezing. She pulled a wool scarf out of her pack, wrapping it around her neck, and then huddled down in her jacket. Remembering her resolve of only a few short hours ago, she had a talk with herself—it was time to pull herself together, trust her own intuition and stop relying on everyone else. *Get a grip,* she told herself firmly.

The darkness around her seemed to thicken and grow heavy. It was getting close to the time when she must act—the prisoners had to be released tonight. If she waited, there was the possibility of Brandubh's return and she didn't relish the feel of his hands around her neck again. This time he would use the knife without a second thought. Why couldn't she get control of all these disturbing thoughts? Had the wind done this to her? At least the dog-beasts had quieted down for the moment. Closing her eyes, she leaned her head back against a tree trunk trying to come up with a plausible plan. Possibly during the dinner hour there would be fewer guards outside.

The wolf was silent in his approach; Maeve only looked up when she saw a dark shape out of the corner of her eye. When Finiche came to a stop in front of her, Maeve's arms went round his neck—she buried her face in the thick ruff of fur. *I'm so happy to see you,* she whispered into his ear. He gazed at her out of his intelligent amber eyes, his mind reaching out to her, and although it wasn't in words she understood. The wolf had been traveling with Eron and Catriona, had heard Maeve's call and found his way to her.

Maeve's thoughts went to her grandparents—she longed to see them, but right now she had to keep her mind focused on the task at hand. "I have to release the prisoners down there." She watched the wolf, waiting for a sign that this was a bad idea, but he only stared back at her with an alert expression.

Finiche followed her down the hill to her former hiding place, taking care to stay in the shadows. As Maeve had suspected, the moment came when most of the guards left their posts, heading inside for supper. After his eyes met hers, the wolf moved away, slinking toward the back of the fort while she crept toward the front. When she arrived at the gate there were only two guards left on watch. When one of them called out some guttural utterance she flattened herself on the ground. A few minutes later she heard an eerie howling from the back of the fort and both guards left their posts to investigate the disturbance. A minute later there was shouting and the yips of wolves.

There was no time to lose. She ran to the gate, fit the little key into the lock and swung it open. The Crion looked up in surprise as she sprinted toward them. A few recognized her from her trip with MacCuill and an audible sigh went through the group. She fitted the same key into the padlock and undid the chain, pulling each one free. She was almost to the end of the chain when the Oillteil guards returned. "Go," she whispered to the ones who were free, but they didn't want to leave their friends.

"Aieee!" came a loud shout as one of the guards spotted her. She had a moment of paralyzing fear as she realized they were blocked in. A second later the wolf came running through the gate. His lunging snarls kept the Oillteil back while she and the Crion made their way quickly around them. Two more wolves appeared, circling the guards with teeth bared. Horses were trotting around the side of the fort. Had Finiche released them?

There was another surprised shout and a group of Wildmen appeared, the beasts circling around them. The wolves attacked the beasts and in the ensuing chaos Maeve inched her way toward the gate, motioning for the Crion to follow. When a group of Wildmen blocked her way she shouted for them to move, her only thought getting the Crion to safety. The wolves circled around the Wildmen, jumping forward to nip at their legs. From the other side of the gate an arrow whizzed in, hitting Maeve in her upper thigh and making her fall. "Go, go!" she cried to the Crion, pushing them away as they tried to help her up.

By now the shouting had grown in volume, and the wolves and beasts were rolling on the ground. It was hard to tell who was winning. The Crion were trying vainly to get away but a lot of them were too weak and sick, barely able to walk, much less run. More horses appeared, Finiche driving them toward the gate. Maeve got his message—to put the small ones on their backs. Struggling to stand, Maeve worked her way to the gate, pressing herself between the fighting animals and the fence. Her leg was forgotten in her fervor to help the Crion, lifting them onto the horses, two on each one. Once they were secure she whistled and Finiche reappeared, nipping at the horses heels as he urged them into the night.

Arrows were still flying, coming from Oillteil outside the pen and Maeve watched in horror as several Crion were hit. She watched them fall, realizing she could do nothing to help them; the gate was completely blocked with Wildmen. When another bolt from a crossbow dug deeply into her hip, she went down without even breath enough to cry out. This time she could not get up. The Wildmen watched her, their frightening eyes the last thing she saw before sliding into unconsciousness.

Chapter

17

When Maeve woke again she was surrounded with Crion men and women. They were camped deep in the woods, a fire burning close by. When she tried to move pained seared through her. "Twella, twella," one of the Crion men said, hurrying over. As she struggled to get up, he pushed her back, pointing to the wounds in her leg. They had stripped off her jeans and gotten both the arrow tips out, but the gaping flesh needed to be closed and stitched. She moaned as a fresh wave of pain hit her and then motioned for her pack. A Crion woman brought it to her and then the others made a circle around her. Their faces were lit up by the fire as they crooned their sympathy, their eyes trained on Maeve. The sight of their reed-like bodies, tattered clothes and pale faces brought Maeve to tears, overcome by their selflessness. They drew closer, the soothing purr-like sounds calming her until she fell back, unable to do anything more for herself. The pain had obliterated everything from her mind. When one of the men handed her a piece of willow bark to chew on, she didn't argue. As the pain receded a bit she was able to extract yarrow leaves from her pack, which she placed on both wounds. The Crion came closer and closer, forming a tight circle around her. They rocked back and forth making the strange purring sounds as they stroked her lightly with their hands. Maeve's eyes closed.

It was the next morning before Maeve woke up again. She was lying on her back next to the fire, her body covered with a thick sheepskin. The Crion men and women sat together talking, their melodic voices like a lost song on the edges of her consciousness. Seeing she was awake a few of the women came to sit by her, one of them handing her a gourd filled with tea. Gingerly, Maeve pushed her self into a seated position and reached for the gourd. When she removed the sheepskin to check out the wounds, she was surprised to see they were closed, with only a thin red line to indicate where they had been. And, she realized as she changed position, her hip was barely painful. "How?" she asked, pointing.

They all smiled widely and then one of the women spoke. "We have a special gift but you are a true healer."

"I didn't do this."

"With our help you healed the wounds."

"The sounds? That's what you do?"

"The sounds are a vibration that encourages the body—it is our way. But where you found us, the guards would not allow it. That is why we are all sick now. I am Rea." The small woman smiled, her eyes nearly hidden by straight copper bangs.

Maeve took the small hand she held out, thanking her. After finishing her tea, Maeve tried to stand, but a wave of dizziness came over her.

"The Willow should rest today. The healing is not complete." Rea's upturned amber eyes regarded Maeve gravely.

Nikki Broadwell

"I just need to check on the wolves." Rea held her hand out to help Maeve up, the diminutive woman surprisingly strong. Maeve patted her arm before heading away from the fire.

She found Finiche with the rest of the pack a short distance under the trees. Examining each wolf in turn she discovered a few minor scratches and a cut ear or two, but other than that they were unscathed-their thick fur seemed to have protected them. When she came back to the fire, Rea told Maeve that the night of crooning had not only helped Maeve, but the rest of the Crion as well. Maeve surveyed the group, surprised at how much better they all appeared. Their methods might be strange but they worked. She encouraged the Crion to go home where they would be safe from Brandubh and then Rea translated, but when she finished there was low disgruntled murmuring amongst the others. "They plan to remain with you," Rea told Maeve. "After what happened at the pens they wish to help you in whatever way they can."

"What *did* happen? I remember the arrow and being unconscious, but how did we manage to get away?"

"The wolf carried you here. We helped get you up on his back."

Maeve imagined the scene before the last arrow hit her. She thought Finiche had gone with the horses and that she was about to die. "Did the horses bring you here?"

Rea nodded. "They've gone now—off to forage for food. I doubt they will be back."

"Rea, your people can't remain with me. It's too dangerous and beside that I don't know where I'm going."

"We will be safer with you than in our home. The village was ransacked and all our families have disappeared. We hope they've found a safe place but they could all have been taken prisoner at another fort."

Maeve shuddered, wrapping her arms around her body. Rea took one look at her and disappeared, returning with her warm

231

coat. "Thank you," Maeve said, feeling immense gratitude that she and all the others were here and alive. She thought about the tunnels she had visited, the bright weavings hanging on the walls, the tinkle of sheep bells and the sense of solace and community that permeated the place. It gave her a sinking feeling to realize that it was all gone. "Where are your sheep?" she asked.

Rea shook her head. "Most have been killed for meat and the others...they wander lost. It would be good to have their milk right now but to find them would take much time."

"I'm sorry. Maybe we'll come upon them as we travel. Are we very far from your tunnels?"

Rea nodded, her eyes sad. "At least a full day of walking and no one here is up to that. Many of our group died back there and many others are severely hurt."

Maeve thought back to the grizzly scene at the pens. There had been no proper burial—the bodies had been left there to rot.

Rea pointed toward the right where several forms lay close by the fire. "Tian and Sang are the worst hit. Their wounds are deep and I fear for them."

Putting her mind on the present, Maeve followed Rea, the two of them examining Tian and Sang and the others and setting up the purring circles. Maeve used herbs on their wounds as well as her healing hands. A lot of them were dehydrated and had developed nasty chest colds.

Once everyone was resting she went with Finiche in search of food and water. Her supplies of cheese and nuts would not last long with this many mouths to feed. Too bad she had left most of her food back at the settlement.

Finiche led her across the hills to a place where Eron had set snares. Maeve didn't know whether to be happy or sad when she discovered the dead rabbits. They would bring sustenance but she hated the idea of it. But that night when the smell of roasting meat came to her nostrils her appetite surfaced and she was glad to have them. As far as water was concerned, she was only able to find one running stream and it was barely a trickle. At least it filled two large water bottles. At the camp she heated the water, adding one of the iodine tablets that Harold had given her.

Early the next morning she had a bout of nausea, leaving camp to retch under the trees. Her eyes watered and she had to lie down for a moment, waiting for it to pass. The rabbit must have been rancid. Who knows how long it had been dead?

On her way back to camp she heard the distinctive low hum of the Crion women. She followed the sound out of the shelter of the trees and down a short slope leading to a frozen creek. The women straddled the stream, their eyes closed. Maeve didn't move as the sounds grew stronger, reaching a crescendo and then fading away. The silence that remained seemed charged, small waves of energy bouncing against her face. What they were up to was powerful. When the women opened their eyes and rose as one, Rea motioned for Maeve to join them.

"What were you doing?" she asked, scrambling after them. They headed away from camp, following the streambed as it meandered downhill.

"We try to bring back the water spirits."

"Where are you going now?"

"We need to replenish our stores of roots and mushrooms. We will show you how to find these things."

Rea lowered her eyes, her hands in prayer position before turning to follow the others causing Maeve to wonder if this was their way, or if it was a gesture of respect directed at her. If so it made her a bit uncomfortable. When the women turned and climbed the hill and entered a hardwood forest, she followed, struck by the hush under the canopy, the shadows crowding out the meager light. Rea stopped in front of an enormous beech and began breaking off chunks of some large fungus at its base.

"This is agarikon, good for the chest affliction we have. I am glad it still grows here." Rea and the other women removed several pieces placing them in the small woven bags slung over their shoulders. Maeve followed them deeper into the trees where they dug hazelnuts and walnuts out of the frozen ground. In another area they dug deeper under the frozen surface, pulling out some kind of a tuber. Maeve kneeled to help them, her hands going numb as she worked through the hard dirt. "How do you know where to find these?"

"They grow wild in these sorts of woods. Some have rotted now because of being frozen but many can be harvested."

When they arrived back at camp the men had stoked the fire and water was heating. In went some pieces of the mushroom as well as the tubers, leftover bones of the rabbits as well as the watercress. The Crion, including Tian and Sang, seemed to feel better, chatting amongst themselves in their language and leaving Maeve free to think about what she should do next. Somehow the positive energy of these small people had renewed her faith in herself.

After the meal she quietly left the fire, heading into the woods. She whistled for Finiche and then skirted the camp to avoid alerting the Crion; searching for more holding pens was something she had to do on her own. Finiche led the way with his nose in the air. When he caught the scent of fire he was off, running ahead of her and disappearing from view. Maeve didn't see him again until he stopped on the top of a hill. Behind him a barely visible line of smoke rose into the night air. As she jogged his way a twinge went through her hip. It was time to take advantage of his wide back.

The sky had grown dark by the time Maeve and the wolf reached the second fort. Just like the other one, it had been built in the valley with hills on all sides, hiding the structure from view. A well-used road snaked from the entry gates, heading around a bend and disappearing. Maeve listened carefully for the sound of horses but there was only whistling from the chill wind that blew across the hilltop.

In the holding pen a few men and several Wildmen were sitting in groups next to the fire. There was only one Oillteil guard and Maeve wasn't sure if he was there for their protection or to keep them in. She waited for the guard to leave, hoping he would have to relieve himself at some point. After about a half an hour he got up and walked into the woods, yelling something unintelligible over his shoulder. Maeve took her opportunity, climbing quickly down the bank.

The gate was unlocked but when she swung it open the squeak of the hinges alerted the men and they all turned toward her with hostile stares. "Please come with me, I can get you out of here. I have food and water at my camp." No one spoke, making her wonder if they understood. She pantomimed them following her, bringing her hand to her mouth in the gesture of eating.

Finally one of the men stood, his dark eyes trained on her. "Why should we go with you? We get enough food here and after this fight is over we will be rewarded."

"Rewarded? With what?" she whispered, moving closer. "Your homes have all been destroyed. I've seen the villages that have been burned and looted. Your livelihood is gone. Where are your wives and children?"

"Our wives and children are fine. They wait for us to come back with the gold and silver that has been promised. If something has happened to our homes the dark man will rebuild them."

"Where is your village?" Maeve asked, glancing nervously over her shoulder. She thought she could hear pounding hooves in the distance but maybe it was her imagination.

"Our village is where the big church sits on the hill. Our wives wait for us there."

After more discussion, Maeve realized that most of these men were from Sorcha's settlement. She relayed Sorcha's information about the deacons and what was going on there. They stared at her in disbelief until she described Sorcha and the details of their conversation. Angry muttering began as they took in the unwelcome news.

"How do you know this?" one of the men finally asked in a harsh tone, glaring at her from under bushy eyebrows.

Maeve went through the story again, adding descriptions of the individuals that she could remember, describing the coughs and the rashes that covered the women's faces and how thin they all were.

There was a lengthy silence when she finished speaking and then one of the men said, "We need to get home." He stood and gathered his belongings. The others looked at Maeve and then got to their feet as well.

Almost all the villagers left with her as well as a few Wildmen, sneaking out the open gate before the guard returned. It seemed almost too easy. As they climbed the hill she expected an ambush but none came, but down in the valley she heard the approach of horses again, closer this time. Whoever was coming was riding hard.

Uncertain as to why the Wildmen came along, she hoped they didn't have some sort of treachery on their minds. She found their dreadlocks and feral light-colored eyes disconcerting and because of the language barrier she had no way to know what was going on in their minds. From the top of the hill she looked down on the pen, noticing the three Wildmen and two villagers who had remained. They sat around the fire as before, hunched against the cold. In the distance she could see dust from the approaching riders. The guard was nowhere to be seen.

Before dawn Maeve stumbled out of camp to retch in private. This was becoming all too common, she thought to herself as she tried to rinse her mouth out with the tiny bit of water left in her water bottle. What had she eaten last night? Everything here could be laden with bacteria—she couldn't waste their meager supply of water to clean the food before they ate it.

She came back to camp just as a group of Wildmen and Crion headed out to hunt for game. They watched her warily as they slung bows over their shoulders, securing the hand-made quivers on their backs. The Wildmen were expert hunters, skilled in archery and with the knives they used to skin and dress the rabbits and other animals they killed. After they were gone Maeve searched out Rea, asking the woman where to look for more tubers and greens to add to the stews.

"To find the roots you must be in the forests that carry the nuts. There are tubers growing in certain places there, planted long ago by the Amuigh."

"The Amuigh planted them? Rhea, do you know where the Amuigh are imprisoned?"

"The Amuigh move from place to place, planting to harvest the next time they come through. There may be a few at the fort to the east—the holding pen is close to one of the mines. I have not seen many of their kind for some time." Rea turned sad eyes on Maeve. "They are gentle creatures who have no wish to fight and no defenses."

"If they are being held somewhere I would like to find them."

"The wolf could help with this as well as locating the tubers—his sense of smell is acute. This orange food is particularly good for you now," she added with a sly smile, staring pointedly at Maeve's belly.

"What are you talking about?"

"The little one you carry."

"The little one...?"

"And we must find one of our sheep—the milk would be most helpful."

Maeve's mind reeled as she registered the symptoms she had been having. Despite her increasing thinness her breasts had grown larger and had been sore for some time. She placed her hands on her lower belly trying to remember her last period but couldn't come up with a date. It had been over two months for sure. Hadn't they used birth control? She thought back to the intense and passionate encounters, trying to recall if Harold had used anything. He must have thought she was on birth control pills. How could she be so stupid? Adrenaline shot through her at the thought of what she had to do here, the danger for this unborn child. And what would Harold think about this new development? Had *this* been mentioned in the prophecy? She scanned back to the wording but couldn't remember much— only the feeling of responsibility it engendered.

"How did you know?"

"You have a glow about you—light shines from your eyes." Rea laughed, a high tinkling sound. "And I have heard you in the woods before dawn. This new life you carry is special, a gift. We have not been able to conceive."

"No babies? How long has it been?"

"Years—since the spirits began to desert us. But now with your baby there is hope."

Maeve's solar plexus contracted with terror at the thought of miscarriage. How could she carry a baby to term here? According to Rhea as well as the women at the settlement, no women had done so in years. She counted up the months in her mind—at least six more. Would she still be here in six months? Tears welled up as the real meaning of that question went through her mind. This was not part of her plan—but then again, being here in the Otherworld hadn't been part of her plan either.

Rea patted her arm. "This one shall be born."

The sureness with which Rea said these words calmed her. "Is this child mentioned in the prophecy?"

"Yes."

Maeve tried to believe Rea. It was all she had.

As the rest of the camp woke, Maeve made the morning tea, struggling to get control of her thoughts. She pulled out the sack of oatmeal, adding the last of it to a pot of water over the fire. Coughing and moans reached her ears as she stirred the mixture. The people here still needed her attention whether she was pregnant or not.

After breakfast Maeve searched through her stores, supplying the men from Sorcha's village with catnip and ginger root to take home with them, as well as some of the agarikon, which she determined had anti-viral properties. All these herbs could help the poor women in the settlement as long as their condition wasn't due to some horrible spell cast by Brandubh and his mother. The men looked grim as they took her offerings, packing the herbs away in their woven bags. They left without a backward glance, walking into the woods and disappearing into the shadows. Maeve's mind cast ahead to their reunion, wondering what would happen now that they knew all about the deacons. Would they take it out on their women or confront Brandubh and Adair? It was not a pleasant daydream.

The Wildmen and other men who remained conversed with the Crion in their language, elaborating with hand gestures. Maeve watched them, realizing that these men were the ones Eron referred to as the duine fiain—the wild ones who had no leader. These strange-looking men with their wild hair and odd eyes no longer caused Maeve to look away in fear—she didn't know if it was her or them, but it seemed as though their forbidding expressions had softened.

Due to the hunting prowess of the Wildmen, they feasted on fresh rabbit stew that night, giving the bones and entrails to the wolves. After eating, the newcomers stretched out beyond the circle of Crion, kindly allowing the small ones proximity to the fire. The wolves made up the outside circle, keeping watch as everyone huddled close together under whatever coverings they could find to keep out the cold. With no sun to warm the ground, the nighttime temperatures were dropping, growing lower every night.

In the morning Maeve woke at first light, but this time she was prepared for the nausea. She put a small piece of stale bread in her mouth, chewing slowly, her gaze wandering the camp. Despite the hunting and gathering their food stores were nearly gone, the stream dried up and frozen solid. Over a meager breakfast of leftover stew she made her announcement. It was time to move on.

With Finiche by her side, Maeve led the way, staying along the edge of the forest to keep an eye on the canyon below. The valley widened as they traveled north and from their vantage point they had a clear view of the many bodies left to die and rot on the frozen ground. Crows pecked at them, the cawing harsh in the frosty air.

"No, it is too dangerous!" Rea cried, reaching toward her as Maeve started down the hill. "The Oillteil—they are coming."

Maeve gazed into Rea's worried eyes, placing a hand on the small woman's arm. "Finiche will go with me—I'll be fine." Maeve waited for the wolf and then headed away again, but this time a handful of Wildmen pulled out their knives and followed at a crouch. Maeve found a narrow deer trail and followed it to the valley floor where the scene of devastation made her physically ill. Dead Crion, Amuigh, Oillteil, and Wildmen were strewn about like rag dolls amidst their torn and muddied banners. Some were striped yellow, blue and orange, others depicted the auroch in black on a field of green—the emblem of the red-haired men who lived in the east. As she searched through the still bodies, hoping for some sign of life, a sound kept coming to her ears, a horn blown in the distance like a warning—she wondered where it was coming from.

Crows circled, swooping down to land on the bodies. "Go!" Maeve screamed, waving her hands. An angry black cloud lifted into the air, waiting impatiently for the opportunity to resume their feast. While Maeve and the Wildmen searched for injured, the wolves kept the crows at bay, their barks sharp and insistent.

"Here!" Maeve looked up at the cry from the Wildman. She hurried over to see what he had found. Lying at his feet were several men with reddish hair, their eyes barely open. "What is your name?" she asked the Wildman, realizing he could understand her.

"Soru," he said, his finger touching his chest.

"Soru, can you get me some branches from the trees up there? We need a way to carry these people." Maeve reached in her pack, pulling out a ball of thick twine. "We can make some portable beds." Soru watched her, his eyes suddenly lighting up. He nodded, calling to his friends and then heading away from her and up the hill.

While they were gone Maeve found several Crion, Oillteil and Wildmen near death. She placed her hands on them, concentrating to push energy into their injured bodies—a stopgap until she could get them back to camp. When Soru returned with the others, their arms full of pine boughs, Maeve began weaving the twine around the limbs to hold them together. Soru called out something to his friends who then came by her, grabbing the twine and cutting off lengths with their knives. With their help it didn't take long.

With the ground frozen it was not possible to bury the dead, so the Crion scrambled down the hill to speak the special prayers—saying them for all, including the fallen Oillteil. The wolves acted as sentries, strategically placing themselves along the valley floor. When the Crion voices lifted into the air, singing the special chants, unchecked tears made their way down Maeve's cheeks. She didn't even try to wipe them away, her mouth opening to emit her own grief, a sound that surprised her in its intensity.

The litters were not strong enough to carry the large bodies of the Oillteil and so the Wildmen took it upon themselves, picking them up and slinging them over their shoulders like sacks of meal, their arm muscles bulging. She shook her head in wonder, surprised by their strength and generosity; she no longer thought of them as frightening or even dangerous. They were part of her group now, helping in whatever way they could. Once they reached the top of the hill, the crows rose from their roosts, flying down to settle on the remaining bodies. Maeve turned away from the grizzly sight, afraid she might be sick again. By tonight the bones would be picked clean and after the cold night they would be gone, dragged away by the foraging wolves, lynx, foxes, and other meat eaters.

Late that night when they finally came upon a suitable place to camp, the Wildmen built a shelter to house the sick and injured. It resembled a beaver den when it was completed, with a hole in the center to let out the smoke from the firepit. Maeve and the Crion women worked together to treat the wounds of two Oillteil men as well as the injuries sustained by the tall ones with russet hair. They were known as the Tuatha De Danann, Soru told Maeve, fierce warriors who were not to be trifled with.

One of these men, who introduced himself as Dirg, spoke to Maeve quietly as she worked. He told her that the name Tuatha De Danann referred to their race being descended from the goddess Danu and that they came from the far northeastern section of the Otherworld, on the other side of the deer forest. Long ago they had fought with the Sons of Mil who came up from the south, and had been driven underground, their clans or 'tuaths' scattered. Because they lived in barrows and cairns, the name for them changed to People of the 'Sidhe', a word which translated to 'mound' or 'thrust'. They were the first people, and had defeated the evil ones long ago, chasing them back into the underworld. His weathered face and blue eyes held pain as he spoke of the return of the Oillteil and the recent destruction of the sacred lands. He told of the way things had been, how all was held in reverence, the beings living together in mutual harmony. Maeve listened as she dressed the deep wound on his upper arm, placing yarrow leaves there to help close the ragged skin. She was struck by his stoicism, the way he held himself proudly but without ego. He seemed the epitome of the true warrior.

That night after everyone had fallen asleep Maeve lay awake thinking about what Dirg had told her. Each time Brandubh fomented the hatred that led to killing, he diminished the natural resistance of this place. As his men cut down the forests, ripped apart the earth and extracted the gold and silver and sold it outside this world, it weakened the invisible web that held the Otherworld together. The land itself was where the real riches lay, and each time it was ravaged and destroyed it lost a little bit more of its essence. The spirits had fled, the gods and goddesses were almost ghosts; no one remained to heal the damage.

She sat up, her gaze going to the different factions of the growing camp. The shelter held the very sick ones, keeping them warm. Around the firepit on the outside, her original group banded together, sleeping in a close circle made up of Wildmen, Crion and villagers. They had become friends. Behind them were a few injured Oillteil and Wildmen who were not known to the others. She assumed they worked for Brandubh and kept a wary eye on them. Even further from the fire were the Tuatha De Dannan, or Sidhe. What would happen once the members of the enemy were healed—would they turn on Maeve or would they join her cause? She needed to bring many more to her side to succeed. As night deepened she allowed her thoughts to stray to Harold, imagining telling him about the baby. When she finally fell asleep, close to dawn, she had a vivid dream.

Ahead of her, going down a steep tunnel were several Oillteil. She looked back, noticing that others followed her. They looked grim holding clubs, their eyes focused on her.

"Where am I?"

Behind her one grunted, pushing her in the back and making her stumble. Trying to right herself she was able to see ahead where the tunnel ended, opening into a large cavern filled with more Oillteil. She heard a voice that sounded familiar speaking English.

It was only a moment or two before they reached the opening. She was pushed violently from behind, landing in a heap at the speaker's feet. Looking up she realized it was Brandubh. A cold shiver went through her body.

"Glad to see you here," he said, reaching down to help her up.

"Where is here?" she asked, looking around. There were niches in the stone walls filled with statues of gargoyles and other demonic looking icons. In the distance she could hear moans and cries of pain and the splash of water.

"You are in the underworld. And I hope to convince you to stay." Brandubh looked around and then called out in a loud voice. "Mother? Are ye back there?"

"I'm here. What do you want?"

"We have a visitor, an important one."

A moment later Adair appeared, her eyes fastening on Maeve. "Ha! What a surprise. Come, my dear, let me show you around."

When Adair reached for her, Maeve was unable to stop herself from grabbing the older woman's hand.

"Isn't this nice." Adair pulled Maeve forward, heading into the dark recesses where the noise was coming from. At the edge of a precipice Adair stopped. "Down there are the souls of those who have died." Cackling, she led Maeve to a narrow and slippery flight of stairs carved into the rock. "The section down there holds the souls of the damned.

The Oillteil make their home here in the underworld in a deeper chasm leading to tunnels they use to access the surface."

Maeve followed the older woman down, the horrible noise becoming louder with each step they took. "You can hear them now, can you? They are the lost, full of misery and despair—and will remain like this for eternity. And you, my dear, will be joining them very soon."

Maeve wanted to pull away from her but it was as though she was linked to the woman, with no will of her own. She followed obediently, her terror rising the closer they came to the origin of the voices.

"Here we are," Adair said suddenly, letting go of Maeve's hand. "Look down there and you will see your new home. That is what we've planned for you, my dear. Instead of being killed, your torment will go on for eternity—exactly what you deserve." Adair pushed Maeve in the back, sending her tumbling down a steep rock wall. She landed at the bottom, her gaze going to the endless throng of people just ahead of her. Their pale faces were distorted in expressions of anguish, their arms lifted as though in supplication. They all gazed upward as though some benevolent entity might come to their rescue. Behind her the sheer wall of dark rock rose like a pane of glass. There was no way out.

Maeve stood and headed toward the people but when she tried to talk to them they paid no attention to her. Before she knew what was happening she'd been pulled amongst their milling bodies, sucked along as they moved to and fro. Terror entered her like a dark angel, her thoughts scattering like frightened birds. Her mind was numb, filled only with despair and fear. She became part of the group, her own arms going up in supplication, her pitiful cries joining theirs.

A long time went by before she noticed the roar of water as it disappeared into a maw of black. The group had brought her close to the edge and now she slipped away from them, letting herself fall into the dark depths. At first she was sucked into a sort of vortex but then she realized she was moving away from the pleading cries of pain, breathing in air despite being under the surface. Reaching the falls she let herself go, relaxing completely as she fell with the rushing water. She landed in a warm pool that overflowed, heading in rivulets going in different *directions. She cupped her hands, taking a long drink, soothing her parched throat.*

Climbing onto the dark rock surrounding the pool she gazed at her surroundings, trying to get her bearings. Several yards from her another wall jutted into darkness. Searching at its base she discovered a narrow ledge of rock. Below her, a chasm yawned into inky blackness and from it came clanking and the sound of heavy objects being dragged across a hard surface. Hugging the wall, she edged along the ledge, following it until it ended. To her right a river ran by noisily and in the distance on the other side she could see a slight glow. She had to find a way out of here.

At the river's edge she contemplated her next move. She could follow the water downstream or swim to the other side. A voice came to her, silvery and melodic. Female, she thought, and singing. It seemed to be coming from the other side of the river. She stepped in, expecting it to be warm, but the water was ice cold, numbing her feet and legs. There was no choice but to immerse herself and swim. Once in the river, her breath was sucked away. The cold current took her downstream and it was everything she could do to reach the other side.

It took a long time before she reached the bank, and she was barely able to pull herself out of the water. When she stood up, jagged rocks cut into her bare feet—her shoes had been lost somewhere along the ay. Trying to catch her breath she sat down to take a look at her feet, surprised to see blood coming from several places. A minute or so later she heard the voice again, looking up to see a ghost-like figure moving toward her.

"You have reached the realm of the gods and goddesses," the woman said, taking her hand to help her up. "Not many make it this far."

"But where is this? I thought I was in the underworld."

"This is Annwn, but you have gone deeper, beyond the fear of death and the hell that is Uffern. Here we wait for our opportunity to rejoin the world. This is not a terrible life; it is only the darkness that is hard to take. Everyone must come here to discover the hidden, to understand what lies beneath the surface. Unfortunately most are trapped

higher up. This is where the spirits wait for mankind to wake up. I am Cerridwen, the keeper of the cauldron in which knowledge and inspiration reside. If you would like a drink, I will lead you there."

Maeve gazed into her golden eyes, amazed by the benevolence shining out. " I…don't know…"

Cerridwen nodded. "Now is not the time. You will return to the surface and when you do, remember all you have seen here. It will empower your journey."

Maeve woke suddenly. Her body was cold, as though the dreamscape of dark rock and icy water had entered her veins. A sound escaped her lips before she could stop it, sort of a low moan, bringing Rea running.

"What is it?"

"I had a terrible dream." As Maeve recounted the dream to Rea, the Crion woman took Maeve's cold hands between her own. By the time the story was finished Maeve was calm, her hands and fingers tingling with warmth.

"That is a good dream, Maeve. You have now visited the underworld, spoken with the goddess of the cauldron." Rea's eyes sparkled with merriment. "Next time you might even take a drink."

When Rea left, Maeve examined the bottoms of her feet, surprised to see tiny cuts all over them.

Chapter

18

The cold increased with each day, making it impossible to ever feel warm enough. Firewood was damp and sputtered without giving off ample heat. The frost, a spiderweb of gray that coated everything, lent its special ugliness to the landscape. Dark clouds scudded across the sky looking heavy with promise, but by now Maeve knew nothing would come of it. Oh how she longed for the salt tang of the sea, a gentle rain, even snow or sleet would be welcome. Everyone was constantly thirsty, searching the crevasses and creeks for ice. Maeve's water bottles had been empty for many days. The wolves scouted ahead, always on the prowl for water and game. Maeve and the others followed them into the deep gloom of the forest, sometimes coming upon old homesteads that had been burned and looted. They searched through the rubble for useable items—tools, potatoes and apples—withered and dry but edible.

As they traveled northward, earth tremors became a regular occurrence, sending rocks and debris flying, scaring the animals and opening up deep chasms in the frozen ground. Brandubh's armies marched in the valley below in alarming numbers. It was difficult to keep going, to not be taken over by the despondency that rode the air. Maeve was exhausted and could not seem to let go of her rising anxiety. It didn't matter how far into the forest they got, she could still hear the steady drumbeat of the marching troops, her own heartbeat keeping time in her ears, and all she could think about was what in the world she could do to stop the killing and heal the land. Her attempts to connect telepathically with Catriona had failed. Most of the time her mind was so agitated she could barely think.

Their retinue had increased, with several wandering farmers and their wives joining them. Their homes had been burned, their livelihoods gone along with their animals and all their household goods. They gave horrific accounts of the looting and killing going on across the land.

With all the mouths to feed, food supplies were at an ebb and Maeve despaired of what to do. She discussed this with Dirg, who was still with them, as well as Soru and his Wildmen friends. Dirg seemed to know about some secret hoarding places, saying he thought he could lead them to one of them if he could get his bearings. Much to Rea's dismay, Maeve, Soru and Dirg had headed out after dark several times, scouting for miles, but so far Dirg was at a loss. He told her that if they reached the river he would know where he was. The Wildmen were still able to find an occasional squirrel or rabbit but they were becoming increasingly scarce. Out of desperation they had begun heading into the valley to pick up deer and other animals that had died of starvation, bringing them back and cooking them before the crows had a chance to pick their bones clean. Maeve was as hungry as everyone else and didn't turn away from the slightly rancid tasting meat.

What would happen when this was all over--if it ever was. She shuddered at the thought of spending her life in this gray and frozen wasteland. And what of the child she carried? Fresh tears filled her eyes as Harold's face loomed in her mind.

"Catriona?"

The surprised question was in a man's voice. Maeve had been scouting ahead and turned to see a gaunt old man with sunken eyes staring at her. He had seemed to appear out of nowhere, putting Maeve immediately on the alert.

"I'm Maeve," she answered carefully.

His back was bent as if from arthritis and gray hair lay in filthy tangles around his drawn face. "Ye look so much like her, but that was years ago." He scrutinized her, running dirty fingers through his hair.

"Catriona is my grandmother."

His eyes brightened. "Of course! You're the one, are ye not? I'm an old friend of your grandmother's—Duncan Kincaid." He held out a hand.

Maeve took it, surprised by the strength of his grip. "Where did you come from?" she asked looking around.

"I live in a cave just down there," he said, pointing to the escarpment that led along the edge of the cliff. He chuckled. "I've grown adept at secreting myself in these times of war." He gazed away his expression turning sad. "My village of Tiadhan has been decimated and most of my friends killed. 'Tis a wonder I've managed to stay alive. Where are ye headed?"

"North. We're searching for victims of Brandubh and trying to stay alive. I have quite a few people traveling with me."

"I would be pleased to come along. I have nae food but I can tell stories to entertain or help with whatever ye set me to. Do ye ken where your grandmother is? I havna seen her for many a year."

"Of course you can join us. I'm not sure where Catriona is now—I haven't had time to search her out."

"Your grandmother and I...well, we go back a long time. And the last time I laid eyes on your mother she was pregnant. With you, I would imagine."

Maeve noticed that his eyes had lost some of their dullness and he was not quite as bent over as he had been. "Yes, Finna's my mother. Where did you see her?"

"It was when Finna and Catriona were on their way to the Glass Mountain for the blessing ceremony. They spent a night with me on the way." He stared into the distance. "My life was wonderful back then. Now I have lost everything to the pillagers who burned down my town."

Maeve had a sudden memory of the conversation, it seemed like years ago, between her mother and grandmother. This was the man who waltzed all over the square with Catriona. It made her sad to see how old and decrepit he'd become. Her grandmother seemed so young in comparison. "I travel with others in the same plight, Duncan. Maybe there are some with me whom you know."

"Where is the rest of your group?"

"They are a short distance behind us. I wanted to scout out a possible camp place before night. My wolf is up ahead."

"Your wolf? Aye. Catriona had an uncanny gift with wolves as well. You must have inherited it. If you follow me I might be able to find you a safe place to shelter," he added, picking up his walking stick.

Maeve watched him hobble away. "What happened to your leg?"

Duncan turned. "I was in the wrong place at the wrong time—I got caught in a fight about six months ago and the wound has never properly healed."

"Can I take a look?"

A confused expression passed over his features. "If ye wish to. 'Tis only a slight bother. I've become used to it. Do ye have some medicine along?"

Maeve held out her hands. "Just these."

"Ah ha...so ye take after your grandparents." He sat down and pulled up his ragged trouser leg, showing her the swelling and purple bruising around his knee. "Catriona has always been good with herbs, but Eron...now he had a knack."

Maeve squatted next to him, attempting to clear her mind. It had been a long time since she'd used any of her 'powers', if you could call them that, her attention taken up with the growing group of people depending on her. Maybe it wouldn't work.

"Now Eron, he was a right good man. Have ye met him? He..."

"Duncan, I don't mean to be rude but I need to concentrate if I'm going to do this."

"Ach...how stupid of me. I'll keep my big maw shut for a while then."

Maeve placed one hand on each side of his knee, asking the spirits to aid her. Her hands grew hot as she focused on removing the swelling. For a long time nothing happened and then something seemed to shift.

"Ahhh...much better," came Duncan's comment. "I think ye've done it, lass." He looked up at her, his eyebrows raised in surprise.

"You didn't think I could."

"Well...let's just say I had my doubts. I've only known one real healer and he is your grandfather."

Maeve smiled. "So why wouldn't you think I might have inherited the gift?"

Duncan shook his head sheepishly. "These last years have turned me into a pessimistic man. I used to be the happiest person ye would ever meet, but lately...I dinna trust anyone."

"I understand completely. Let's test your leg, shall we?"

Duncan stood and then took a couple of tentative steps. "Like new. I dinna think I need this anymore." He threw his walking stick into the bushes, did a couple of dance steps and then strode happily away from her into the forest. He began to whistle a dance tune, the lively sound dispersing the gloom.

Maeve called out to Finiche, and then followed him, a tendril of joy making its way into her psyche. No wonder Catriona loved this man.

Chapter

19

arold looked carefully at the map. He had been walking
for a day and a half and felt like he was getting
nowhere. Nothing too strange had happened so far,
other than the weather being very nasty and cold. Wind was a
constant, the landscape depressingly bleak. He traveled along
the edge of the forest trying to keep warm but he was afraid to
go too far under the trees in case he missed the approach of an
enemy.

There had been lots of time to puzzle over what the boatman had told him about Kenneth's participation in the battle
that drove the Oillteil out of this place so many years before. It
didn't make sense but then nothing Maeve had told him about
this place did either. He believed in reincarnation but he didn't
have a feeling one way or the other about Kenneth MacAlpin.
But he had to admit the strange thoughts he had on his trip
from the airport seemed to spring out of nowhere and the pictures in his mind had been pretty vivid. Right now he just
wanted to get to the spring and figure out how to find Maeve.

He was fairly certain that the two of them were not going to be using the return tickets home and that her father would worry. He wished he had thought to call someone before he came into the Otherworld. His cell phone did not work here.

Finding a small stream, frozen like all the others he had encountered, he stopped to break the ice to get a drink and fill up his water bottle. He threw in an iodine tablet and then scooped water until the bottle was full. When he stood up again there was a man riding toward him from the hill on the other side. He was leading another horse and heading directly for the stream. Harold didn't know whether to run for the trees but some inner sense told him to wait, so he stood his ground, trying not to feel nervous. The stranger was middle-aged, stocky with gray hair and a beard covering part of a lined and ruddy face.

"Halloo!" he called out loudly.

"Hello," Harold called, raising a hand in greeting.

The man crossed the little creek, breaking through the ice with the horses and then dismounted to let the horses drink. "I'm Mikdal," he said, extending his hand as he came up to Harold.

"Harold." Harold grasped Mikdal's calloused hand, racking his brain for name recognition. Had Maeve mentioned this person? She had given him so much information that most of it hadn't stuck.

"Should I ken who ye are?" Mikdal asked.

Just what I was going to ask, Harold thought. "I'm Maeve's boyfriend, if that means anything to you."

Mikdal's face lit up, a wide grin creasing his weathered cheeks. "I should say it does. I have yet to meet her, although I'm told she is among us now."

"I'm trying to find my way to the spring—Corra's spring. I have a map that Maeve gave me..."

"I will accompany ye," Mikdal said brightly. "I've just now run off from Brandubh's men. They've been forcin' me to make weapons for 'em, takin' advantage of my skills with a forge and iron. After my escape I went back to my village to find my horses. The place has been ransacked but the people are driftin' back, at least the ones who survived. Thank goodness these beasts remained close and didna get taken." He reached over, affectionately slapping the rump of the horse he had been riding. "Now I'm on my way to find my wife."

"What happened to your village?"

"Burned to the ground. Why don't ye get on Argyll here and we can make it to the spring a bit faster."

Harold looked at the big piebald. He was enormous, black and white, with feathers on his fetlocks and a tangled mane of white and black that hung down his muscled neck. A halter and lead rope was the only thing he wore. It was obvious by the padding on his flanks and his heavy muscling that he had been well cared for.

"Dinna worry about this one," Mikdal added, chuckling, noticing Harold's dubious expression. "He's as gentle as a bairn. Take him over there to mount." Mikdal pointed to a large boulder close to where the line of trees began.

Harold took the proffered lead rope and led the horse up the hill. Argyll waited without moving as Harold climbed on the rock and then lowered himself onto the wide back. He held the lead rope in his hands wondering how this was going to help steer the big guy, but as Mikdal put his foot in the stirrup and swung onto his horse again, Argyll turned to follow.

It was early evening before they reached the narrow path that led down the hill to the spring. Harold had learned all about Mikdal and Herska, how they knew Maeve's mother and grandmother and some of the past history. The time had passed by quickly with the companionship of the loquacious older man.

"We can leave the horses here." Mikdal dismounted and tied the reins in a knot to keep them from slipping over the horse's head.

Harold slid off, wincing as his feet hit the ground. He left Argyll and followed Mikdal down a steep and winding trail.

"What happened?" Harold cried in dismay as they arrived at the bottom of the hill. The spring the note had described in considerable detail was no more. All that remained were charred stumps and a jumble of rocks and rubble. A caustic stench lingered in the air.

Mikdal looked puzzled, his hand over his beard. "It looks like an earthquake but it also seems manmade. I doubt that this fire started by itself." He walked over and examined the hole where the spring had been. "Look at the spring itself. Someone has deliberately ruined this place."

Harold examined the broken pieces of rock that seemed as though they had been destroyed with an enormous sledgehammer. No water trickled from anywhere. "I wonder if Catriona and Finna have been here yet. If they haven't, I don't want to wait around for them. I don't like the way this place feels." He glanced nervously in Mikdal's direction.

"I agree. 'Twas hopin' I would find my wife here since last I heard she was travelin' with Finna and Catriona. Maybe there's some way we can leave a message."

They discussed what to do and Harold finally decided to write a short note explaining that he was heading north as Maeve had suggested. He placed the small piece of paper under a rock in a conspicuous spot and then followed Mikdal up the path. They mounted the horses and headed left along the edge of the woods.

"Kenneth, you are awake!"

Harold heard the meliflous and familiar voice as he opened his eyes. A transparent body floated toward him like a diaphanous cloud. The woman went in and out of focus as she came up to him, gazing into his eyes. He had an odd sensation of being two people at once as he recognized Rhiannon, the horse goddess. He watched himself get to his feet and then go down on one knee in front of her, taking her hand in his and placing his lips there. This woman was his lover, his heart friend.

"This is not your current life. Please rise," Rhiannon entreated with a sad smile.

Harold felt caught in the middle of emotions he couldn't sort out and stood staring at her in confusion: deep sadness and regret at what she had just revealed and then a sudden flash of relief. How had he ended up here? The last thing he remembered was riding along the edge of the forest with Mikdal. He looked around. He had been lying on a settee that was broken down and covered in tattered brocade. The rest of the room was in the same disarray, tables overturned, broken bits of pottery and other debris scattered across the floor.

"Where is Mikdal?"

"The poor man is having something to eat. At least I am still able to provide food for my guests. I have something for you Kenneth, something you left behind the last time we were together." She went to a long table against the wall behind him and picked up a leather scabbard and brought it over. As he watched her she began to solidify, her golden gown coming into focus as well as her lovely violet eyes he had marveled over in the past.

"Your presence here has made me stronger," she said, noticing his rapt expression.

Harold pulled the sword out of the ancient leather scabbard. It shone dull silver in the muted light drifting through the narrow windows and had several nicks from previous battles. He had an unexpected image of himself on horseback fighting in some long ago battle with Rhiannon by his side. He had loved this woman. He felt his face grow hot with the memory of their intimacy.

"I see that you have remembered," she said, her beautiful eyes filling with tears. "I had not expected to see you again. I will not tempt you, as I know that in this life you are pledged to the one who calls herself Saille, the willow. You have your own destiny to follow."

The door at the end of the room opened and Mikdal appeared. "Glad to see ye back in the land of the livin'," he commented as he came over and sat down. "Thought I had lost ye."

"I can't remember what happened."

"'Twas the fog. The nasty stuff takes over your mind and wipes it clean. Lucky we were so close to the castle here."

Rhiannon had left the room and now returned with a platter that she put down on the low table in front of Harold. "Eat, Kenneth, and then be on your way. This food will give you strength for what you have to face. I must warn you that my son Pryderi is involved in the evil that has taken over here. He is in league with Brandubh and will stop at nothing to get rid of me and the other gods and goddesses. He lusts for power."

"Isn't your son also a god?" Harold asked, remembering his mythology class. For one horrible moment he thought that he might be the father of this man, his heart speeding up as he waited for her response.

"He is a demi-god, half human, and this is why he has not lost himself as I have." A smile curved at the corners of her full lips, as she seemed to take in his expression. "Not for want of trying, my dear one, but you are not his father. His father's name is Pwyll. Unfortunately Pryderi has many powers and will use them to destroy our way of life. You must ride north to find Saille. She needs you by her side."

Harold picked up some cheese stuffing it into his mouth. He felt muddled and confused as images raced through his mind: battle scenes and he and Rhiannon engaged in a lot more than kissing. He felt split and strange. "How many days ride?" he asked, not recognizing the sound of his own voice. He watched his left hand pick up some bread, putting in his mouth--last he remembered, he wasn't left-handed.

"Many days. Go now and head toward the farthest mountains. You have not a moment more to spare." Rhiannon rose, smoothing her golden dress before she led the way outside to the keep where Argyll and Mikdal's horse, Mistral, stood waiting. As Harold turned to say good-bye she reached up and kissed him on the mouth. His arm slipped around her back, drawing her close as his tongue sought hers. Desire swept through him as he felt the warmth of her full-breasted body against his. He fought for self-control as the Kenneth personality bent to pick her up and carry her back to the bedroom, this other half of him ready to jepardize everything for a roll in the hay. Somehow he was able to contain his desire to the kissing, aware that his hands had strayed to her bottom, both palms firmly held there.

When they pulled apart she stared at him with eyes full of unshed tears. "You must go now, my dearest Kenneth. Know that I will never forget you."

A pang of regret went through his chest as he tore himself away from their embrace. "Nor I you, my lady," he said in his new, unfamiliar voice. He lifted his arm in a wave as he mounted Argyll and led the way out of the castle keep.

"Ye have nae recollection of what happened, do ye?" Mikdal asked, as they left the castle behind.

"No, I guess not," Harold replied, feeling puzzled and slightly dizzy.

"Ye insisted that we find Rhiannon and would nae be dissuaded. 'Tis how we ended up here."

Harold stared at him. "Why would I do that? I thought we were heading to the

North."

"I dinna ken, perhaps it was so ye could retrieve that sword," Mikdal observed, pointing to where it hung from Argyll's saddle. "Or maybe 'twas to get the tack. Riding bareback can be painful after a while as I ken ye've found out." He chuckled. "But in all honesty I fear 'twas Rhiannon herself ye were lookin' for. Ye've obviously *known* each other."

Harold's face grew hot. "I don't understand any of this," he said in confusion.

He looked at the saddle and bridle Argyll wore. "So we got these from Rhiannon?"

"Aye. So what should I call ye now, Harold or Kenneth or m'lord?"

"I'm Harold. At least for the moment." They rode on in silence, images invading Harold's mind. He was with Rhiannon in her castle—it was beautiful then, filled with light from the sun streaming through the tall windows. He lay in a high bed, his arm stretched out toward Rhiannon by his side. Her dark hair spilled across the pale pillow her violet eyes trained on him. They had just made love and he was getting ready to leave her once again—something that happened often. He shook his head—this was not him, it couldn't be. He reached up, grabbing his head with both hands.

"What is the matter, man?"

Harold turned to face Mikdal, wondering if he should share his thoughts but then he decided that if he talked about it, maybe the images would go away. "It's the memories. All this stuff with Rhiannon—it's totally freaking me out."

Mikdal laughed. "It didna seem to 'freak ye out', if I take your meanin', back there. In fact that good-bye I witnessed was not what I would call restrained. Enjoy it while ye can, 'tis nae every day ye can kiss a goddess, especially one as comely as that." He raised his eyebrows suggestively.

Harold had to laugh at Mikdal's expression. The man was right. All of this was in the past anyway. As Rhiannon had reminded him, Maeve was his woman in this life. When he thought of Maeve's crazy spiky hair, the feel of her touch, their amazing intimacy at the cottage, he was finally able to let go of Rhiannon.

"I can accompany ye nae further," Mikdal said an hour or so later, reining in his horse. "I must find my wife. I have the sense that she may have gone back to Clachencreid, especially after what we discovered at the spring. In any case my destination lies in the opposite direction."

They had crossed the fog valley safely and were now headed due north. Harold turned toward his new friend. "If you see Finna and Catriona please tell them I've gone to find Maeve. And thank you, Mikdal, for the loan of your horse and for your help."

As Harold swung his leg over to dismount, Mikdal put his hand up. "Keep Argyll. He's my plow horse and I have nae use for him at the moment. And besides, he eats too much." Mikdal chortled.

"Are you sure?"

Mikdal nodded. "He's strong and can help with all sorts of tasks. I'd feel better knowin' ye had him. I hope ye ken what ye're doin'. This has become a very dangerous place."

"Maybe Kenneth can help me." Harold grinned, and then watched Mikdal turn and ride away in the other direction.

"Good luck, M'lord," Mikdal called over his shoulder. Harold heard his laughter as he disappeared into the trees.

That night Harold camped in a hollow surrounded with boulders and tangled briar bushes. He made a small fire and huddled close for warmth, eating a hunk of cheese and bread. When he checked Argyll, the big horse was standing in the open with his back to the wind. There was no food for him and Harold wished he had asked Mikdal more questions. Where would he find hay for this beast? When he finally fell asleep a disturbing dream plagued his rest, and when he tried to wake himself it felt as though he wasn't truly asleep. It seemed that he had to endure the movie-like scenes from start to finish.

Harold rode through a forest on a silver gray horse. It was before dawn and he had left Rhiannon at the castle after a night full of robust lovemaking—the sweet memory of her body was still fresh in his mind as he followed the trail through the trees. Armed with a crossbow as well as a broadsword, he was alert for noises and anxiously watching the underbrush for danger. Engaged in a scouting trip for his father, the king, his job was to determine the whereabouts of the enemy. The sound of shouts had him kicking his horse, riding out from under the canopy. From the top of the hill he scanned the valley where a huge battle waged. Screams of rage and pain and the heavy metal sound of swords clanking rose on the wind.

He hesitated for only a second before he left the hill spurring his horse to gallop down toward the battle. It was hard to tell what was happening in the confusion, but once in the midst of it he pulled out his sword and did as much damage as possible. His sharp blade was brutal in its ability to inflict pain, cutting off limbs, gouging and tearing flesh. Blood flowed copiously from the wounds he inflicted and the agonized shrieks of agony filled up his ears. An arrow struck him in the arm and he reached down and pulled it out, rage making him ignore the pain. His father would have to be told of this outrage. His tunic turned red but he ignored it as he worked his way through the mass of riders. A fire had started in the village close by and his eyes began to tear from the acrid smoke billowing across the battlefield. As he fought he began to feel the futility of it all as more and more men fell, their deaths going unnoticed. Sick and disheartened at the bloodshed and mayhem around him, he was finally knocked from his horse and fell to his knees in the mud, tears flowing freely down his face.

Harold woke from the dream, horrified at what he had been involved in. He knew this was something from his past life as Kenneth and it was all he could do not to scream out loud. He didn't want this, not the memories, nor his violent nature as that other man, not even the confusing realization of his past love for Rhiannon. He could never be involved in that kind of battle again and he hoped and prayed that he wouldn't need to be. But he also knew that if it came to it, he would do anything to protect Maeve. He struggled with his impatience—he had to find her and soon.

Harold peered into the gloom. He knew it was morning but it may as well have been night considering the amount of light there was. There was a feeling of despair here that had crept inside him, curling around his heart. His fire had long since burned out and it was bitter cold. He nibbled cheese and tried to make a plan. The day before he had ridden by places where the land had been torn up, where trees had been felled and left to rot, barren hillsides with stumps and not a blade of grass. Dried up and frozen stream beds were everywhere and sometimes he came upon dead animals that looked as though they had starved to death. Argyll snorted and shied in fear, aware of the stench long before Harold picked up the rank aroma. From a distance he had watched men working in mines with pick axes and shovels. They were chained together to keep them from running away and strange creatures kept guard over them. Oillteil, he figured, from Maeve's descriptions. The feeling in the air was one of pain and suffering and Harold felt despondent as he watched them going in and out of the mines to drag out the heavy carts of ore.

Sounds in the distance brought his attention back. He heard talking and the squeak of wheels. He slid off and grabbed Argyll by the mane, pulling him under the low hanging branches as a raggle-taggle group of people appeared around the side of the hill. Thin horses were hitched to carts filled with all manner of household goods. Their progress was not quiet, as pans banged and rattled against each other, the people conversing loudly. Harold watched until they were very close and then he stepped out.

"Hello."

The two men leading the group stopped. "Who are you?" one of them asked pulling out a knife.

The sword Harold carried was out of the scabbard before he could register what he had done. "I'm Harold and I have come to help the Willow."

The man's face relaxed and he held out his hand. "I am Iain Cormac and this is Caleb Dougall. We're on our way to the Caer Sidi. Brandubh's men have destroyed our village. Will ye come with us for protection? I see that ye are well armed." Iain stared in admiration at the special sword in Harold's hand.

Harold returned the sword to its scabbard and looked over the small group. The five men, four women and three small children looked tired and hungry. "I will. I would like to enlist your help though, if I may."

Harold, Iain and Caleb ran through the dark night. The three men looked very much alike since Harold had borrowed some of their clothes and changed out of his jeans and bright plaid shirt. Now he wore homespun trousers and a deerskin tunic, his long hair tied back with a strip of leather like theirs. His belt held the sword and he carried a small knife he had borrowed from Iain. Once they reached the mine they set to work to destroy the shaft. It was difficult and dangerous work and took close to two hours before they had pulled out enough supports to cause the roof to collapse. After that Harold convinced the two men to help him search for the prisoners who worked the mines—they must be held somewhere close by.

They found the place by the pale smoke that lifted into the night sky. It was small, a pen more than anything else, and in a remote area which made the situation easier. The prisoners were under a lean-to, of sorts, that was surrounded by a high fence. At least there was a fire going to keep them warm. Two men with filthy matted hair stood watch at the wide gates. Harold found that he knew exactly how to manage his rescue. He sent Iain to one side, Caleb to the other and then sauntered up to the gate. "Hey, let me in!"

One of the men opened the gate and peered at him. "Who are ye?"

"Do ye nae recognize me?" he asked in a scathing tone. "Get out of the way and let me by."

The other guard came to look at him as they opened up the gate. About that time Iain and Caleb ran around the corner throwing rocks. One guard fell and then Harold hit the other one, bruising his knuckles and surprising himself with his own ferocity.

"The chains are locked."

"One of the guards must have a key—I'll get it," Caleb said, running back to rifle through their pockets.

The released men were weak but managed to follow them back to where the others had set up camp waiting for their return. The other creatures held in that pen—ape-like beasts-- disappeared into the night as soon as the chains were unlocked. Harold was told that they were a tribe called the Amuigh and would not hurt a flea. It was horrible to see them in this condi- tion, Caleb added. They were part of the spirit keepers and their kind was nearly extinct.

In their absence the women had cooked up a meal and Caleb's wife, Maggie, served them all, her smile welcoming. After wolfing down the food the men settled around the fire for what was left of the night. Harold, however, was hot to go out on another foray but Iain and Caleb were not eager to accompa- ny him. He finally decided to keep watch while the others slept for a couple of hours; he was too keyed up to rest.

Chapter

20

G ertrude stopped at the same spot where she had camped earlier with Catriona, Finna and MacCuill. It was a protected circle of stones along the route that led to Brandubh's fort and would give her shelter for the remainder of the night. She had been traveling through the night for what seemed like hours but of course it was impossible to tell since she had no watch. Somehow she'd remembered several landmarks from that earlier trip but still it amazed her that she had found the place at all. Brandubh must be psychically leading her to him.

A sense of urgency had awakened her in the middle of the night, causing her to pack her things and take off. The vivid dream had been about something happening or about to happen to Brandubh. She had to find him. But first she should consult the cards, she thought rifling through her pack with cold and frozen fingers. It seemed like ages since her time with Brandubh at the fort. Ever since the burial ceremony, the memory of which still gave her the creeps, Catriona and Finna seemed bound and determined to find Maeve, even though Finna was catching a cold and there didn't seem to be any clue as to where the young woman was. MacCuill had disappeared after they left the Dolmen saying he had matters to attend to—Eron had appeared for a day or two and then headed off again, much to Catriona's annoyance. The older woman groused around for two full days before accepting the fact that her husband was off on his own and wouldn't be back for a while. For someone who seemed so independent, Catriona seemed oddly clingy.

It was later that same day that Mikdal had wandered upon them, regaling them with lengthy details about Harold's arrival in the Otherworld. He also mentioned something about past lives and some goddess named Rhiannon that Gertrude tuned out, her mind focused on the priest. Mikdal was searching for his wife Herska, the wiry-haired woman Gertrude remembered meeting at the cottage. But Herska was off searching for Mikdal, so they might never find each other in this godforsaken wilderness. The man left the next morning, riding out before dawn.

Gertrude was sick to death of going in circles and listening to the two women grouse about how horrible Brandubh was. All she could think about was her time with the priest—and hearing about the man's exploits from those two was making matters worse. She had to find the truth out for herself.

Pulling out the worn cards, she found the Queen of Pentacles and put it in the significator position. It was the one that represented her: the dark-haired, dark-eyed woman. As she shuffled she thought about the question. *What was her connection to Brandubh?* That was a good place to start. Cutting the deck into three piles, she picked them up in the opposite direction.

A deep shiver went through her as she turned over the first card, placing it across the Queen. *The Devil.* It was the card in the placement representing the atmosphere and influences at work around her question. The devil symbolized domination of matter over spirit: black magic, exactly what was happening here in the Otherworld. She stared at the card nervously, wondering whether to continue, but decided she had to know what was going on.

She drew the next card and placed it across the first: *The High Priestess*. This card represented the opposing forces, whether for good or evil. Maeve came into her mind as she stared at the image. This was a card of knowledge: instinctual, supernatural and secret. And the fact that it opposed what Gertrude was asking made a lot of sense. A feeling of guilt went through her. She was involved with Maeve's enemy. The third card represented the foundation or basis of the matter, something she had already experienced. She drew the card and turned it over: *The Lovers*. So they *had* been together before. This card proved it. But then she realized it could be referring to their very recent encounter. Reading her own cards was so much more confusing than reading for others.

The fourth card represented an influence that had passed or was now passing. She drew the card, holding her breath: *The Moon*. It had to do with intuition, dreams and deception or secret foes. But it was reversed and so had an entirely different meaning. She was not sure what it signified. Maybe it had to do with spying for Brandubh—being used by him. She didn't really care whether he was using her or not because she felt their deeper connection and she was positive that he did too.

The next card represented an influence that might come into being. She turned it over: *The Tower*. This card could spell disaster for everyone and then again it could refer to the changes that were necessary to bring back the balance. It stood for the war between lies and truth and signified that any false concepts were going to come tumbling violently down. But what did it mean in terms of her connection to Brandubh? She hated to think.

The sixth card signified what would operate in the near future: *The King of Pentacles*, a dark-haired, dark-eyed man.

Brandubh. But it was reversed and in this position it referred to the perverse use of talents. Double-dealing. This was not looking good.

She drew the last four cards and placed them on the right side in a line above the cross. The seventh was the *Nine of Swords* and represented her fears. It pictured a woman grieving with nine swords hanging over her. It meant doubt, suffering and could sometimes mean the death of someone you love. Did this mean Brandubh was going to die? She wished she had never started this. All she really wanted to know was whether they had been together in some previous life but so far that question had not been answered.

The next card represented the opinion and influence of friends and family. She turned over the *Two of Swords*. The picture was of a blindfolded woman surrounded with swords and a castle in the background. The interpretation could vary but in this case Gertrude was pretty sure it meant she was going to be ostracized, either by Brandubh or the others. By now this had probably happened, considering she had run away to get back to Brandubh. She hoped they did not come looking for her this time.

The next card represented her hopes and ideals and she knew what it would be. The *Two of Cups*, a card that represented the beginning of a love affair: harmony and cooperation.

The tenth card would tell the outcome of the matter and Gertrude waited for a moment wondering if she even wanted to know. When she finally turned if over she was prepared for the worst. It was the *Eight of Cups,* which could mean several things: rejection or decline of an undertaking...maybe disappointment in love. It was not encouraging.

There was still no answer as to whether they had been together before. Once she reached the fort she hoped to get some answers from him. Did he feel the same way she did? But what if he wasn't there? She didn't want to be captured again by the Wildmen or Oillteil. He might not ride to the rescue this time.

As night deepened she took off her warm jacket and put it underneath her and then slipped Brandubh's warm robe over her clothes, curling up in a ball with her feet tucked inside. She tried to sleep but images kept going through her mind: Brandubh's angry face, the Wildmen in some kind of weird clothes, maybe armor? Wild-eyed horses, a dark sky full of storm clouds. Well, that was nothing new. As she drifted into a restless sleep she had the strangest feeling that her mind had been taken over by something far beyond her control.

Gertrude was dreaming about wet dogs. She opened her eyes to see two wolves lying next to her. Their warmth had probably kept her from freezing to death, she thought, registering the frost that lay over her body and the chill wind that had her teeth chattering. When they noticed she was awake the wolves jumped up and nosed her, as if to say 'come along with us.' "No, I'm not coming with you. I'm heading the other way," she said as they stared at her out of lambent eyes. She tried to ignore them as she collected her things and got ready to go.

Thick fog had settled over the surrounding landscape. She was already cold and the prospect of this day did not appeal. The wolves followed her down the hill and then stopped and whined, turning back toward the forest. For a moment she considered going with them.

"No," she finally said as Brandubh's warm body came into her mind. "Go back doggies." She walked purposely away and when she glanced over her shoulder they had disappeared.

The following morning Gertrude woke to find herself in a small cell with her hands tied behind her back. The details of the day came back, along with a racking headache and terrible thirst: the Oillteil had grabbed her the minute she had come in sight of the fort, taking her roughly and dragging her the rest of the way down the hill. They had thrown her in this dank space despite her insistence that she was a friend of Brandubh's, acting like they couldn't understand a word she was saying. A lump had formed on the side of her skull where one of them had hit her. So far no food or water had been brought and there was not only no place for her to pee, there was also no way she could, with her arms pinned the way they were. She called out until her throat was hoarse, to no avail. She was dozing when she heard someone opening the heavy door and the next moment a backlit form stood over her.

"What in hell are you doing here again?" Brandubh sounded angry. "One of my men managed to get a message to me. I was engaged in the north and I am not at all happy about this diversion."

Her original feeling of elation fled as she opened her mouth to respond. "I had to come. After what happened between us...I..."

Brandubh interrupted. "What do you think happened between us?"

The timbre of his voice seemed different. Gertrude moved so she could see his face. His brows were pulled together in a deep frown, his lips forming a thin line. A cold feeling went through her chest. "Well, we..."

"Come on then," he responded in a tone of resignation. "I can't leave you here. We better have a little chat and it's too damn cold out here to think." He grabbed her by the arm, none too gently, and she staggered to her feet. He pulled her from the cell and untied her bonds.

"How did you get here so fast? I was planning to come to you but then these people here didn't understand that I was on your side."

"I have my ways," he answered, ushering her through the door and pushing the guard out of the way with his elbow. "Are you really on my side, Gertrude? I find that hard to believe. And by the way, do you know the whereabouts of Maeve or her mother and my sister?" He frowned down at her as he gestured toward the chair.

"Yes, of course. I was just with Catriona and Finna and a man named Mikdal. I haven't seen Maeve but a friend of hers has come into the Otherworld. A man called Harold." She sat down and rubbed her wrists where red welts had appeared.

"Harold? What does he have to do with anything?"

"He's Maeve's boyfriend and according to Mikdal he seems to think he's a reincarnated king called Kenneth."

"Kenneth MacAlpin?" Brandubh stared into space for a moment. When he turned back she didn't like the expression in his eyes. "And where is this Harold now?"

"I don't know. Mikdal left him on the north side of Rhiannon's castle, he..."

"Shut up for a minute! I need to think. Rhiannon's castle... and then what are his plans?"

"The only thing I know is that he's looking for Maeve."

"It was stupid for you to come here. You're interrupting my plans—don't you think they'll try to rescue you?"

"Well...maybe...I hope not, but I suppose they could..."

"Of course they will. They're not going to let you get hurt, even if it puts them in danger. That's the thing with these do-gooders, they're very predictable. You may have to accompany me."

Gertrude looked up at him eagerly. "That's what I was hoping. In my vision I saw something that may have been in the future...but..."

"Saw something? You mean you're psychic?"

"I thought you knew."

He looked puzzled for a moment. "What did you see, my dear?" he asked in a sneering tone.

The pain in her heart was back and her fingers went there. This was not the same man she had been with two weeks ago. She clasped her hands together trying to stop their shaking. "I thought you had been hurt in some way…I wanted to…"

"Wanted to what, Gertrude? The only way you could help me is to…oh never mind. Tell me what you saw."

"I didn't really *see* anything. It was more of a feeling, like you had been hurt in some way, but I don't know the details."

Brandubh frowned. "We need to go soon. The battle has begun and I must be there to direct my men." When he pulled her up she lost her balance, stumbling into his arms. For a moment she could feel his strong heartbeat, the heat from his body making her weak. He pulled away from her abruptly and strode toward the door. "Come on," he said impatiently.

"Can I use the facilities before we…?"

"Go," he said, waving her in the direction of the bathroom as he turned to the Wildmen and beasts waiting by the door.

She ran inside, finding her way to where she had taken her shower. The toilet was not much more than a hole in the ground but it would do. A shelf against the wall held a straight razor and a small brush and a bowl for lather, a round mirror hanging on the wall above it. The reflective glass showed a woman with wild eyes, dark hair full of tangles and bits of leaf and twig; she looked like the gypsy she had always pretended to be. Her hair was too full of knots to run her hands through and she gave up, practicing instead some facial expressions that would hide the fear she felt. A minute later she hurried outside. It wouldn't do to keep this man waiting. As she came though the door, John appeared from the back of the fort leading three horses.

"Get on," Brandubh ordered gruffly. "It will save us time if we ride." He held the reins out to her and then he and John mounted the other two.

Gertrude struggled with the stirrup trying to hoist herself up. "Oh for God's sake! Don't you know how to ride?" Brandubh dismounted and gave her a boost, remounting his own horse quickly. He glared at her and then kicked his horse viciously with his heavy spurs, urging it into a gallop. John spurred his horse after him, leaving her behind.

Gertrude was terrified. She knew nothing about riding, had never been on a horse. But as the men got further away her horse paced and then took off, rapidly closing the distance between them. She held on to the pommel with both hands trying to stay on, her knuckles white by the time she caught up with them. The two men had come to a stop on a hill where they talked together and scanned into the distance. Gertrude searched behind her for signs of Catriona, Eron or MacCuill, realizing that this time she would be relieved to see them. Unfortunately there was no one in sight. She pulled her poncho out of her pack slipping it over her jacket, but the chill she felt penetrated through all her layers. Brandubh glanced her way and then he and John took off again and before she could settle herself, her mount galloped after them. By the time they stopped again she was exhausted from trying to stay on, her thighs weak and trembling. She slid off and crumpled to the ground wondering if she might be sick.

When John led the horses away, Brandubh sat down on a flat rock waiting for the rest of his men to arrive. He did not glance her way or make any acknowledgement of her at all. After some time the Wildmen arrived, out of breath and tired from running. The beasts lolled around them panting with their tongues out. Before they had a chance to catch their breath Brandubh yelled, "Make yourselves useful! Go hunt for something for our evening meal." They took off again, sprinting into the trees without a word of complaint.

Gertrude summoned her courage and walked over to Brandubh but just as she was about to speak he turned his dark eyes on her. The look in them chilled her to the marrow.

"Leave me alone. I only brought you along because..." His face turned hard. "Because it was that or kill you, and you may still be of use to me."

He stood up and strode away, heading into the forest. She started to follow him and then thought better of it. He was angry; she needed to let him work through whatever was bothering him. Maybe this had nothing to do with her. A few minutes later she watched him conversing with John, saw John glance at her with an expression of pure hatred. The man was jealous of her. A large flock of noisy crows arrived suddenly, landing in the tree branches just above her head. When Brandubh saw them he came over and waved her away. "Get out of here Gertrude. I have work to do."

After walking down the hill she turned to watch him. The birds were silent now, regarding him with their heads cocked, dark eyes gleaming. After a few minutes of silent communication Brandubh walked away and the loud cawing began again as they lifted into the sky, dispersing in several different directions.

"Better have a snack if you're hungry," Brandubh called out to her. "We still have a long way to go."

Gertrude's heart sank—she had been sure this was the end of the day, her trembling legs protesting even the thought of more riding. In her pack she searched out some leftover crumbs of bread and cheese, stuffing them into her mouth unceremoniously. The food seemed to calm her churning stomach as she watched Brandubh. It was only a few minutes later that the priest stood, ordering everyone to get ready to move on. When he and John mounted the horses Gertrude found a rock to stand on, pulling herself clumsily onto the saddle. The Wildmen had returned empty handed, hanging back away from John and Brandubh with expressions of terror on their faces. She heard yipping as the beasts appeared from under the trees, scaring her horse as they ran in excited circles.

Her horse followed the other two, stopping when they did. Gertrude made sure to keep the mare some distance away, sure that she would be yelled at if she came closer. Brandubh and John were talking again and when she heard the word 'spring', a fleeting image of savage destruction flew through her mind, unnerving in its intensity. Brandubh had been involved, hurling rocks with the others, wielding iron mallets to smash out a natural pool and stopping up the flow of water with mud and rock. The violence of the devastation frightened her and she wondered if this terrible act was in the past or yet to come.

The day dragged wearily on, Gertrude keeping as far away from Brandubh and John as her horse would allow. By the time they stopped again it was late afternoon and she was so tired she could barely keep her eyes open. A cold wind had begun to blow, sucking the heat from her body. Wrapping her poncho close she slid to the ground, letting her horse go.

"We will camp here," Brandubh announced as he dismounted, handing the reins to John. He turned to the Wildmen. "I want meat tonight and I expect to have it."

His tone was harsh and Gertrude watched the men scurry into the woods. For all their wildness they did not seem able to stand up to him. She hoped for their sakes they were successful this time.

John came back from settling the horses for the night and set about making the fire. The crackling wood and warm flames drew Gertrude and she sat as close as she dared, trying to get warm. A short time later a shout of greeting went up as six or seven men appeared out of the trees. They were dressed in priest's robes and headed straight for Brandubh and John, greeting them with handshakes and smiles.

"Where have you been?" Brandubh asked them after they were all seated around the fire.

One of the men threw off his hood revealing a bald pate and pockmarked wrinkled skin. His fleshy lips and nose were red from the cold. He loosened the tie around his enormous belly, his eyes fastened on the priest. "We've just come from the settlement. One of my favorite assignments, I have to say," he chuckled.

"And what else have you done to help the cause, Dan?" Brandubh asked. "I do hope that pleasure has not been your only focus in this war. I didn't bring you here for fornication."

Dan looked abashed and then turned to the man next to him. "Gary and I were just having a little fun. You told us this was acceptable," he added defensively.

Brandubh stared at him for a moment without speaking. "I asked you a question," he finally said in a low menacing tone.

"Of course not," Gary answered. "We've been rounding up the ones fighting against us and putting them into holding pens, at least the ones who survive." He laughed. "Some of them are just too weak to make the trek, if you know what I mean."

"No Gary, I don't know what you mean. If you're telling me that you've killed these men or tortured them, you will know my wrath. We need all the manpower we can get. I can't afford to leave a trail of dead across this land. More mines are being built every day and we have to have workers."

"The lack of water gets them, your lordship," Dan said. "We haven't enough water to share and there are only two springs that still run."

"I've told you where to get water, you fools! Don't you ever listen? I have stores of water hidden all over the place in the souteraines. Food is stored there as well. I think I was wrong to bring you men here. You don't take what we're doing seriously, think it's a lark to fuck the women and kill people."

Gertrude flinched at the coarse word. She watched Brandubh turn away and retrieve a worn map from his saddlebags.

"Come with me, John," the priest ordered, heading away from the fire. John followed him, glancing back once with a sneer on his face. Gertrude had been sitting some distance away and now she crept forward, hiding behind a tree to hear what the priest had to say. From the few words she picked up, it sounded as though they were planning another attack on a village to the west. Leaving her hiding place, she headed back toward the fire sitting as close as she dared to the newcomers.

"He told us to do what we wished, didn't he? I distinctly remember him saying that this was a place where anything goes," Gary said, with a furtive glance toward where the priest stood talking with John.

"That's how I remember it," Dan agreed. "Now he's changing his tune and I'll tell you, something has to make up for this hellhole. I wouldn't have come had I known."

"Are you men really priests?" Gertrude asked, coming to sit on the log next to them.

Gary looked at her in surprise and then glanced at the other men. "We've been recruited to the cause. We call ourselves the deacons."

"So the answer is no?"

"We consider ourselves men of the cloth because of our connection to Brandubh. Our lives outside this world were not in the priesthood, if that's what you're asking."

Gertrude nodded and then turned back to the fire. It was as she suspected. These men, with their American accents, were nothing but weak-willed scavengers taking advantage of the situation. It was disgusting. She added a few twigs to the flames and listened to them crackling, watching the sparks fly up and disappear. A short while later she noticed that a shadow had come across the already dark sky and looked through the trees. Brandubh and John were also watching the gigantic raven approaching from the north. Gertrude froze in fear as the bird shape-shifted into a larger-than-life woman as she landed.

Her body was not completely solid, her blue-black feathery dress shimmering in and out of focus, but her words were clear, booming into the silence.

"Mortal, I am here to exact the payment that you promised twenty-six years ago when my powers helped you with your destruction of the settlement. From this moment the crows and ravens are no longer under your power. Their part in your schemes is finished. I share them with Nantosuelta the Goddess of the valleys and streams and she is very angry. We are all angry at what you've done here. You have loosed a power that does not belong in this world. You have disrupted everything we hold dear."

Gertrude watched Brandubh's cowed expression. She had never seen him look so fearful.

"I gladly give them back, Morrighan."

"The second payment will not be so easy for you to accept."

Her dark eyes were riveted on Brandubh's face, her brows pulled together in a frown as she spoke.

"From this day forward you will feel all the pain that you inflict on others. I have given you free rein for too many years. Look at the destruction you have wrought! You should be ashamed!" She pointed toward the bleak landscape, the bare eroded hills across the valley where abandoned mines lay like open wounds. *"I should have taken your powers long ago. The third and last payment I have not yet decided on. But know that it will be terrible."*

Brandubh paled but he did not speak.

"Do you understand me?"

"Yes," he said meekly.

An expression of fury came over Morrighan's features as she bellowed, *"Bow down to me this minute or I will kill you on the spot!"*

Morrighan lifted the heavy spear she carried and pointed it at Brandubh. He quickly knelt down and bowed his head. Gertrude could felt his humiliation like a sharp pain inside her own chest. A moment later Morrighan began to transform and then she rose into the air on black wings and took off across the valley.

Gertrude ran toward Brandubh as John came out from his hiding place behind a tree. When one of the Wildmen approached from the woods proudly carrying a dead rabbit, Brandubh backhanded him, sending him sprawling. As the man hit the hard ground with a shriek of surprise and pain, the rabbit flew out of his hands and a moment later the beasts were snarling over the carcass. A second or so later Brandubh doubled over and cried out.

"What is it?" John asked, kneeling next to him.

"Pain...my hip, I feel..." he answered in a strangled voice.

"You mean it's real? The curse that scary witch just put on you?" John placed his hand on Brandubh's shoulder.

"Not a curse. I owed her three things for her help in the past. I'm surprised she even remembered." He shook off John's hand. "Get away from me!" he screamed.

Gertrude had been planning to comfort him but instead she retreated to a place out of sight. The deacons looked down as Brandubh sat on a log next to them in front of the flames.

A short time later another man appeared out of the darkness, walking with elegant movements toward the fire. He would have been handsome, with masses of golden curls that hung to his shoulders, but the expression in his eyes marred his good looks. Brandubh stood and bowed his head and the others followed suit. Gertrude stayed where she was, watching the men in conference, noticing the way this newcomer seemed to be the one in control. She wondered who he was.

Later that night Brandubh seemed his old self, making sure she had a place by the fire, bringing her food. His anger seemed to have fled, replaced by a solicitude that was very welcome after his recent nastiness. John and the other men, including the newcomer, sat a short distance away talking together quietly as they ate cheese and bread and drank from a bottle of some sort of alcohol. Their low laughter took on a dangerous edge as they finished the bottle and opened another one. Gertrude tried to ignore them, asking Brandubh who the new man was. Pryderi, he answered, Rhiannon's son, and he was going to come in very handy in the upcoming days.

When it was time for sleep he took her by the hand, pulling her with him to where he had made his bed away from the others. She didn't want to sleep with him but when she saw the look on his face she decided she better go along. After he covered her with the warm sheepskin he took his clothes off and climbed in beside her. Her entire body was trembling from the cold and fear that had lodged itself under her breastbone.

"You aren't afraid of me, are you?" he whispered in her ear.

She pulled back to see his expression. His face was mostly in shadow but there was a glitter in his eyes, the fevered look of desire. She thought back to their time at the fort and felt herself begin to melt. His hand slid underneath her sweater. "Let me in, Gertrude. You need this as much as I do." She sucked in her breath.

"Your body is so lush, my dear. I can hardly help wanting you. But I won't continue if you say no."

After a few moments she put her hand on his. She felt hot enough to melt ice. He was her dark lover, the King of Pentacles, and she was his queen.

Chapter

21

At first light Maeve went into the forest to meditate. It was becoming a morning ritual, a time to clear her mind and let her intuition take over. The morning sickness was under control now due to the ginger root Rea had produced. The woman had become her friend as well as a mothering influence during the time they had been together. She smiled, thinking about the many times Rea had counseled her, rubbing her back and feet. The woman insisted on taking care of Maeve because of her condition, plying her with foods she dug up and searching every area they traveled through for the missing sheep. The other Crion women and men did everything in their power to help heal those who were ill and maintain a cheerful attitude. Maeve was beginning to understand why the Crion were known as the keepers of the wisdom here in the Otherworld.

Where they were camping was an unfamiliar wood, a place where they had decided to spend the night only because she and her group had become too exhausted to continue. Wind whistled through the higher branches and she had the sense it knew they were there and was not happy about it. Every day she discovered another strange thing about this place. She sat down beneath a tree and closed her eyes, breathing slowly and watching her thoughts as MacCuill had taught her. When a twig snapped her eyes flew open, surprised to see a beautiful woman walking toward her. Maeve stared at her gown of spun gold, the long golden hair that flowed like silk down her back and around her oval face. Her eyes were light blue, the color of the sky that Maeve could barely remember.

"Saille," she began in a light mellifluous voice. "Please accompany me, I have something important to show you."

"Who are you?"

The woman hesitated, her eyes flicking to the right. "I am Agrona, goddess of the waterways."

Why wasn't she wispy and indistinct like the others? But the winning smile on the woman's face set her mind at ease. Maeve stood, following the goddess deeper into the forest but as they continued on she became confused and disoriented. It was as though circuitous paths were forming in front of them and then disappearing behind. She would never find her way back on her own. "Where are we going?"

The woman turned. "You will see."

A tiny prick of fear went through Maeve's midsection. She stopped. "I don't think I can continue," she said. "My people are waiting for me."

Agrona walked back and took hold of Maeve's arm, steering her down yet another path. "You will come with me."

Maeve tried to loosen her grip but the fingers were strong, digging into her flesh. Agrona did not look so beautiful anymore, in fact there was a hideous smile on her face and her features seemed to be shifting into another configuration. When she pulled back, the woman grabbed her around the waist. "Only a bit farther. Do not worry, it will be soon."

"What will be soon?"

A weird cackle came out of the woman's lips. "You are too smart for your own good."

A second later a clearing came into view and Brandubh was standing in the middle of it. His stance was that of a commander, legs spread, hands behind his back, dark brows pulled together as though in concentration. Looking around Maeve spied Gertrude cowering behind a tree a short distance away. It was a surprise to see her, especially in the company of this man. Remembering what MacCuill had told her about the psychic's infatuation she wondered what was going on between them—had Gertrude taken leave of her senses? On the other side of the clearing Wildmen and Oillteil milled about, gathering wood and talking amongst themselves as they cast furtive glances toward Brandubh. And there was Adair, dressed in a stylish fitted robe of red, watching her closely from a seat beside the fire. The woman looked quite young now, her skin unlined and very little gray in the glossy hair that hung around her shoulders. Adair caught her glance and waved.

"Thank you so much, Pryderi," Brandubh drawled. "I couldn't have done it better myself." He moved to a log in front of the fire, gesturing. "Come sit next to me, Maeve. We need to have a little chat."

Pryderi shape-shifted back into his male body, pushing her roughly toward Brandubh. Maeve shuddered as she realized how easily she'd been tricked.

"I think you know Gertrude, don't you?" he pointed toward the psychic and then leaned over reaching for Maeve's neck before she could move away. A second later the ribbon ripped and he put the moonstone in his pocket. "Time for that stone to go." He leered at her, showing large yellow teeth. "And of course you remember my mother, do you not? Say hello to your great-grandmother."

When Maeve didn't say anything Brandubh took her roughly by the arm. "I said say hello to her," he growled.

Maeve glanced toward Adair, mumbling hello.

"Nice to see you again, dear," the older woman said. "The last time we did not have a chance for a chat. And I'm afraid what Brandubh has in mind for you will keep this from happening today as well. Too bad."

"Come here, Gertrude, and tell your friend what you have done, how you've turned on her," Brandubh said, signaling to the frightened-looking woman.

"If you're wondering, Maeve, Gertrude is my lover now—maybe she even carries my child." He stared at Gertrude, his eyebrows raised in question. "She will never help you with Tarot or anything else ever again." He laughed and then stood and strode toward Gertrude and grabbed her by the hand, pulling the woman toward Maeve. "Sit, sit, my dear. Now isn't this nice?" When he bent down to nuzzle Gertrude's neck she shrugged away from him. "Oh come on, woman, don't put up this false front. You know you like it." He gave Gertrude a little push toward Maeve. "Greet your friend," he ordered harshly.

Maeve gazed into Gertrude's wide, frightened eyes. The formerly beautiful thick hair was tangled into dreadlocks, the olive skin mottled and broken out. Her full lips were cut and bleeding from being chapped. The woman looked as though she'd lost at least ten pounds. "I...I don't know what to say," Maeve said, picking up one of Gertrude's cold hands. "I'm sorry you had to get mixed up in this."

Gertrude looked down. "I'm sorry too. I didn't know. You have to believe me." When she looked up again, her face was white with fear.

"I believe you."

"Okay, enough girl talk. Let's have a little tête-à-tête, Maeve. I want you to get the hell out of the Otherworld. None of this is your concern. You have a life elsewhere. If you agree to this I won't kill you today, but if not, John is waiting to put a knife in your heart."

"Yup." John walked into the clearing, a glittering hunting knife in his hands, blood dripping from the tip. "I've been using it to skin rabbits. It's sharp as can be." He pressed the tip of his finger to the blade and a thin line of blood appeared. "And if you run, well, that's even better because I'm an expert with this thing. Shall I demonstrate?"

Maeve stared at him, trying to make her features neutral. His glittering, half-crazed eyes scared her more than Brandubh.

Gertrude grabbed her hand and squeezed. "He'll do it. I've seen him."

"So? What's it to be? Are you staying or going?" Brandubh asked.

Maeve weighed her options. If she lied and said she was leaving maybe she could get away from here. She had no defense against these men without the moonstone. But why would they believe her? She was sure they would provide an escort. What she couldn't fathom was why Brandubh didn't hold the knife— it seemed that he had turned the dirty work over to Pryderi and John.

She put a little worried frown on her face. "I'll go."

When she stood up, Brandubh said, "Not so fast. Pryderi and John will accompany you to make sure you're safe."

A second later Pryderi grabbed her, slipping a rope quickly around her arms and fastening it behind her back. He began walking, pulling her like a dog on a leash.

John laughed. "This is too perfect."

"Good luck, Gertrude. I would help you if I could," she called just before being hauled out of the clearing. Pryderi went quickly, making her stumble, John right beside her with the knife held at the ready. Maeve thought about her powers and wondered what might work right now. Without the moonstone nothing came to mind. When Pryderi began to run she hurried behind him but her foot caught on a root and she lost her balance. She fell with no ability to break it, landing directly on her face. Her nose was bleeding, trickling down and into her mouth but there was nothing she could do.

"Get up!" John screamed, grabbing her under the arm. "We don't have time for this. I should just kill you despite what that old fart says." He stuck the tip of the knife under her chin, his eyes glittering. "Bet you didn't expect this back when we met in Milltown, did you?"

Maeve's mind traveled back to her first meeting with John. He had seemed slightly disengaged the day her next door neighbor, Naomi, introduced them, but this behavior was extreme. He watched her without blinking as he pressed the knife in, breaking the skin. An involuntary shudder went through her body—this man was a psychopath.

"What about Naomi and Katherine, your daughter?" she asked through clenched teeth.

"What of them? They mean nothing here in this world where I can do whatever I want," he sneered.

"John! Let it go. This is not a simple villager. I would like to kill her too but with the prophecy in play I think it would be ill-advised."

"Why? What could possibly happen?"

"Just get a move on."

They continued down the trail. Maeve's mind refused to work and she wondered if Pryderi had done something to her. He certainly had several powers. Rhiannon's warning was loud in her ears—*stay away from my son*, she had said. They moved forward silently, the only sound the snap of branches and their labored breathing. Maeve knew better than to try to wheedle her way out of this one. Pryderi was not someone to mess around with. Her mind went to Finiche and she called to him in her mind, hoping that the desperation she felt wouldn't hinder the telepathy. He should be on her trail by now; it had been many hours since she left camp.

When they emerged into the open again a hill stood out ahead of them, the dark slash of a mine a wound in its side. Maeve heard the workers, the sound of pickaxes and the steady rumble of wheels. A Crion man appeared from the darkness, pulling a cart way too heavy, his thin body straining against the weight. When he collapsed the cart rolled backward a shout went up and a moment later Oillteill guards were beating him with their massive clubs. His screams rent the air and then there was silence. Maeve turned away, tears flowing from her eyes. They trickled down her face, burning her chapped cheeks, the salt taste coming into her mouth. She retched and almost threw up, her insides churning with horror.

"Jesus, woman—that's disgusting," John said. "Get it together, it's just one of those dwarves. Who gives a shit about them?"

"Can we rest for a moment?"

"No. We have a long way to go," came Pryderi's curt reply.

"Why don't we kill her and leave her here in the mine?" John asked. "The Beithir would enjoy a good meal, although come to think of it there's not much meat on her bones." John prodded her in the ribs with the butt of the knife, laughing.

Pryderi didn't answer, just kept moving forward past the mine and down a steep hill to a dry creek bed. They walked another quarter mile or so, heading up another steep hillside. Maeve could hear John panting, as though he couldn't get enough air.

"I have to stop for a minute," John said a moment later. "I'm not a demi-god like you. Also I'm fucking thirsty." He pulled the water skin off his shoulder and took a long drink.

"Can I have some?" Maeve asked.

John looked at her through narrowed eyes. "I don't think so." He took another long swallow and hung it back on his shoulder, regarding her with a mocking smile.

A few minutes of rest and they were walking again. Maeve strained to hear any sign of her wolf. Her head ached, her eyes were unclear and she couldn't seem to focus on calling to Finiche or anything else for that matter. Pryderi never seemed to tire, nor did he drink water or eat anything. He didn't talk or look in her direction. What was he thinking? Her legs were shaking now, and the cold had seeped inside her body, making her teeth chatter.

It was an hour or so later when Maeve was about to collapse that she began hearing a rhythmic sound, like galloping hooves hitting frozen ground. She perked up scanning the area. They were moving across a desolate endless valley and she shivered when a gust of wind whistled through her clothing. So far no sign of the rider, but the sound was growing more pronounced. When a rider appeared over a small rise, Pryderi stopped, a look of surprise on his features. John seemed nonplussed, his sneering face just as before. Maeve's heart lifted as she recognized Rhiannon on her beautiful gray mare, Finiche loping beside her. The goddess was no longer indistinct—her powerful stature very clear. For the first time Maeve took in the woman's strength, the unusual color of her luminous eyes.

Pulling the mare up right in front of them she looked down on her son. "Pryderi! What are you engaged in here?"

"This is none of your concern, Mother," he answered sullenly.

"How dare you say this? The Willow is everyone's concern and most particularly mine. Let this woman go immediately!" Her eyes flashed and Maeve saw a small bolt of electricity head toward Pryderi. When it hit him he dropped the rope and fell to his knees. John looked terrified, moving backward to get away. "Cut the rope," Rhiannon ordered, her eyes focused on her son. Pryderi stood up and pulled out a knife, slicing neatly through Maeve's bindings. "Now go!" Rhiannon ordered, her voice booming into the silence.

Pryderi stepped back and turned away, signaling to John, and then the two of them were running in the other direction.

Maeve rubbed her wrists and then gratefully accepted the water skin Rhiannon handed her. She rinsed out her mouth and then drank deeply of the sweet water. She held out the water-skin and then climbed onto Finiche's back, leaning exhausted onto his neck.

"You must go now," Rhiannon told her. "And try not to succumb to my son's deceptions in the future." Rhiannon smiled and pushed her heels into the horse, moving past Maeve.

A second later Finiche took off in the other direction and when Maeve glanced over her shoulder, she got a glimpse of John sprawled on the ground, his arms held protectively over his head. Bolts of electricity passed from Pryderi to Rhiannon and back again. Finiche didn't pause, his feet flying over the frozen ground.

The closer they came to the camp the uneasier Maeve felt. Something was not right. They had been gone for a long time, anything could have happened in her absence. Finiche slowed and then stopped, his ears pointing forward. Maeve slid off, moving ahead of him to peer through the trees. She sucked in her breath, a hand over her mouth and then ran as fast as she could toward the scene of devastation. The camp had been attacked, clothing, blankets and cooking utensils scattered across the ground around the smoldering firepit.

"Hello!" she called frantically. There was no answer. Finiche moved through the chaos, his nose to the ground. When he took off into the trees, Maeve ran after him.

To Maeve there was no sign as to where her people had gone, but Finiche continued, winding around trees and heading under brush. When he stopped to sniff a snag of material that had caught on a limb, Maeve took a look. It was a piece of woven wool from one of the Crion tunics. Her fear mounted.

It seemed a long while before Finiche located them them huddling around a fire next to a deep cave. Many were hurt and bleeding and according to Rea others had never shown up. Maeve surveyed the area, feeling satisfied that they were in a place of safety, at least for now. When Duncan appeared from within the cave Maeve hurried over. "My god, I can't believe this!" she cried, grabbing hold of the older man's arms. "Can you tell me what happened?"

Duncan rubbed his eyes wearily. "It was a few hours after ye left. I worried somethin' might have happened to ye, so I took a couple of scouts with me and went to search. Well, they must have been lurkin' in the forest because once we got back to camp they attacked--'twas like the hounds of hell, those beasts of theirs. The Wildmen here tried to subdue 'em but those horrible animals paid no attention. And then the men arrived, Wildmen from Brandubh's camp and some of the biggest Oillteil I've seen so far. They were carryin' these clubs that looked like tree trunks. Of course by that time half the camp was runnin' around like chickens without heads. I had to take control. I told 'em all to follow me and took off. Everyone was beatin' their way through the woods, screamin' like all get out and so Brandubh's men didna ken which way to go. Should they follow this group or that? Controlled chaos is what I call it—in any case some of our lot were taken and others are just plain gone. What ye have here are the ones who made it, but as ye can plainly see, many have been hurt."

Looking down Maeve noticed the bleeding cuts on the older man's arms, the welts from brambles on his face and neck. "And you're one of them," she said, checking in her pack for salve. "I'm so glad you were here, Duncan, and able to take control— without that I'm sure these people wouldn't have made it," she added, gesturing toward the hollow-eyed Crion and others in the immediate vicinity.

Maeve made the rounds, checking everyone over. Several Crion, a couple of villagers and two Wildmen were unaccounted for, but the others seemed cheerful enough despite their cuts and bruises, glad that she had returned unscathed. It took most of Rea's herbal supplies to treat the wounded and by the end of it she was utterly done in, especially coming on the heels of her own ordeal. She sank down next to the fire, her head in her hands.

"So what in hell happened to ye? Why were ye gone so long?" Duncan asked, sitting down beside her.

Maeve walked through a deep and verdant forest. Singing birds and the rustling of foraging animals was all she could hear. Through the thick foliage, the soft eyes of a stag peered out at her. His antlers were huge. As she walked on, another animal appeared—it looked like an enormous cow with giant horns growing out of the sides of its massive head. She felt a deep connection with each one in turn as their eyes met hers.

The sky she could see through the branches was cerulean blue, the air warm, moist and fragrant. The need to follow this path to its con-clusion kept her walking. Finally she arrived at an outcropping of pale gold rock, a pool at its base. Water trickled from above, filling the pool and spilling over to meander away in the form of a stream. Centuries of cascading water had molded the deep hollow that beckoned to her, send-ing wisps of steam rising into the air. She sat down on a ledge of rock next to the pool, letting her mind float, open to whatever would come.

Maeve woke herself with an intake of breath and sat up. The spring held a message. And from what she had gotten from the dream, it was close by, or at least she hoped it was. It made sense

with the camp being next to an escarpment and the caves that
ran along the edge of what used to be a stream. The geology in
her dream was the same.

These visions were becoming more frequent, leading her
on a certain path, but half the time she wasn't completely sure
about them—were they from the future or were they current?
Or were they just from her imagination? She pulled on her
boots and scanned the area. Yes, over there by the conspicuously
gnarled pine was the path she'd seen. Was it safe to leave again?
Best to let Duncan know what she was doing. He'd done a pretty good job the last time.

Quietly waking the older man, Maeve whispered her plans,
telling him where to look if she wasn't back in a couple of
hours. He tried to protest, saying he could come along, but she
shushed him—this was something she had to do on her own and
besides that he was the one she trusted to watch over things in
her absence. He smiled at that, an expression of pride lightening his features. Leaving everyone else asleep, she made her way
into the trees, heading down one twisting trail after another,
following the route in her dream. A deep gloom hung below the
branches, a feeling of hopelessness that seemed to emanate from
the dank air. This was not at all like the forest in her dream—
this forest and its inhabitants were wounded.

When she finally reached the spring, she was glad to see it
still intact. It was the same as her vision with the exception of
the majestic willow tree that sprang up from the far side of the
rocky bank, its branches falling gracefully over the water. The
atmosphere felt charged here, making her aware that the tree
and the spring repelled the darker forces that had invaded the
rest of the forest.

While she gazed at the rough bark of the tree, examining
the many branches that curved over the little pool, a voice,
like the tinkle of bells, entered her mind. "We are the Ghillie
Dhu, the spirits who guard the trees. You have answered our

call." A sigh went through the branches and when Maeve looked again she saw a tiny flash of silver and the movement of translucent wings. It was gone before she could get a proper look. Scanning back to her early days in the Otherworld, she thought of the web that had kept her dry on her night under the birch trees, the little light beings that led her to the Rowan Village. Why had they called her here—what was it they wished to tell her?

When a glint of light caught her eye she looked down, spying her moonstone lying next to the pool. For one horrible second she was afraid this was another trick—that Brandubh or Pryderi had hidden themselves in the luxuriant foliage and were planning another ambush. But when nothing happened, she relaxed, picking up her necklace and tying it back around her neck. This time the stone did not reach her breastbone, instead it reached to just below the hollow of her throat. She laughed to herself—if this happened again she would have to replace the velvet ribbon.

A small stream from above trickled down the rock face, falling gently into the hollowed out pool. Maeve breathed deeply of the moist air, thanking the tiny beings for keeping it safe and for the return of the stone. She placed her open lips on the water trickling down, diverting it and letting it cool her mouth and trickle down her throat. It tasted sweet. She put her arms into the pool trying to soothe the inflamed skin from the rope burns of two days ago, but when she bent over to gaze into the water, the ribbon came untied and the stone sank to the bottom. In alarm she reached for it, but the surface began to bubble and turned white. Pulling her hand out, she sat back on her heels, watching it foam and froth for several long minutes. When the water finally cleared she could see the necklace on the bottom, the glowing stone sending shafts of cool light in all directions. A scene came into view, projected clearly on the bottom of the pool: red-haired men standing side-by-side with their arms linked. The light from the moonstone was refracted by the movement of the water and encircled the tiny red-haired figures who seemed to glow from within. And at the front of the group a dark-haired man and a woman with red hair stood together--Maeve and Harold. Before she could make sense of it all, the scene faded and then was gone.

Once she could see the bottom again, she reached in to get the moonstone, but a lengthy search brought up nothing. The stone was simply not there. While contemplating this, there was a rush of air and when she turned around MacCuill was standing in front of her. With him was an enormous man, naked except for the deerskin he wore around his lower body. Curly brown hair hung to his shoulders, vines twining around the antlers protruding from his head. His chest was as wide as one of the old growth tree trunks, his skin the warm golden-brown of bark. *The Green Man.*

"This is Cernunnos, god of the forest."

Maeve stood up, staring in awe at the man who resembled the pictures in Harold's book of Celtic mythology. He seemed to be part goat or ram or maybe bull. He towered over her, and she nodded to him, unsure how to greet a god, especially one as impressive and stern looking as this one.

Into the silence MacCuill's voice said, "Cernunnos has come to help you. This is his forest and he is concerned for the many aurochs and deer being killed by Brandubh's men. If the destruction is not stopped, this spring will be dry and frozen like all the rest and many more animals will die."

When Cernunnos turned toward her and she caught a glimpse of his untamed light golden eyes a shiver went down her spine.

"I pledge to stand by you against the dark forces." The voice was deeply resonant, more like the sound of a bull than human. "I will not allow any more of my forest to be destroyed, my animals killed."

Maeve felt his power on a visceral level. He had not lost his strength as the other goddesses had. "Thank you, Cernunnos," she uttered respectfully, finding her voice. She bowed and then turned toward MacCuill. "I have just seen the future in this pool—the answer to the dilemma that I've been trying so hard to figure out."

Cernunnos stood motionless, a gleaming statue made of marble.

Maeve recounted what she had just seen, telling MacCuill her interpretation: that bringing balance to this world had to be accomplished without violence.

MacCuill lifted his head from where he had been staring at the ground. "You cannot count on this, Maeve. The vision in the pool is one possible outcome. This battle could take the path you saw or it could go any other way. The reason for the vision is to give you a direction."

"But MacCuill, this has to be what I'm meant to do. I got a message from the tree spirits—they led me here. And my moonstone disappeared. It's not in the pool—I searched everywhere."

MacCuill's expression registered neither surprise nor concern. "The moonstone did what it was meant to do. It kept you safe and protected until the inception of the wolf moon. Now that you have come into your own power the stone is no longer needed. The circle is complete."

The circle is complete. The same thing Brigid had told her. MacCuill's interpretation made her doubt her intuition, but she had to trust herself to succeed. "The people with me are starving and dehydrated. I can bring them here to drink and we can fill our skin bags but we'll run out again within a day or two."

"Water is stored in the souteraines. I can tell you how to find them but you must be extremely careful. It is Brandubh who has placed the extra barrels there and I am sure he has guards to watch over the supplies."

"What is a souteraine?"

"The souteraines are underground dwellings built hundreds of years ago, now only used for storage of foodstuffs and, more recently, water. Did you say Harold was beside you in this vision? I have yet to meet this man."

"Yes, he was standing right next to me."

"He must be part of the prophecy," MacCuill observed, as though to himself, "the 'one of noble birth'."

"How is that possible? He isn't...I mean, he's just... Harold."

"If he was part of your vision he belongs here. What did he look like? Was he dressed differently?"

Maeve thought for a minute. Yes, Harold had been dressed in some sort of protective leather vest rather like armor and had an enormous sword hanging by his side. "He looked like a warrior from the distant past."

"I'm very much looking forward to meeting this man. I see how much you care for him; it shows in your eyes. You will be reunited soon."

She looked away for a minute to hide the tears as her thoughts went to Harold and the love that resonated in her heart, the baby that grew within her. "Is he close by? I'm surprised we've haven't found each other."

MacCuill smiled. "If I come upon him I will certainly let you know."

Maeve stared into the distance. How would they find each other? Without the moonstone she couldn't just say 'take me to Harold' and be whisked away. Every day she discovered how big the Otherworld was, how extensive the forests and the now dry waterways. "I wish I hadn't lost the moonstone," she mumbled.

"You did not lose the stone, Maeve. You have its power within you."

When Maeve opened her mouth to ask how that was possible she noticed Cernunnos staring at her. "This will summon me," he announced, handing her an enormous horn.

Maeve reached for the horn, admiring its delicate curve, the gleam of almost translucent bone. As she put it to her lips his enormous hand came onto her arm.

"Only when you need me," Cernunnos ordered. "I will leave you now. I must tend to my animals."

Maeve turned to say good-bye but he had already disappeared, melting into the trees like smoke.

"Where have you been all this time, MacCuill? So many things have happened since Rowan."

"I told you I had to meet with my queen." MacCuill smiled. "I think you have been managing quite well on your own."

Maeve thought about everything that had happened in the past weeks—she could have used MacCuill's calming presence and council during some of the more hair-raising episodes. "And Brandubh? Have you seen him?"

"I have not, but I have heard rumors. Morrighan has taken from him what he owes her."

"Morrighan?"

"The goddess of war. From what I hear, Brandubh has been severely hampered by this." MacCuill chuckled. "It is very good news."

"But if she's the goddess of war wouldn't she...?"

"No, Maeve. She has always been aligned with the Tuatha De Danann. She may be a war goddess but she is not stupid. She is able to see how out of balance this place has become and the catastrophic effects of this."

"Would she fight for our cause?"

"I thought this was to be accomplished without fighting." He gazed at her quizzically.

"I don't mean that kind of fighting. I just thought...you know...the goddess of war...I thought she could put an end to it, once and for all."

"Not without much bloodshed, and besides, this is for you to sort out. If it were that easy it would have been achieved by now. Nothing that is accomplished with violence 'will put an end to it once and for all', as you put it."

Maeve looked down, feeling ashamed. "Yes, I know this-- now more than ever. But then why did you say what you did about my vision?"

MacCuill stood quietly, his hand running across his beard. "I only wanted to warn you not to assume that your first thought is correct. Things are not always what they seem and especially visions, as you should know from your time here. Don't think too hard; instead let your unthinking mind make sense of it over the next few days. And since I have pledged myself to you, is there anything I can do to help?"

The day in the dreamtime when he went down on one knee seemed like a story she had read years ago; so much had happened in the interim. Her mind went to her latest dealings with Pryderi and Brandubh, the tricks they employed to ensnare her—turn the tables, she thought to herself, looking at him. "Use your magic to confuse and delay as much as you can."

MacCuill's eyebrows went up, an expression of delight on his weathered face. "I can do that."

As soon as MacCuill disappeared Maeve realized she hadn't gotten instructions for how to find the souteraines. "Wait…" she called. But he didn't return. After a few minutes she stripped off her filthy clothes and climbed into the warm water to soak and allow the creative side of her mind to work on the problem. It had been a long time since she had bathed, she thought, longing for the feel of the pulsing stream of her shower at home, but for now this would have to do, despite the lack of soap and towels.

She broke off a willow twig to use for a scrubber, rubbing it across her body as she contemplated the situation. The only way to bring balance was to effect a change in the people who were now following Brandubh, to sway them to her side. This meant convincing them that the riches they had been promised were not worth the sacrifices they were making. So far she had managed to free a few prisoners but she needed to do a lot more than that. She needed to win the hearts and minds of those who had been brainwashed into working and fighting for Brandubh. The next question was: how would she find these people without getting herself killed?

Her group had become integrated, the disparate beings united in service to her and saving the Otherworld. Even the injured Oillteil worked with the others to support the camp. The language barrier had been dismantled as everyone made an attempt to communicate. They would help to sway others of their kind if they came upon them. Her idea was possible. And if Harold was truly mentioned in the prophecy she needed him. She stilled her mind, trying to connect with her inner knowing, breathing in and out slowly until her thoughts turned into wisps and disappeared. After a few moments, a clear image appeared: Eron and Harold running together through the forest. Had they already found each other or was this vision in the future? She puzzled over this for a while and then climbed out of the pool. It was time to get to work.

Back at camp she summoned everyone and then told them of her meeting with MacCuill and Cernunnos, the path that had been laid out for her in the pool. Looking around she noticed some skeptical expressions but most seemed to accept her words. When some questioned her, she was unable to answer, because, as she explained, it was all new. She needed time to process before she could communicate to them clearly what it all meant.

When she arrived back at camp she enlisted the help of Soru and Duncan, the three of them heading back to the spring to fill up the water skins. By the time they returned in late afternoon her need to find Harold had grown from a seed into an urgency that she couldn't ignore. The vision in the spring had shown him standing beside her—he was part of what was going on here and they needed to be together now. Her meditation in the pool had indicated that the man was close by, although where was not clear. She had to trust her instincts on this and let the spirits guide her—the Ghillie Dhu had drawn her to the spring, maybe they would help her find him. Reaching up to her neck she had a moment of terror—no moonstone. But MacCuill had seemed very sure that she no longer needed it. She hoped this was true.

That night her sleep was filled with shadowy images of Harold in the distance, as though some magic was conjuring him and keeping him just out of her reach. When she woke her mind was made up. It was time to find him and she was certain that the spiritis would help her. While she ate a bit of cheese Rea fussed over her, plying her with a special tea that she insisted would help the baby. The small woman was distraught when Maeve conveyed her plans, warning against too much exercise and stress after what had happened recently.

"I can't wait around until this baby is born, Rea. If he or she is part of the prophecy, as you told me, then I have to go on with my mission."

When Maeve left the fire to find Duncan Rea handed her a small bag of tea leaves. "Promise me that you will drink this while you travel."

"I promise," Maeve said, putting the bag into her pack. She was touched by the woman's concern but at the same time she didn't want to start worrying again; there was too much at stake right now. Her main focus at the moment was food supplies, a need that included everyone in camp. Finding Harold and Eron was part of her plan to remedy this—surely her grandfather would know how to locate the souteraines.

She consulted with Duncan, asking him to take care of things in her absence. It could be a full day before she returned. This place where they had ended up seemed safer somehow, protected. The caves were deep and if something happened, her people could hide within them. Dirg and Soru could stand guard. She also told Duncan that the wolf would remain at camp. Finiche would definitely alert them to any danger.

Duncan stared at her, his mouth agape. "Ye plan to take off again without anyone to help ye? I think you're mad, lass. At least take Dirg or Soru if ye refuse to take me. Think, lass—did ye nae get picked up by Brandubh's people? What makes ye believe things will go any different this time?"

"I can't be bogged down by two men trying to protect me. Harold is close—I can feel it. And besides that, this is really my responsibility—I have to be the one to decide. I'll be fine, I promise you. And I have a job for you while I'm gone. MacCuill told me that there's water stored in the souteraines. I knew we've been taking water from the spring but if we found a souteraine there might be some food there as well. Do you think you could take a couple of men and Finiche and try to find one of these?"

Duncan's expression lifted. "I'd be happy to do this for ye. And I ken the wolf can smell the water."

Maeve nodded. "But be very careful. According to MacCuill these are Brandubh's storage places and will be well-guarded." Maeve smiled, patting the older man on the arm. Lately he seemed younger, as though the excitement and danger had revived him. He was a good man and an asset to the group.

Someone or something was on her trail. Maeve could feel waves of anger pouring toward her. The sharp crack of twigs breaking behind her had her sprinting down the path. They certainly weren't trying to keep quiet, but then again her hearing had become very acute in the last week or so. Her decision to leave Finiche behind was beginning to seem somewhat unwise. Without him she was much more vulnerable, but then again, the tangled brush was hard enough to navigate without a large four-legged animal along. It was safer for her camp with the wolf there to alert them to danger and lead them to safety if something happened in her absence.

This route, this path she was on, had come to her as soon as she left camp, propelling her forward—her entreaty to the Ghillue Dhu had been heard. Harold must be close by. The news about the baby burst in her chest, a feeling of excitement causing her to hasten her pace.

Her mind went back over the pregnancy, revisiting the moment when she became aware of it. She was still in the first trimester, a time Rea had told her was critical. The Crion woman always managed to bring her something green to eat as well as finding nettles and dandelion root for tea. It seemed miraculous that anything managed to grow in this desolate place. Two days before, a lactating sheep had wandered into camp and since then Rea had brought her fresh milk every morning. Maeve had worried about the lamb—where was it? But Rea told her not to concern herself with that—that maybe it had been eaten by some of her people who still roamed the hills. Maeve drank the milk but insisted that Rea share it with the others, especially those still healing from injuries.

A snapping twig brought Maeve's mind back to the present. She stopped for a moment to look back. When a shadow disappeared behind a tree trunk she took off, sprinting through the brush. A knife was the only weapon she carried. After a few minutes of running she stopped to listen again, but all was silent. She continued on, slower this time, her breath coming in gasps. A few minutes later a shout rang out and she turned to see three men emerging from the forest: Brandubh, Pryderi and John. *Not again!*

"Maeve, my dear, no need to run from us. I was hoping you would be gone from this place by now, but apparently Rhiannon had a bit of a contretemps with her son. Too bad she didn't let Pryderi take you out of danger. Now we have come upon you again, and this time I think there will be no escape."

Maeve turned away and ran, heading out of the trees toward the river. Luckily this one had not yet been dammed up; her only hope was the boatman. At the bank she scanned up and down. There was no wading across this deep and icy expanse. Brandubh and the other men were right behind her and then all at once Brandubh stood next to her. She shrieked and took a step backward.

"I still have a few tricks up my sleeve." He moved forward and grabbed her roughly by the shoulder bringing a knife blade across her forearm. The blade penetrated through her clothing, blood oozing onto the material. "See, you bleed like anyone else." He leered at her, pressing the knife blade deep into her arm.

Maeve let out a scream of pain, clutching the wound with her other hand. She struggled to get away from him, but his arm came round her waist, holding her there in a vise-like grip. Blood gushed from the wound dripping down her arm. "Let me go!" she shouted. In the next moment his features collapsed in a grimace—he let her go, grasping his forearm.

Maeve moved away from him wondering what was going on. Looking up she saw John heading toward her, an ugly grin on his face.

"Let me do the honors," he said, bowing to Brandubh. "Now I can have the pleasure denied me during our last encounter. Dark Raven believes in the one true God," he called to Maeve, pointing reverently toward the priest. A trickle of blood ran down Brandubh's hand, dripping darkly onto the ground. "Who do you worship, little girl?"

Maeve felt as though her feet were stuck in cement. She gazed into the very thin layer of ice, her attention taken by the roiling dark clouds reflected there. When she placed her foot on the frozen expanse a sharp crack rippled across the smooth surface. It was not thick enough to hold her weight. Out of the corner of her eye she caught the gleam of the knife as John walked toward her. Beneath her feet something began to materialize—she could clearly make out what looked like an underwater bridge. Should she trust this image to carry her across?

John was so close she could smell his foul breath and Pryderi was coming up on her left. She stepped gingerly onto the ice, her foot breaking through to connect with something solid. When she moved forward, John's knife whizzed by her ear, falling with a clatter and sliding away. Taking another step she looked back to see Brandubh's bewildered expression.

"How in the hell are you doing that? That ice is way too thin to hold you."

"Come on Pryderi, you ineffectual demi-god—fucking DO something!" John yelled, pulling another knife from his belt.

Maeve continued across as quickly as she dared, the bridge forming under her boots. Behind her Pryderi waved his arms and a moment later a blue spiral whirled toward her with terrifying speed. When she held up her hand to deflect it a shout of rage came from Pryderi, a look of pure hatred on his face as he waved his hand in an angry circle above his head. A second later a black cloud formed above her and a torrent of ice, like small knives, hit her head, shoulders and arms. She lost her balance, bruising her recovering hip as she landed. Blood flowed down her face blinding her for a moment. Struggling to her feet she wiped it away with the back of her hand, her heart pounding in her ears. Moving one foot carefully in front of the other, she concentrated on getting to the other side.

John yelled a string of obscenities as he and Brandubh fell through the ice. "Stop her!" Brandubh bellowed. Maeve could hear splashing and swearing but she dared not turn around, focusing only on the shore in the distance. In her peripheral vision she could see Pryderi moving his hands in waving patterns bringing spirals of blue light whirling around her. The earth heaved under her feet throwing her up onto the bank. A sharp pain shot through her leg as John's knife made purchase. Her jeans were ripped, blood flowing copiously down her leg. She stood shakily and limped slowly away, heading for the trees.

"Goddamn it!" she heard Brandubh yell as he and John worked their way through the ice chunks back to the bank.

The sing of a knife whizzed by her ear.

"What the hell, John? Can't you hit the bitch some place where it counts?"

Under Maeve's feet the ground tilted, icy wind whirling and spinning around her. She fell hard, pain searing through her leg, making her cry out. She heard someone laughing. Using all her will power she forced herself to stand, staggering toward the trees.

Chapter

22

arold and the villagers traveled a well-worn path at the edge of the valley. Behind them were the fifteen men they had rescued. A few were on horseback, riding next to Harold, but many walked, guarding the carts that carried the women and children. Oillteil and Wildmen had been spotted in the distance and so they were careful to stay out of sight and go quietly.

"Are there mines or bridges close by?" Harold asked Iain. Ideas were surfacing from his past life as Kenneth—clever ways to use his skills to undermine Brandubh's plans. Apparently it was the type of warfare he had enjoyed immensely in his previous life.

"There are bridges and dams all along the river. Mines are being worked everywhere. If we stop and listen I'm sure we will hear the sounds of the pick axes. What did ye have in mind?" Iain's eyes were bright, his eyebrows raised in interest. The recent rescue they had conducted had given all of them a sense of accomplishment.

When the group found shelter under the cover of trees on a low rocky ridge they could see where the wide river had brought water for the farms. Now it had been dammed and lay like a bruise along the valley floor, the dried out crops blackened from the cold.

"Why do so many follow Brandubh?" Harold asked, gazing across what used to be fertile land planted with corn, potatoes, beans and squash. Earlier in the day they had spent time out there gathering the few vegetables they could find.

"He promises wealth, especially to the ones who are intelligent and would otherwise rise up against him and his cohorts. He manipulates the others with only the promise that the god he's always talking about will reward them for their service. He speaks of heaven where they will end up once they have given their lives for him."

"So he's brainwashed them."

Iain looked at him quizzically. "I do not know this word."

"It just means he's taken over their minds."

"Aye, that is correct."

When it grew dark Maggie and Iain's woman, Clara, brought some potatoes to roast over the fire, sitting down with the men as they discussed plans for the night. When a man appeared out of the darkness they all looked up in surprise, knives at the ready. With sword in hand Harold stood. "And who might you be?"

"I'm Eron, a friend of the one known as the Willow."

"You are very welcome. Come by the fire and share our meal," Caleb invited, moving over on the log to make room.

As he sat down, Eron looked around, his eyes coming to rest on Harold who was still standing with folded arms. "Your face is familiar. Have we met?"

"No. I'm Harold or...possibly you know me as Kenneth...?" Harold looked curiously at the man. There was something familiar about him as well.

"Harold, of course! I am Maeve's grandfather." He held out his hand.

"It's good to meet you," Harold said, smiling. He remembered Maeve talking about this man and how he figured in the story of her family.

"I'm searching for Maeve. Have you seen her?" Eron asked.

"No. I was hoping you had. I've been traveling with these people who have been kind enough to feed me."

A voice piped up from the back. "And launching daring rescues." It was a red-haired boy named Addis, around twelve years of age. The children had already made up an exciting tale about the men's exploits.

Eron glanced at Harold, his eyebrows raised in question.

"I seem to have some skills as a saboteur, or at least Kenneth does."

"Kenneth?"

Harold sighed. "Apparently I am not only Harold Fitzhugh from Halston, Massachusetts, but also Kenneth MacAlpin, the first King of Scotland." As Harold told his tale, the men clustered close around the fire. This was fast becoming part of their oral history.

An hour later Eron, Harold, Iain, Caleb and two other men were running down the hill toward the valley. It was a very dark night with heavy clouds. Icy fingers of wind blew on them as Iain led the way upriver toward the dam. It took most of the night to dislodge the heavy rocks and dirt ramparts that kept the water back, but finally a trickle broke through and after that the heavy weight of the water scattered the rest of the boulders like pebbles.

It was two days later that Iain and Caleb informed Harold that their group was moving on. As much as they had enjoyed their adventures, the women wanted to get to the Caer Sidi where they would be safe; they were tired of worrying every night as their men disappeared into the dark. Iain gave Eron his horse, Taranis, named after the god of thunder, with the condition that Eron would bring the beast to the Caer Sidi at some time in the not-too-distant future. Eron thanked him profusely and waited until the caravan was safely on its way before he and Harold headed on horseback toward the valley.

Harold led the way across one of two bridges spanning the river. They dismounted and set to work on the east side, removing several critical supports from beneath, taking turns checking for Wildmen, Oillteil or other men in Brandubh's employ who had been spotted marching toward the north. After they were finished, Harold left Eron with the horses and scouted up the valley. He found the enemy camp under the trees, recognizing Brandubh's distinctive dark cassock where he stood talking with a group of Wildmen. The second bridge they had planned to dismantle was dangerously close.

When Harold joined Eron an hour or so later they discussed a plan, deciding to begin their work on the west side of the bridge. That way if Brandubh and his men discovered them they would have to cross in order to attack. The bridge was heavily built, made to carry horses and carts, but with Argyll's talents as a workhorse they were able to remove enough of the supports to be confident of its imminent collapse. This river now flowed because of the their earlier efforts at the dam but the water was already beginning to freeze over. Hopefully the water beneath the ice would soon be available to the people and animals that lived along its banks.

Both bridges looked perfectly normal as they rode away, but with any luck the next group to cross would be Brandubh or some of his men; not only were they the only ones arrogant enough to travel out in the open during the day, but Harold had also done some reconnaissance and planned to draw the men with a series of diversionary tactics starting with an echoing call with one of Eron's small flutes. They rode the horses into the forest and left them to forage, creeping back toward the river. Both men began to yell as loud as they could, Harold also clanking his heavy sword against tree trunks to simulate a fight. After a short time at this, Eron cried out in a falsetto, "Maeve, Maeve!", as the two men moved off into the forest. From their hiding place, Eron and Harold heard excited yipping as the beasts and a couple of scouts came to investigate. As soon as the Wildmen were in sight, Eron and Harold sprinted away, making as much noise as they could. They wanted the Wildmen to believe there were enough people here to pursue. Reaching the horses, they mounted and galloped off, feeling assured that their plan would succeed.

Early the next day the two men headed to the shallow mountain range that lay close to the western valley. They crossed the low-lying hills making good time, finding their way to the large loch glistening with ice at the deepest part of the valley. From the hills they could see the two villages that flanked each end of the loch.

"I hope Brandubh has not been here," Eron muttered, scanning into the smokeless distance.

Harold noticed the grim set of the older man's mouth as they came down off the hills. At the bottom Eron held up his hand to signal Harold and then brought his horse to a halt. The older man dismounted, kneeling to examine the animal and human tracks in the nearly frozen ground around the loch. "A day or two old, I would say," he said, turning to glance at Harold. They left the horses in what had once been a fertile valley and made the rest of the trip on foot, walking through freezing fog that left a gray coating on their jackets. When the first village loomed into view they stayed low, skirting the houses at a crouch. An eerie quiet surrounded the deserted place.

"He's been here all right," came Eron's angry mutter. A trip through town brought them to an old man who had been injured. He cowered from them until Eron told him who he was.

"Eron! 'Tis been too many years. I am Dougal, do ye nae recognize me? How is Grita, that lovely wife of yours—and the child?"

Eron's face darkened. "Brandubh killed them—burned them up years ago."

"By the spirits, man. I am sorry to hear that. My wife, my grown daughter and my grandchild were all taken during the slaughter that went on here." Dougal's bloodshot eyes filled and he turned away.

The wound on Dougal's leg still bled and the two men helped him back to his house, helping him onto the bed. Eron pulled herbs out of his pouch, placing them directly on the wound. To Harold's surprise he then placed his hands over the wound and began to chant. Harold moved away, trying not to form an opinion about his healing methods, instead going to the hearth to make a fire. After a few moments, Eron joined him, whispering that the old man was sleeping.

"I'm going to scout around and see if I can find us something to eat," Eron said, heading to the door.

Harold nodded, and then turned back to the fire, placing several logs on top of the kindling. He pulled out a box of matches and lit it, sitting back on his heels. As the wood began to burn, his thoughts went to Eron—had Maeve mentioned that he was some kind of a shaman? He shook his head. He knew that Eron was Finna's real father, hadn't met his daughter until she was grown, but other than that the man's past was a complete mystery. He obviously knew his way around here and could fight with the best of them. So far the two of them had managed quite well together.

A half hour or so later Eron burst through the door, his arms filled with bread, cheese and a couple of apples he'd discovered in someone's root cellar.

"I found these and something even better." He grinned, holding up a handmade crockery jug. "Beer," he announced.

Eron's arrival awakened Dougal who sat up rubbing a weary hand over his eyes. Harold followed Eron over to the bed, watching as he checked the wound. It had completely healed.

"How did you do that?"

"What?" Eron asked, puzzled. "Oh, you mean that," he answered, pointing. "I have a knack, I suppose."

"That's more than a knack—I'd say it's bordering on the supernatural."

Eron laughed. "Hardly. Have you not met a healer before this? There are many here and I'm sure in your world too. It is not so unusual. It's all about energy and moving it where it needs to go."

"Hmm...I guess the Chinese work that way, don't they?" Harold looked up, watching Eron for clues.

"I have no experience with the Chinese but I do know that Druids and many others are adept in the healing arts. Catriona, Finna's mother is one of them."

"I haven't met her yet, but Maeve told me about her—she sounds amazing."

Eron smiled. "She is that. I love that woman." Eron's eyes turned misty for a moment and then he turned toward Dougal. "How 'bout some beer, old man?"

As the three men took turns drinking from the jug, Dougal recounted the events of the day before: Brandubh's men had arrived before dawn and laid waste to the place, taking all the livestock and able-bodied men. The women and children had been slaughtered like cattle. Somehow he had been spared. He figured it was his age that caused them to ride off without him.

Once the jug was empty, Eron and Harold set out to find the mass graveyard, hoping to find some survivors. With the circling crows it didn't take long to find the bodies. They had been thrown behind a stone wll at the back of the village and obviously had been providing food for the crows as well as other marauding creatures. Harold was violently ill, retching until there was nothing left in his stomach. The slaughter was complete, bodies hacked apart, bloody clothing strewn across the frozen ground. From the looks of it they had been driven from their homes to the place of their death, with no way of defending themselves. There was zero chance of any life still existing here.

It took hours to dig graves to bury the dead. Once they had covered them with dirt, the two men gathered stones and placed them on the graves and then went back for Dougall. The old man sobbed quietly as Eron said a few words about speeding them into their next life. After a moment of silence Eron took his flute from his pack and put it to his lips, playing an eerie and mournful song.

By this time the dim light had leached out of the sky leaving streaks of dark cloud. They would stay the night and leave early the next morning. When Harold asked, Eron assured him that the horses would be fine where they left them; there was still a bit of grass up that way for them to munch on. Once they had added a couple of logs to the fire Harold went in search of another jug of some kind of alcohol, feeling the need to get beyond the gruesome images lingering in his mind.

Walking down the silent street gave him the willies and Harold entered each house warily, not sure what to expect. Many of them had been burned, the foundations compromised and he didn't fancy falling through the floor into some root cellar and being trapped there. His imagination was working overtime and he kept seeing shapes in his peripheral vision, deciding after a while that they were ghosts. They seemed to float around the houses, disappearing inside to reappear through a window or a door. It creeped him out and made him wish for the Kenneth personality, but right now he seemed solidly Harold. A few houses had been left intact with dishes laid out on table as though the people would be coming back shortly for a meal. At one point he had to sit down, feeling the horror again, imagining the terror of these poor people as they were rounded up like cattle and slaughtered without mercy.

With another jug in hand, he headed back to Dougal's house. He had been drinking steadily since he found the hard cider in someone's root cellar and his journey back was none too straight. He wiped at the tears that had formed in the corners of his eyes as he walked through the door, knocking it against the wall noisily.

"I see you've had a bit already," Eron said smiling.

Harold grimaced, putting the jug down on the floor in front of the fire. "What's it to you?"

Eron looked surprised. "I'll not begrudge you your alcohol, Harold, just making a comment is all."

"Well, don't." Harold grabbed the jug, tipping it up to take a good swallow.

"Hey, man, leave some for us," Dougal called from the bed.

"Take it all!" Harold yelled, anger bursting out of him. He turned and ran through the open door, tears filling his eyes. He ran down the road, his hollow cries echoing into the distance. At some point he stopped and collapsed, letting tears course down his cheeks. My god, what if they had Maeve? What if they had done to her what they'd done here? Terror shot through him as an image of her crumpled body came into his mind. Now he knew the true horror of this place, the pure evil that had infested Brandubh and everyone who worked for him.

When Harold finally got back to the house, he felt completely done in. Dougal was already asleep, stretched out on the bed. He let out a long sigh as he came over to the fire and sat down next to Eron. A long silence went by as both men stared into the flames.

"This is a very hard thing, Harold," Eron said quietly. "For someone who hasn't seen it before, death like this can change a man forever."

Harold looked over, meeting the older man's sympathetic stare. He shook his head. "I wouldn't have believed this of any human being. Of course I know all about the Nazis and all that but seeing this…it brings it home. From what Maeve told me this used to be a wonderful place." Harold stared into the fire, his thoughts on the last time he and Maeve had been together. He didn't want to ask the question but it came out before he could stop it. "What if they've killed her?"

"They have not killed her, Harold. She's very resourceful and if she were dead I would know it."

"How can you be so sure?"

"Think about it. If they killed Maeve, the war would be over, no need for this kind of destruction and killing. No, this was done in a blind rage and I have my suspicions that Maeve has thwarted them once again."

"I have to find her."

"You will. Now try and get some sleep. We have a long way to go tomorrow." Eron stretched out on the floor using his pouch for a pillow.

Harold watched him for a while, thinking about what he'd said. Jesus, he hoped the man was right. He wouldn't want to live if Maeve was gone. After a point his head began to nod and he lay down, curling himself into a ball next to the fire.

They both slept badly, waking in the morning with a sense of urgency, certain that Brandubh had gotten to the next village ahead of them. Harold was frantic, terrified of coming upon another grizzly scene. His head ached and there was a searing pain behind his eyes; he hadn't drunk this much alcohol in one sitting since his college days. Before leaving they checked on the old man, begging him to come along, but he said, no, he wouldn't want to slow them down. He waved them off with good luck wishes, assuring them he had what he needed right here.

"We'll come by on our way back," Eron assured him.

They found the horses nibbling on sparse grass close to where they left them and saddled up, heading toward the far end of the loch where another village lay hidden under a blanket of fog. It wasn't long before they noticed dark smoke billowing into the sky. "We're too late," Harold said, his eyes meeting Eron's.

The village was burned to the ground, the charred remains still smoldering. They spent a long time searching through the rubble for survivors, but found no one. As far as animals and food, there were none. It was with a feeling of bitterness and despair that they left, heading northwest toward another village. Eron had friends there as well and the look in his eyes told Harold he was very worried.

An empty souterraine sheltered them for the night but there was no protection for the horses as they stood shivering with their backs to the wind; in the morning, a breakfast of barley collected from the depths of the souterraine gave them back a little of the energy lost to the cold night. With no way to make a fire, the men huddled close together drinking cold tea brewed the day before. Wind continued to whine through the hills, chilling them and bringing an even darker mood.

After breakfast they saddled up, pushing the horses more than on any other day. By nightfall they had reached the western forest that stretched to the sea. It was filled with ancient yews, firs and larch interspersed with elder, low-growing hawthorn and brambles. The smaller bushes made riding difficult and they dismounted, leading the horses through the thick undergrowth. According to Eron, foxes, rabbits, wild boar and the small wild horses known as Tarpan, lived in this forest, using the underbrush for cover, but on this day there was no sign of them. There was a desolate feeling under the trees, ice dripping off the needles of the trailing branches as though they were weeping.

"I don't like the feel of this place," Harold mumbled, looking around uneasily.

"The energy has changed here. I'm afraid of what we might find at the village."

Harold's mind immediately filled with a gruesome scene of destruction. But with it came a feeling of resolve. He was Kenneth again, his hand going to the scabbard hanging by his side. They would get through this and, if necessary, they would fight.

While they walked, Eron told Harold that the village they were heading toward was called Bannee, a word meaning blessed because of the sacred yew that grew here. It was one of only two places in the Otherworld where you could find it. Many of the villagers were proficient bow-makers, using the yew wood and carving special decorative symbols into the ends. The bows from Bannee were well known all over the Otherworld for their grace and beauty.

They walked single file, trying to follow the narrow trails made by the Tarpan. It was dark under the trees and fog clung to the bushes and swirled around them in strange eddies. By the time they reached the end of the forest, all of them were on edge, including Argyll, who snorted and jumped at every little noise.

"We're almost there. It's just over the next hill." Eron pointed into the distance.

They mounted the horses and rode on toward the top of the hill where they could see the little village below. Beyond it gray sea stretched into the distance, a fog bank obscuring the horizon. Thin smoke rose from the chimneys.

Eron let out a long sigh of relief. "I don't think Brandubh's men have been here."

The tension eased and they pushed the horses into a trot, covering the distance quickly.

That night they stayed with Tannith, a handsome woman in her fifties, dark-haired and buxom, who raised goats for the village. She was an old friend of Eron's and was very happy to see them. They dined on fresh goat cheese and freshly baked bread. It was as though this little seaside village had been forgotten in the battle for the Otherworld.

Eron and Harold stayed up long into the night talking to Tannith, impressing upon her the importance of going north to the Caer Sidi. They told her that her village might be safe now but would certainly be found by Brandubh's army in the upcoming days. It was the gruesome account of Dougal's village that finally convinced her.

In the morning Harold took charge, helping Tannith organize the other villagers for travel, getting the carts and horses hooked up, the food supplies loaded, including a number of bales of hay to feed the horses. He told them to destroy what they left behind. There was no point in letting the enemy get anything of value. Each man carried a longbow of exquisite design and their quivers held as many arrows as they could fit in them.

The preparations took most of the day and were made more difficult because of some of the villagers' reluctance to leave their safe haven. They had seen the decimation of the surrounding countryside, had heard horrific tales from travelers coming from other areas. Harold was finally able to convince these farmers to ride with Eron and Harold, to help them warn other villages and to disrupt Brandubh's troops in various devious ways as they traveled. He explained what they had already accomplished at the river, bringing some levity to the somber group as everyone imagined Oillteil and Wildmen falling into the icy water as they tried to cross the bridges. The raucous laughter that ensued was a welcome relief, releasing a lot of the tension of the past days.

By mid-afternoon Eron and Harold were ready to travel, accompanied by ten men on horseback. They made sure the rest of the villagers were on their way, with instructions to get them safely to the Caer Sidi, and then headed out, trotting along the western edge of the forest. The conversation was light and lively, and despite the dismal weather the spirits of the men were high as they rode along companionably. Harold had taken charge in his assumed role as leader, riding the big horse at the front of the line and discussing strategies to employ in case of possible attack. Eron filled them in on what had been happening for the past few weeks. They felt united in their sense of purpose as they headed north.

They camped in the forest that night, making a fire and eating heartily from the fresh food the men had brought with them. Harold was pleased to be able to give Argyll a substantial meal of sweet-smelling hay, the first he had had for many days. The western sea was farther away now but they could still smell the salt tang and feel the heavy fog that rolled inland off the water. They spread out around the fire, and then Harold took the first watch, standing guard at the edge of the camp.

As he sat with his back against a tree and his sword by his side, Harold thought about the strangeness of the situation. The Kenneth personality seemed to have taken over and he was grateful for it as his senses came alive. He felt no fear sitting alone in the dark, only the knowledge that he was a strong and able warrior, capable of defending himself and those whom he was guarding.

Harold woke in the morning with an anxious feeling in the pit of his stomach after dreaming about Maeve. He didn't say much to Eron about it until they had eaten breakfast, hoping the feeling would dissipate, but if anything it grew stronger.

"You've been very quiet Harold, is everything all right?" Eron asked when he and Harold were away from the other men.

"I have the feeling that Maeve is calling to me, as though she's close by."

"We're headed north and I'm sure we'll run into her in the next day or so," Eron replied with his usual calm.

When the two men joined the others a few minutes later, Harold called out, "Let's get a move on!" He headed to Argyll, heaving the saddle up on his back as the other men jumped up , rushing to ready their horses.

Harold had his back turned when he heard Eron exclaim, "Moon grand-daughter! We had a feeling you were close by!" He turned in time to see Maeve enfolded in Eron's arms. His heart lurched and skipped a beat as he took in her familiar form—her hair had grown out a bit and curls had appeared where the tufts had stuck up straight.

When she and Eron pulled apart she spied him, her mouth opening in surprise. "Harold! How...?"

Before she finished her sentence he had seized her around the waist, lifted her and spun her around. "Maeve, you're all I could think about." He put her down and looked into her over bright eyes noticing the trickle of dried blood that lay on her cheek, the decided limp as she moved. "What's happened? Are you all right?"

"Just a little cut, don't worry. I must have gotten your message, Harold. I came to find you. I have something very important to tell you."

Before Harold could ask her what the important thing was, a couple of men began asking him questions: what formation to ride in and whether they should have weapons at the ready. Should they cover the horses' feet with rags to keep them quieter? What was their mission today?

Maeve listened to the exchanges with a puzzled expression on her face. "What's going on?" she asked softly after Harold finished giving the men instructions.

"Long story. We can fill you in as we travel," Harold answered, glancing over at Eron. "It's time we were on our way."

Eron nodded briefly in agreement and then turned to their traveling companions introducing Maeve as the Willow. Their eyes widened and some bowed their heads.

"I am glad to meet you," Maeve said formally. "I have others that you may know at my camp a little to the north. Together we make quite a sizable group." She smiled and then turned to Eron. "Where are my mother and Catriona? I thought they would be with Harold."

"Catriona is taking your mother back to the cottage...she... she's very ill."

Maeve blanched. "What's happened?"

"She has pneumonia, a virus that never existed here until very recently. She'll be all right once she's out of the cold. I did what I could for her but it was beyond Catriona's and my healing abilities. Finna is not strong and the stress of the trip overwhelmed her immune system."

Harold saw Maeve's stricken face and put his arm around her shoulder, pulling her against his side.

"What about Gertrude? Has anyone seen her or is she still with Brandubh?"

"I don't know when you saw her last but Gertrude took off again a while back. We went to find her but the fort was deserted by the time we got there. There were prints in the ice indicating three riders and a number of people on foot as well as many beasts. It was then that we made the decision to take Finna home. Your mother wanted to stay because she was worried about you, but we finally convinced her that if she didn't go she would not get over her illness and would impede our progress. I rode north and Catriona and Finna headed south on the horses we found wandering around the fort. Gertrude will have to find her own way, I'm afraid."

"Poor Gertrude. I was captured by Pryderi a while back—he tricked me. He took me to Brandubh's camp and Gertrude looked terrible. I felt so sorry for her—you wouldn't know she was the same woman. I honestly don't know how long she'll survive under those conditions. And Brandubh was hideous to her. If there was any love between them, it's gone now."

Eron shook his head. "We tried to tell her, to warn her. I think she was bewitched or something along those lines. How else could she have stayed with him?"

"He must have tricked her in some way. She's a smart woman—she's psychic. If we come upon their camp I want to try and get her out of there. He'll kill her without a second thought."

"If the man has a fraction of the charm his sister has, I understand her initial infatuation. Unfortunately he's the opposite of Catriona, only concerned with himself."

"I had another run-in with Brandubh, John and Pryderi on my way here. But I didn't see Gertrude. I'm really worried about her."

Harold looked at her in alarm. "Is that how you got these bruises on your face and the cuts?" He traced his finger gently along her jawline.

Maeve nodded, showing him the deep cut on her leg.

"Let me take a look at that before we go," Eron said. "No need to strip down, we'll just rip the hole in your jeans to make it wider. Do you have others?"

"Not with me but I have some back at camp."

As Eron worked on Maeve's leg Harold asked, "How did you escape?"

"It's another story to tell as we ride. I seem to have acquired some new abilities." Maeve looked down. "Ooh...that feels weird."

Eron stood. "That should do it. Try and keep out of trouble, would you?"

Maeve laughed. "It's good to have a healer at the ready. Thanks, Granddad."

Eron let out a whoop. "That's a new one for me!" He turned toward Harold and the other men. "If we want to stay ahead of Brandubh we better get a move on. Maeve, why don't you ride with Harold? Argyll can easily carry the two of you."

Harold put his foot in the stirrup and swung nimbly on while Maeve stared at him with a look of disbelief. "Yes, I can ride," he said, noticing her expression. "I'll answer all your questions soon enough. Put your foot in the stirrup there," he ordered, taking his boot out to give her room. Once she did as he asked he reached down and took her hand firmly in his and pulled her up. After she settled in front of him she turned to look over her shoulder. Her face held a worried frown and he put his arms around her, burying his head next to hers for a moment before he picked up the reins.

Chapter

23

Gertrude camped with Brandubh and his men along the eastern side of the valley. A group of Oillteil had joined them, as well as defecting villagers and more Wildmen. In the wide valley below, marching men headed north and it gave Gertrude a chill to watch them. Every day Brandubh was down there giving orders and drilling them in preparation for the final battle that he said would take place in the far north. A man of stature carrying an iron pike led each battalion and all wore swords strapped to their sides. They looked formidable and Gertrude couldn't imagine how Maeve could possibly defeat them.

It had been a cold and nasty couple of days of travel and Gertrude was ready to drop. She hated the weather and the fighting and the cruelty she had witnessed from Brandubh's troops. Brandubh himself had not been involved in the killing but it was his orders that sent the Wildmen and others out to kill and plunder in the small villages they had passed by. Pryderi, John and Brandubh had headed out together on more than one occasion, leaving her to fend for herself. It frightened her to be left alone with the Wildmen, but they ignored her, going into the forest to hunt or lying around on the ground with their huge ugly beasts.

After hunting one night the Wildmen had brought back some kind of creature that looked like an upright ape. They had put a collar around its neck, dragging it along with them as they traveled north. They gave it no food or water. One evening when Gertrude happened to walk by and glance its way she noticed that there was intelligence behind the dark eyes. When she spoke to Brandubh about it he told her that, yes, the Amuigh were sentient, but if the men needed food they would kill it just as easily as anything else.

It took two more nights for Gertrude to summon her courage, leaving Brandubh asleep and slipping away to release it. The look in its eyes before it lumbered into the trees was enough for Gertrude to know she'd done the right thing. The next morning there was great consternation about what had happened to it, but in the end they decided the creature had merely escaped.

Gertrude had not been able to penetrate beneath Brandubh's shell during their recent time together. Even the nights had not afforded her a chance to feel close to him. When their coupling was over, because that's all it felt like now, he turned away and fell asleep. She thought about the comment he had made, that she might be carrying his child and wondered if it could be true. She was over forty and the possibility worried her. She had not bled since being in this horrible place. But then again she could be in menopause for all she knew. Her body had changed, her feminine curves gone, breasts sagging and hipbones jutting—not that it stopped Brandubh from his nightly rutting. Lying under him felt so impersonal now.

Adair had appeared the day before, arriving without preamble. She had stopped in their various camps once or twice before to confer with her son, but this time it seemed she planned to stay. Her hateful glances had Gertrude moving far from the fire, hoping the woman wouldn't bother her. Several times in the past weeks Adair had done something to her that had Gertrude feeling like she had the flu, with absolutely no energy. Every time it happened it seemed to take longer to recover. It only occurred if she let the woman come too close—it seemed connected with her breath. The last time she'd thought the woman was being friendly, her hand on Gertrude's shoulder, a sweet smile on her face, but when Gertrude began to feel ill and the woman seemed to age backward, Gertrude realized that something was up. But by that time it was too late. She remembered crumpling to the ground, Brandubh's harsh laugh and Adair's cackle in the background. It had taken her nearly a week to recover that time and she noticed Brandubh's irritated looks as she fought to keep up as they traveled, barely able to get on and off her horse. It had even affected his desire for her. He had yelled that she needed to clean herself up, to eat more—she was getting too thin which made her look old.

From her place away from the fire she watched Adair speaking with her son, asking him why he was keeping the woman around...she assumed Adair was referring to her.

"You are a man of the cloth. Celibacy is part of the vows you took."

"You must be kidding, Mother. Do you think I give a damn about that? I will do as I please."

"She's nothing but a whore!"

"At least whores get paid for their services," Gertrude said, walking toward them.

Adair and Brandubh both turned. "Your payment is allowing you to live," Brandubh answered, his dark eyes trained on her. He turned back to Adair. "I've noticed that you've retained your youth over these past weeks. Don't tell me you haven't enjoyed what she has to offer."

Gertrude backed slowly away as Brandubh and Adair glared at each other. So her suspicians were true—the woman was sucking energy from her.

"You will not speak to me in that tone!" Adair yelled. "I'm the one with the power here—you've been castrated by Morrighan. No wonder you have to rut every night to prove you're a man. We had a good thing going—if you hadn't abused Morrighan's generosity this would never have happened!"

"I didn't abuse anything. It was you who convinced me to use the crows, you who insisted we burn the village and kill all those people, you who used your connections with the underworld to bring back the Oillteil—and for what? How much money have we netted from the gold and silver we've managed to extract? Wasn't it you who insisted that we could be rich beyond our wildest dreams—enough to have power over things outside this world, you said. Well, where are we now? From my calculations the people you contacted 'out there' have backed away, afraid of where the gold is coming from. They think you're a crook, Mother!"

Gertrude watched in mounting nervousness as the two of them faced off.

"You've been mismanaging things since Milltown and I blame it on your ridiculous infatuation with this woman. My contacts do not think I'm a criminal—they are merely waiting. And I should never have allowed you to bring in those outsiders. It was my magic that broke the defenses here, allowing them in—and now I wish I had never seen their faces. They are desecrating the tenets of the church."

"Oh Mother, would you get off it. As though a sorceress like you gives a shit about the tenets of the church. You are a hypocrite and I have a mind to prevent you from any more of your youth-enhancing magic." He glanced toward Gertrude. "Look what you've done to this woman—she's aged ten years because of your insistence on remaining young. Stick to the ones at the settlement. They're younger and can take it. I need a beautiful woman to take to my bed, not one drained and haggard due to your meddling."

"You can scream at me as much as you wish—it does not change the fact that you are impotent now, less than a man." Adair turned, walking away to speak with Pryderi who was watching the proceedings from under the trees.

Gertrude felt Brandubh's rage and frustration as though it was her own. In a way she felt sorry for him, but even if he hadn't initiated things he had gone along with everything his mother put before him—he was equally responsible for what was happening here. She thought about their time together in Milltown, wishing he were still the consummate gentleman, the priest who was 'sorely tempted' as he put it. Instead he was cruel with no love inside him to give.

The days passed wearily by. Brandubh spent a lot of time with John and Pryderi, only joining Gertrude at night to release his frustrations. Adair did her own thing, disappearing for hours, only to appear looking more youthful than when she left. It was as though she visited some fountain of youth every day. Since Brandubh's accusations the sorceress had not approached Gertrude.

Adair participated in the drawn out conversations with the men every evening and a few days back Gertrude had overheard some story about Brandubh, Pryderi and John almost catching Maeve, and then something about Maeve being able to walk on water. The entire episode sounded made up and she was afraid to question Brandubh about it later because of his mood. There was frustration among the men due to sabotage that had been discovered at several local mines. Also John had gone out on some wild goose chase the day before, insisting he saw Maeve again in the forest, but when the men joined him they found nothing. Gertrude wondered if Maeve was really close by or if it was some magical conjuring done by Maeve's champions. Obviously Brandubh had not succeeded in getting her to leave the Otherworld.

The memory of that meeting with Maeve still plagued her—the way the younger woman had scrutinized Gertrude, worry lines creasing her wide brow. Gertrude hadn't looked into a mirror in a long while—she knew she'd dropped a lot of weight, that her hair was a rat's nest. But the main thing was the shame she felt for what she'd done. Maybe the deprivation was lessening the grip of whatever bewitchment she was under.

Maeve seemed thinner too, but there was something about her...a glow that seemed to shine from her eyes. Brandubh had been awful to both of them, trying to convince Maeve that Gertrude was a traitor. Maybe she had been back then, but now all she wanted was to get out of this horrible place and home to her warm apartment and her cat. After Pryderi and John had lassoed the woman like some kind of beast and dragged her off, Gertrude had questioned Brandubh—what would they do with her? Would they really let her leave this place? He stared at her without answering and then told her to shut up—it was none of her business what they planned. Her only job was to fulfill her nightly duties in his bed.

Today the Wildmen and their beasts had managed to catch a couple of very thin rabbits, one of which had been eaten by the wild dogs before they got it away from them. The other one Brandubh had skinned, placing the carcass on a spit over the fire. The smell was making Gertrude's mouth water, it had been a long time since she had eaten meat and her body craved it.

They shared the meager rabbit with the others, extending the meal with some nuts Gertrude had managed to gather from the hazelnut and walnut trees that grew around the area. Some cheese, bread and homemade beer was produced, looted from the last village they had ransacked. There wasn't much conversation and after the meal the Wildmen went off to wrap themselves in their blankets surrounded with the beasts to keep them warm. It was a good thing they were downwind because the dogs stank like dead animal. Gertrude was sure they had rolled in something. The Oillteil and the villagers headed off as well, bedding down in separate areas.

Gertrude glanced at Brandubh who was picking his teeth with a toothpick he had whittled out of a twig. John sat next to him, leering at her, his teeth yellowish in the gloom. Adair sat across from them, her gaze focused on her son. She was dressed in black, her low-cut dress managing to show off some cleavage that she had recently acquired. Tonight she seemed quite young, somewhere between thirty and forty. Some of the men were giving her furtive glances their expressions salacious. Gertrude almost laughed trying to imagine what would happen if one of them put the moves on her—it would not be a pretty sight. In the distance she could see Pryderi. He seemed to be communicating with someone but there was no one there that she could see. A minute later he loped off into the trees.

"How many more days of travel before we get to the north?" Gertrude asked, glancing at Brandubh.

Brandubh looked up. "The main battle is already in full swing and our troops are winning," he answered, glancing toward his mother. "It's three days from here but before that we need to find food. These Oillteil are pigs, they eat everything in sight. Tomorrow we raid the villages across the river—besides food, I need to recruit more men." His eyes glittered in the firelight.

"I'll come with you," Adair offered. "You never know when my services might come in handy."

Brandubh stared her way. "I know exactly why you want to join us, Mother. As far as your help, I doubt that we'll need it with Pryderi along."

Gertrude had witnessed firsthand what 'recruit' meant to Brandubh. She waited for the exchange with his mother to end and then whispered, "If you're winning why do you need more men?"

Brandubh smirked, his gaze going to John. "Everyone has not yet come out of the woodwork. We need to be prepared."

"And from my understanding you've had some defections, have you not?" Adair stared at her son, a small smile hovering around her full rosy mouth. She turned her shoulders girlishly letting the dress slip lower and drawing more stares from the men at the other end of the fire.

Brandubh frowned. "It's to be expected. Not every man, woman and child is going to choose our way."

"What about the women and children, Brandubh—what will you do with them?" Gertrude asked.

"What about them? If they get in the way they'll be killed."

"The undevout need to be culled. If they cannot be convert-ed they are of no use to anyone," John added.

Gertrude was surprised. John seemed to honestly believe he was on some religious crusade, doing God's work. She had tried to talk to Brandubh about this—that killing the women and children was unnecessary, reasoning that they would become his followers if he took care of them. But he told her in no uncertain terms to keep her opinions to herself, that he was the one in charge.

"I tend to agree with John," Adair said. "It does no good to argue with them."

"I never argue," Brandubh said.

John seemed particularly adept at taking over for him. Gertrude had witnessed his cruel methods firsthand. Maybe his religious fervor was blinding him to what he was actually doing or maybe he was a psychopath. Possibly Brandubh was as well. She couldn't imagine anyone getting that much pleasure out of something so horrible. The one time she tried to intervene, John had turned the knife on her and she had known that he wouldn't hesitate. When the slaughter was over and the poor people lay bleeding and dead she had retched and retched until there was nothing coming up but bile. Afterward when she lay weak and exhausted on the ground, John had walked by. "Don't worry, they were all heathens," he had said, looking down on her with a satisfied smile.

Gertrude had lost any remaining attraction to Brandubh. Just the nasty way he spoke to her was enough, not to mention the killing that the others were doing in his name, and also how he had all the Wildmen and villagers bowing down to him each morning as he said prayers for them. She found him utterly loathsome and sincerely hoped he wouldn't approach her tonight. It didn't really matter who was doing the killing, it was still Brandubh who was ordering it. She had hoped that his inability to inflict pain might have made him think more about what he was doing, but obviously it hadn't. Adair's arrival seemed to have heralded some new, even viler attitude.

When Pryderi arrived back at the fire, there was a lull in the conversation. Gertrude watched him sit down next to Adair, his eyes on her décolletage. When Adair turned toward him with a flirtatious smile Gertrude's mouth opened in surprise.

"Mother, what are you doing?" Brandubh asked.

"Why nothing, dear. Why do you ask?"

Brandubh abruptly stood, leaving the fire to wander toward the trees. Gertrude rose as well, unable to stomach what was going on. She stayed far from Brandubh, following a small deer path that led to the edge of the forest. When she turned back, Adair and Pryderi were hand in hand walking in the other direction.

That night Brandubh did come to her, but this time she was not welcoming and told him she wanted nothing more to do with him. His face turned ugly.

"This is the only thing I ask of you, Gertrude. It helps me let go of all the other worries and dealing with these stupid Oillteil and Wildmen. If you can't allow me my pleasure then I have no other use for you. For god's sake, you should be happy I still want to—you look like a filthy slut with your dirty hair, tattered clothes and wasted body. What happened to all your enticing curves?"

Before she could stop them, tears filled her eyes. He had made her into this—he and his mother. He wasn't talking about leaving her behind, he was talking about killing her. And she knew just the person he would choose to do the dirty work for him. She tried to wipe the tears away but they just kept coming. "Why are you like this now? When we first got together I felt...I thought there was a connection between us."

"I don't know what you expect, woman. I only brought you along so that I could lie with you. I told you right at the beginning that I was planning on using you. Didn't you hear me? I gave you that necklace in payment for your services. Shall I take it back now?"

When he reached for the necklace, Gertrude pulled away, making him laugh. "If you imagined some great love affair then I'm sorry for you. Your services have been paid for in advance. I would imagine that necklace is worth a lot more than what you have to offer, especially now." He looked down at her with a sneer. "If you want to be warm you will let me in your bed, otherwise you can sleep without a sheepskin." He picked up the cover she had been using and wadded it up to take with him.

"What choice are you giving me?"

He crouched down next to her, staring at her with an expression that froze the blood in her veins. Her body and mind recoiled as she watched him slip his boots off and lie down. "Now that's better, isn't it?" he asked, pressing against her.

The sour smell of his breath assaulted her as he leaned close and began to fumble and pull at her clothes. She struggled away from him but he held her firmly with one large hand as his rough knuckles raked across her body. "The alternative is a lot worse," he growled. When he was finished he turned away, immediately falling asleep and leaving her alone and sickened by this new reality.

She dressed and went to huddle next to the fire trying to warm up her shivering body. The past weeks whirled through her mind—her denial of reality, insisting that this man actually loved her, making excuses for his unforgivable behavior. How could she have kept the truth from herself for so long? There would be no sleep for her this night.

As the cold gray days passed by Gertrude felt more and more revolted by Brandubh and his men and their brutal and sadistic ways. Adair was no better, giving directions and lording it over everyone. Pryderi and she seemed to have become an item, as long as she sipped from the fountain of youth, that is. There was one day when she hadn't found a victim to suck dry and had returned to camp old and haggard. Pryderi had taken one look at her and then disappeared until the following evening.

Maybe when they got to the north she could find Maeve and the others, or slip into the Caer Sidi where she might find some protection. She would never find her way out of here on her own. Early on she'd hoped that through their physical intimacy he would open up to her, share his inner demons. Clearly he'd had a difficult childhood, as evidenced by Adair. What had happened to the man's father? It was too late now for these pointless meanderings. It was time to escape this place before she ended up dead.

Brandubh, Adair and John dismounted. Gertrude watched them untack the horses and turn them loose. They had been riding since daybreak, and it was time for a rest. Her mind was on alert, her nerves frazzled from hunger, lack of sleep and fear. Something had changed since the last camp and whatever it was had everyone rattled. Even Adair had been silent during the long trip.

"Too bad we didn't think of this earlier, we could have eaten them," John remarked, watching the horses trot off into the trees.

Gertrude slid off her horse and removed the saddle and bridle. Maybe now the poor thing could forage for food. The mare trotted after the other horses making Gertrude suddenly aware that they would be continuing this trip on foot. Every day she saw more troops heading down the valley. How could she escape without her horse? Because that was exactly what she planned to do. She couldn't stand one more night of Brandubh's abuse.

"Don't worry, John. Pryderi's magic and our dams will bring more animals into the open trying to find water. We're getting closer to the great forest where the aurochs and deer live. We'll have plenty of meat soon enough. Mother, you can handle Cernunnos, can't you? Better get yourself some young energy before we come upon him, you're looking a bit haggard." Brandubh laughed in a bitter way, turning back to John. "Right now we need to find that witch before her powers are solidified."

"What do you mean, 'solidified'? I thought she was the Willow, the one in the prophecy."

"Do not speak that word in my presence!" Brandubh bellowed. "There is no such thing as prophecy—it's blasphemy. She is only a witch like my sister and I'm stronger than both of them."

"So glad to hear you speaking as a priest again," Adair said, coming to place her hand on Brandubh's arm. "You may have lost your power but I am stronger than both you and my daughter. Catriona has succumbed to love, which diminishes her ability to see. Just think how much the two of you together could have achieved—your power would have been unstoppable! This child, Maeve, is a different case—I must admit she has some strengths but ultimately she will lose this battle as surely as I'm standing here."

"But how does she keep escaping?" John asked, his glance going from mother to son.

Brandubh's face turned scarlet. He didn't speak as he went over to John and grabbed him roughly by the shoulder. His arm came back and he closed his hand into a fist, working to get himself under control. "Maybe I will allow you to do it, John. You lust for blood, don't you? How would you like to see her die? Slowly? Or with a stab to the heart with that sword you have hanging there? Think about it, plan it, imagine it in your mind until you feel like you've already done the deed." He turned away as Pryderi emerged out of the trees.

Gertrude was now aware that it was Pryderi's dark magic that held the water back, not just the dams Brandubh's men had built. He and Adair conferred for hours now, their heads close together. At night they disappeared, his arm around her tiny waist. She knew that Brandubh was furious about what was going on between the two of them but there was nothing he could do. Pryderi seemed to bask in Brandubh's discomfort, making it very obvious in front of the other men what his intentions were. For her part Adair reveled in the demi-god's advances, her girlish laughter making Gertrude almost physically sick. Gertrude wondered where she was going during the day to maintain her gloss of brown hair, her rosy cheeks and full lips. Even the clothes she wore had changed, the dour suits replaced with velvet and silk, with lowcut laced up bodices. The idea of young vibrant women being drained and probably dying from this woman's craving for youth was appalling.

Sometimes Gertrude would notice Pryderi staring at her with his expressionless cold eyes. He could send her to her death with a flick of his hand; she had seen him do it to Oillteil, Wildmen and villagers who dared to disagree with him. But somehow he couldn't kill Maeve, or so it seemed from what she had witnessed so far.

Pryderi let a few minutes go by before he walked over to Brandubh and whispered something in his ear. "Come on, John!" Brandubh called over his shoulder a moment later.

"What about me?" Adair called.

"You too, Mother."

Gertrude stayed back as Adair and the three men headed toward the bridge. Oillteil and Wildmen cowered behind them glancing furtively toward John. Lately John had been taking his anger out on the Oillteil and Wildmen, beating them for no reason that she could see. And Brandubh thought it was funny, egging him on and clapping. It was a wonder they hadn't all deserted by now.

A yell brought her attention to the bridge—it seemed to be collapsing under their feet. At the same time there was an earth tremor that shook the ground so hard she couldn't keep her balance, landing on the ground just in time to see Brandubh and the others splash into the river, their screams of rage splitting the silence. In the mayhem she couldn't spot Pryderi—he must have jumped free. It was hard to imagine the demi-god succumbing to such humiliation. When the rest of the bridge collapsed, sending splintering wood flying in all directions shrieks filled the air as Brandubh and John and the others struggled with the ice and freezing water. Only their heads were visible now as broken chunks of ice hit them, carried by the released water that pushed wildly downstream.

"Use your magic, Pryderi!" Brandubh screamed. But there was no response.

Gertrude moved closer, crawling on her hands and knees trying to spot Adair. Her heart skipped a beat when she saw the youthful-looking woman standing on the other side of the bridge. Adair was watching her son and the others being carried away. When she turned her head, Gertrude followed her gaze. Pryderi was up the hill away from the river, his focus on Adair. A second later they both disappeared.

The few who had been left on shore ran along the riverbank trying to help, but to no avail. Brandubh's dark garments rose like sodden bird wings before they rounded a bend and were gone from sight. Gertrude began to laugh, all the pent up emotions rising to the surface in a rush. A few of the villagers stared at her with dark looks but no one bothered her as tears rolled down her face.

She finally got up and made her way into the shelter of the trees. As she watched the skinny horses searching for something to eat she felt a wave of sadness. They had been ridden too hard and not fed and now they were barely able to hold their heads up. She thought about the killing she had witnessed. How could she have gone along with this? She had chosen to ignore her psychic visions and the cards that pointed out the darkness inside this man. All the evil acts she had condoned came rushing back in a wave and she bent over to throw up. Her insides heaved, thoughts rushing by with dizzying speed—images of their coupling, the priest's leering face as John handled the killing at the villages, the Oillteil bowing down to him, Morrighan's pronouncement. All of it came up and out as she retched and retched. Afterward she lay on the ground, dizzy and unable to move. It was as though she had just awakened from a dark and horrible nightmare.

Chapter

24

It was dark by the time Alex reached Bailemuir. He had worked himself into a fever pitch with all sorts of strange scenarios. All he wanted was a beer. He pulled up to the curb and got out, heading across the street to his friend Calum's pub. He went through the door, bombarded with the noise of conversation, music from a fiddle group in the back and the calling of orders to the kitchen. It felt like home. He went up to the bar and ordered his favorite ale on tap, John Smith, savoring the creamy flavor so lacking in American beers. It was the way they were pulled here that did it, with a hand pump without pressure. He didn't feel even a twinge of guilt at going off the wagon as he sat there with his pint.

"Alex, could that be ye?" came a booming voice from the other side of the wide bar.

"Calum, my man! Good to see you!" he said, reaching across the bar and clasping the older man's meaty hand.

"Hey, I met that friend of yours, what's his name? Goes with your daughter, Maeve."

"Harold? He was here?"

"Aye, the day he arrived."

"That's why I'm here, Calum. Maeve and Harold were due back to the States on the eighth and I haven't heard a word from them."

"Canna help ye there. I havna laid eyes on 'em." He turned away to help a customer and then turned back to Alex. "Make time for a chat, will ye? 'Tis way too many years."

"I will, you can count on it. Right now I better go see Rose or she'll be in bed."

"With ye arrivin? She'd stay up all night for ye, Alex."

Alex finished his beer and put some coins on the counter. "See you soon," he called over his shoulder.

The door opened before Alex had even knocked. "Alex! You're finally here!" Rose hugged him, tears spilling from her eyes.

"Mother, please don't cry. Everything is going to be all right."

"I'm nae cryin' about that, dear boy. I'm cryin' with joy at seein' ye again. Come in out of the cold. Ye can sleep in your old room at the top of the stairs if ye like. I'll just go and put the kettle on." She left him standing in the hall and disappeared. He set his suitcase on the floor and followed her.

"Don't make a fuss, Mother. It's late and I know you're tired." Alex was shocked by the changes he saw in Rose. Her hair was thinning, her cheeks gaunt. Her eyes had lost the sparkle he remembered.

"It's nae trouble," she said, bustling around the kitchen. "Would ye like some biscuits with your tea or something more substantial? I have some cheese or I could cook up something."

"Biscuits are fine. I stopped in at the pub for a beer on my way in and it filled me up."

"Ach, Alex…I thought ye were in AA!"

"It's okay mother, I just had a pint."

She looked at him worriedly and then turned to pour hot water into the teapot and put it on a tray. "Can ye reach the cups? They're right there in the cupboard."

He knew where they were, in the same place as the last time he had been in this house over twenty years ago. He lifted two of them off their hooks, located the saucers and followed his mother into the other room. As they sat down together in the dimly lit cold room, Alex asked, "So tell me mother, when was the last time you spoke to Maeve or Finna?"

The next morning Alex woke early, his stomach churning with anxiety. Jet lag combined with anticipation had interfered with his sleep and he did not feel rested. He snuck down the steep stairs hoping to have tea alone but when he opened the door to the kitchen Rose was already there.

"Good mornin'! I've made tea and there are some muffins toastin'. Are ye still partial to marmalade?"

"Yes, Mother, and thanks." Alex sat down on a wooden chair by the small kitchen table. "You're up early, aren't you?

"I dinna sleep much these days, I guess 'tis old age. I'm usually up by first light. I was hopin' ye could sleep in, ye look so tired, dear."

"I guess it's the jet lag. I'll be all right after a couple of days. I need to drive out to the cottage this morning. Have you contacted the police?"

"Nae, I thought I would wait for ye. Ye ken how Finna goes places sometimes—I havna been back since the day I called ye. Maybe they've returned," she added hopefully, gazing at Alex.

"The fact that they didn't take their scheduled flight home and didn't contact me is what worries me. I can understand if they wanted to stay a little longer, but Harold has a phone that supposedly works in Europe, so why didn't he call?"

"That I canna tell ye. Can I come along to the cottage?"

"Of course. Can you be ready in half an hour?"

The day was cold and threatening snow and they were glad of the car heater, which was working overtime. Alex left the rental in the middle of the drive, staring in surprise at all the cars parked there. He recognized the mini that had belonged to Finna's father from years ago, but the others looked like rentals. When he and Rose went around the side of the cottage to the front door, Alex remembered the last time he had been here. All the emotions rose to the surface, making him want to cry. That was the last time he had seen Finna.

He tried the door, finding it unlocked and he and his mother went inside. Not much had changed in the twenty some years since he had been here. She still didn't have electricity, using oil lamps instead. She was a stubborn one, his Finna. Oh my god, he couldn't believe the emotions that were churning around inside him. He could barely breathe as his buried feelings surfaced.

"Nothing has been changed since I was here, Alex," his mother stated, startling him out of his reverie.

Alex took a look around, noticing Harold's guitar lying by the fireplace. A pile of clothes were also on the floor and it looked as though someone had bedded down here, he thought, noticing the comforter and blanket. He examined the clothes, noticing a fancy red velvet dress that had been torn and muddied. He picked it up. "What's this, do you think?" he asked his mother.

"Looks like some ceremonial garment that Finna or her mother made. They get dressed up at the winter solstice." Rose came over and examined the ripped and muddy hem, the uneven strips missing from the bottom of the dress. "It looks like it's been through a war."

348

"I know. I wonder how it got this way."

"This is new since I was here last," Alex observed, walking toward the open door on the other side of the fireplace.

"She added it a number o' years ago," Rose answered, following him into the room.

"This is obviously where Maeve stayed. Her clothes are all here." Alex walked around the room, picking up different objects that were familiar to him. The candle holder that he remembered from the house in town, the antique mirror and brush and comb set Finna had gotten from Angus, the antique table that held the water pitcher and bowl that he and Finna had purchased together. "Why would she leave all her clothes behind?"

"I've been wondering that myself. Alex, I hate to bring this up since I ken how ye feel about it, but.... do ye think 'tis possible they went into the Otherworld?"

"That's not a real place."

Rose caught his eye, not speaking for a minute. Finally she said, "I didna believe in it either, but...over the years... Finna has told me too many stories...things that couldna be explained."

"But I thought we agreed that she just made the place up to explain her own weird behavior—like kicking me out for instance." Alex did not want to revisit this. It had been painful enough at the time.

"Alex..." his mother began.

"I don't want to talk about this, there has to be a rational explanation about where they are. What did you say about this wild dog or something? I think we need to get the police out here to do a search."

"Ye may be right. I suppose we should start with that, but..."

"No buts, mother, let's go into town and get the police."

By mid-afternoon the police had conducted a thorough
search of the surrounding area and found nothing to suggest
foul play or any other clues as to where Harold, Finna and
Maeve could be. All they could say about the disarray in the cottage was that it looked like someone had left in a hurry. They
told Alex and Rose that there had been a large party outside
the cottage fairly recently and remnants of a bonfire. They also
observed many animal tracks but assumed these had been made
more recently. As far as the wild beast went, there had been no
more reports of anything and they had never found the animal.
They were as confused about the cars as Alex, and suggested he
call the companies to find out exactly who had rented them.

Alex and Rose drove back to town and Alex left his mother
at home, heading to the pub for dinner and a beer. Screw AA.
He wasn't going to miss out on this special Scottish ale, the
non-alcoholic ones just did not taste the same. And besides, he
needed something to calm his nerves. It was too late to call the
car rental companies and he was anxious to find out as much
as he could from Calum about the past twenty years and what
Finna had been up to. He told himself he hoped to glean some
information that might help locate his lost daughter and of
course that was true, but there was definitely something more
working in him.

He and Calum sat together in a booth, catching up. Calum
had not seen Finna much over the years and said that she stayed
to herself, not even coming to town very often. Ned made sure
to come to the pub when he was there for a visit, and always
filled Calum in on what Alex was up to. Alex felt frustrated by
the lack of information about Finna, asking Calum if there was
anyone else in town who might know what had happened to his
wife, daughter and her boyfriend. Calum thought for a minute
or two and then shook his head. His only suggestion was Ned's
family, since Ned always visited Finna when he was in Scotland.

Alex was surprised to hear this since Ned never mentioned anything to do with Finna.

Alex walked home lost in a fog of frustration. He had spent two hours talking with Calum and was no closer to finding Maeve then the day before. It was late and he was exhausted and depressed, not to mention a little bit drunk. He got to Rose's cottage and tried the door, finding it locked. Damn it--why hadn't she left the door open for him? He really didn't want to wake her. He walked around the side, heading toward the back door. He found a window unlatched and pushed it open and crawled through, trying not to make too much noise. He crept up the stairs to his room and fell on the bed, falling asleep in his clothes.

Rose woke him around 10:00 a.m. with the news that she was going to church. He was surprised to realize it was Sunday. His head was pounding and after Rose left he went to take a shower. When she arrived home around noon he was just finishing his second pot of tea.

"Mother, I'm going to go stay at the cottage," he announced as she came into the kitchen.

Rose took off her hat, gazing at him in surprise. "Why Alex? What good will that do? I won't see ye if you're there."

"I just think I might be able to figure something out if I'm there—maybe someone will come back."

"No one has been there in over two weeks. I'm going to say it again whether ye like it or not, I think they're in the Otherworld, there's just no other explanation for their disappearance."

"Why do you keep talking about that? What has Finna told you anyway?"

Rose poured herself a cup of tea from the pot on the table. "She hasna said anything directly—just stories she's alluded to a number of times over the years. Catriona lives in the Otherworld."

"Oh for Christ's sake, Mother—that's ridiculous!"

"Alex, do not blaspheme." Rose turned away from him and began to take things from the refrigerator for lunch.

"What exactly has she said?"

Rose turned from where she was preparing sandwiches. "Finna gave birth to your daughter there. That I believe because she appeared out of nowhere when Maeve was just a wee thing. Ye havna memory of that?"

Alex looked at his mother, surprised by the vehemence in her voice. "I guess so but…I always just assumed…I don't know what I assumed. I think I just put it out of my mind."

"That's exactly right. Ye have a blind spot when it comes to this. Ye've somehow managed to push all of it out of your mind. Finna tried many times to talk with ye. If ye hadn't been so stubborn ye'd still be together."

Tears filled his eyes. Jesus, was this true? He put his head in his hands feeling an overwhelming sadness. Finna was his first real love, the mother of his only child. His only true love, he thought as he sat there. Where the hell were they? And how was he going to find them?

"I'm sorry, dear boy, I didna mean to upset ye," Rose said, coming over and placing her hands on his hunched shoulders. "By the way, did Father McDuff ever visit ye?"

"What do you know about him?"

"He was the priest at the church in town for a number o' years. I was sorry when he left. He was my confessor for the time he was there—a wonderful listener as well as a good speaker. I always liked his sermons. I ran into him in town a few months back and he told me he was takin' a short trip to New England. I told him I finally had your address. He said he wanted to look up Maeve for me, try to talk her into visitin' her grandmother."

Alex shook his head. "You have no idea what you've done, Mother. He came by and asked for Maeve's address. Brandon

McDuff is not a good man. How much did you tell him in the confession box?"

"Well, everything, Alex. He's a priest. I told him all about the sadness in my heart about ye and Finna. I told him about my granddaughter bein' so far away. I told him my misgivings and feelings of guilt about your departure from where ye belong. He was by here just recently and brought me a present. I'll just get it." She disappeared into the other room, coming back with something in her hand. "I canna imagine where he got it and I think it might be valuable." In her palm was a small gold nugget.

Alex decided to go back to Finna's cottage one more time before he tried to figure out how to get to the Otherworld. He thought there might be some clue, a map or something to point him in the right direction. He couldn't believe that he was starting to take this stuff seriously.

He parked his car in the same place as before, noting that the other three cars had not been moved. As he walked around the side of the house the smell of the fresh sea air thrust him into the past. It was a memory from when Maeve was a baby and he and Finna had decided to work on their relationship. He sighed as he recalled Finna radiant with motherhood. It had been good for a while, their love for the child overcoming most of their differences.

He looked out at the flat expanse of dark water. It was rough today, waves booming as they hit the beach. The weather was unusually cold and nasty for the time of year, everyone in town was complaining about it. When he came to the door, the smell of burning wood reached his nostrils. Looking up he saw a thin line of smoke coming out of the chimney. His heart leapt into his throat as many thoughts flew through his mind all at once. Who was here? Was it Maeve? Finna? Or was it some stranger that found the cottage, maybe the same person that killed that woman? He opened the door, tentatively looking around.

"Hello?" he called. "Anyone here?" There was no answer. He stood on the threshold, letting his eyes adjust to the dark room. That's when he saw the form in the bed. He closed the door quietly and tiptoed over and looked down. The face was turned away but chestnut hair threaded with strands of gray lay across the pillow.

"Finna?" he asked, in a strangled voice.

She turned her head toward him and opened her eyes. "Who are ye?" she asked in a raspy voice.

"Finna! It *is* you! What's happened? Are you sick?"

"Alex?"

"Yes, I'm here." He sat down on the bed next to her, picking up her hand. Her skin was hot. "You have a fever."

Finna closed her eyes and seemed to fall asleep.

"Finna!" he called, shaking her. When she didn't respond he felt her brow. She was burning up. He wasn't sure what to do, whether he should take her to the doctor in town or just let her rest. Then he remembered it was a Sunday. Nothing was open now. He also remembered Finna's attitude about doctors in the past, how she disliked going, didn't trust their methods and treated herself with herbal remedies, roots and teas. What could he do to bring down her fever? He ran out to the car and got the bottle of aspirin he had stashed in the glove compartment, and rushed back. He went to the sink, pumped water into a glass and then came back to the bed. He placed his arm under her upper back. "Finna you need to swallow these."

When her eyes opened they were unfocused and glittering.

"You need to take this aspirin to get your fever down."

She placed them obediently on her tongue and he held the water glass to her lips. After she swallowed the pills she fell immediately into a deep sleep. Alex looked down at her pale thin face, frantic about what to do. He finally decided to wait until the aspirin had a chance to work and then if she wasn't better he would take her to the doctor first thing in the morning. He went over to the fire and added a couple of logs and then went outside to chop more wood. The cottage felt cold.

He heard her coughing when he came back with an armload of wood. She had a lot of mucous in her lungs. He put the load of wood down and went to her, held her up while she coughed and then rolled her onto her side so that she could breathe a little easier, leaving her there while he made tea: ginger and angelica leaves with honey, something he remembered from their years together. He waited until her breathing had become less noisy and then brought the tea over.

"Finna? Can you drink a little tea?"

She opened her eyes and looked at him. "Alex? I thought I was dreamin'."

"I made you tea. I think it might help." He helped her take a few sips before she closed her eyes again.

She was still asleep when night fell but her breathing seemed easier. She hadn't had a coughing fit for an hour or so. Alex found some cheese and bread in the pantry and sat down in the chair in front of the fire. When he was finished he went into the kitchen and rinsed his dishes, putting everything neatly away. When he went to check on Finna he realized she was shivering so hard that her teeth were chattering. Maybe the aspirin had worn off. He looked around for an extra blanket and then thought that his body heat would probably help her more than anything else. He climbed into the bed and wrapped his arms around her.

Alex woke with a start, unsure where he was until he felt the familiar body next to him. They lay as they had in the past with his knees bent behind hers, his arms around her and her head resting next to his on the pillow. She was sleeping quietly, breathing normally. He placed his hand on her forehead. Her temperature was down. He extricated himself, being careful not to wake her and went into the kitchen. He got water ready for tea, waiting for it to boil as he stared out the small square window over the sink. The view was so familiar, the sloping hill down to the beach, dark stone of the mountains to the right, green hills to the left. It felt so normal to be here after all these years. As the water began to boil he heard Finna begin to stir.

"Alex?" she called, sitting up.

"I'm just making tea, love, stay where you are."

He got the cups and poured boiling water over the fragrant leaves in the teapot. He remembered that teapot. His mother had given it to them when he and Finna got married. He carried two cups to the bed and sat down next to her. "It's ginger and angelica again. I thought that might help with whatever you have."

"Thanks," she said taking the cup and placing her hands around it. "I don't have much memory of anything, when did ye get here?"

"Yesterday. I found you pretty much delirious. But I think your fever finally broke."

"I do feel better. I don't even remember how I got here. In my last memory I was with my mother on horseback."

"In the Otherworld?"

Finna looked surprised. "I thought ye didn't believe in the Otherworld."

"I guess I do now, after everything that's happened. Rose convinced me and there just wasn't any other explanation for where all of you had gone."

Finna sipped her tea.

Alex noticed her furtive glances toward him, realizing how much he must have changed. He was heavier, his hair had gone gray and he had a beard, not to mention the extra lines in his face. He watched her eyes for any reaction but they looked luminous and without guile, despite the dark circles beneath. His heart did a funny little somersault.

"I still canna believe you're here, Alex."

"I had to come. Maeve and Harold were supposed to get back on the eighth and when they didn't show up and didn't contact me I kind of panicked. And let me tell you, when I found your cottage abandoned...well...that just about did me in. I was really happy to find you here this time, even though you're sick. How long have you been here?"

"I don't have any idea."

"The fire was going when I came in yesterday so somebody must have made it, but not you?"

"Did I seem like I could have made a fire?"

"No, it's just that...if not you then who?"

"I'm sure my mother brought me here."

"But why didn't she stay? You're really sick."

"I think I need to go back to sleep now," she said, handing him the cup. "If you want to keep me warm again you're welcome," she suggested, her eyes drifting shut.

Alex gazed down at her sleeping face. She looked so much better today, with a bit of color in her cheeks. Damn, he hadn't even had a chance to ask about Maeve and Harold. Oh well, he would question her further when she woke up again. He crawled into the warm bed, snuggling next to her.

Chapter

25

Angry echoing voices rose up from the valley reaching Maeve and her group on the ridge. There was a battle going on down there between the Tuatha De Danann and the Oillteil and Wildmen. Although well armed, the red-haired men were no match for the stronger forces carrying iron axes and swords. From here Maeve had a clear view of Brandubh, John and Pryderi standing on a low hill to the north. She could tell they were calling out orders but their voices were lost in the din from below. Looking down she recoiled from the dark patches on the frozen ground—spilled blood and a lot of it. Bodies lay in various positions of death, made up mostly of men with russet hair. Maeve's hand went to the horn she now kept on her belt. Was it time to summon Cernunnos?

"Maeve, you need to get dry." Harold's voice interrupted her concentration and she realized she was shivering, soaked through from the cold fog. She got up and followed him under the trees to where her grandfather had made a fire. Duncan and the villagers sat on one side and the Crion the other. The

Wildmen and Oillteil hung back under the trees, using their blankets to keep them warm.

"We need to be smart about our next moves," Harold said, as he brought her some dry clothes from her pack.

She got the feeling he wasn't speaking to her, that he had been addressing Eron and the other men. Taking the clothes she went behind a wide tree trunk to change. Harold seemed like a different person, one who had a lot of experience with war. This new unfamiliar side of him had prevented her from sharing her news. Also they had not had even a minute to themselves since they day they met in Bannee. The trip here had been done quietly since there were so many of Brandubh's troops around. Nights had been spent listening to Harold and Eron talk about strategy and subterfuge with the other men. In some ways it had annoyed her, since she considered this to be her fight, but then again, she was impressed by what the men had managed to accomplish without any bloodshed. Since the bridges, they had managed to send a group of Brandubh's Oillteil and Wildmen on several wild goose chases using flutes and other devices. She chuckled, thinking back on the big oafs crashing through the underbrush in pursuit of nothing. It definitely obstructed their plans, leading Brandubh's men wildly off course.

But what was going on below was something else. There was so much death and pain, a situation she'd been trying to avoid. It wasn't just the Sidhe who were dying, it was also Oillteil, Wildmen, villagers and Crion. This was not what the vision in the spring had shown, and it had to be stopped.

When Maeve came back to the fire, Harold was holding forth again in his new voice. She sat down, listening to the conversation.

"Eron, I think we need to break up what's going on down there. Duncan, how about it? With the three of us I'm sure we can create some kind of diversion," Harold said, his eyes bright. He pushed the hair out of his eyes in a gesture Maeve didn't recognize, and then pulled out his sword, checking it for sharpness.

"What about us?" one of the other men chimed in. "We're set to help ye, just tell us what to do."

Harold nodded to the man and then began explaining strategies for diverting the attention of the enemy troops, ways in which they could confuse them and lead them astray by pretending to be their allies. He talked about grabbing the Oillteil and then releasing them, making them see the error of their ways in following Brandubh. As he spoke he gestured with his hands, making squares and other shapes to illustrate his points. At one point he drew in the dirt with a stick.

To Maeve his face looked different, more rugged and older. His voice was deeper. She had a flash of uneasiness as if she didn't know him at all.

"What do *you* think?" Harold asked her abruptly in his new voice. His eyes looked fierce, his brows pulled together in concentration.

She searched his face trying to find the man she knew, but he wasn't there. She tried to think about what he was saying, whether it made any sense and then answered in a neutral tone. "We need to bring these people over to our cause. Without that there is no chance of success. What you're suggesting could help with that, I suppose." Harold seemed to know what he was talking about. And he *was* mentioned in the prophecy. She had to trust him on this.

Shouts rang out and they ran to see what had happened. A fire had been started in the trees on the other side of the valley and smoke was billowing over the valley floor.

"Come on, now is our opportunity—the smoke will obscure the battlefield. They'll think there's an attack coming from the rear." Harold turned to address the men. "You and you," he said, pointing to two of the villagers. "Take a couple of horses and skirt around the back to the other side and make as much noise as you can."

"I'll go with them," Maeve said, whistling to Finiche. When he got up from where he had been resting and padded over, she pulled herself onto his back and thought her intentions.

"Try to make it sound like a large attack is coming from the other side," Harold continued, ignoring Maeve. "The rest of you come with me. We'll hide on either side of that ravine." He pointed to the steep hillside about one hundred yards away leading to the valley floor. "And you Crion, get down to the stragglers at the end of the Oillteil's lines, let them see you through the smoke and then lead them toward where we're hiding. They should be happy to get away from what they perceive is an attack. As soon as they get close enough, Eron and I and the Wildmen will grab 'em. Duncan, do you think you can help?"

"I'll do whatever ye tell me to do." Duncan had changed in the past week, becoming much more robust. His body had straightened significantly and his eyes held a bright excited look. "This is the most fun I've had in years. I love seein' Brandubh's men go down after what they've done."

"Okay. I want you with us. Do not wound or hurt anyone unless it is absolutely necessary. Remember we're trying to draw these people over to our cause," he called out to all within earshot.

Finiche and Maeve and the men on horseback took off, heading south to get around the rear of the battlefield. The Crion headed down the hill at a crouch. Harold and Eron and a few men distributed themselves along the hillside, lying flat to avoid detection. A minute later Maeve and the men began shouting and galloping toward the rear guard. Out of the corner of her eye Maeve saw the Crion sneaking through the smoke and caught the moment when Brandubh's troops saw them. The ploy worked and a second later the Crion men sprinted away and headed toward the hill. As soon as the Oillteil and

Wildmen came abreast of the hiding men, Harold jumped up and yelled, "Now!" and the hillside erupted in shouting and the clash of weapons. The shouting brought others from the valley floor to help and pretty soon there was screaming and shouting and the harsh clash of metal against metal.

As Maeve and Finiche moved away from the valley floor, she realized that the smoke had cleared. Brandubh, John and Pryderi had a clear view of everything that was happening. She watched in rising alarm as Pryderi looked straight at her and raised his hand, directing the wind in swirling light patterns. A few seconds later she was knocked off Finiche and held down on the ground—as though a giant hand was pushing on her back. She gasped to get her breath and then thought about what MacCuill had told her, that she was stronger than the gods and goddesses—she pushed against the wind with all her might. Rising to her knees she caught a glimpse of Eron and Harold running. Duncan was twenty feet or so behind them. They were in clear sight of Brandubh and the others. A sharp stab of fear went through her as she glanced at the hillside behind her.

Harold sprinted toward her. "You're going to get yourself killed!" he cried, helping her to her feet.

Brandubh watched them from under a tree. John had climbed down the hill and was partially across the battlefield, heading her way. Where was Pryderi? He was the one she was most worried about. Wind began to roar and whip, making it almost impossible to move. Harold was knocked off his feet and inched his way closer, trying to shield her from the Oillteil, several of whom were bearing down on them. A moment later an arrow whizzed by Maeve's ear and then Harold was standing next to her with his sword out. He tried to drag Maeve up the hill but as he turned to face the Oillteil, an arrow hit him squarely in the chest.

A roar started from the valley as the rest of Brandubh's men saw what had happened. Oillteil and Wildmen ran toward them. Some held swords, some shot bolts from crossbows as Maeve tried to drag Harold up the hill. She looked for her grandfather but he was not in sight. Harold was unable to stand or walk. The Oillteil were closing the gap and the arrows were too close. Just as she turned to face them, Finiche appeared. It took every bit of her strength to lift Harold onto the wolf's back, laying him across like a sack of meal. She climbed on behind and Finiche took off.

Maeve's fear made her drive the wolf on, beyond the campfire and deep into the forest. The weight he was carrying was too much, she knew, but there was nothing else to do. When Finiche finally came to a stop, Maeve slid off. The wolf was panting, his sides heaving as he tried to catch his breath. When she pulled Harold off the wounded man crumpled to the ground. "Help me, Harold," she cried, trying to drag him over to lean against a tree. He grunted in pain as he tried to walk and then collapsed against the wide trunk of the oak. The arrow was still imbedded in his chest and he was having a hard time breathing. Maeve was unsure whether to remove it or leave it where it was. Very little blood had seeped out so far but she figured that if she tried to pull it out the bleeding would be unstoppable. Her herbal supplies were not close and her healing hands were not up to this kind of wound. She sat next to him, holding his hand. His eyes were closed and his face looked pale as tissue paper. "Harold, can you hear me?"

Harold opened his eyes and looked into hers. "Maeve, I love you," he gasped, his hazel eyes liquid and soft.

She gazed at his familiar face, seeing the effort it took for him to speak. "I love you too, you don't need to talk right now. I just need to figure out how to get this arrow out."

He looked up at her, trying to keep his eyes open as his lids drooped. "Maeve, I'm dying. Leave the arrow where it is. I wish I could help you but I…" His eyes drifted shut.

"Harold!" she called, trying to rouse him.

He opened his eyes again, smiled. "I love you," he declared hoarsely and then closed his eyes.

"Harold? Harold!" She put her ear to his mouth, listening for his breath but all she could hear was the wind in the tops of the trees. "Harold!" she placed her fingers on his neck, searching for the carotid artery, listening for a pulse, but there was no steady beat, nothing but the residual warmth that still flowed through his body.

"No!!" she screamed, "You can't die! I love you! Harold! I'm pregnant! I'm pregnant," she whispered softly, realizing he could no longer hear her. Why hadn't she told him this sooner? Tears streamed down her face. She felt for his pulse but his hand was limp in hers and there was no heartbeat. She sank onto the ground next to him, put her hands over the wound and concentrated on bringing life into him. For a long time she worked at this and then she stopped. Her healing was useless. She rested her head against his chest, her arms around his inert body. She felt him sliding sideways away from the trunk and supported him, letting his body came to rest on the ground. He was slumped over from the waist and she tried to straighten him, *to make him more comfortable,* she thought, and then a keening cry began. She heard it as though from a distance, thinking it sounded like a wounded animal and then realized it was coming from her. She stretched out on her side beside his lifeless body, placing her head on his shoulder.

Hours later Maeve roused herself. She had fallen asleep and had a dream that she and Harold were walking down some dusty road. In the dream she was barefoot and could feel the softness of the dirt between her toes. In between them, holding their hands was a tiny human being, whether a boy or a girl she wasn't sure. The child was just old enough to walk. In the dream she had glanced over at Harold, seeing the love in his eyes, the joy. The sun was warm on the top of her head and she could hear birdsong in the distance; she was filled with happiness. When she woke up she still had the feeling inside her until the reality hit. Her chest felt compressed and heavy with an aching pain. Her throat filled and tears ran down her face.

She sat up and looked down at Harold's lifeless form. His face was utterly pale and his lips had turned blue. She placed her hand on his cheek. It was cold now. Her tears dripped down her face onto his shoulder where they began to freeze. Her heart ached so severely she wondered if she was having some kind of attack. She couldn't think. It was all she could do to draw in one breath after the other, each one more painful than the last. She placed her hand on her chest, trying to soothe the pain, feeling it lessen a little. What was she going to do?

After a while the pain subsided a bit and she got up and walked over to where Finiche lay watching her. He put his big head into her hand and she heard his sorrow expressed without words. She began to cry again, burying her face in his fur. MacCuill's face loomed up in her mind. He hadn't even had the chance to meet Harold. It was so unfair. The only reason Harold had come here at all was to help her. Why couldn't he be safely waiting for her in Bailemuir or back in the States, for that matter? She had basically killed him. The ache in her heart came back as she glanced to where he lay. He looked like he was asleep, except for the arrow sticking out of his chest. She called for MacCuill, it was the only thing she could think to do. She didn't know how or where to bury him and she didn't have the wherewithal to complete the task by herself. She felt like she wanted to die too…*except she was carrying his child.* That started another bout of tears. She sat down next to Harold, again picking up his limp hand, tracing the pale blue veins that ran beneath the skin.

When she looked up a moment later, MacCuill was standing in front of her.

"What has happened?"

"MacCuill, this is Harold. I'm so sorry you didn't meet him when he was still alive." "Did you forget about the spring, Maeve?" he asked, gently.

"What spring? What are you talking about?"

"Airmid's spring, the healing spring."

Maeve was quiet for a moment. Yes, she remembered, there was something about a spring where the dead could be brought back to life. "Where is it?" she asked, trying not to get too excited.

"It's a good distance away from here, on the other side of the Caer Sidi, in the hills behind the forest on the northwestern side of the valley—at least a two or three day trip by horseback."

"Will it be possible? I mean is it possible...so much time will have gone by."

"Yes, it's quite possible, but you need to go soon. The longer he remains in this state the harder it will be to revive him."

"How will we get there? The valley is full of troops. And Eron has gone missing. I hope he isn't hurt. "

"Eron is fine. He's just arrived back at your camp. You have horses, don't you?"

"Yes, Argyll and the one Eron got from the villagers."

"Leave Eron, Duncan and Finiche here with your people. They need looking after. Take Argyll and the other horse. I'll give you directions."

"Won't you come with us?"

MacCuill ignored her question. "Airmid will ask for something. I don't know what. It could be as simple as the moonstone or it could be something you don't have right now, something from the future."

"I don't have the moonstone so I hope she doesn't want that. Whatever it is, I don't care. I just want to save Harold. But you didn't answer my question."

"This task is for you to complete alone. My place is here with Eron. We need to prepare your followers for what is to come. I'll help you carry Harold back to the camp and get him tied onto Argyll's back. You need to be on your way."

Maeve heard the urgency in his voice and a wave of terror went through her. MacCuill grabbed Harold under his shoulders and Maeve took his feet. As they walked, MacCuill gave explicit instructions to the spring. She tried to focus on what he was saying, knowing that it was imperative to get there quickly, but she was distracted and her heart was pounding from carrying Harold's limp body.

Once back at the camp Eron and MacCuill tied Harold securely onto Argyll's broad back. Eron had tacked up his horse and now held out his cupped hands to give her a leg up. After she was settled in the saddle he put a hand on her thigh. "This is Taranis, named for the god of thunder. He is strong and sure-footed and will carry you safely."

"Try to avoid the enchanted forest," MacCuill said, holding out Argyll's lead rope.

Maeve took the rope, waved good-bye and then skirted around the hillside heading north.

The trip was a blur, a mad dash away from the fighting and then hours and hours of riding through the cold. She rode through most of the first night, only stopping when her exhaustion threatened to knock her off her horse. Leaving Harold tied to Argyll's back she made a fire and brewed some tea, unable to eat any of the cheese and bread she'd brought along. After a few hours sleep she was off again, following MacCuill's instructions.

It was the middle of the second day when she realized she was going in circles. Whether it was black magic working against her, or her own fear and confusion, she didn't know, but the trip had taken her down one circuitous path after another,

MacCuill's instructions making no sense. A narrow canyon had beckoned, hard to navigate and even harder to get out of. Large craggy boulders lined the dry creek bottom that twisted and turned with no end in sight. She had to let go of the lead rope, hoping the big horse would follow Taranis. She'd wandered the canyon, always hopeful that she'd find a way out around the next bend. But when it didn't happen her mind began playing tricks on her—she would see what she thought was a person in the distance, waving her on. She shook her head—she must be hallucinating from exhaustion.

Finally she came to a trail leading out of the deep ravine and pushed Taranis up the steep and rocky bank, hoping Argyll behind her would be able to manage. She lay over Taranis's neck, helping him forward. At the top she stopped, letting the heaving horse regain his breath. Argyll stood beside her, sweat glistening along his neck. Harold lay over his back as before, limp and lifeless. There was nothing to be done about it—they had to keep going.

She pushed Taranis into a trot, hurrying into the forest, realizing too late that this was the place MacCuill had told her to avoid. When she turned to leave, the path behind her had disappeared. After hours of hearing voices calling out to her and seeing shadows moving under the trees, she began recognizing the terrain, realizing she had ridden by here before. She pulled Taranis to a stop and burst into tears. If she couldn't find a way out of this repeating loop she wouldn't make it in time— Harold would never see their child. Wiping the tears away, she let her thoughts slide back to the time with MacCuill, trying to recall every word he had said. Hadn't he told her to turn left at the large oak on the hill? She searched for that tree for hours, finally giving up.

Dismounting she ate some cheese and bread, realizing that her brain needed nourishment. Her hands went to her belly— the baby needed food as well. She had barely slept or eaten, afraid that if she stopped it would be too late to bring him back. Glancing toward Harold's slumped body put her into another fit of crying. The trip had taken longer because her mind had let her down and she was overtaken with terror that she would never be with him again. He looked truly dead now, his features slack and pasty.

When she remounted Taranis an hour later, the remaining light had left the sky. Feeling hopeless she headed down the all too familiar path, surprised when she came to the edge of the wood. A majestic and ancient oak stood directly in front of her. How had she missed it the first time? At the base of the tree, the path branched left and right. She pulled on the left rein, heading in the direction MacCuill had told her to go.

When she couldn't hold her eyes open any longer she stopped again, sliding off Taranis to land in the dirt. Deep gloom surrounded her, the dark night full of strange shadows and sounds. She was barely able to walk, her legs shaky and sore. Too tired to worry about anything, she pulled a sheepskin out of her pack and curled up on the ground.

Up at first light, Maeve headed out, urging Taranis into a fast trot. She had to make it by today or she knew it would be too late to revive him. From here she had a clear idea of where to go. Maeve ducked under tree branches, steering Taranis around heavy brush. Argyll crashed through behind her, the big horse heaving with the quickened pace. Tears flowed down her face, blinding her at times. She didn't even bother to wipe them away. The day seemed to lengthen and stretch, the light dimming and then brightening again as though magic was at work. Maybe this wood was also enchanted—where spirits played tricks on the people who dared enter.

A long stretch of time went by while she maneuvered through the murky dimness. She ignored the voices calling in sultry tones, the flashes of light she could see in the distance. When the end of the forest was in view, she kicked Taranis into a canter. On the outside of the trees was the group of boulders MacCuill had told her about. Her spirits lifted—she must be close now.

Another hour or so of hard riding down a rutted track brought her to a flat wall of black rock. Looking up at the sheer, glass-like sides she thought it looked manmade, or maybe magic had erected the twenty-foot tall edifice. A few straggly trees grew along its base, their misshapen branches covered in a thick layer of ice. It was a desolate place and it was hard to imagine a healing spring being anywhere around, but this was exactly how MacCuill had described it. Looking around she found the narrow path MacCuill had mentioned, the one leading to the spring.

Maeve dismounted, hastily untying Harold. As she dragged him off Argyll, her knees buckled. She sat in the dirt, Harold's body slumped against her, wondering how she would ever manage to get him to the spring. After a minute she roused herself, standing to untack Taranis. She put the saddle and bridle down by the wall, glad to notice a trickle of water going by. The horses would at least be able to quench their thirst.

Using every bit of strength she had, she struggled with the body. Harold outweighed her by more than fifty pounds—it felt like he was made of cement. Going backward she hauled on his arms, dragging him inch by inch down the narrow path. By the time she had gone ten yards, she was covered in sweat, despite the freezing air. Her muscles felt like mush. She stopped and looked over her shoulder to see if the spring was in sight, but there was only the narrow path.

Before starting again she put her hands on her knees, breathing in and out slowly, trying to summon strength. Her arms and back muscles were weak from pulling, her legs shaky. But as her eyes lifted and went to the body on the ground she was seized with determination, adrenaline carrying her forward for more than five minutes. She must be getting close, she thought, peering over her shoulder. The path was barely visible in the gloom as night descended.

Finally the unmistakable sound of bubbling water reached her ears and when she rounded the next corner, the spring was there. It was like an oasis in a dark world: bright green plants crowding around the sides of the pool, vying with one another for the warm moist air. Small trees grew in back of the spring, their branches laden with some kind of sweet-smelling red fruit. The water was singing as it ran into the deep pool. There was an aliveness here that was missing in almost every other part of the Otherworld. She rested next to the pool, trying to catch her breath. She could feel the healing atmosphere here; it seemed to fill her with light. Now if she could just find Airmid....

After fifteen minutes or so of mentally calling to Airmid she began to call out loud. She projected her voice as much as she could, but the tall walls of stone muffled the sound. Finally Maeve decided to take matters into her own hands, pulling Harold over to the pool. She removed his clothes, dismayed by the gray-blue pallor of his wrinkled skin, the stiffness of his body. She was crying now and could barely stand to look at him. After he was undressed she placed his sword and scabbard carefully on the ground and then stripped her own clothes off. She pushed him partially over the lip of the pool and then got in, pulling him in behind her. His body undulated, his face disappearing beneath the dark water. Frightened, she gripped him under the arms to keep him from sinking, letting his head rest against her upper chest. As long as she didn't look at him, she could almost imagine he was alive as the weight of his head came against her, his long dark hair waving across her chest. She tried to stay focused and to keep her fear at bay as her arms began to protest.

The warm water felt good on her cold skin, and as the minutes went by, she relaxed, allowing Harold's body to rise and fall with her breathing. She said a fervent prayer to the spirits of the spring, thanking them for being here and then thanked Airmid, even though the goddess had not yet shown herself. She closed her eyes, willing Harold to come back to her, saying, *I love you,* over and over in her mind.

Soon it was pitch black and all she could see was the silver glint of the water as it spilled over the lip into the pool. The wall of stone hung above her like a dark curtain. Hopelessness went through her and she knew he was not going to come back. She began to cry silently, letting her tears fall freely onto Harold's face, her hand stroking his pallid cheek. A shimmer on the other side of the spring startled her, bringing her attention to the gauzy pale dress that had picked up light where there was none. Her heart sped up when a shadowy form came into view.

"Maeve, I see you remembered my spring." Airmid's oval face and brown curls emerged as her willowy body slipped into the water. Her dress floated around her like flower petals, her body ghostlike and ethereal. "Give him to me," she ordered, reaching toward Harold.

Maeve pushed his floating body toward Airmid. *I love you, I love you I love you.*

Airmid held Harold with one arm and pulled the arrow from his chest. A gush of blood came with it, turning the pool dark. After that she pressed him down under the water, holding him under for so long that Maeve was frightened, despite knowing he was already dead.

Airmid began to chant:
Bone to bone
Vein to vein
Balm to balm
Sap to sap
Skin to skin
Tissue to tissue
Blood to blood
Flesh to flesh

Sinew to sinew
Marrow to marrow
Pith to pith
Fat to fat
Membrane to membrane
Fibre to fibre
Moisture to moisture.

After several minutes, bubbles began to rise to the surface of the pool. A minute or so later Harold's head pushed forcefully up as he reached for the surface and gasped for air. Maeve watched in disbelief as his eyes popped open.

"Maeve!" he cried out, reaching for her. "I thought I was a goner."

"You were gone, Harold," she stated, as tears of joy flowed down her face. She cradled his head against her, kissing the top of it over and over. She was overcome with emotions that she had never felt before: deep gratitude and relief beyond anything she could have imagined.

"My work is finished," Airmid's sweet voice pronounced, as her shimmering form moved gracefully from the pool. Her dress clung to her, revealing her long legs and arms, her narrow hips and small breasts. Her wet hair hung dripping to her waist. She turned back to look at Maeve and Harold, her liquid eyes filled with fractured light like stars. "You must promise me one thing. If it's a girl I want her to be named after me." She smiled and then disappeared like a wraith into the vapor behind the pool.

"If it's a girl? What did she mean by that?" Harold asked, staring at Maeve.

All Maeve could do was smile at him as tears of joy and relief continued to fall from her eyes.

Chapter

26

"Finna?"

"I'm in here, Alex." Her muffled voice came from the other side of the kitchen wall, followed by a splash of water. That set-up had not been here when they lived together. They had devised a complicated way of warming water from the well and used hoses to create a makeshift shower. He remembered how irritating this had been for him and how it didn't seem to bother Finna at all. *She was a strange woman, his Finna,* he thought, smiling.

"Do you need anything?" he called, putting the kettle on for tea.

"No, I'm fine thanks, I'll be out soon. Shall I leave the water for ye?"

He ran his fingers across his unshaven face, realizing what he must look like. "Yes, please, I could definitely do with a wash."

He busied himself in the kitchen making tea, eating some cheese and bread. As he was cleaning up she came through the front door. She had a towel wrapped around her hair, a sky-blue

375

woven tunic covering her body. His eyes wandered across her familiar form, the roundness of her breasts pushing against the fabric. When her eyes met his, he turned away, afraid to show what lay in his heart.

"I'll just get the fire going—why don't you sit down there and dry your hair." He went over and added a couple of logs and then got a pillow off the bed for her to sit on.

Finna sat down, running her fingers through her thick hair, lifting it off her neck to get out the tangles.

"Can I get you a comb?"

"No thanks—why don't ye go and take your bath? The water will be cold."

"I thought of that. I'm heating a bit more on the AGA. I can't believe I'm here, you know...in Scotland...with...you..." He gazed at her sitting there. She really hadn't changed very much at all. When she lifted her hair up again, he took in the pale graceful neck, the little fuzz that grew at the base of her hairline. Her profile was turned toward him, her lashes lowered as she bent her head toward the fire. She was just as beautiful as he remembered and he liked the contrast of gray threading through her chestnut hair. He found himself in a past memory, the soft shell curve of her ear...the sweet rosewater smell of her hair... he heard her voice from a distance answering him.

"I canna either. I have a lot to tell ye but why don't ye take your bath first?"

Alex came back from his bath just as Finna was climbing into bed. "Oh no you don't," he cried, shutting the door behind him. "You need to fill me in on what's going on before you disappear into dreamland again."

Finna laughed, "Well, since ye put it that way, I'll try to stay awake for a little while—but I really am tired, ye ken."

Alex sat down next to her on the bed. "I know you're still getting over your illness, I was just trying to be funny—but seriously, we do need to talk. If you're not up to it right now, I'll wait, but I would at least like to hear about what's happening with our daughter, if she's all right."

"I would have told ye right away if she wasn't. But who knows now? Considering what she's up against." Her gaze went out the window.

"What are you talking about? Where is she exactly?"

"There's a war going on in the Otherworld and she is the one they call…" Finna stopped and looked at him.

"The one they call…what?"

"Alex, if I tell ye this ye have to promise me that ye won't do your usual…your usual dismissal. What I have to tell ye is serious and real, as real as ye and I sitting together on this bed. Well?"

"Well, what? Will I shut up? Is that what you're asking me?" Anger rose in his chest.

"All I'm askin' is for your suspension of disbelief. There's a lot ye dinna know and will have a hard time with. I guess the fact that ye've finally accepted that the Otherworld exists is a good first step."

"Just get it over with, for Christ's sake!" Alex yelled.

Finna stared at him for a full minute, her disappointed expression making him feel like a heel. Finally she said, "Maeve is known as the Willow."

"The Willow? What the hell does that…?"

"Remember that I talked ye into havin' her middle name be Saille? As I'm sure ye ken, 'tis Gaelic for willow. I wanted to name her that because of the prophecy."

"Prophecy?"

Our daughter is part of a prophecy that was written many many years ago. She was always meant to come here to Scotland to lead the fight against the dark."

"I'll buy the part about the Otherworld but what is 'the dark'? And a prophecy—really, Finna?"

"Maeve is supposed to be the one to bring the balance back—remember Catriona's brother, Brandubh?"

"I've met him."

"He's killed more people than I can count, good people, men, women and children, he's a horrible evil man and has to be stopped. He's been tryin' to kill Maeve."

"What? Finna, we have to get her out of there!" Alex stood up and began to pace.

"'Tis way too late for that and besides our little girl has become a very different person, a woman with all sorts of amazing abilities...she can definitely take care of herself."

Alex came to a stop next to the bed. "This sounds very far-fetched and it's reminding me of some of our arguments. I met Brandubh back in Halston—I didn't like him but it's hard for me to believe that he's done what you say—he is, after all, a priest."

"I asked ye at the beginning of this discussion if ye were ready for it, that ye needed to keep an open mind. What I'm telling ye is the truth. Now sit down and listen."

Alex was shocked into silence by the vehemence in her voice. He sat on the edge of the bed, his gaze focused on the floor. He didn't want to believe what she was saying but he knew there was no reason for her to lie. Calm down, he told himself and pay attention to what this woman is saying. There may be some action we need to take and denying it isn't helping. "Okay, I'm ready."

Finna continued, her hand on his arm. "The fight is very far from here, in the northern- most part of the Otherworld. 'Twould take us a long time to get there traveling by normal means."

"By normal means? What other way is there?"

"Well, there are all sorts of magical ways to move around in the Otherworld, but I don't have those abilities. Your daughter does though."

Alex looked up, his attention taken into her gray-green eyes. "What should we do?"

"Right now I'm going to take a nap. I'm still too tired and weak to think straight. Maybe ye can ruminate on what I've told ye and we can discuss it later." Finna moved down under the covers and closed her eyes.

Alex watched her, his mind rushing in circles. He was very keyed up and wished Finna wouldn't keep falling asleep, he needed more information to make a plan. Maybe he should take the car and go into town. He had to do something—waiting around wasn't going to help anyone. He paced around the small cottage and finally put on his jacket and headed outside. When he reached the cedar log he sat down, staring out at the dark water.

Memories rose in his mind about the last time he had sat in this spot. It had been a cold wintery day very much like this one, and he and Finna had been arguing about something he couldn't remember. Now when he thought back, it all so seemed so silly and such a waste. They could have spent those years loving each other and raising their child instead of miles apart, not having any contact. He knew it was his fault. He was the one who took Maeve away and didn't get back in touch with Finna. And had she really been so crazy? Ned seemed to think so. And now finding out that Ned visited with Finna every time he came to Scotland...was there something going on between them? Maeve had asked and he had assured her no, but...he had to admit he felt betrayed by the man who professed to be his good friend.

He scanned back to the past. With Catriona living with them, their physical intimacy had disappeared, as well as any meaningful relationship. Finna and her mother just seemed to shut him out. And then all the talk about the Otherworld—it was why he decided that Maeve needed to live with him. And Ned had heartily agreed. But Finna had kicked him out way before that. He lived in town, having to fight to see his child. Maybe he should be angry right now instead of feeling guilty, but all he felt was worry about his daughter and sadness about his failed relationship with the one woman he had ever loved.

He decided to make a quick trip into Bailemuir to get some supplies and also let his mother know what was happening. When he went in to ask Finna if there was anything she needed, she was sound asleep. He left the house and closed the door quietly behind him.

Chapter

27

Maeve and Harold spent the night next to the spring wrapped in each other's arms. Many hours had gone by talking about their unborn child and the newest plan that had come to Maeve at the spring. Harold filled her in about his former life as King Kenneth, what this meant in terms of the prophecy. The 'one of noble birth' finally made sense. Very early in the morning Maeve woke to his lips on hers and felt her heart stop for a minute. They had gotten a second chance. Her arms went tight around him as she pressed herself against his very alive body. They reconnected slowly, searching out the places that gave the most pleasure, savoring one another like never before.

"Wow!" Harold observed when they lay spent and breathless. "I should die more often."

Maeve gave him a sharp look. "Don't even joke about that. We still have a lot to get through."

Harold reached for her, his hands moving across her belly. "I can feel it," he said, his eyes growing wide. He put his ear to her belly. "The baby's talking to me, he says…"

"He?"

Harold shrugged. "Fifty-fifty."

Maeve laughed. "All you feel is the slight bulge of my stomach—it's too early for anything else."

Harold bent to kiss her belly, murmuring sweet nothings. When he looked up, his eyes were shining. "I can't wait to see him...or her," he added. Laughing, he pulled her close. "Jesus, Maeve, this is just amazing. A month ago I was in my house in Halston, thinking about some kind of nonsense, like how I was going to make a living, and now..." he spread his hands out in an expansive gesture. "I'm going to be a father and I've discovered a most incredible part of myself...not to mention a prophecy and a strange and wondrous world!" He shook his head, staring at her with his eyebrows raised.

They moved into the water heading to the tree on the other side. When Harold picked a piece of fruit and handed it to her, Maeve said, "I feel like Adam and Eve."

"But I'm the man and I handed it to you—will it be men now who come from the rib of a woman?"

Maeve laughed, sinking her teeth into the succulent red fruit that she couldn't identify. "This place is so idyllic, I don't want to leave."

Harold nodded, his chin covered in juice. "I could use more time to recover from my demise, but I guess we'd better get back."

They dressed, walking together up the path to find the horses. Taranis and Argyll had scattered pebbles and stopped up part of the stream with their footprints, creating a small pool from which they had obviously partaken. Now they munched on a tiny bit of grass growing at the base of the rock. Seeing Harold and Maeve, they looked up for a moment and then resumed their meal. Harold laid his hand on Argyll's neck, affection in his eyes. "This is a great horse," he said, turning toward Maeve.

"I know it—he carried you all the way here without a word of complaint." Maeve laughed, swinging the saddle up on Taranis. "Looks like you're going to have to ride bareback."

Harold grinned. "I've done it before—not the most comfortable thing in the world, but after dying, I think I can handle it."

Away from the spring the day was cold, a mass of solid gray clouds in the sky above them. It was a shock after the warmth and the sweetness of their intimacy. There was a palpable desolation here that clung to everything, but their joy of being reunited and the news about the child kept any despondency at bay. They rode side-by-side, keeping a good pace but not rushing. The horses had not eaten properly for several days and Maeve didn't want to overtax them, especially since there might be a time when it would become necessary. She didn't relish the idea of the fight looming ahead of them.

When they got closer to the valley, they noticed many druid guards all along the border of the Caer Sidi. Maeve scanned carefully for MacCuill but didn't see him among them. He must still be with Eron and the men. She wondered what had happened in her absence. The second full moon was almost upon them, just another day or two, and they needed to have their plan in place before that. From what she'd heard from MacCuill, this full moon would herald in something new, although he neglected to tell her what that might be. Hopefully it would mark the end of the fighting and the beginning of balance here in the Otherworld.

Glancing over at Harold she noticed that his face looked stern, his hand waiting on his sword. "What's the matter?" she asked.

When he turned her way his features changed a little, coming back into the Harold she knew. "There's something going on here. I want to be prepared."

"What is it?" Maeve looked around, trying to feel whatever he was talking about.

"Look over there," Harold pointed to the druid guards who now seemed to be agitated, rushing around to form a tight line.

A bolt of lightning hit the ground, followed almost immediately by a resounding boom that had the horses jumping sideways. Maeve grabbed the saddle to keep herself from falling off. When she glanced over at Harold he had his sword out of the scabbard, his body ramrod straight. It amazed her that he could look like that without even a saddle to keep him centered. Following Harold's gaze she spotted a group of Oillteil in formation heading toward the border.

"The sky gods must be angry," Harold stated, staring up at the roiling dark clouds. "We need to be on the other side of this valley before those Oillteil arrive."

"We also need to avoid being attacked." She pointed toward the masses of troops in the valley below them. "Those Oillteil are only half our problem."

Their eyes met. "What do you suggest?" Harold asked. "We can't outrun them, we're too far away. I think we should lay low and watch what happens here. If the druids can hold the line we can sneak behind them and make it across."

"You mean go into the Caer Sidi?"

"Do you have a reason not to?"

"I guess not. I've always thought of it as the last bastion of safety and wanted to prevent any of Brandubh's troops from getting through—but you may be right, the druids could hold them back. And I hate the thought of being down there," she added, pointing toward the valley. "Especially after what happened to you."

"You cannot protect me. Besides, I've already died—what else could happen?"

Maeve laughed nervously. "I just don't want to lose you."

"How do you think I feel now that I know you're pregnant?"

Maeve stared into his eyes for a full minute, unable to respond.

Harold grabbed Taranis's reins. "Maeve, we need to focus on what we're doing here, not on what might or might not happen. I have Kenneth inside me, and you're the Willow. This is our destiny. Now is not the time to worry."

"I know all of this but…"

"You haven't shared your plan with me yet, don't you think it's time? Or don't you believe what the prophecy says?"

Maeve looked over at him. His voice had changed, and his features had rearranged themselves slightly. For some reason this time it really unnerved her. "Harold? You don't look like yourself."

"I'm here, it's just that Kenneth is here too. Don't worry, we both love you." He laughed, a deep, rich chortle that did not sound at all like his usual laugh.

"Well, lass? Are ye going to tell me the plan or do I need to beat it out of ye?"

"Stop it Harold, you're scaring me now," she exclaimed, but then she noticed the teasing look in his eyes. This Kenneth thing worried her and she found herself putting off telling him what she'd been thinking—for one thing Kenneth was a warrior and might not want to go along with it. But then again, he was mentioned in the prophecy.

When she glanced at him again, Harold was staring at her with a decidedly irritated expression. "Sorry," he said, "just attempting to make light of a serious situation and trying to impress upon you who I am in this scenario." When she didn't respond, he added, "I'm still waiting."

While they rode side-by-side toward the border of the Caer Sidi, Maeve began to relay the plan that had been forming in her mind since the vision in the spring. The way to fight without fighting.

They crossed the border about an hour later, slipping into the Caer Sidi behind a hill. The fight between the druid guards and the Oillteil was in full swing—they could hear it from where they waited. Harold slid off Argyll, and then came to help her off Taranis. "We need to be careful here, there may be some Oillteil who've managed to get through the line." Harold headed away from her, finding a trail up a slight rise where they could watch the proceedings. "It looks as though the druids have managed to hold them back, at least for the time being."

Maeve stared into the distance, her ears picking up the shouts and clanking of swords. It looked as though fire was coming out of the druids' hands, keeping the underground dwellers at bay.

"What is that?" she called to Harold, pointing toward the blue flames.

"Ah yes, I remember reading about this somewhere—the druids control the elements."

"I've never seen MacCuill do that."

"Have you been in battle with him?"

"Well, no, at least not until now."

"Come on, we need to get across the valley before dark." Harold did a vaulting leap, landing squarely on Argyll's back. "Don't look at me like that," he said, noticing her astonished expression. "It just comes with Kenneth," he chuckled.

Maeve mounted her horse and followed Harold down the hill. She felt like she was losing control of the situation, giving over to the Harold/Kenneth duo. Was this the way things were supposed to go or was she losing connection with her own wisdom and intuition? She puzzled over this as her horse broke into a trot, trying to keep up with Argyll.

They reached a flat boggy area and Harold stopped the big horse with a pull on the lead rope. "This does not look good."

Maeve rode up beside him following his gaze. "I know nothing about this area but I wouldn't want my horse to break a leg in there."

"Breaking a leg is the least of our worries. Look." Harold pointed ahead to an area of sinkholes.

In the center of one Maeve thought she saw two yellow eyes. "Okay—that isn't what I expected to find here in this place that's supposed to be so safe."

"Ciamar a tha sibh?"

Maeve and Harold both turned to see a druid walking toward them, his gray robe nearly dragging in the bog.

"'S fhada bho nach fhaca mi thu," Harold replied.

The druid stared at him for a moment and then reached up to clasp his hand. "Kenneth!"

Maeve watched this interchange with amazement. She knew what the Gaelic words meant but she couldn't speak it herself. The druid had said hello and Harold had just said, 'it's been a long time'....how much time—thousands of years? How old was this druid?

They both turned toward her and Harold said, "Maeve, this is Tadg, he's a Danann druid from long ago. I knew him then, as you probably surmised."

Maeve turned to take a closer look at the bearded man. Yes, he did look fairly ancient with his weathered skin and heavy beard, but held himself proudly, his back straight. She took his hand when he proffered it, surprised by his strong grip.

"I'll escort you past the sinkholes," he said in English. "The serpents are very active during this time."

He turned, leading the way down to the bog. Maeve glanced warily toward the green-yellow eyes watching as they rode by. Harold and Tadg kept up a running dialogue in Gaelic, laughter punctuating their exchanges. She heard the names Muirenn, Bodhmall and then MacCuill.

"Does he know MacCuill?" she asked, kicking her horse forward to ride next to Harold.

"They're related—Demna is his daughter's son."

"Demna?"

"Another name for MacCuill."

"That means Tadg is way older than MacCuill."

Harold nodded, turning back to continue his conversation with Tadg.

Maeve turned her attention back to the bog and keeping Taranis from shying. Apparently the water and the serpents made him nervous. Her own reaction had become one of mild interest—she wasn't afraid and felt a strange link with them. When she asked Tadg about them, he told her that the serpents were a transformative force, symbols of rebirth, representing immortality and the creative life force, but were dangerous to those who did not belong in the Caer Sidi.

It was getting close to midnight by the time they reached the other side of the marsh. Tadg suggested that she and Harold spend the night in MacCuill's cottage since it was very close by. They said good-bye and then she and Harold backtracked for about a half a mile, and then headed north, coming to an area of rolling hills and stone fences. A few bedraggled sheep huddled in groups trying to keep warm from the winds that had begun to howl.

They dismounted and untacked the horses, leaving them to munch on low scrub grass along with the sheep. When Maeve opened the door to the cottage it was obvious that no one had been there for quite some time. It was cold, with the lingering scent of rot, as though food had spoiled. Harold set to work making a fire, leaving the house to gather firewood while Maeve found water and a pot in which to brew tea. She pulled out the little bag Rea had given her, throwing in the last of the leaves.

There wasn't much to eat so they made do with tea and a bit of dried fruit. While they sat in front of the fire Maeve began telling Harold the rest of the plan that had come to her during the time he and the druid had been talking.

"I didn't mean to leave you out," he said defensively, interrupting her. "It felt good to reconnect with the man. He was a close friend in the old days."

"Don't worry about it. I was miffed at first but I got over it. Besides, I needed time to think." She smiled, putting a hand on his arm. "Anyway, the plan has to do with tapping into my connection with the moon."

"What?"

"Oh, I guess you don't know about that—it happened when I was still at Finna's cottage. I had a vision of the moon, tendrils of energy kind of went into my body—I know it sounds weird."

Harold shook his head. "Nothing sounds weird anymore. Go on."

"I told you about my vision at the spring, right?"

Harold nodded.

"Well, the Sidhe are a big part of it—I need to talk with them. It also includes relying on the superstitious nature of the Oillteil and Wildmen. And, there will be no fighting involved."

Harold frowned. "How is that possible?"

"All I know is that this is how I'm supposed to manage it."

"And what about me? I'm part of it too, you know."

"Do you want to kill people, Harold? All I'm saying is that I want to do this without violence—how can you go against that?"

"I'm not going against it, I just don't see how it's possible. Have you forgotten about the heavily armed troops in the valley?"

Maeve sighed, putting her head in her hands. "No—how could I?"

"If you really want to go through with this, I can help with troop placement and timing. I'm good at that, at least Kenneth is. But I still don't have a clear idea of what you intend to do."

"All I know is that it has to happen on the night of the full moon. My moonstone played that part when it fell in the water at the spring. And the red-hairs were all there with their arms linked, but they didn't have their swords out."

"And was I in this vision?"

"Yes, Harold, I told you that already. You and I were standing together at the head of the line."

"Wish I had a better idea—it would be great if I could do a mind meld with you. It would make things easier."

Maeve laughed. "But you're not a Vulcan and neither am I."

His eyes glittered. "But I am Kenneth and Kenneth knows a lot about battle formation, sabotage and all sorts of devious shit. Hopefully you can explain this plan in more detail before we go through with it. I need to have it clear in my mind."

"We still have a couple of days to work out the details. My first order of business is to talk to the red-hairs and see what they have to say."

They slept in front of the fire that night, feeling the little stone house shake as the wind grew to gale force, making a sound like whining animals. Lightning strikes woke them periodically, rolling thunder rumbling in its wake. Maeve worried all night about the horses' lack of shelter and food. She was glad when morning came and they could continue on their way.

After a meager breakfast, they rode out, anxious to get on with their plans. Harold had seemed to accept her ideas, only adding some advice about possibilities they might face. He told her it was hard for him to imagine winning without any violence, but he would bow to her authority if she wished it. Maeve laughed at the absurdity of Harold bowing down to her, but then she thought of MacCuill and what he'd done. Maybe the Kenneth personality would bow at some point but even that made her feel uncomfortable. They were equals in this place— he was part of the prophecy, just as she was. They needed to work together.

At the eastern border, the druid guards pointed them in the direction of the Tuatha De Danann camp. After leaving the guards behind, Maeve glanced furtively at Harold, glad to see the familiar expression that she knew so well. The hood on his jacket was pulled partially over his face to keep out the cold wind and as he caught her eye he gave her a crooked smile. A second later a jagged streak of lightning hit the ground very close to them and both horses shied.

"Come on, Maeve!" Harold called, urging Argyll into a canter.

"That's got to be the camp," Harold yelled over his shoulder, pointing toward a dark line of smoke snaking into the sky. Wind whipped against their faces, making their eyes tear as they galloped on. Maeve finally caught up to Harold and then they rode side-by-side, navigating the treacherous ground and going as fast as they dared. As the storm moved toward the west an earthquake struck, opening up a wide fissure. Maeve screamed as Taranis slid sideways toward the gaping hole.

Harold reached over and grabbed the reins, pulling the horse back. "Jesus! Be careful! Just hang on to the mane!"

Maeve righted herself and pushed her freezing hands into the thick coarse hair, holding tight. She bent low on his neck, shielding her eyes from the wind. "Harold, look!"

They had ridden to the top of a high mound overlooking the valley. As the wind shifted, the clash of swords and the sounds of screaming came to their ears. People ran in all directions, slashing and killing one another in a frenzy of war. Too many to count lay unmoving on the ground while around them arrows whizzed and swords found purchase in soft flesh. The screams were terrible, full of anguish and pain. Maeve buried her face in her arms and began to cry. "I can't stand it!" she screamed. "I hope my people are safe, I shouldn't have left them."

"Maeve, you've got to be strong. You told me you left Eron in charge. I've ridden with the man, he knows what he's doing. This is why you're here, isn't it?" Harold rode up next to her and grabbed her by the shoulder. "I don't like this anymore than you do but we've got to keep our wits about us. We need to get to the Tuatha De Danann camp. The sooner we do that, the faster your plan can be implemented."

Maeve gazed into his determined eyes. His strength of mind revived her and she turned away from the terrible scene. They had to continue. They rode on, passing by villagers with carts pulled by exhausted horses, Crion with looms on their backs, all heading for the Caer Sidi. Lyrics from a song went through her mind, 'when there's doubt within your mind because you're thinking all the time, framing rights into wrongs, move along move along'...did that mean to ignore her thoughts or did it mean to go on despite her thoughts? It had been a long time since she'd meditated. Without clarity she could get off on the wrong track and really screw things up. Nerves shot through her stomach—people were dying down there and she was doing nothing about it. Her tears started again, blowing off her cheeks as the wind hit her face. She reached up to wipe her eyes, hoping Harold hadn't noticed.

Closer to the forest, hanging back nervously from the villagers and Crion, Maeve spied a group of injured Oillteil. When she stopped, they told her they were defectors and asked if they could stay with her; they were terrified that they would not be allowed into the Caer Sidi. She glanced over at Harold but he only shook his head in resignation and rode on.

Having the Oillteil along slowed them down and they didn't reach the eastern forest until the end of the day. They finally made camp in an area on a wooded hill southwest of the Tuatha De Danann camp. Harold made a fire while Maeve treated the Oillteil injuries with her dwindling herbal supply. Luckily she'd picked up a few more from MacCuill's cottage. It surprised them all when Eron and Finiche suddenly appeared. Behind him she saw Duncan and a long line of villagers, Crion, Wildmen and Oillteil.

"I'm glad you are back, moon granddaughter," Eron said, hugging her tightly for a moment. He turned toward Harold. "And that you are alive, my friend!" Eron grasped Harold's arm, pulling him close.

Rea ran up to Maeve and grabbed her by the hand. "I am glad you are safe." She examined Maeve from head to toe and then smiled. "Look how many more have joined us," she cried, pointing to the disparate groups still continuing to appear from under the trees. "It happened right after you left. The Oillteil and Wildmen who got separated in the mayhem decided it was safer to remain with us."

Maeve watched in amazement as they continued to appear. There were at least fifty more than when she had left. They formed a large circle, all eyes trained on her, as though waiting for some kind of declaration. She saw Soru with several Wildmen she had never seen before, their eyes seeking hers as they came close.

Maeve acknowledged Soru and all the newcomers with a nod and then began to speak. "If some cannot understand my words, ask this man," she said, noticing Oak, the Oillteil she'd worked on in Rowan. She put her hand up in greeting, acknowledging the enormous creature.

Oak watched her with a crooked expression that she thought might be a smile, and then raised one hand, pulling his meaty fingers into a fist. "Aa-aag!" he yelled. All the other Oillteil repeated the odd guttural phrase, a roar going through the crowd.

Maeve waited until they had quieted and then said, "We have a plan now for how to fight without fighting. Is everyone in?" another roar went up, this time everyone participating.

"I will be speaking with the red-hairs as soon as I can. I hope they will agree to be part of it." Maeve looked around, noticing that Dirg was not part of the crowd. Too bad, she could have used the Sidhe warrior as liaison. In any case he had probably headed home and would be her ally once she approached them. "Now let's make camp—we need to eat and rest in preparation for the full moon."

Maeve stepped out of the circle, Harold on her heels. "That was good," he whispered.

Maeve and Harold led the way into the forest, choosing a somewhat level area big enough to accommodate them all. An old firepit remained from some previous occupant and a few pieces of wood had been left behind. Before she had a chance to ask, Oillteil and Wildmen were heading into the forest to search for game and wood.

Eron kneeled to make the fire, talking in low tones with Harold while Maeve made the rounds, checking in with everyone. Rea helped her, chatting about who had been sick and who had injuries and what had been done about it. Several Crion had been killed after Maeve left camp, as well as ten villagers. Maeve was saddened by this news. The Crion were innocents with no weapons. When she questioned Rea about how it happened, the Crion woman turned away, her eyes filling with tears.

The other Crion women milled about, crooning their happiness at seeing Maeve again and showing her the baskets of tubers and greens they had collected. They all pointed to her stomach, pantomiming eating. "They think you are too thin,"

Rea translated. "And I do too. If you want a strong and healthy little one you must eat more."

"I didn't have any food, Rea—or at least not much."

"You do now," Rea retorted in a tone that could only be described as annoyed.

Maeve smiled to herself, touched by the small woman's mothering.

When Maeve came back to the fire, Eron, Duncan and Harold had settled next to it. Wildmen, Oillteil and villagers stood around, taking part in the conversation. Eron related that after Maeve's departure, Brandubh's scouts had found them, that without the careful maneuvering of Duncan and the Wildmen they would all have been captured. "And you, Eron," Duncan added, his bright hazel eyes filled with admiration.

Eron smiled at Duncan and then his expression turned serious as he repeated the news Maeve had just heard from Rea, naming each of the ten villagers in turn, and explaining how heroic they'd been. Most were from Bannee, men with whom Harold and Eron had become close. "And the Crion deaths are particularly upsetting. They hold this place in their hearts, their only purpose to keep the spirits alive." He shook his head, staring into the fire.

It was a few minutes before conversation resumed, each person lost in their own thoughts about recent events. It was Eron who broke the silence, gazing at everyone with an expression of pride. "We made a good team. The Wildmen have an innate ability to keep themselves hidden as well as being able to travel without making a sound. And these Oillteil are the strongest people I've ever had the pleasure to work with." There was a repetitive grunting sound from the Oillteil that threw Maeve back to her first encounter with them. It seemed a miracle that they were on her side.

"We now have food and water because of several raids made on the souteraines. It seems that Brandubh intended to starve us out." Eron laughed. "Now we've turned the tables on him!"

Rea made tea in a large cauldron that had been confiscated from somewhere, and then managed to produce several cups. She poured tea for the immediate group, assuring the others standing around that they would have the next batch. When she brought over a cup of sheep's milk, Maeve grinned. "Is this part of my new diet?"

Rea laughed. "It is. And I expect you to drink every bit of it," she added, holding up a finger with a mock frown.

After the tea had been consumed, everyone moved closer to the fire. One of the Wildmen known as Claif spoke up, asking about the plan. His friends clustered close, waiting for him to translate as Maeve and Harold discussed strategy. The consensus was that it was too late to do anything tonight; they would wait until the following afternoon to connect with the red-haired men of the Sidhe.

About an hour later, Soru and two other Wildmen appeared with several ruffed grouse, handing them to the Crion women to pluck and prepare for cooking. A short time after that, the Oillteil emerged, their arms full of heavy branches and twigs. The fire would burn long into the night.

While meat cooked, conversations continued. Sticks were used to draw pictures in the dirt to illustrate upcoming actions and there were long discussions of what had happened during Maeve and Harold's absence. It seemed that the fighting in the valley had been nearly continuous, with many casualties, described by all as a bloodbath. And many of the dead belonged to the eastern clan of the Tuatha de Danann. Maeve recoiled, trying to hold back tears and hoping that Dirg was not one of the lost. When she glanced toward Harold sitting beside her, he took her hand, squeezing it. It was very late by the time everyone bedded down, their bellies full of meat and tubers as well as cooked grains collected from the souteraines.

Lying close to Harold, his arm protectively around her, Maeve dreamed about Catriona and Gertrude. They were together, on their way toward the north. When she woke in the morning she sat for a long while trying to tap into her grandmother's mind and was given a quick vision of Finna being taken home to the cottage and then a strong feeling of Catriona's determination to reach Maeve before the full moon. At least her mother was safe, she thought, with a huge sigh of relief.

By late afternoon of the following day Maeve was on her way, hoping that by this late hour the Sidhe warriors would have traveled back to their camp. The cries of battle had continued in her ears long after she had fallen asleep the night before; she hoped there would be men left to help her after what she had witnessed and heard about. She knew now that the clan had lost many of their men and been pushed back to this remote area.

Despite Harold's protests she had decided to make this first trip by herself. Finiche had not left her side since their arrival and followed at her heels as she moved toward the line of smoke, making her way down a steep and rocky hill to cross a narrow valley. On the other side was another hill to climb before she came to the camp. She had dressed in local garb, afraid that these strangers might be put off by her filthy jeans and ripped down jacket. Homespun wool pants designed by the Crion and Eron's leather tunic provided the impression of someone who belonged.

Her approach revealed the community fire with a large iron pot hanging from a wooden tripod over the flames. They had placed their tents beneath a grove of oak trees that, despite their leafless limbs, seemed to be giving them some reasonable amount of protection. They were tall men, well built with wavy gold-red hair and smooth faces. Swords hung in tooled leather scabbards at their sides and they were dressed in battle gear: heavy leather armor over long-sleeved homespun shirts, the image of the auroch, black against green, painted on the leather.

Strong voices rang out as they recited poetry, verses that were designed to invigorate, full of courageous exploits of former members of their race. In the shadows away from the fire Maeve could discern hundreds of faces. A flash of nervousness went through her. She had never addressed a gathering of this nature and she wasn't at all sure these men would respect a lone woman, even if she *was* mentioned in a prophecy.

Maeve told Finiche to wait and then announced herself in a clear voice, walking into the circle of firelight.

"Who are you?" a man asked, deftly pinning her arms behind her back.

"I'm Saille, the Willow."

There was silence as everyone turned to stare at her. "Better get Dagda," another man stated. "He'll know what to do." Her captor let go and disappeared into the shadows.

"Come warm yourself, 'tis a cold and nasty night." He motioned to a log set in front of the blazing fire. "I am known as Aedh," he added, leading the way. Steam was rising from the cook pot, sending out the mouth-watering aroma of stew.

A moment later a tall broad-shouldered man appeared. He looked about forty years old, with curly shoulder length hair the color of honey. His eyes were the pale green of sea foam, his long straight nose set a little off center, deep lines running from nose to mouth. "I'm Dagda, son of Danu—how may I be of service?"

"I've watched your men fighting in the valley. You have lost many."

"Aye, 'tis true. Our numbers dwindle as we defend our territory. The Oillteil burn our trees, harm the animals and the plants, and kill our women and children. There be nothing left of our forest if we do not defeat them."

Maeve looked directly into his tired eyes, straightening her back. He was the one in charge and she knew she must convince him of the rightness of her plan. Before she could open her mouth, Brigid appeared in her mind and she found herself speaking in the goddess's voice, saying things she didn't intend. "I am born of Brigid, and my strength comes from that eternal source. I daresay you know this woman?"

Dagda raised his eyebrows. "You are born of this woman? I have lain with Brigid and she has born my children. We are mated." He stared at her, his eyes registering surprise. "What does she bring me here on this cold night?" he asked, cocking his head to one side.

"She brings you her wisdom through me and assures me that you will remain her lover forever."

Dagda looked away. "'Tis many lifetimes since we have been together. I would be deeply in your debt if you could...if you would ..." He gave her a bleak look, one hand on his heart.

Maeve stared into his pain-filled eyes. This had not been part of her plan, and how was she supposed to...before she could finish her thought, her mouth opened and words flowed out. "I will find a way to bring you together again, my lord," she said, and then clamped a hand over her mouth. She was making promises she couldn't keep. But then she registered that it was Brigid's voice, Brigid's thoughts she had just spoken—of course there was a way, and Brigid would show her.

Dagda focused into the distance for several long moments seeming to struggle with his emotions. When he turned to her again his expression had closed, his face that of a warrior. "We are all tired. Just this day we have lost many. We mourn for them."

"I know how heavy your hearts must be. I have met one of your warriors. His name is Dirg—he spent some days with us after he was wounded. I hoped to see him here."

Dagda's eyes met hers. "Dirg was one of our best, but sadly he is lost, killed down there with the others." He pointed toward the valley, his eyes opaque. "We wish to avenge all these deaths—they should not have been made in vain." A murmur of agreement went through the crowd.

Maeve thought of the bright-haired soldier who had talked of the Tuatha De Danann, given her some of their history. Sadness went through her for his loss. She tried to think of some words to express this, but nothing came. "We have also lost people to the troops in the valley. But the moment is upon us and we must act—the time of the second full moon is tonight," Maeve continued. "My strength and power come from this wolf moon's intensity. It is imperative that we use this potent time to defeat our enemies. Will you stand with me and my men?" She watched him, thinking about her words and how they didn't express her true intent. *Wait until I have agreement*, she said to herself.

"Who fights with you?"

"We are a group of five-hundred strong. With us are Harold, who carries King Kenneth MacAlpin inside him, my grandfather Eron, as well as the many Crion, Oillteil, Wildmen and villagers who have joined our cause."

His eyebrows lifted. "King Kenneth? He lived long ago."

"His name in this life is Harold, but he remembers his life as Kenneth and carries the wisdom of that earlier time."

Dagda didn't speak for a moment as he seemed to ponder this news. "Please bring these men to our fire where they can share our stew. The Cauldron of Plenty is never empty. And when your bellies are full you can tell us more of this plan of which you speak."

Maeve nodded, heading away from the circle of firelight. With their minds intent on revenge, it would be difficult to convince these men of her plan. At the edge of camp, freezing wind swirled around her bare head. She wrapped her wool scarf around her neck and over her hair, tying it securely, and then went to find Finiche, whistling softly for him in the dark.

When Maeve returned later with Harold and the others, many more stumps had been placed around the fire. Flames crackled and spit from the new logs that had been added in her absence. Dagda's men looked wary, giving the Wildmen and Oillteil a wide berth as they arrived. Maeve waited while her people helped themselves to the stew, amazed by the cauldron's capacity. How could this one pot contain that much?

As the long line moved slowly past, Maeve scanned the faces of Dagda's troops. There were many women, long hair cascading down their backs, their features resolute. They talked amongst themselves, whispering and pointing toward the Oillteil and Wildmen with expressions of doubt. Maeve had a moment of uncertainty, hoping she had the wherewithal to pull this off— her idea would have to be carefully explained, put in such a way that they would all accept it.

Once everyone had eaten their fill, Dagda and his men crowded close to hear what Maeve had to say. She put her bowl down, motioning for a few Wildmen hanging around the edges to come and eat and then she stood on a stump so that everyone could see her. "What I'm about to ask may be hard for you and your men," she said, addressing Dagda. "I know how courageous and what fine warriors you all are, but this plan is not about fighting. It is about strength through the power of trust and the full moon which will shine above us tonight."

"The moon has not been visible for many seasons," a voice said from the shadows.

"Yes, this is true, but nevertheless, it is there, only covered with thick storm clouds. My plan is to lead all of us to the battlefield and draw out Brandubh's men. I believe that with our combined energy and clarity of purpose that the clouds will melt away and expose the bright moonlight on this special night."

There was a ripple of laughter and then one of Dagda's men said, "You are quite certain of this, my lady?" Behind him the group broke up, laughter overtaking all of them.

Maeve waited until she had their attention, trying not to react. She began again. "Many of Brandubh's troops have never seen the moon. The sudden appearance of this enormous bright sphere in the sky will be frightening indeed. We will raise our voices in a cheer as the moon appears, making them think it is our power that has brought this gigantic orb."

One of the women in the back stood up. "But how can you guarantee that the moon will show itself? It has been obscured by cloud since I can remember. The moon goddess has become just as weak as the others and will not come to our aid."

Maeve waited until the woman sat down, allowing a moment to go by. When she spoke her voice rang out with authority. "I have seen this in a vision. *I* am the one named to bring this world back from the brink of darkness, not the moon goddess. Shall I recite the prophecy to prove my point? You must open your hearts and minds and trust that what I say will come to pass."

There was utter silence for several minutes and then Dagda spoke. "If we do what you ask, we will be slaughtered like animals." He stared at her, his eyes like green opals in the flickering light of the fire.

Maeve took a deep breath and summoned her strength. "We will only prevail if we are willing to stand for what we believe. Have you defeated this enemy with your swords? Have you not lost many of your men? Brandubh has more than a thousand troops now. The magic that he and Adair and Pryderi wield far outweighs your swords or your bravery. You will die tonight if you go against them with weapons. What I propose is a new way—a way to fight without fighting. There will be no use of swords unless to save yourself. We will use the power of love and acceptance to bring these forces to their knees. This is written and will come to pass."

No one spoke, including Dagda. When he finally looked her way, his face was an unreadable mask. "I need to think about this, talk it over with my troops. And King Finvarra must be consulted."

"Where is this King Finvarra?" Harold asked, standing up to face the Sidhe warrior.

"He is with his wife in our camp to the east. Shall I summon him?"

Harold turned his head to look at Maeve, who nodded her agreement. "Yes," he answered.

While a messenger was dispatched they all remained around the fire talking with Dagda and his army, explaining what they had seen the past months. Harold got into a lively discussion with one of the men about long ago battles, their laughter pleasant after the seriousness of the evening. Maeve moved through the group, stopping to talk with men and women alike. These people were big-boned and handsome, with straight noses, their eyes green or blue. It seemed that the women were warriors too, their long hair pulled back, their bodies covered with the same leather armor the men wore. Yes, they had children back at their homes, no, they did not worry about being defeated. Their lives had been filled with war since time immemorial.

When the King stepped abruptly into the light there was a hush, and then everyone bowed their heads. He wore a long blue velvet robe studded with jewels over his leather pants and jerkin, his bare head covered with thick strawberry blonde curls. Heavy boots rose up to his knees. If it hadn't been for his beard and the strong masculine features of his face, he could have been considered pretty.

"What is the meaning of this?" he asked gruffly, looking around. His piercing blue eyes lit on Maeve coming toward him. When their eyes met she stopped and bowed, waiting a full minute before meeting his gaze again. "And who is this?" he asked, his eyes traveling from her face down to her feet.

"I am Maeve, born of Brigid, and known as the Willow."

He frowned turning to Dagda standing next to him. "Is this one of your brats, Dagda?"

Dagda shook his head. "No sire, she is from this time, come to fulfill the prophecy."

"The ancient prophecy that speaks of the return of balance?" He turned to Maeve again, his eyes flickering with interest. "And are you not to be wed soon?" he asked, with what seemed to be a flirtatious smile.

"I haven't planned...I mean..." Maeve stuttered, surprised by the odd question. She turned to find Harold in the crowd but he was facing the other way. "I would say, no. I am not planning a wedding."

"I am sorely disappointed," the king said, turning away.

"And what exactly are you scheming about this time?" a female voice asked from the shadows. A woman stepped into the light, her wide almond-shaped eyes trained on Finvarra. Ringed fingers smoothed the hair back from her forehead and then she shook her head, making the mane of russet ripple down her back. Her black brocade dress, studded with what looked like diamonds, shimmered as each jewel caught the firelight. "I should have known what you might be up to," she said with a frown and then turned to glare at Maeve. "You cannot be trusted for more than a minute with another beautiful woman around, especially one about to be wed. You are to wed, are you not?" she asked, her eyes boring into Maeve's.

"I have no plans to marry," Maeve answered in the strongest voice she could muster.

"Well, then, what is all the fuss? Will no one introduce us?" she asked, looking around angrily.

Dagda walked over, bowing before he spoke. "Donagh, my queen, this is Maeve, known as the Willow, who has come to fulfill the prophecy."

"Ah! Now that is good news!" Donagh went to an empty stump and pulled out her long skirts, settling herself. "Continue," she said with an expansive gesture of her hand.

"As I was saying earlier," Maeve said, gazing around at all the men and women who now focused on her, "we will stand together as one. We will not use violence unless we are in danger of losing our lives. We will use every bit of our will to keep the anger at bay. Concentration is our best weapon to deflect the waves of darkness that will be hurled at us from Brandubh and the others. We will prevail."

A younger man appeared out of the shadows. "Pryderi stands with Brandubh and he has all the power of a god. How can we stop him if he moves against us?"

Dagda turned to him. "This is my son, Aengus Mac Oc. What he says is true. How do you respond?"

"And what of Adair? She has all the powers of a sorceress. I have witnessed firsthand what she is capable of." The speaker, a woman dressed in leather, stepped forward. "She and her son control what little is left of this place and they will stop at nothing to bring all of us to our knees. I have lost two children to this evil and I do not relish losing more."

Dagda glanced toward King Finvarra and then turned toward Maeve. "What say you to my son and Eithne?"

"I say again that trust and love are the strongest weapons in the world. And the god of this forest, Cernunnos, has pledged to stand with us."

"You dare to speak of *our* deity, the mighty Cernunnos?" Finvarra demanded. Frowning he ran his fingers through his beard, his gaze going from Dagda to his men. When he laughed, a nervous low chuckle moved through the group.

Donagh stood, her voice strident as she addressed Maeve. "You have no right to send these men and women to their deaths. Cernunnos is our god. Finvarra and I will decide our future." She came to stand by the king, looping her arm through his.

"Let the woman speak," Finvarra said, turning to Donagh. "Let this 'child of the prophecy' verify that what she says is true." He turned to face Maeve. "What proof do you bring?"

Maeve reached down and untied the horn from her belt. "I am to call him," she answered, raising the auroch horn so that everyone could see.

"Demonstrate the truth of what you say, Willow. Call him now," Donagh challenged.

When Maeve glanced at Harold, his face held the warrior expression of Kenneth. His eyes met hers and he nodded. She took a deep breath and raised the horn to her lips, forcefully pushing air into the opening. The note seemed to magnify in tone and loudness as it ricocheted off the hills and reverberated across the valley, hanging in the air for long moments.

When it finally died away, Cernunnos appeared as though by magic and stood before Maeve. "You summoned me?"

There was a ripple of sound through the assembled crowd and some stood, bowing low to the deity. Even Finvarra bowed, his thick curls falling across his face. When he raised his head, he glanced around at the assembled crowd and then nodded to Dagda.

"We will stand with you tonight," Dagda announced, his admiring eyes trained on Maeve.

"We'll be back before moonrise," Maeve replied. "And then we will discuss the particulars."

On the way back to their camp, Maeve asked if anyone knew what was going on with King Finvarra and his wife. The discussion of weddings had mystified her.

Several men laughed, including Harold/Kenneth and then Eron answered her. "You should be careful, Maeve. It seems that Finvarra has his eye on beautiful red-haired women who are soon to be wed. Why this is, is a mystery, but it angers Donagh greatly. The King has taken many soon-to-be brides to his bed."

Maeve turned to Harold walking beside her. "Good thing we don't have marriage plans."

He turned toward her, his eyes unreadable in the dark. "Yeah, good thing."

Chapter

28

T he hour was growing late and the wind had come up, becoming stronger as each minute went by. Maeve and her entire group had arrived back at the Sidhe camp, the extra numbers spilling out around the outskirts. Another fire had been made and Oillteil, Wildmen and Crion huddled around it, trying to keep warm. Maeve, Harold, Eron, Duncan, Oak plus Dagda and King Finvarra and several other Sidhe soldiers sat together under the trees discussing what was to come. When the first lightning struck, thunder less than a second later, a shiver went down Maeve's spine. Surviving this night would not be easy. When the rumble had died away, MacCuill appeared, as if escorted by the electricity. Maeve was glad to see him but did not want to embrace him in front of the Sidhe. Her image as the strong warrior woman must remain intact.

As if responding to her unspoken thoughts, MacCuill came to her and took her hands, going down on one knee. After he bowed his head in respect, he rose to greet the others, bowing low to Cernunnos and then to King Finvarra. After that the druid turned to Dagda, acknowledging him by name with a special elbow-clutching handshake.

"It is good to see you, my old friend," Dagda declared, grinning.

"What is the plan you have concocted here?" MacCuill asked, coming to sit by Maeve.

"I've told all these men about my vision and instructed them on what to do, but," Maeve lowered her voice, "I hope it works."

MacCuill stared into her eyes, and in that moment of silence, all her earlier resolve returned. Despite his seeming lack of support at the spring the message she got was that her plan was exactly how it was meant to go. Now, if only the others would trust her and do as she instructed.

Near moonrise Harold mounted Argyll and led the way toward the valley. Maeve was right beside him, riding the wolf. Cernunnos had gone ahead. It was so dark they could barely see and Maeve was shaking with cold and apprehension. The wind had now turned into a gale, the force of it whipping around them making it hard for the animals to keep their balance. MacCuill, Eron and the Crion were right behind Maeve, and the Sidhe warriors fanned out around and behind her, at least a hundred or more. The Oillteil and Wildmen were dispersed among them, part of their army now, but easily spotted because of their physical differences. A cry from the woods made Maeve turn back. "What's that?"

It came again, an anguished shriek. "I've to see what that is—it sounds like someone's being hurt."

"Do you want me to come with you?" Harold asked, reining in Argyll.

"No, just go ahead. I'll catch up."

"Be careful, you don't know what could be lurking about during this night of the full moon," Harold said in his Kenneth voice.

Maeve nodded once and then urged Finiche into a lope, heading back they way they had come. She rode by her group, who turned to stare at her nervously. "I'll be right back," she called over her shoulder.

The cry came again just as Maeve entered the forest. Finiche barked once, his hackles raised, but Maeve ignored him, slipping off his back to continue on foot. When Finiche nosed her arm, she pushed him away. "I'll be all right," she whispered.

Several minutes later she entered an unfamiliar clearing. Surprised, she tried to place it. She must have been through here at some point. But the trees that grew here were not the pines and cedars she was used to—these were huge and majestic, with roots that crawled above ground forming a thick spiderweb. In the midst of the roots a woman lay sprawled on her side, her long skirts ripped, the brocade bodice pulled off one shoulder. Her face was turned away but the beauty of her golden hair had Maeve stopped in her tracks. This must be a goddess.

Maeve approached cautiously, wondering who or what had attacked. Following at her heels, the wolf growled. "Go Finiche, I don't need you here," she whispered. His whine made the hair on the back of her neck stand up. "Go with the others," she ordered, pointing to the trail. "I'll catch up with you in a minute." Finiche watched her and then turned and trotted away. Maeve waited until he was out of sight before approaching the poor woman. It wouldn't do for her to awaken to such a scary sight.

Kneeling next to her, Maeve shook the woman's shoulder, hoping there was still some life in her. The skin of her neck had a bluish cast, reminding Maeve of Harold's recent demise. Getting no response, she reached around her body to turn her over and then moved the strands of hair away to see her face. She had expected youth but this woman was ravaged, with haggard, gray skin revealing very advanced age. When she suddenly opened her eyes, Maeve jumped back.

411

The woman sat up, her hands pushing her long hair back. Maeve stared at the pale unblemished flesh, the tapered fingers. On her forefinger a heavy gold ring caught the light revealing an intricately wrought Celtic knot design, but this knot had been broken and didn't connect the way it should. A flicker of fear went through her mid-section, her hands going reflexively to her belly.

"Ah...Maeve," the woman said as though she'd been expecting her. When she stood she towered over Maeve, her hooded eyes staring down. "I am so glad you heeded my call. I would not want to keep you from your duties on this night."

Maeve backed away as the woman came toward her.

"When will it be born?" she asked, her untroubled gaze going to Maeve's belly.

Maeve couldn't seem to move or speak. She stood rooted, watching the woman move toward her and wondering if this was another of Pryderi's tricks.

"Now my dear, we wouldn't want another of your kind to be born here, would we?" She cackled, her hand going coquettishly to her mouth. "'Tis quite astonishing that you and I are both born of Brigid. Why was I not chosen for this exalted position, can you tell me? You do understand that I am your great-grandmother, Adair, do you not? You are not a stupid girl, just ill informed about the way things work here." Her eyes turned dark, obliterating the white. She put her hand on Maeve's arm, the fingernails digging into Maeve's flesh.

When Maeve looked down, the nails had turned into talons, and they had drawn blood. Maeve watched in horror as Adair's hand moved toward her mid-section, the black eyes paralyzing her. She was an insect caught in amber, unable to move or scream.

Watching her, Adair laughed. "Before I end your life and that of the little one inside you, I need a tiny bit of energy from you. You see I'm feeling somewhat old at the moment, and we can't have that, can we? I need my strength to help Pryderi and my son down there after you're gone. Of course, without you the fight will end very badly for your followers. Now don't worry, this won't hurt a bit."

Adair's hands circled Maeve's waist, her mouth close to Maeve's mouth. For one horrible moment Maeve thought the hag would kiss her, but that was not what she had in mind. When Maeve breathed out, Adair sucked in air noisily through her mouth, as though sipping some delightful nectar.

"Ahh...just what I needed. Youth is wasted on the young," she muttered, in between her lengthy inhales. Her face began to change, first looking middle-aged and then younger still, her cheeks turning plump and rosy.

With each breath Maeve felt more energy drain from her body. Adair's long inhales and licentious utterings of delight went on and on until finally Maeve crumpled to the ground. Watching her blandly, Adair straightened her dress, arranging the bodice to reveal her voluptuous bust line. She shook out her curls, reaching for a small mirror in her pocket. "Now that's better," she said, pulling her hair up to peer at her smooth neck. She pouted, examining her full red lips and then threw the mirror aside.

When the sorceress looked down on Maeve, her features rearranged themselves into a worried frown. "Oh my dear, I hope I didn't overdo it. But you cannot imagine the wonderful sensations, the vitality running through my veins." She smiled, wiping her lips with the back of her hand as though after a meal.

"Well, no matter. You would have been down there soon enough." She bent over Maeve, her talons poised over her heart. Maeve felt the prick as it slid through the leather tunic and entered her skin. When she met Adair's eyes, it was like looking into the darkest recesses of hell. All at once MacCuill's words were in her mind: *You have everything you need within you; it is only a matter of tapping into it.* She stilled her mind letting go of the fear, sending a mental burst of current toward Adair.

"Aaach!" Adair screamed, pulling her hand away.

"You will not do this," Maeve said, her eyes trained on Adair's. She stood, moving backward toward the tree roots.

Adair straightened, her face moving back and forth between youth and age. She moved toward Maeve, her eyes like black holes.

Maeve stepped between two tree roots and held her hands up. "You will not come any closer."

Adair moved forward and then stopped, her expression contorting into an ugly grimace. "Come now, dear. We are of the same blood."

Maeve watched her try to get through the invisible shield, her features rearranging themselves into a hideous, witch-like crone. "Let me IN!" she shrieked.

Maeve's mind was on her people, and how much time she'd wasted here with Adair. The moon would be up very soon. There wasn't another minute to spare. MacCuill's face appeared in her mind and she concentrated on it, her hand moving to her neck. But there was no stone. *Please*, she said silently, thinking of Harold, Eron and Finiche. *Please*. In the next moment she felt herself whirling through misty color.

"You are back," MacCuill said calmly, reaching a hand down to pull her up. "Did I not tell you the stone was no longer necessary?"

Maeve dusted herself off, surprised by his bland expression. She was still reeling from the horror of the encounter. "Weren't you worried about me? I was almost killed."

MacCuill laughed, his indigo eyes twinkling. "I have a hard time believing that. How did you leave things with Adair?"

Maeve frowned and shook her head and then turned, whistling for Finiche. When he arrived he didn't greet her, just stood obediently, waiting for her to climb on. *Does everyone, including my wolf, assume I'm an almighty goddess now?* she muttered under her breath. But then an odd thought went through her mind—*maybe I am.*

"What took so long?" Harold asked when she caught up with him. "Was it one of the villagers caught in a trap or something?"

Maeve nodded, unable to meet his eyes. "It was definitely a trap, but it's over now."

The trailing group made their way along a small side valley, heading to where it opened onto the wider plain. Lightning flashed every few minutes now, followed by the echoing reverberation of thunder rolling across a malevolent sky. The wind hit them sideways, and it was vicious, full of stinging ice crystals that clung to their hair and clothes. The wind pushed back every time they took a step forward. Something supernatural was certainly at work. Behind her MacCuill had taken out his flute and seemed to be waiting for some sign. Maeve had witnessed first hand how these guardians of the Caer Sidi could control the elements. This ability would come in handy, she thought, as another strong gust hit her, making her eyes water.

Scanning ahead, Maeve was relieved that Brandubh's men were not yet on the battlefield. From what Dagda had told her, the enemy troops would surely have come up this valley tonight to attack the Sidhe at their camp. She stopped and addressed the crowd, her strong voice projecting. "Remember what we've spoken about, how our only purpose is to save this world—and to manage this without doing harm. Do not let your fear or anger obscure our purpose here. Keep your minds focused only on love and bringing this wonderful place back to what it once was. But remember, if your life is threatened you must defend it. I want no casualties among you. If, during the course of our actions here, unfamiliar Oillteil, Wildmen or villagers attempt to join your ranks, do not turn them away. I expect a lot of defectors once the moon rises."

When Maeve finished her speech a shout went up—'*buaidh!*' pronounced *bway*, the Gaelic word for victory the Crion had yelled during her trip to the Otherworld in the dreamtime. After the noise had died down, Maeve signaled to her people by holding up her hand, putting a finger to her lips—it was time to employ stealth.

Once they reached the valley floor, Dagda placed himself at the front of his men, a guard on either side. The rest of the men and women of the Sidhe got into place behind him with their arms linked, just the way they had been in Maeve's vision. Eithne was there, a determined expression on her lovely features. Catching Maeve's eye she smiled, her hand going up in a salute.

Maeve was impressed with how formidable they appeared— standing as one, their waxed leather armor glistening. King Finvarra and Queen Donagh came into view at the back, their twin crowns picking up some glimmer of light where they waited on their black horses. Guards made a circle around them, swords at the ready. When the Crion went to join the Sidhe, dis- appearing among the larger race, Rea's small face drew Maeve's attention. The woman's smile was a tiny light in an otherwise dismal world. Maeve had a moment of misgiving, wishing she had not put the small ones into this dangerous situation, but she knew if she had tried to stop them they would have insisted on coming along. At least they were warmly dressed. Rea and the other women had spent long hours working to skin the deer found rotting in the valley, as well as every rabbit and squirrel they had trapped and eaten. Tanning the hides with their own urine, rinsing and drying them afterwards, the Crion women had managed to fashion the pelts into vests, sewing them to- gether with needles of bone and flax thread.

Cernunnos appeared out of the shadows, taking his place in front of Dagda, his impressive stature reassuring. Behind Cernunnos and a little to the right, MacCuill's grey robes billowed. Eron hurried forward to stand next to the druid, bending his head to whisper something. Looking around, Maeve noticed Taranis at the edge of the formation, Duncan on his back.

Just before Maeve took her place beside Harold at the front of the line, Catriona appeared, running toward Eron. When she reached him, Eron picked her up, burying his face in her hair. When he released her a few seconds later, she linked her arm with his and then turned to do the same with the Sidhe warrior on her other side. Catriona fit right in, looking like a war goddess herself with her wild grey hair blowing every which way, her eyes bright with determination. When Maeve scanned the crowd for Gertrude she couldn't find her.

A second later a tremor rippled across the valley, followed by a jagged flash of lightning. The boom of thunder followed, echoing on and on. The earth heaved, throwing Finiche sideways—he let out an eerie howl that was answered by several others. Maeve righted herself, patting the big wolf on his neck and then glanced over at Harold next to her. He and Argyll were perfectly suited, she thought, both calm and focused. When Harold turned toward her she saw the Kenneth personality shining out through his eyes. One hand held the reins and the other was on the scabbard, ready to pull out the heavy sword if necessary. He was a warrior through and through, exuding strength and courage.

Behind her, Cernunnos had the horn in his big hand, waiting for her signal. She glanced back once more at the Sidhe and others of her group dispersed through their ranks, noticing the glow that was beginning to radiate from all of them. Her mind went back to the village of Rowan and Janus and Sara—the rose auras that seemed to expand with the emotion of love. She had a moment of pride before she raised her hand to let Cernunnos know it was time. He nodded once and then placed the horn against his mouth. The enormous sound filled the valley, and reverberated, echoing back and forth. Seeming to materialize in response, heavy gusts swept down the valley, slamming against her body. She swayed for a moment and then felt Harold's hand grab hers. Her gaze went to the sky where dark and ominous clouds shoved against each other—the embodiment of the fury of Brandubh and his men. Wind began to whirl in patterns, moving through the crowd behind her. She heard sharp cries and some swearing but dared not look back.

A rhythmic thumping began, growing steadily louder. When Brandubh's men appeared out of the darkness, they were daunting, organized into groups of Oillteil, Wildmen and villagers, marching in rows of eight. They continued to come into view, row after row—surely more than two thousand strong. In their hands bright swords and crossbows gleamed out of the darkness, armor clanking rhythmically as they advanced. Maeve heard the whining of the beasts and then saw them spiraling through the lines, weaving in between the men. Their eyes glowed red, like burning coals.

When Brandubh was only a hundred yards away he put up his hand, bringing his men to a halt. He faced Maeve and the others, gray hair blowing wildly, his features twisted into a mask of rage. "Prepare yourselves for the last battle!" he shouted, raising his fist. His ranks were silent, waiting for his command. When a claw-like hand appeared on his left arm he turned, bending to speak to whoever it was. Maeve heard each word, as though they were being whispered in her ear. "She has a shield now and we must find a way to pierce it. Call to Pryderi."

Brandubh shook Adair's arm off, focusing his gaze on Maeve. He moved toward her, his steps measured as he assessed the situation. Adair watched her son, her wizened features filled with outrage. Maeve could almost hear her thoughts of frustration, the feeling of powerlessness that the woman's recent encounter with Maeve had left behind.

A low rumbling growl came from Finiche as Brandubh drew closer.

"Don't worry, Maeve. He can't do anything to you," came Gertrude's voice behind her. "Morrighan has stripped his powers because of his arrogance." Her gaunt face was oddly serene as she headed toward the priest.

"No, Gertrude!" Maeve cried, moving forward to intervene. But the woman had already placed herself between Maeve and Brandubh, her attention on the priest. Energy shimmered between them, crackling like electricity gone wild.

When a few of Brandubh's men rushed up to help, he waved them off, keeping his gaze focused on Gertrude. "You really believe you can defeat me?"

Gertrude smiled. "I do indeed, and you know exactly why."

Brandubh seemed taken aback for a moment. As he glanced over his shoulder, a whisper of uncertainty went through the men standing behind him.

"Do not let her unnerve you!" came Adair's scream.

"Shut up, Mother!"

Maeve glanced over at Harold, but he seemed unaffected, his hands folded over the pommel of the saddle, as though watching a play. Another streak of lightning hit the ground, turning the scene into garish green before dissipating. The resounding thunderclap a second later was deafening.

Brandubh moved forward, his cat-like motions putting him in a position to knife Gertrude. It was like a choreographed dance as Gertrude moved in to block him, her back arched. He turned like a ballet dancer, going up on his toes to grab her and hold her against his body before twisting her away from him with a shove. When she came at him again, he seized her around the waist with one arm, his other hand circling her neck. When he squeezed her throat she gave a garbled, strangled cry.

Maeve was just about to rush into the fray when Brandubh suddenly let go and fell to his knees, coughing uncontrollably. Gertrude took the opportunity to attack, pushing him backward where they grappled on the ground. Gertrude's high-pitched shrieks rent the air. "You evil bastard—I wish I had never met you!"

Brandubh stood, pushing into her with all his force. Gertrude was now on her hands and knees, Brandubh standing over her. "Do it!" she cried. "Kill me! I'd like to see you die with me you son-of-a-bitch!" Brandubh backed away, and Gertrude staggered to her feet, bringing a shout from within his troops. "You are beaten by a mere woman?" someone called out. In the next second chaos ensued, fights breaking out within the ranks as tempers flared.

Gertrude ran toward Maeve and the others, raising a cheer from within the Sidhe. Brandubh was now trying to regain control of his men, his voice rising in anger. "You will **not** question my actions. I am in charge here. Have you not filled your coffers from my gold? Is it not my actions that keep you safe? Bow down to me now!" he shrieked. Most of his troops bowed their heads, a few going down on one knee, but others seemed reluctant, with furtive glances toward the men behind Maeve.

Out of the shadows Pryderi appeared, heading toward the priest. They conferred for a moment and then Pryderi raised his hand, creating a swirling blue-black cloud above his head. It grew and grew, going faster and faster until he straightened his arm, pointing his fingers toward Maeve. The angry cloud unfurled, heading her way at a terrifying speed. At the same moment a tremor shook the earth, knocking Maeve off Finiche, and luckily putting her out of its trajectory. Behind her chaos ensued as the winds whipped through her people, knocking them down. Frustrated cries from the Sidhe joined the sound of growling beasts and screams of rage coming from Brandubh's troops.

Buoyed by Pryderi's success, a large group of Brandubh's men left formation and headed toward her and the Sidhe. By this time Maeve had found her balance, standing with her hand on the wolf's back. Finiche remained rooted to the spot and when she glanced to her right, she saw that Argyll and Harold were also planted. Maeve looked back to see the Sidhe standing like an impenetrable wall, their expressions resolute. What would happen when these Oillteil and Wildmen reached them? The sharp swords pointed toward them would surely penetrate their leather armor. All Maeve's visionary ideas came crashing down in her mind…how could she protect them?

As Brandubh's troops closed the distance between them, the glow faded, her people moving out of formation as panic set in. She saw hands going to swords, bows and arrows at the ready. Her plan had failed completely. A moment later a yell from Pryderi brought Brandubh's men to a screeching halt. The demi-god had his hand up, keeping them back, as if to say *this is my fight*. His handsome features distorted into an ugly grimace as his fingers circled above his head creating a spinning cloud full of dark magic. It came at Maeve before she had a chance to move aside, digging into her flesh and pinning her to the ground. She tried to clear her mind, tried to summon her strength, but she couldn't move, her face pushed into the earth, making her gag when she tried to suck in air.

In the distance a strange and eerie sound had begun— MacCuill was playing his flute. A second later she was released from Pryderi's grip and rose to her knees. Pale mist spiraled toward Pryderi, knocking him violently off his feet. A cry of rage came from the demi-god and he moved toward MacCuill, both hands in the air. A battle began between the two of them as they sent winds toward each other with increasing force. A high-pitched whistling became a shriek as the currents of air shot back and forth. Maeve watched them, awe-struck by the power coming from both of them, the anger and fury on the demi-god's face. MacCuill's expression was neutral, his gaze completely focused on Pryderi.

"Watch out, Maeve!" MacCuill suddenly shouted. Pryderi had turned from MacCuill, sending an ice-filled blast that hit her squarely in the chest. She went down, all the wind knocked out of her. Her chest ached from the cold, tiny knife-like crystals stuck in her tunic.

A bellow went up from Brandubh's men as they cheered Pryderi on. Maeve watched the wolf run toward Pryderi, his teeth bared, but when another tremor hit, the wolf lost his balance, falling onto his side. Maeve watched in horror as one of the Oillteil stuck a sword into him, the enormous creatures swarming over the wolf in their rush to get to Maeve. She struggled to her feet, falling again as tremor after tremor rolled across the valley. Icy wind blinded her and when she checked for Finiche he was completely lost from sight. Scanning behind her frantically, Maeve realized that MacCuill had disappeared, along with Harold and Argyll.

When the Oillteil were nearly upon her she held up her hand, hoping she could create the shield again. "NO!" she screamed. They seemed shocked for a moment, their ugly features confused as they came against the invisible wall. But in the next second they turned away, heading toward the Sidhe again, their weapons at the ready.

When the Oillteil reached the first line of the Sidhe there was a sudden clash of metal on metal. Maeve watched in dismay as the enormous Oillteil grappled with the smaller men, pushing the red-hairs backward and pressing swords deep into their flesh. Maeve screamed, her voice loud and desperate. This couldn't happen. When she called out for help, her voice was taken away by the screeching wind that raged across the battlefield. So far the first line of her men was holding, but it wouldn't take much for the stronger Oillteil to bull their way through. Everyone would be killed. Tears flowed down her face as she tried to figure a way out of this.

On the northern hill above the battlefield a gray horse had appeared, the dark-haired rider intent on the valley floor and Pryderi. Rhiannon was no longer wispy and out of focus, this woman looked like a goddess and a very angry one. Behind her other goddesses appeared, their beautiful features clear—she recognized Corra and Airmid, but the imposing one dressed in black was not familiar. But then Maeve noticed the enormous raven on her shoulder—this must be Morrighan, the goddess of war. Beside her stood a small golden-haired woman, her gaze fixed on the sky. That had to be Arianrhod, the moon goddess. Something had changed to bring them here—maybe all was not lost after all.

A collective shout from the hill brought Brandubh's at-tacking troops to a standstill, everyone turning to watch the fight between Pryderi and his mother. From the hill a battle cry came, a bolt of lightning hissing toward Pryderi. He deflected it easily, sending it back. After the strike, Maeve was blinded for a moment, unable to see what was going on, but a minute later Pryderi was no longer where he had been. For a moment Maeve thought Rhiannon had killed him, but when another bolt struck, mother and son were illuminated on the hill, circling each other like cats. A sharp crack of electricity hit the ground between Maeve and the Sidhe, opening several fissures and send-ing Brandubh's men cowering. But after the brightness disap-peared, shadows deepened, the only evidence of the continuing battle on the hill the shrieking curses and tremors that were becoming more and more extreme. Looking toward the Sidhe Maeve was glad to see them re-grouping and tending to their wounds. The Oillteil had backed away now, trying to put dis-tance between themselves and the gaping holes in the ground.

Brandubh's remaining troops focused all their attention on the hill above the valley as the fight between Rhiannon and

Pryderi grew more and more intense. Every lightning strike brought it into view, the other goddesses staring down at the humans with expressions of fury and disdain. Sparks showered over the valley, landing on Oillteil and Wildmen alike and sending them screaming in circles. "Where is the one true god now?" someone shouted, bringing a rumble of assent. "Aye!" someone else screamed.

"Get back in line!" Brandubh roared. "These are but women on the hill, they are NOTHING!"

In response to that there was a deafening shout from Morrighan. *"Is that what you think, mortal? Has nothing I have said or done had any affect on you?"* Morrighan's laugh echoed across the valley causing many of Brandubh's men to cover their ears in terror.

"You will suffer greatly when the time comes for your last payment," she cried out, sending a bolt of flame raining down on everyone.

Shrieks of pain and fear rang out as Brandubh's men caught fire. Brandubh had been struck and was rolling around on the ground, his screams bringing Adair running. The sorceress bent over her son, doing something with her hands and a moment later Brandubh was standing, a smoldering dark cloud rising from his robes.

A flash caught Maeve's eye, taking her attention toward the Sidhe. Somehow in the past few minutes, Maeve's people had reorganized themselves and now blinding light streamed from them, radiating into the darkness and meeting the luminescent rays sent across the valley by the goddesses. Brandubh screamed at his men, ordering them to attack. Wind shrieked down from the hill, obliterating the priest's words, his hands waving as he tried to get his men to obey. They refused to move.

Maeve watched the pale luminosity flowing across the valley growing brighter and brighter. This was unexpected, a gift from the goddesses who had now gained back their strength. Lost in the beauty of it she didn't see Brandubh running toward her until he was nearly upon her, his knife held out to impale her on the razor-sharp blade. She rushed backward trying to keep a certain distance between them but he quickly closed the gap. In the next second, black fog spiraled into the valley obliterating every bit of her view. She moved away as quickly as she dared hoping Brandubh wouldn't find her, her mind reeling at the man's arrogance and bravado after what she'd just witnessed.

Maeve could hear screaming but couldn't figure out what was happening. Everything was going too quickly, like a sped-up movie. Finiche was not beside her. At least she'd lost Brandubh in the fog. Another earthquake struck and she slipped, falling heavily and when the fog parted Brandubh was bearing down on her. She rose to her knees trying to manifest the shield but her mind was muddled and nothing seemed to materialize. Her mind flew in circles wondering what was happening, as shrieks and screams continued unabated. Her people were being massacred. Brandubh was nearly upon her when John rushed out of the fog, leaping ahead of the priest.

"Don't do it!" he yelled. "I'll do her for you."

John looked deranged, his lips curled back in an eager smile. He held a sword, the tip of the blade set to sink straight into her heart. She knew without a doubt that she could not get away in time, and that for some reason the shield would not come into being. He would kill her. A flash went through her mind of everything she had planned and hoped for; her love for Harold and the others here she had come to care so deeply about, the Otherworld and what could have been. Tears flowed down her cheeks as an enormous sadness engulfed her: the knowledge of what she was about to lose. She clutched her stomach convulsively thinking about the baby who would never be born. And then calm came over her and she watched John with a feeling of acceptance, waiting for the inevitable pain, hoping it would be over quickly. She closed her eyes, bracing herself and saying a little prayer of gratitude for her life.

Just before John reached her, there was a shout of rage and then Harold rushed out of the fog, his eyes wild as he plunged his sword deeply into the other man. John fell, his hand going helplessly to the handle sticking out of his chest. "You!" he cried, his eyes wide with surprise as his life ebbed quickly away. He lay on his back in a pool of blood, his eyes still open, his own sword abandoned on the ground beside him.

Maeve turned away, afraid she might be sick. When she searched for Harold a minute or so later, he had disappeared again, lost in the mounting hysteria caused by the fog. John's sword had gone with him.

Terrified shouting, snarling beasts and swearing came out of the ever-swirling mist; there was no way to tell what was going on. When Maeve rose she was attacked and thrown backward by one of the Beithir. The raging animal bit into her arm, drawing blood, but she managed to curl into a ball to prevent the ceature from grabbing her throat. She concentrated every bit of her will on having the beast leave her alone, surprised when it slinked away.

The fog began to disperse bringing a yell from the Oillteil. Maeve's attention was taken to the sky where the moon appeared and disappeared as the clouds thinned. With the moon's emergence Maeve rose to her feet, a feeling of power entering her body. The line of goddesses standing like marble statues on the hill were linked to her—she was one of them. Suddenly she was chanting Gaelic words that she didn't know the meaning of, archaic words repeated over and over, the goddesses joining in, the swelling sound echoing across the valley. *Sir-ee-ee-ee ha-all*. But then it came to her. *Sirheadh Thall* was an ancient prayer that meant 'seek beyond'. After a few minutes the chant drifted away on its own leaving the valley bathed in stillness. Looking up she lifted her arms, waving away the rest of the heavy clouds and bringing a low guttural moan from Brandubh's troops. When the remaining wisps scattered like so many frightened birds, bringing the bright orb into full focus, an audible sigh went through Brandubh's men, some falling to their knees, others rushing to join the Sidhe.

"It's only the moon, you idiots!" Brandubh bellowed. The priest made a motion to one of the Wildmen, ordering him to kill one of the defectors, but the man ignored him, heading away from the troop formation. Adair stood next to her son, her fixated stare directed at Maeve who could feel the dark energy cascading toward her. But her shield was in place, her power glowing around her body and she didn't move.

"Get back in line!" Brandubh yelled. "We've all seen it now!" As his words rang out there was scuffling as some of his men returned, their focus again on him. They pulled out their swords, ready for his next command. Adair whispered something in her son's ear, pointing toward Maeve. Brandubh glanced at Maeve over his shoulder and then looked up at the sky. He addressed his men, his voice deep and carrying. "Do not be fooled!" he shouted. "This is all a trick conjured by a heathen witch! You must kill her to be free of the curse she brings down on us!"

In the sky things were changing, the bright moon growing dark. There was a muffled yell, fingers pointing toward the sky as the earth's shadow began to eclipse the moon's face. Maeve gazed upward, as surprised as anyone else. She watched it progress, the sphere slowly turning to the color of blood, and scattering six-hundred men, most of them running to join the Sidhe. Many were on their knees, arms held up in supplication, some simply covered their heads, trying to keep out the strange and eerie sight. Wildmen and Oillteil ran in circles, their voices adding to the general pandemonium, but there was no escape. When the beasts began to howl, utter panic ensued. Screams rent the air as men and beasts took off into the night.

"Kill her!" Brandubh ordered. Beside him, Adair performed some intricate hand movements, as if to compel the men to do the priest's bidding.

A rush of men left the ranks. Like automatons, they pulled their swords out, charging toward Maeve. Wildmen loosed arrows that hissed toward her with unfailing accuracy. Trying to keep from being hit, Maeve stumbled backward. Her gaze went to the hill above the battlefield where Cernunnos now stood, flanked by the goddesses. Others had seen him now, causing more mayhem as defectors rushed toward the Sidhe. People were being trampled, others standing still, their mouths open in a perpetual scream.

Maeve hurtled toward her troops, finding a spot on their northern flank. Oillteil and Wildmen struggled with her people, shouts ringing out. More arrows whizzed by, and Maeve watched in mounting alarm as several of her men went down. Into the utter pandemonium a sound began, building and building until it filled the valley, thundering and reverberating through the forest. On the hill Cernunnos stood with arms spread, his mouth wide open. Stronger than the auroch horn, his cry of rage and pain echoed on and on.

Once it died away, silence spread across the battlefield, bringing everything to a stop. Many of Brandubh's men kneeled, their foreheads pressed to the ground, hands over their ears. Others stood as though turned to stone, gazing toward the hill.

In the next moment there was a deafening roar as a fifty-foot wall of water surged down the valley heading for the sea. Maeve stood transfixed, unable to believe her eyes as the water came toward her, a curling lip of white at the wave's top. Glancing around at the Sidhe, her heart contracted. They stood as before, their glow still strong. Cowering in their midst were newly arrived Wildmen and Oillteil, their arms raised to the sky. She couldn't see the Crion at all. Brandubh's men were in panic, fighting with each other to escape. Some hurtled toward the sea, others were knocked down, trampled in the mad rush. Brandubh and Adair were nowhere to be seen. Tears brimmed in Maeve's eyes, spilling over to track down her cheeks. "Save yourselves!" she screamed to her people, trying to be heard over the roar. Would anyone survive?

The water was nearly upon them, sticks, rocks and debris tumbling inside the gray green mass. She turned, tripping in her haste to get away, seeing the expressions of terror and disbelief on the faces all around her. And then the water slammed into them, engulfing everything in its wake. Maeve was lifted roughly off her feet, the cold water snatching her breath, turning and twisting her body as it swept forward. She was struck with rocks and tree limbs, turned over and over as she was carried violently downstream. Flailing bodies were under the water, all struggling to rise to the surface, but there was no surface to this heaving mass, the depth beyond her wildest imaginations. She wondered if this was it; that all this was for nothing. But just when she felt she couldn't hold her breath another second, she somehow found her way to the top, drawing in air with a gasp.

Sucking in mouthfuls of air she struggled to stay afloat; her clothes were heavy and dragged her down, making her heart race. Kicking, she got her feet free from her boots and then pulled the leather tunic over her head, her panic subsiding as her body became more buoyant. A large shadow appeared in what had become a lake and she looked up to see an owl gliding silently overhead, it's eye trained on her. The eclipse had now passed, the full moon luminous and huge, brilliant in the black star-filled dome of the sky.

Floating on her back to catch her breath, she glimpsed the quiet radiance of the moon reflected in the gently lapping wavelets. It was like a lake of molten silver. She swam in a circle, feeling the icy numbness starting to creep into her limbs, and trying to determine where Harold and her friends were. There were heads bobbing in the water but she couldn't see their faces. Cernunnos and the goddesses were no longer on the hill. And where was Brandubh?

Just as that question went through her mind a loud splash took her attention. Not far from her, her grandmother and the priest wrestled in the water. Catriona's white face was pinched in anger as Brandubh clawed at her, his heavy wet hair hanging in his eyes. It was the first time Maeve had truly recognized the resemblance between the two of them. They looked almost interchangeable, long gray hair plastered to their skulls, green eyes flashing. "Stop...stop it...it's over!" she cried, swimming toward them and trying to be heard.

They never looked up or even seemed to notice her in their intense concentration on one another. Treading water she called out over and over and then watched in rising horror as Brandubh raised his hand. The knife blade caught the light, turning bright silver just before he plunged it into his sister. Catriona let out an unearthly scream, sinking below the surface. In the next moment Brandubh screamed, the eerie echo rippling across the water. His struggling body rose and fell, disappearing under the surface only to reappear a second later.

Maeve was suddenly caught in the priest's mind, the barriers to her broken. She knew that what he had just done to Catriona was also killing him—it was like they were the same person. As he struggled in the water an image come toward him, a beautiful woman with dark luminous eyes. Dark wavy hair hung loose around her shoulders, shining in the light from a sun only visible in his mind. On a visceral level, Maeve felt his enormous happiness when he saw her, his heart almost bursting with love. Gertrude was smiling, moving toward him with her hands held out, her diaphanous long blue tunic sliding back and forth over the obvious swell of her belly. She was barefoot, her hips swaying gracefully as she drew closer and closer. When she reached him Brandubh took her hands. And in that moment Maeve could feel his anticipation and desperate longing for the feel of her body against his. Wonderful memories surfaced in his mind of his full life with her. He smiled as he pulled her close, but in that second she began to fade, bringing a sharp pain in the middle of Brandubh's chest. Maeve clutched her own chest and then cried out as an agonizing wave of regret and yearning for what might have been went through the priest's mind. This was all unreal and his life had been wasted. Brandubh's mouth opened, no sound coming from his throat as he realized too late that this was his last payment to Morrighan. The horror of it bit into him and then seared into Maeve, making her clutch her stomach. His wide-open eyes stared into the beyond as death claimed him, the water closing solidly over his body. He sank to the bottom, and was sucked into the currents and eddies heading toward the sea, his black garments spread around him like drifting seaweed.

Maeve was sobbing now, her body shivering with cold and sorrow. The anguish was too much—it would be so easy to slide under the water and let herself go. The water was calling, seductive voices pulling at her. And then she saw the ghosts, their translucent limbs reaching out to her from Annwn. Her body went limp and she let herself sink, reaching for the entreating hands. But a second later she was jerked from the dreamlike reverie, Harold's voice in her ear. "Maeve, thank everything that's holy." His arms were around her, worried eyes staring into hers. "I thought you were gone, I couldn't find you…"

"Harold." It was all she could manage to say as stinging tears mixed with the cuts and bruises and muddy streaks that ran down her face.

Chapter

29

F inna sat straight up in bed. "Something's happened."

"What is it?" Alex asked, his voice muffled by the pillow. It was the middle of the night and he had been deeply asleep.

"I don't know, it's just a feeling...an absence...like...I don't know how to describe it."

Alex sat up, immediately wide-awake. Finna's skin had an odd greenish tinge where the moonlight touched it. "Is it Maeve? Has something happened to Maeve?"

"I don't think so..." She stared at Alex. "No, it isn't Maeve."

He took her hand. "What then? What's happened?"

Finna was crying without making a sound, the bright tears tracking down her cheeks. "Don't cry," he said, his arms around her. "We don't know what's going on, do we?"

She pressed her face into his shoulder. "I wish I was psychic, Alex, I want to *see!*"

"You obviously are psychic if something woke you out of a dead sleep. You just haven't gotten all the details yet. Just sit here, love. I'll go make us some tea." Alex got out of bed and pulled his trousers on, padding barefoot into the kitchen. He knew there would be no more sleeping tonight. God, how he loved this woman—he couldn't imagine life without her. Just sleeping together in the same bed was enough for him. He put the kettle on and came back to the bed.

Finna touched his face. "I'm very glad you're here." A moment later she slumped against him and began to sob.

"Finna? What did you see?"

"It's my mother," she gasped. "My mother's dead."

Chapter

30

"**M**aeve are you sure you're okay? And the baby?" Harold had carried Maeve up the hill to their former camp after they managed to drag themselves out of the water.

"I got bumped a bit, bruised here and there, but I think everything's all right." She smiled wanly, pulling on a pair of jeans from her pack and attempting to button the top. "Or maybe it's just my imagination," she added, tears starting again. "It's too early to actually feel anything, isn't it?"

Harold pressed her hand. "I don't have any idea—how far along are you? Was it from our first time?"

"I think so."

"Well, he's showing now," he smiled, watching her strain to close her jeans. He put his ear to her belly, listening for a long while. "He just told me he's fine."

Maeve laughed through her tears, her fingers leaving muddy streaks as she wiped her eyes. "You seem to be convinced of the gender."

Harold raised his eyebrows, a wry smile on his face. "Maybe I have some psychic abilites too. After all this reincarnation stuff I wouldn't be at all surprised."

When the wolf appeared with a deep wound in his side, Maeve turned away and set to work, applying yarrow from her pack and then using her healing hands. While she worked the moon set, the sky turning to deep purple velvet and then lightening into violet as dawn approached. The colors seemed acutely vivid and breathtaking.

"You need to rest."

"Not yet, there's too much to do. We don't know where anyone is. Dagda hasn't

checked in, or the Crion, Oillteil or the Wildmen who were with them. Have you seen Rea? And where's MacCuill? I haven't laid eyes on Eron or Duncan since very early on—I hope they're all right. I should have made Duncan stay back at camp—he's far too old for this."

"And how would you have managed that? The man's not any older than Eron.

It could be a long while before everyone's accounted for," Harold added, putting his hand on her shoulder. "They could have been washed down toward the sea. That's miles from here. Remember where we ended up and how long it took us to get back up here."

Maeve hugged her knees, her head going to her chest. She felt drained, as though everything had been sucked out of her. The grief she felt was like a heavy weight pressing down on her heart.

"I'm so sorry about Catriona," Harold added, as though reading her mind.

Maeve stared up at him. "Maybe it was inevitable. The boatman told me Brandubh had come from the Underworld. I didn't understand at the time, but now I do; he wasn't meant to be." Maeve's pale face contorted in pain. "When I saw Catriona and

Brandubh fighting in the water...it was so weird, like they were the same person...all that anger coming from both of them! And I knew that Brandubh felt every single bit of pain he inflicted. I could almost feel it myself. It was horrible. Poor Eron--I wonder if he knows about Catriona."

"I'm sure he does. Those two are really connected. But we don't know for sure—she could have been washed away after the fight."

"You didn't see him stick that knife into her chest. I can't imagine anyone surviving that. Oh Harold!" she began to cry, pressing her face into his shoulder.

"Maeve, you're exhausted--just lie down here for a few minutes and close your eyes. I'm going to scout around, see if I can find anyone."

"But..."

"Please, Maeve," he pressed her gently down next to the wolf, placing the dry coat from his pack over her. "It'll be dawn soon. We can take a look together once the sun comes up, but you're very pale and I don't want you fainting on me." He smiled and kissed her hand.

"All right, but just for a moment," she agreed.

A few minutes later Harold stood up, extricating his hand from hers. He looked down on Maeve, noticing the dark shadows under her closed eyes, the hollow of her cheeks. Her breathing was deep and regular—already asleep. He checked on the horses before heading down the hill; Argyll and Taranis had managed to find their way back and were lying under the trees with their eyes closed. Most of the valley was covered by water now, the battlefield completely obliterated. He thought of what he'd seen, the panic and insanity. He thanked the spirits for the Kenneth personality—he couldn't have managed without it. But as his mind went back to John, he knew he would have done the job as easily as Kenneth—in fact he wasn't sure which personality had been in charge at the moment he plunged his sword into the man. He shuddered, the horror of it making him feel ill.

He hadn't wanted to leave Maeve but the Sidhe needed him and he figured that Maeve could take care of herself now that John was out of the picture. He had seen the woman do amazing things during those endless hours. His memories now were of a chaos so complete that it was hard to tell friend from foe. His mind returned to that awful moment when he pulled a sword out of one of the Wildman's hands, turning it on him. Several others had attacked after that and he had slain them all without even knowing if they were defectors. Killing to save Maeve was one thing but this was something else altogether. He shook the images from his mind, telling himself it was over. Now he could be Harold again, the man whose main purpose in life was to love Maeve and be a good father to their child. He smiled at the romantic sentiment, wondering if it was true. Surely there was something else in his future...but then he had an image of the three of them, a baby boy walking between them with his tiny hands in theirs. He shrugged, acknowledging the reality.

A very faint orange band had appeared at eastern horizon, sending streaks of bright color into the purple and mauve sky. He hadn't realized until this moment how much he had missed the sun. As the sky began to lighten in the east something in his heart lifted in response. He thought of this place and the people, all the friendships he had forged in his short time here. His life in Halston seemed utterly remote, removed from his life like a story in a book. To the west the moon was sinking fast and soon would disappear. Sun and moon—both had been invisible for months, maybe years.

A faint mist hung over the surface of the water as dawn broke, the scudding wisps of clouds reflected in the unruffled surface. Most of the area where the Tuatha De Danann camp had been was flooded, but a large group of men had gathered on the side of the hill. They looked exhausted, with sodden clothing and cuts and bruises all over their faces and arms. Many were barefoot. Dagda was there with his son Aengus and many others who had stood with them. The Oillteil, Crion and Wildmen were not among them. Had they washed down to the sea? He hoped they were alive.

Moving closer to the group, he spied Duncan and Eron talking with Dagda. He drew closer hoping that Eron knew about his wife, because if he didn't, Harold did not want to be the one to break it to him.

Eron looked up as Harold approached, reaching out to clasp his hand. "It's good to see you in one piece. Where is Maeve?" he asked, his gaze going toward the hill.

"I left her resting. I told her we could search for people later when the sun comes up. She's done in."

"I can imagine—I think we all are."

"Hello, Duncan. Glad you made it."

"And you, Harold. I have to tell ye I caught sight of your prowess with a sword—very impressive."

Harold shrugged, feeling uncomfortable. "I did what I had to do, I guess. Have you seen the others? MacCuill? Gertrude?"

Duncan shook his head.

"We were hoping you had." Eron turned away, his eyes flooding with tears. "Catriona is gone."

"I know. I was there."

"You witnessed what happened?"

"I was in the water searching for Maeve when she and Brandubh fought."

"What? I thought she had drowned. I found her body washed up just a little while ago."

"No, it was a lot more than that."

Eron stared into space. "She had some blood on her chest but I assumed she had been hit with a tree limb or something. Tell me what happened."

"He stabbed her, but if it's any consolation, Brandubh died of the same wound."

Eron frowned. "What do you mean by that?"

"Morrighan made a bargain with Brandubh a long time ago. One of the men who defected told me all about it, how the goddess asked for three payments for what she had helped him with in the past. Apparently she had given Brandubh control over the crows and ravens—they acted as his messengers. In any case, the man told me that recently Morrighan appeared at their camp and announced that the crows were no longer at his disposal. But after that, she told him that if he inflicted pain on anyone else, he would feel it in his own body. According to this man, the goddess was terrifying in her fury."

Eron shook his head. "The crows were part of what happened to my first wife. They came into her village and attacked with no mercy. No crow in its right mind would act in such a manner. After killing and maiming many, the crows flew away, but then Brandubh and his mother torched the town, killing all the rest."

"I remember hearin' about that horror. The settlement was never the same," Duncan added, frowning.

Eron looked down letting a long moment go by. When he raised his head again his eyes looked bleak. "So he killed himself at the same time he killed my wife."

"Yes, I'm sorry to say that's exactly what happened."

"And he knew the outcome of this?"

"Oh yes, I'm sure he knew."

"So killing his sister was worth his own life," Eron muttered.

Harold didn't reply. When Eron walked away, he followed him, leaving Duncan talking with Dagda. He knew the man needed him right now, even if Eron hadn't said so. He was the color of ash, his eyes raw from crying—he looked as though he had aged fifty years.

Harold followed the older man down to the water's edge where Catriona's body had been placed with care. Her hair had been combed and smoothed back revealing an unmarked face in repose. Eron had manged to find clean clothes for her, a long woven skirt of sky blue and one of his deerskin tunics. Pale and beautiful in death her chiseled features reminded Harold of a marble statue—a goddess. Harold knelt next to her struggling to control himself and trying to come up with some words of sympathy, but nothing came to mind. He had never even met the woman. There were no words for this kind of tragedy.

"Did you find anyone else?" he asked after a few minutes.

"No, but I'm sure there are many dead."

They sat together in silence, listening to the soft lapping of the water, watching the sun rise over the eastern mountains. The sky turned brilliant orange and then pink and then the orb of the sun appeared, dazzlingly bright against the dark trees. It was a beautiful and welcome sight. Already the ground had begun to thaw and small patches of green were showing underneath.

Finally Harold got up. "I need to go and wake Maeve. I promised her we would search together after dawn. I'm sorry she missed this sunrise. Before I go Eron, what can I do for you?"

"There's nothing anyone can do for me, Harold. I just need to be here with her for a while longer, see if she has anything to say to me."

Harold reached down and patted Eron gently on the arm. "See you in a while."

When Harold reached the top of the hill he found Maeve sitting with her back against a tree, her face to the sun. At his approach, she opened her eyes, smiling up at him in welcome.

"I thought you would still be asleep."

"And miss the first sunrise? I woke up as soon as the sky began to get light. I will never take the sun for granted again."

Harold sat down next to her and picked up her hand. "Are you warm enough?"

"Oh stop fussing. I'm fine."

"It's not about that, your hands are cold that's all. And we need to find you some shoes," he added, looking down at her bare feet.

"My hands are always cold. Remember? Cold hands, warm heart."

"I found Eron and Duncan."

"How are they? Does Eron know?"

"Yes, Catriona's body washed to shore. He's devastated." Harold couldn't stop the tears that filled his eyes.

"My poor, poor grandfather."

"He has her body down there. He's trying to communicate with her."

Maeve sighed, sadness passing across her hollow eyes. "What about Gertrude? Did you see her? I hope Brandubh didn't kill her too."

"I would have told you if I had."

Maeve was standing now, a look of determination on her face. "Let's go."

On the side of the hill below them the Sidhe were preparing to leave. Maeve hurried ahead, Harold trailing behind. When she reached Dagda, he went down on one knee, bowing his head. "Willow, we are taking our leave now. We thank you for your guidance, your wisdom and for what you have accomplished here."

"Dagda, I thank you and your courageous men. Without your light we would have failed completely. And please convey my deepest gratitude to King Finvarra and Queen Donagh. I am so sorry I let you all down."

"You did not let us down. What happened this night was part of the prophecy. Have you not read it, my lady?" Dagda smiled sadly. "It did not say that no lives would be lost, only that if you succeeded the light would return. Look around you." He pointed toward the sun, now fully risen, the bright light spreading across the water down in the valley. "A lot of my men have not returned. I hope they were washed down further, into the Caer Sidi, that they did not perish."

"I hope this too." Maeve said. "I have yet to see many of my friends. The water could have taken them miles from here."

"The sun has come back because of you. The water has healed the land, restored the waterways. The balance is returned, daughter of Brigid."

Maeve froze, her mind on her earlier promise, but Dagda was already turning away.

"I thank you, my lady, " he called, leading his straggling group of soldiers to the east and home.

Maeve watched them, her mind far away. It had been Brigid who promised to bring them together, not her. She stared into space for a while imagining Brigid and wondering if the Brigid who had appeared before her was her ancestor or the goddess. Or maybe they were one and the same. Maeve walked slowly down the hill. When she turned back for one last look at the Sidhe, she noticed a tall, bright-haired woman in a long gown walking next to Dagda. Her head was bent to his as she adjusted the dark shawl around her shoulders and then looped her arm through his. He must have felt Maeve's gaze because Dagda turned, raising his right arm in a fisted salute. Maeve smiled and waved, watching them until they rounded a bend and disappeared.

"Do you want me to carry you?" Harold asked when she caught up to him. "Your feet must be freezing."

"I'm okay, I would rather feel the earth, even if it's a bit cold."

Harold took her hand, leading her to the place where Catriona lay. Eron was still there, sitting cross-legged next to her with his head bowed. Next to him Duncan cried silently, his head in his hands.

"Maeve," Eron said, rising.

Maeve went to her grandfather, falling easily into his arms. "I'm so sorry," she whispered into his shoulder, tears tickling down her face.

"Some part of me knew this would occur," Eron said. "I don't know why, I guess it was Brandubh and her unfailing connection with him. At first I thought she had drowned, but Harold told me what really happened." He gazed down at Catriona's body. "I wouldn't have known, otherwise." He lifted her right hand, examining the fingers. "Look how beautiful her hands are...were," he amended. "I'm not sure I want to go on without her."

Duncan stood up, reaching out to grasp Maeve's forearm. "I'm very pleased to see ye both unharmed. So very sorry this happened. I was hopin' for some good talks with Catriona about the past when this was all over and done with. I suppose I will have to share my memories with ye and Harold." He tried to smile but failed miserably.

When Maeve hugged him, the older man stiffened, but she didn't care. She was just so glad he was alive. "I was worried about you, Duncan—I didn't see you during the battle at all."

"I was there, lost in the chaos. Somehow I managed to keep out of harm's way—somethin' was lookin' after me."

Eron worried at Catriona's clothes, straightening the tunic and smoothing her skirt.

Duncan put his hand on Eron's shoulder. "I loved her just as ye did, Eron. We had a relationship back in the early days. She was the most free-spirited woman I have ever known." Streaks of dirt lined Duncan's unshaven cheeks where tears still trickled down. "She would wish ye to go on for your great-grandchild, Eron, not give up because she's nae longer with us."

When Maeve kneeled on the ground next to her grand-mother a lump formed in her throat, the enormity of everything that had happened rising to the surface. She looked so peaceful, as though she was simply asleep. "I didn't get the chance to re-ally know her." Tears trickling down her face making dark spots on the tunic. "Mamo," she whispered. She ran her hands lightly in the air over Catriona's body, searching for some small spark of energy, but there was nothing. This was not a wound she could heal.

Maeve glanced up at Harold. "I thought that maybe...but it's no use."

Harold's brows furrowed. "What about the healing spring?"

Eron glanced his way. "I don't think so Harold, but I would certainly be willing to try."

"But why not?" Maeve asked, excited now. Harold had been resurrected and he'd been dead longer than her grandmother. "MacCuill would know."

Eron stared into the distance, his eyes dull. Maeve could see the effort it took to keep himself under control. He bent over Catriona's feet, pulling off the deerskin boots he had made for her. "Take these moon granddaughter, your feet are bare."

"I don't need these, I'll find some others."

"She would want you to have them, Maeve. Please."

Maeve sat down and pulled the boots over her cold feet. They should have been sopping wet but instead they were dry and warm inside. They fit her perfectly as she knew they would.

"Find MacCuill," Eron said after a moment, and then reached down and lifted Catriona's body, cradling it against him. Her head rested in the crook of his elbow, her long hair streaming down over his arm. He turned away from them and started toward the hill without looking back.

Harold and Maeve watched him until he faded into the light mist that hung over the saturated earth.

"Should we follow him?" Maeve asked. "I'm afraid of what he might do."

"No, he said to find MacCuill. If there's any possibility of bringing her back, the druid will know."

The water had receded, leaving a muddy and meandering path that led toward the low hill between them and the Caer Sidi. There were no guards now, no people anywhere. The wall of water must have swept them all down toward the sea.

"Call to MacCuill, Maeve. We need to find him as soon as possible," Duncan urged.

Duncan's voice reached Maeve through what felt like layers of cotton wool. Everything had taken on a dreamy quality, as though time had slowed down. She didn't know how long they had been standing at the top of the hill, and had no memory of climbing it, didn't know how long her grandmother had been lying at the bottom before Eron had carried her away. She thought she might be in shock. Her thoughts went to MacCuill, conjuring up his face in her mind's eye. Visualizing the druid brought her back into her body—she took a deep breath, feeling the solidness of the earth beneath her feet, warm now in her grandmother's boots, Harold's hand in hers. Her eyes rose from where they had been focusing on the ground, her gaze taken into the distance, making her breath catch in her throat.

Before them the shoreline curved gracefully, a pale shell against blue-green water sparkling with millions of tiny lights from the sun. The bright azure sky looked domed, with streaks of pink clouds above where the sun hung suspended over the eastern horizon. The vivid green of growing things was already visible where there had been nothing only a few hours before. A shallow silvery lake lay in the valley, stretching down to the sea.

"Oh look!" Maeve cried, pointing to the island where a castle of ice clung to the mountain, shining blue in the glint of the sun.

A second later she heard a deep voice behind her. "That is the castle of the moon goddess. We need to pay her a visit."

"MacCuill!" Maeve flung herself into his arms.

He chuckled and then laughed. "It's good to see you, and you as well, Harold," he added, glancing his way. "And Duncan—glad you made it through all of this."

"We were looking for you because of Catriona…"

MacCuill's eyes turned opaque. "Yes, Catriona," he said sadly.

"Can we take her to Airmid's spring?"

"This is not possible."

"Why not?"

"Her death was part of what needed to happen. She accepted this."

Maeve frowned. "I don't understand. Did she say this to you?"

"Yes, she told me this many times. Brandubh and Catriona were linked. As twins there couldn't be one without the other. Brandubh and Catriona each represented one half of a whole— that is why they both had to die. Remember, the prophecy spoke only of bringing back the balance, not the light—the darkness is part of all life and must be acknowledged. You should know this by now, Maeve. Did you not pay a visit to Annwn, the Underworld?"

447

"It was only a dream but how did you know about it? I don't remember telling you."

MacCuill smiled. "Are you sure about that? I spoke with Cerridwen after your meeting—it was she who brought you there so that you would understand the hidden, so that you wouldn't fear it."

"She offered me a drink from the cauldron of knowledge and inspirtion but..."

"It wasn't the proper moment for that."

Maeve thought about what she had witnessed during Catriona and Brandubh's fight in the water: the dark and the light. Like the earth as it went around the sun, night and day. She thought of her time in the underworld, what Ceridwenn had told her. She thought about her grandfather, how he seemed to accept Catriona's death even though he was devastated by it. He must have always known it would come to this. An ache went through her chest as she realized the sacrifice Catriona had made, the deep loss to all of them.

"She never spoke of her brother," Duncan said quietly as though to himself. "There was always this part of her that she kept hidden despite her free-spirited attitudes. I will miss her greatly."

Maeve looked up her eyes seeking MaCuill's. "I tapped into Brandubh's mind at the end, the few moments before his death. He had a vision of Gertrude—he really loved her. His last thoughts were of the life he could have had with her. She was pregnant in his vision and I could feel all his emotional pain—the guilt and misgivings. It was so terribly sad."

MacCuill nodded. "This must have been his final payment to Morrighan. I know how this goddess operates and this would be her style—to show him the life he could have had, make him long for it and then take it away at the last moment. Do not feel sorry for the man, Maeve. Think back on what he did to this place, all the death and destruction he's responsible for."

"Do you think Gertrude's all right? Could she really be pregnant?"

"Under the circumstances it is certainly possible. Morrighan may have known the truth of things when she presented that vision. When we find Gertrude you can ask."

"And what about Adair? I didn't see her at the end."

MacCuill didn't say anything for a moment, his eyes lowered. "Adair lives," he finally answered.

There was silence for a moment as everyone took in this news. Maeve had a moment of panic, remembering her encounters with the sorceress. But with Brandubh gone what could the woman do? It seemed that all her energy had been wrapped up in her son. And besides that, Maeve had a shield now to protect herself from harm.

A minute or so later another question bubbled up in Maeve's mind. "MacCuill, why did we have that incredible flood? It happened right after Cernunnos made that unbelievable sound. That wasn't Adair, was it?"

The druid shook his head. "Cernunnos poured himself into that call, Maeve. It was his way of letting the forest and all the spirits know his outrage about what had been wrought here. As far as the water goes, the strength of the call must have broken Pryderi's magic, releasing every dammed up stream and river in the Otherworld all at once."

"Did Cernunnos plan that?"

"I highly doubt it—I think he was merely expressing his own feeling of impotence."

"And yet he was the least affected—all the others were indistinct the first time I met them but Cernunnos was solid as a rock."

"Maybe so, but that did not change his fury and powerlessness. Many of his animals perished during this dark time."

They walked on, each lost in their own thoughts. At a rocky outcropping the group stopped to rest, pulling out water and some cheese MacCuill had managed to salvage. MacCuill and Duncan sat down next to each other, talking about the battle and what they'd been involved in. Behind the two men Harold placed his hands on Maeve's shoulders and slowly turned her around to face him. He leaned down and kissed her on the lips with such tenderness that she began to cry. He reached forward to touch MacCuill's shoulder. "Did you know we're having a baby?"

MacCuill turned, chuckling. "I would love to tell you this was a surprise, but I have been aware of this since your death, Harold. Maeve screamed it to the heavens."

While they rested, they heard the sound of galloping coming up the hill behind them. When Argyll and Finiche came into view, Maeve let out a delighted cry. She laid her hand on the wolf's wide head, gazing into his expressive and luminous eyes. "No, I would not have left you behind," she said aloud, as she received his message. Maeve glanced over to see Harold patting the big horse on the neck and crooning something into his ear. She smiled.

"Where do you think Taranis is?" she asked.

"Probably hanging around waiting for Eron," Harold replied. "Your grandfather promised to return him to his proper owner—they were to meet in the Caer Sidi."

"Will we have a burial ceremony for my Mamo?" she asked, turning to MacCuill.

He nodded. "Catriona would want that—a proper send-off with all the goddesses in attendance. It would make her proud of her part in all of this—her sacrifice. Once you meet the moon goddess we'll reconnect with Eron and plan the trip to the Dolmen. Hopefully we will find the ones who are missing. Catriona would want everyone there, including your mother. Someone will have to be dispatched to fetch her."

A pang went through Maeve as she thought of Finna. They had barely connected before all of this started. She wondered idly if her father had come looking for them or if he was still in Halston. More than likely he was in Scotland—he would have been worried when they didn't show up. Was he with Finna at the cottage? She smiled to herself, imagining what that might be like.

"And in a few days it will be Imbolc, Brigid's day," the druid continued. "This celebration of fertility and the first signs of spring couldn't be more perfectly timed. And now that Brigid walks among us once again the festival will be especially momentous." He made an expansive gesture toward the valley, including the sky. "This renewal of the sun will bring all to the bonfire in the Caer Sidi. There will be many bairns conceived on this special night after all the years of infertility."

Maeve thought of Rea and the other Crion women, the women at the settlement. Would they be able to conceive now? Her thoughts went to her life back in the States, the gallery, and her friends. None of it seemed real—it was this place that made her heart sing. Down in the valley animals were coming out of their hiding places, drinking at the shallow lake and feeding on the tender shoots that were beginning to come up. The sun was high, the warmth of it taking away any lingering doubts about what had happened here. The sky had turned a brighter blue, a few puffy clouds moving sedately above them. The Otherworld was again the place it was meant to be.

Catriona was gone but they were here, they were together, they had survived. Maeve was sure they would find Rea, Gertrude and their other friends along the way. When she turned to Harold she saw her face reflected in his clear eyes. Love and gratitude washed over her as she picked up his hand. He grinned, twining his fingers through hers. No words needed to be spoken as they followed MacCuill and Duncan down the hill and into the Caer Sidi.

Read the exciting beginning of 'Temple of the Moon', sequel to 'Wolfmoon Trilogy'!

Prologue

Brandubh struggled to get his wits about him. His thoughts were scattered, diffuse and he couldn't seem to remember most of the recent past. For instance, where was he? The terrain surrounding him seemed incased in a milky fog, indistinct and soft around the edges. He knew he had been in a terrible battle, one that he had orchestrated, but somehow that didn't seem as important as his last clear memory of the woman coming toward him dressed in a long blue shift. Even now the thought of her sent a delighted shiver through him. Her large belly strained against the muslin fabric— she carried his child. Her face was smiling, dark eyes on his when she held out her hand…but that's when things became confusing. Water, he remembered water, a wave had washed over him. What had happened to her? Fear gripped him and he coughed as the sensation of drowning surfaced. He put his hand out noticing that his fingers were also fuzzy around the edges. And walking seemed oddly easy, as though he was floating rather than putting his feet down on solid ground. He had to get out of this fog.

Rest, he needed rest. He found a rock and sat down trying to make sense of things. He knew he was a priest. He looked down at his clothes to corroborate this but his body seemed almost transparent—and going in and out of focus. A very disturbing thought niggled at his consciousness but he pushed it away. Better to think about the woman and his life with her. But there was something wrong with that particular memory as though it had been planted in his mind. He frowned, puzzling over the predicament he was in.

He wasn't sure how long he stayed there. It could have been a few minutes a couple of hours or a day but the next thing he was aware of was gliding along a wide dirt path that seemed to appear as he moved forward. A familiar female voice echoed inside his mind, but this was not the woman he had been thinking of earlier. "Brandubh, pay attention," he heard clearly as though the woman was speaking into his ear. "Who is this?" he asked, looking around at the swirling mists. Was he in a dream?

"Brandubh, you have to find your way to me. I'm your mother, Adair."

"I can't see anything. Where are you?" Brandubh peered into the fog, squinting and moving his hands to push away the curtain that separated him from the rest of the world.

Adair. That name did seem familiar. He nodded once and then recalled some more of the past. He had a twin sister, Catriona. They had fought in the water before...or was it after the wave? He had stuck a knife in her chest—killed her with not a moments hesitation. He recalled the feeling of satisfaction it gave him. Why would he kill his own twin? He shook his head trying to clear the mustiness from his thoughts. "Mother," he called. "If you're around here please help me. I'm stuck in fog."

"I can only help you if you find your way to me. Try and recall yourself before you disappear forever."

"Disappear forever?" A shiver of fear went through him as the realization finally burst its way into his mind. He was dead.

I watched the pale horses run by, their glistening bodies appearing and disappearing as waves rolled in and out. From their dark hooves spray lifted, iridescent rainbows of color. The tide pulled seductively, urging me into its blue-green depths and I succumbed, my mind going blank.

Chapter One

The flat soles of my leather sandals were not made to navigate rock-covered trails and I stubbed my toes, stumbling more than once as I headed down the path. I needed my hiking boots but they were gone, along with my most recent memories. When I stopped to remove a pebble lodged under my foot I turned for one last look at the sanctuary where I had spent the night; the Temple of the Sun glittered like gold where it nestled between two mountain peaks. The rising sun bathed the sandstone walls in dazzling color, the sky behind a contrast of vivid blue. But once the sun reached the top of the structure the Temple faded into the landscape, belying its existence. I wondered if this effect was intentional since the ascetic monks who practiced there did not encourage outside visitors.

One night among the monks had given me a chance to regain my strength, but they refused my request to remain longer. Their vows did not allow women—they had bent the rules allowing me to stay. I had noticed the shocked expressions when I showed up to ask for shelter. Not only was I a woman, an outsider with olive skin, but also I was pregnant and conspicuously alone. When the solid wooden doors closed behind me this morning I felt more afraid than I had for all the weeks I had traveled. Kindly they had given me some food and a heavy monk's robe to keep out the cold wind and swirling fog that had recently arrived in the higher elevations. A hard kick took my mind to my belly and I cupped my hands around the growing girth of my middle. It would only be another month or two before this one would be born; I had to be in a warm and safe place by then.

Of course who knew if there was any safe haven in this godforsaken wilderness? How I had arrived in this alien land was a mystery I had yet to solve. My last coherent memory was landing at Edinburgh Airport. After that it was as though a curtain had come down over my mind. All I had since that time was the information gleaned from the villagers in Tolam, where I had been living for the past six months.

A low rumble had me crouching against the uphill side of the trail. A shower of rocks and pebbles careened by, disappearing over the other edge. Below me a few larger boulders loosened and I watched them tumble away and disappear into the deep crevasse that gaped threateningly below. I wouldn't want to fall into that dark place. As things quieted I stood and shifted my woven bag to my other shoulder. It was heavy with oat and barley cakes, the cheese the monk's had given me as well as my talismans, extra clothing, knife, wooden bowl and cup and other bits and pieces of my life. My fingers traced the silver triple spiral around my neck. I was wearing it the day Dia and Lars found me unconscious on the sand close to their village. And although the necklace felt familiar I had no idea where it had come from.

"You were battered to bits and nearly drowned," was how Dia explained my arrival. She showed me my shredded clothes and I smiled thinking about how she must have viewed my down ski jacket with feathers escaping from the rips, the torn metal studded blue jeans. There was nothing of that sort here where clothes were handmade out of flax and wool or knitted. My feet had been bare of the waterproof boots I know I must have been wearing, lost forever in the cold ocean.

Dia told me she and her man Lars had been walking the shore that day, searching for mollusks to put in the stew. "'Twas a wonder you were alive," she told me shaking her head. "That water would freeze a witch." I smiled at the saying, wondering if I qualified since I had once possessed psychic abilities. But during my time here the second sight had disappeared, leaving me bereft and unsure. Somehow my Tarot deck had survived the harrowing trip in the water, making me wonder if I had fallen off a boat close to the shore. Whatever I had gone through had left me completely emaciated. It took months for me to put on weight and lose the strange pallor that lay under my normally olive skin.

I had traveled to Scotland because of a client of mine in Milltown, Massachusetts. The young woman had come to me for a psychic reading and I had seen several disturbing events in her future. My sudden rush to get to Scotland seemed out of character for me but something must have prompted the trip. Apparently whatever happened in between then and when Dia found me unconscious along the shore had been traumatic enough to give me a major case of amnesia. I had the sense that I had been severely depressed for some time, as well as being near starvation. It was a wonder I hadn't miscarried.

My psychic work in my home in Milltown included the Tarot, crystals and palm reading and I had an extensive client list. I owned an apartment and had a cat named Lucifer. But with all my psychic ability I could not recall the father of the child I carried. Nor could I fathom what had brought me to this desolate and backward place. If I believed in time travel I might think I'd been transported into some earlier period in history but I was more practical than that, even though I dabbled in what might be referred to as the occult.

My early months in the small village of Tolam were pleasant enough, despite the hard work and the villager's superstitious ways. I lived in an extra bedroom in Dia and Lar's house, sharing meals with them. These people had no electricity, no indoor plumbing, they cooked over wood fires in iron pots, milked the sheep and goats to make cheese. Work began before the sun rose and ended long after it went down. Gathering wood, searching for mushrooms and greens to add to the one-pot meals took most of a day. Chickens ran loose and occasionally ended up in the stewpot, but mostly it was their eggs that provided protein, that and fish the men caught in rope nets. Rudimentary bread was made from nuts ground into a fine powder, mixed with eggs and butter and cooked over the fire.

They had odd spiritual habits that I didn't recognize despite my knowledge of pagan festivals and holidays. According to them there were elves living underground who would appear periodically and steal your children. Everyone in the village was terrified of these creatures and had stories from the past. No abductions had happened in recent memory but still they fretted, keeping all the children under close guard and scaring the wits out of them. They had bonfires at certain times of the year, sacrificing animals to appease these underground dwellers.

When I showed them my Tarot deck they forked their fingers in the sign to ward off evil, refusing to even look at it. However I noticed that they used Runes for their own divination, which led me to believe that I had traveled far northward from Scotland; when they spoke of deities it was of Odin, Frigga, Freyja and Eir, and they often referred to Asgard, the home of the gods as well as Outgard where the monsters and giants lived.

After I recovered from my injuries I was constantly hungry. Dia laughingly referred to me as the bucket that was never filled. I helped with milking and cheese making just to fill my belly with the leftovers. It was several months before I realized that the reason I hadn't had a period was not because of trauma or menopause, I was going to have a baby. The shock of this had me reeling. I had always been so careful to use birth control—I had never wanted children. How in the world had this happened? I remembered being attracted to a priest I met in Milltown right before I left for Edinburgh, but there was definitely no sex between us. I had a vague notion that things had ended badly—knowing me I could have tried to get the poor man into bed; I never had much respect for the priesthood.

As the pregnancy progressed a certain amount of contentment and even joy filled my heart, no doubt brought on by the hormones coursing through my body. At night before sleep I listened for the extra heartbeat in my center and felt a deep connection with this tiny being growing inside me. Despite my earlier feelings about motherhood, I could hardly wait to cradle this child in my arms.

Around my fourth or fifth month, when the pregnancy became obvious, the villagers began looking at me askance. Having no husband made me a *hora*, an adulteress, they said. Colum, a man who had lost his wife, offered to marry me but I declined. Why would I want to saddle myself with a husband, especially a man I didn't love who didn't love me?

Dia tried her best to convince me to go ahead with the marriage. Colum was a good man and according to their laws I would have to leave if I remained single. She told me that with winter coming on I would never survive. So far the days had been warm enough with the sun peeking through the clouds more than fifty percent of the time. From my estimation the average daytime temperature was in the fifties, dropping lower at night and spreading frost across the grass for the morning milking. From what I heard winter came early and was fierce, bringing freezing fog, snow and gusting winds that went on for a very long time.

Most of the men in Tolam exhibited a decidedly condescending attitude toward the women, but when I tried to speak to Dia and her friends about it, their eyes grew wide and they turned away; they were not allowed to control their fates, living under their father's roof until they were married and then under their husband's tyrannical control afterward. Of course some men were kinder than others and from living under the same roof for so long, I knew that Dia and Lars had a good relationship.

After lengthy discussions with the town elders, all men, I was told that I would need to be out of Tolam within a fortnight. I packed up my things in a state of panic. All I wanted was a hot shower, a real toilet, not a hole in the ground, a bed with a thick mattress and a doctor to deliver my baby. At the age of forty-one I was concerned about complications. But where would I find these things?

As I prepared for my departure I questioned Dia and Lars and several others once again about ships, planes, cars or buses, but their expressions remained blank. Yes, small sailing vessels came to shore occasionally bringing merchants and traders and sometimes thieves, but as to the other things, they'd never heard of them. The day before I left Dia told me of the larger towns to the west on the other side of the mountains. There, she said, I might find what I was looking for. It was sweet Dia, with tears in her eyes, who escorted me to the edge of the village to say good-bye; she seemed the only one who didn't want me to leave. It was she who told me of the Temple of the Sun where I might find shelter and more information.

Looking out over the ochre crags that seemed to go on forever I wondered how much longer it would take to get to these mythical towns. Did Dia know what she was talking about? She was young and I was certain she hadn't ever been away from Tolam. The monks had little to add, only telling me to head toward the valley.

The familiar green forests of the lower elevations were long gone as well as the streams where I filled my waterskin and plucked greens to supplement my steady diet of cheese and hard bread. I missed the soft ground underfoot, the call of birds, the smell of pinesap and mushrooms. Up here water was scarce and I was glad the monks had provided me with several days worth, even though it added considerably to my load. For almost a month I had been traveling west and this area was not where I wanted to end up. It was fall now and snow would come early in this high desert place. Luckily this day was fairly temperate, warm enough to do without the heavy hooded robe that I had managed to stuff into my pack.

I looked up, startled to see a man approaching from down the trail. He was dressed in homespun trousers, leather boots and a thick woolen sweater. His skin had the deep coppery look of someone who spent a considerable amount of time in the sun, his hair bleached to reddish-gold. Suddenly nervous I pulled my shawl protectively around my body. He gaped at me, his eyebrows raised in surprise.

"Are you on your way to the temple?" I asked as he came close, trying not to stare into his startling turquoise eyes.

He nodded and then smiled, revealing straight white teeth. "I did not expect to run into a woman on this trail, especially one as exotic as you. Occasionally the nuns come this way. They're the only women allowed in the Temple of the Sun."

Exotic was not a word I would use to describe my dusty sweat-stained clothes, my hair loosened from its braid and hanging around my face in damp wisps. "Are you a monk?"

He laughed until his eyes teared up. "Hardly. I'm a trader. I come this way every year. It's the easiest route to the many villages hidden in these mountains. Where did you come from?"

A trader—I hoped he wasn't one of the thieves Dia had described who robbed people along the trails and sometimes knifed them. "I lived in Tolam."

"Ah yes, Tolam. The people there are a bit hard. I don't often go there because of the attitude. You're a long way from home." He looked at me quizzically for several moments. "This is not a place for a woman alone, especially in your condition."

When his gaze traveled across my body my cheeks grew hot—I smoothed my skirt over my protruding belly. "The villagers threw me out," I said before I could stop myself. I covered my mouth with my hand. What was I thinking trusting this complete stranger? I looked carefully to see if he had a knife on his belt but his sweater covered the top of his trousers.

"Well," he said after a moment, leaving the unasked question hanging in the air. "I lived in Tolam for a year when I was younger—they are a superstitious bunch who are full of strange stories. You're heading into the valley?"

I waited for the inevitable look of disdain, the judgmental stare but his expression was only one of concern. "The monks were kind enough to let me stay one night at the temple. I've been told there are towns in the valley where I can make a living."

"A fire came through the valley one moon ago. I'm surprised the monks didn't tell you. There's not much left of Tadsell, but Fell remains unharmed." He sat on his haunches and pulled a small pipe from his pack. As he tamped the tobacco down and lit it with a match I looked around helplessly. Shelter for the · night was imperative—the sun had already disappeared behind the peaks.

"Would you like a smoke? It's very calming and it won't hurt the baby," he said, holding out the curious pipe. I took it from him examining the swirls and patterns carved into the stem. The designs were very much like the necklace I wore.

"It's very old," he said watching me. "Belonged to my great, great, great, grandfather." He laughed again and the bright sound echoed into the valley.

I took a puff and coughed. "Try again," he encouraged, grinning.

The second time was better—smooth and cool. When I breathed out, the smoke swirled in patterns and I watched them until they faded into nothingness. Memories of my smoking habit came to me—I hadn't had a cigarette in a very long time. My body tingled. Everything looked bright and I could smell the sea. But how far away was that? It must be a hundred miles from here.

"Can you tell me where we are? Is this some remote island off Scotland?"

"Scotland? No. This place is known as Far Isle." He held the pipe out.

"Far Isle. I've never heard of that." I took the proffered pipe again and drew in the fragrant smoke. I felt strong and full of energy, ready to take on the world. He watched me, his eyes bright and filled with humor.

When I handed it back he puffed a few times and then dumped the ash on the ground. "That's better," he said, standing up and stretching with his hands high above his head. He twisted from side to side, loosening his shoulders. "Maybe you should accompany me. These hills hold many unseen dangers."

I studied him carefully. His face seemed familiar with his kind eyes and easy laugh, but I didn't know him—I didn't want to put myself into someone's care. It was the main reason I was out here alone in the middle of nowhere. "I'm heading the other way. Besides, I have my talismans—I'll be fine." Why had I said that? Now he would think I was as superstitious as the people in Tolam.

He raised his eyebrows. "What do you carry to keep you safe?"

"I have a few herbs and crystals and my spiral necklace." I pulled aside my shawl to show him my one piece of jewelry.

"A proper witch then," he said, leaning in to take a look at the triple spiral. His fingers grazed my breast as he picked it up to get a better look.

"I wouldn't call myself a witch, although I...."

"I swear I know this necklace." He looked up at me, his forehead creasing into a frown.

"It's an ancient emblem, the triple goddess. The villagers told me it was a potent symbol."

"And so it is, but what I meant is this particular one seems familiar to me. The way the silver is worked, the artistry in the embellishments. Where did you get it?"

"I don't know. I was wearing it when I washed up..."

"Washed up?"

I nodded. "I was in Tolam because the villagers took me there after they found me on the sand. It was the place where the river meets the sea. I don't know how I got there."

He gazed at me thoughtfully. "Yes, I know this place where the boats bring in their cargo. What's your name?" he finally asked.

"I'm Gertrude."

"Gertrude? That's an unusual name." He cocked his head and put his forefinger on his chin. "I'm Kafir," he finally said, holding out his hand.

I took his hand in mine feeling the roughened skin of his palm. *Hands of a sailor* came to me but from where I didn't know. "Do you know me, Kafir? My recent memories have been lost." I looked at him hopefully still holding his hand.

"I once knew a woman many years ago who went by that name, but ..."

"Where was that?"

He shook his head, letting go of my hand. "It's all in the distant past. I was a different man then. I'm fairly certain the Gertrude I knew is long dead."

"But if you can tell me..."

"I must be on my way," he interrupted. "Keep to this trail and you will come to a place to shelter by nightfall. It is a perilous journey you have undertaken." He raised his hand in farewell. "May the goddess keep you and your child safe."

He moved past me and headed uphill. "I hope our paths will cross again," he called over his shoulder.

I watched him until he was out of sight before I turned back to the trail. Suddenly I felt very alone.

464

About the author

Nikki's college education centered on English and Art and she graduated with a B.A. in both. While her children were in middle school she began a greeting card business and then later, when they were out of the house, she began painting on silk, selling her scarves and wall hangings to high-end galleries in California and Oregon.

Now she writes full time, working on a sequel to Wolfmoon as well as a fictionalized version of her parent's life based on journals her father kept during his time as a POW during WW2.

Having recently located from Portland Oregon, Nikki has become a resident of Tucson, Arizona where she lives on a hill at the base of the Catalina Mountains with her husband, and a standard poodle, Buddha, and Eesa, the cat.

To visit her website please go to: www.wolfmoontrilogy.com

Nikki's blog address is: http://niksblog-authorinprogress. blogspot.com/

You can find a glossary of terms and characters on Nikki's website.

www.ingramcontent.com/pod-product-compliance
Lightning Source LLC
Chambersburg PA
CBHW030534260626
47157CB00006B/2032